The Great British Potato War

30/01/24

Dear Ian,
Hope springs eternal.
Regards,
Jamie

This book would not exist without Richard Maurice. From imagining the world with me, to hunting down the grammatical crime spree of stray apostrophes in the final draft, he was there. Deepest thanks.

Additional thanks to my wife, for designing the cover art, so that people can judge the book by it.

The Great British Potato War

J. I. McLaren

This is a work of fiction. Names, characters, organisations, places, events, and incidents are either products of the author's imagination or are used fictiously, and satirically.

To contact the author please email :
jmclarenscripts@gmail.com

Cover design by: R. Bankston-Thomas

Contents

One

A Tuber

"Before the war there was before the war. And before before the war there were other wars, and all the wars were won by England, alone, against tyrannical Europeans."

– 'A History of Modern Britain' (Completion Date TBA) by Prime Minister Mark French, Second Prime Minister of the Democratic Monarchy of Great Britain.

Mark My Words

How did I become your Prime Minister? When you find out write to me at 10 Downing Street and let me know.

I'm sure the answer lies in this exhausting essay collection, just as there is wisdom in my bestselling book, *'Fruits and Vegetables, and Their Correct Patriotic Ratings' by Prime Minister Mark French.* If you do not own my premier guide to eating patriotically, don't worry, it will soon be mandatory. Better to voluntarily get a signed copy. Today. Study it well. When you take your next Great British Citizenship Test (revised) you will be able to answer the first question,

Q1. What is the most patriotic Great British Vegetable?
A. …

And,

Q2. Which vegetable was fought over at the Battle of Surrey Hills?

A. …

The Battle of Surrey Hills was one of the first hot engagements of The Great British Potato War, although the war was cold long before it was hot, like all good wars. I was promoted in the field from Private to Lance Corporal, after the death of Lance Corporal Carrot. He was shot between the eyes, staring death in the face, as Englishmen have always done. We leave it to Continentals to be shot in the buttocks, while on the run.

No stone marks LC Carrot's final resting place. There was only time to promote me and carry on the struggle against The Enemies of the People.

Dead superior officers were waiting in front of me, stacked up like tattered football cards, with me at the bottom. Each time fate removed the second last card from the pack I climbed closer to 10 Downing Street.

I have contributed chapters to this book, which I definitely wrote myself. They deal with my life before high office. Like you I look forward to reading the other chapters, when I have time. I have confidence the book is patriotic, because its cover has the Union Flag on it.

Indeed, I am told all the chapters deal with the past, which is what Great Britain deals in best. Newer nations like Germany, or France, run about unnecessarily increasing the speed of trains, blotting their land with solar farms or neglecting to teach infants to forage. We leave them to it. We have more productive obsessions, like bunting.

For the Spaniards a sympathy lingers, as they beg us to

save their tourist economy, but they allied with Brussels and must make do and mend. Let the Dutch fill the showy hotels of Torremolinos, the Norwegians the crumbling towers of Benalmadena, the Poles the tacky party boats of Malaga.

Charity begins and ends at home.

Britons must spend their leisure time in national service. A few weeks on a soft fruit farm, or driving a Class 1 vehicle, is better than any sloven's sunburnt week by a salty Euro pool.

"When Britain was Great the noble Cockney cared not for a cheap flight over the English Channel to Hôtel Mont Doom." – from "Musings Whilst on Sabbatical in Calais", by Prime Minister William Bunsen, First Prime Minister of the Democratic Monarchy of Great Britain.

We observe Mother Earth's bawling, infant countries from behind our sovereign borders. They can only learn by studying our example.

At Bosham we hold our bunting taut. A wall no Frenchman or German can break, so formidable the tide itself does not rise above our line of tiny flags. This is because our bunting is measured in Imperial. What good a puny metre against a sovereign yard?

The Great British Potato War followed the overwhelming, democratic decision by the British people to break free of Brussels' chains. To once again be a sovereign, free trading nation cutting our own lamb deals with Australians, and deciding the safe, approximate amount of effluent for bathing beaches.

The saboteurs among us lost and never got over it. We cupped their salty tears in our hands and sipped. We strived for unity for years, to no avail, as The Anti-Growth Coalition determined to damage growth. England's war against

England was the inevitable outcome. But at least it was to be a civil war, and not some foreign nonsense.

Not so long ago I endured the temporary shortages of canned beans on supermarket shelves. I stared in vain for toilet paper, my shopping trolley willing but the shelves empty. I fumbled in quiet despair for a root vegetable, and I inwardly raged at Brussels over the escalating price of salted butter. But hunger is a great motivator and hard work set me free.

The Democratic Monarchy of Great Britain is now world beating in motivation. Like my predecessor William Bunsen, I promise you a cornucopia tomorrow, all you need to do is keep the faith with me today.

Yours patriotically,

Prime Minister Mark A. French

Two

The Brussels Cramps

"A is for Apple – The Apple, unlike The Banana (which will be dealt with later), is a dedicated public servant. Witness the Great British wasps of late summer, drunk on fermented, fallen fruit, and know we are abundant.

For this reason, The Apple receives a patriotic rating of 300, 033 973, 999 out of a possible top score of 300, 034 974, 000"

- 'Fruits and Vegetables, and Their Correct Patriotic Ratings' by Prime Minister Mark A. French.

Mark My Words – The Day I left Raylee

Mary stood on the pavement twisting a damp dish cloth in her hands.

"Don't miss me," she said, in-between sobs.

It was a red, white and blue cloth.

"I won't," I reassured her, but she looked doubtful, twisting the cloth tighter. Red liquid trickled out. "Mary French, I will look after myself."

"The dye is running," she whimpered.

She only had eyes for me. Her hero. And her eyes were burning.

Around us Raylee's less fortunate women carried woven baskets filled with red, white and blue confetti, which they flung into the air.

"It's like our wedding day," I said.

A skinny, blonde girl stood on the corner singing quietly, but determinedly, a song composed by our Prime Minister William Bunsen,

"Heart of oak are our heads, heart of oak are our legs,
We always are ready, steady, boys, steady!
We'll fight and we'll conquer ourselves again and again."

"She looks like one of Prime Minister Bunsen's kids," I noted. The girl was wearing a unicorn costume. The filthy horn wilting to the right.

Mary just shrugged and replied, "That's one of the Jelly twins. Pandora."

"Oh! I thought the Jelly girls were older. Don't they feed them?"

Mary didn't care.

"Is it heavy?" she asked, touching the rifle on my shoulder.

"No."

I lied.

"The burden of compulsory military service is light."

"For King and country," she replied.

"That's right."

"Get War Done."

"That's the spirit."

I knew I would be fine.

"The war needs me more than I need it."

"It's a long way to Surrey," Mary worried, "be sure to stop for tea and cake."

"I'm going to war. Not a picnic. The Enemies of the People must be purged."

At last.

"That's no excuse for not having a good cup of tea."

I moved to embrace her and she moved back, her head down, shaking like a cow.

"Go Mark. Just go."

I did.

I turned back to make sure she was staring after me. The dish cloth pressed to her mouth, stifling her sobs. Her greying hair in a bun with a pointless HB pencil through it.

There must have been other mothers, other wives, other sisters on the street, other tearful goodbyes. I only remember my wife, Mrs French. It was the last time I saw her alive.

She's still alive today. She never stops writing to me from the Great British Re-Education Facility. But this book deals with the past, so let us stay there, where memory is a tonic.

I had responded to my England's call. I had walked away from home comforts and the certainties of village life, much as a crusading knight must have done. I was looking for the heretics. I would find them.

There were chaps exempt from the fight. They worked in government. They made the slogans that keep us warm at night.

Because the answer to any Great British Dilemma was, and still is, a slogan.

"British Fish Are Sovereign Fish!" gave our fishing boat purpose.

"Get War Done!" helped us to fight ourselves, once we understood that having defeated Brussels, we were now looking inward.

"Get Farming Done!" fed us, enough.

"Patriotic Children Work!" emptied school classrooms and revived our bunting industry.

Prime Minister William Bunsen understood all the British people need to be happy are a few well chosen words, and an enemy. And what better enemy than a domestic enemy?

"It saves on queues at the border," Mary had noted, with a smirk.

And as I marched forwards, I looked backwards, and mined my memory for the ore of his inspiration. Who can forget the television broadcast which started the war?

***

THE TELEVISION BROADCAST WHICH STARTED THE WAR

EXT. 10 DOWNING STREET SUNSET

The lectern is out. Union Flags hang either side of the famous black door. It's a windless day, so giant fans make the flags ripple. And Elgar plays from a sound system. Always.

TWO SOLDIERS stand next to the flags.

RAT ONE emerges from under the lectern and scurries out of shot. RAT TWO follows.

The black door opens.

RAT THREE races out, and then back under cover.

PRIME MINISTER WILLIAM BUNSEN (BUNSEN) walks to the lectern. Haystack hair. Military uniform heavy with medals. The jacket is buttoned up wrong.

FIANCE ONE stands in the doorway. Side on. She is heavily pregnant. She gazes lovingly at BUNSEN.

BUNSEN

My fellow Britons. It is now clear that having won our freedom from the Continentals we have failed to make good on the opportunities seized.

RAT THREE runs out from under the lectern again, changes its mind again, runs back under.

BUNSEN

But it is not our fault. Among us are some who never reconciled themselves to defeat.

***

Those idiots who wanted German cars, French wines and Italian sausages.

"As if proper British sausages with a minimum of 5% meat aren't good enough," I shouted at the television.

Mary sat next to me, knitting, the click-clack of her needles sounded like a Lewis Gun.

"We need purging," Bunsen declared, both hands raised, palms to him, fingers spread. *"We need a Great British colonic. We must break the chains of varied thinking. For British democracy to succeed it must be of one mind."*

"He needs to call the exterminator," Mary muttered, pointing with one of her needles at the television.

"What are you going on about?"

"There's rats in the lectern."

"You must leave your homes!"

Yes!

"You must go to the next village and find the enemy there. Lock him up! And when your villages are free you must march on London!"

Get War Done!

"Rats, Mark French. Rats. And big ones at that."

"I see no rats," I replied.

Although before national mobilisation other strategies were tried. Operation Big Society (Revived) for one.

Raylee was exuberant the day our Member of Parliament opened our food bank inside an empty Halifax Bank. The building had been vacant for years. The windows boarded up. German Shepherds left inside to keep out people too lazy to pay a landlord rent. For years we'd watched jealously as other towns and villages opened these public larders of plenty, for the people, by the people. Finally, the dogs were led out and the crate of tinned tomatoes and beans taken in.

"We must make bunting to hang over the entrance," I told Mary.

"No need silly. Raylee Infants School is doing that," she replied.

We were ecstatic the day our MP visited from his townhouse in Westminster to open our clothing bank in a disused dentists.

"What will we take to the clothing pantry?" I asked my Mary. She was mending my jeans. Patching the buttocks.

"Um..."

"Let's have a look in the wardrobe."

"We're more likely to withdraw clothes than deposit," she worried, but I soon found a few of her old dresses to take down and donate. We weren't going to miss out.

Take that Brussels!

And we were beside ourselves the day our MP opened our heat bank, our medicine bank and converted our public library into a workhouse for two shifts a day. The school children during the afternoon and the welfare scroungers in the night. This was Raylee being levelled up. This was a manifesto promise fulfilled by Bunsen.

This was Blitz Spirit!

But it wasn't enough.

Always there were saboteurs undermining the national effort. So saboteuring was outlawed. No longer would the hardworking British taxpayer be bothered by some yoghurt knitter in a rainbow vest blocking our way to work, screaming incoherently about whatever.

When the end of public protests didn't give us the edge in the great game of international trade, something more was required.

So the government organised the shaming of traitors, first in the best newspapers (standard for years) and then by reviving traditional British public ceremonies, like the stocks and the pillory.

Imagine our pride when public shaming returned to our village square with a sticker bellowing "Made in Britain", over stamped on the "Made in China" sticker on the pillory. Now everyone knew that if you ran your country down you would find your ankles and wrists secured in oak.

"If we had stayed under the thumb of Brussels we couldn't punish ourselves!" I shouted in front of the pillory. That first glorious day. Now we could take direct action ourselves. No more just reading in The Daily Parrot who to hate and tutting. *

I hefted a replica rotten tomato and turned in a circle so everyone could see the replica juice as I squeezed.

My people cheered.

"Why isn't he using real tomatoes?" a one-eyed boy asked and was swiftly taken away by his mother. The pair of them were so skinny you could tell there was insufficient belief in their diet.

In the pillory Raylee's last postman waited with his grey-haired head hung low. He was testing the strength of the justice wood, his arm muscles bunched, his hands opened and closed. His breath came in snorts like a cornered bull. I'm sure he would have pawed the ground with his feet too, but they were held tight.

I looked at the pillory and thought "Walls of oak".

The postman had been found guilty in the court of public opinion and he would pay the price.

Clarence, Raylee's butcher, strode out holding the charge sheet. His apron brown with dried blood, his big face flushed, his cleaver swung from his belt and how it shone as the sun flashed on the blade.

"Pat Patrick McPatrickson," Clarence read out, "you have been charged with undermining the will of the people."

Worse than murder.

"You have been caught red handed placing a copy of 'Unotesticular' in a public waste bin."

A gasp from the crowd. There was only one public waste bin in Raylee. I was staggered Pat had been so dumb. Mary gripped my elbow.

"Unotesticular is the patriot's bible!" I shouted out. I was seeing red.

The edition in question had a wonderful cover too. It was a cartoon of The White House with the hammer and sickle flying over it. Famous communist leaders exploded out of the broken roof like firecrackers. Mao. Stalin. Simon de Montfort. It was a searing condemnation of the explosion of renewable energy use across The Atlantic.

If ever you doubted our nation's destiny you need only open any copy. Week in and week out Unotesticular is there to remind you that Britons are exceptional.

"Why didn't he just use the magazine as toilet paper?" Mary whispered.

"He could have torn up the sheets and flushed them away."

"There's no helping some people," I told her. "Now shush."

"I didn't do it!" Pat shouted. We shook our heads.

"Take responsibility for your crime," Ms Formaldehyde, the pharmacist, spat at him.

"You're my cousin!" he screeched.

She crossed her arms and looked away.

Clarence produced the copy of the magazine. It was still in its weatherproof wrapping with the address label stained by trash.

"Guilty," Clarence declared, "Guilty!"

Pat looked up at him.

"What the fuck Clarence," he shouted.

Clarence rolled the magazine into a tube and inserted it into the criminal's mouth.

"Special delivery!" he shouted, spitting the words at Pat.

How we all cheered!

The replica fruit flew from the buckets. Everyone had a go. Except my wife. I saw her hold back, scowling at Raylee's patriots. How many little red flags like that did I ignore? I just did not want to see that she was a Europhile.

But then I saw a dark haired girl weeping at the back. She's missing out. I took a foam tomato and knelt before her.

***

EXT. RAYLEE - VILLAGE SQUARE DAY

POSTMAN PAT is in the PILLORY.

The PILLORY is metres away from RAYLEE'S WAR MEMORIAL. The sun is high behind the bronze soldier's head. Halo of light. The immortal warrior leans on his rifle.

A furious crowd surrounds POSTMAN PAT. MARK and MARY FRENCH. Ms FORMALDEHYDE the pharmacist, CLARENCE the butcher, and many others. Buckets full of replica, rotten fruit are spread about. The locals grab at the fruit and hurl it at the pilloried man.

A DARK HAIRED GIRL stands weeping in the melee. Huge, wracking sobs. MARK FRENCH goes to her, tomato in his hand, and kneels.

MARK FRENCH
Wipe your tears child. Everyone
gets a turn.

DARK HAIRED GIRL
That's my dad.

MARK FRENCH
You still get a go.

MARK FRENCH pushes the tomato into her hands. She resists. The crowd gathers around. Tighter and tighter.

DARK HAIRED GIRL looks up at the terrifying ring of red faces.

CROWD
Throw! Throw! Throw!

DARK HAIRED GIRL is petrified. Half starved. Filthy. She stares at her father. He nods to say it's okay. She throws.

A poor throw which falls well short.

MARK FRENCH presses another tomato into her hands.

MARK FRENCH
That was just a warmup. Try again.

DARK HAIRED GIRL presses her hands to her face to make them all go away.

Ms FORMALDEHYDE
What did you expect?

CLARENCE
The fruit didn't fall far from the tree!

MARK FRENCH laughs. MARY FRENCH pushes through the crowd, bodily shoving people aside.

MARY FRENCH
Mark French! You son of a bitch!

MARK FRENCH, suddenly sheepish, lifts DARK HAIRED GIRL and places her in MARY FRENCH'S outstretched arms.

***

The pillory was back where it belonged in public life and there was nothing the woke could do but hide from it. The BBC made a documentary about the day called, "A Very British Public Shaming Ceremony", so we could all be proud.

If we'd never left the EU, we could never have done it.

But, strangely, this had not done the trick either. The rot was too deep. The fear of potato shortages a constant and no matter how often we punished ourselves, and no matter how often we played "Land of Hope and Glory" the harvest weakened. The trees withered. The lambs sickened as the Continent jealously guarded its vets.

Yes, Brussels was to blame. That much was obvious. But it was our fault too. We hadn't faced ourselves in the mirror.

"You might pillory one nurse, one teacher, one GP [if you could find one], one postman, but there was always another traitor waiting to spread the sickness of negativity. Some fool in your local pub saying just because today was worse than yesterday, they did not believe their government when it promised them a lovely day tomorrow." – Editorial, The Daily Parrot.

A total effort was needed to capitalise on Great Britain's freedom from cross channel tyranny.

At last, we turned the spotlight on ourselves.

"Saboteurs from the Continent are embedded in our communities," William Bunsen told us day in and day out. *"For years our porous borders let them in because we believed they came as friends to fix our gutters and mend our broken limbs. But they were all sleepers. Anti-Great British Growth was their real aim. Building side returns on Victorian terraces was just the cover story dreamt up in the years Great Britain's money leeched across The English Channel."*

For months we heard broadcasts like this on radios. We were being prepared for the struggle.

I needed no preparation. I was ready. I left Mary to wage war against ourselves the moment I was given the red, white and blue light.

When the soldiers under my command whispered in the black fondant nights, "When will the proper British potatoes run out?", I would close my eyes and think of the fluttering flags outside 10 Downing Street.

I would crawl between the pickets on our perimeter whispering, "Get War Done!"

"What?" the men would mouth back.

"Believe in British Fish!"

"Oh. Okay."

(I imagine it would have been exactly like this, had I been alive to fight in WW2. I can't believe I would have been in the Pacific. I would have been somewhere perpetually ungrateful, like France or Spain. The classic English breakfast would now be called 'The Full Marky', instead of the 'The Full Monty'.)

My men would throw their caps high and cry it too. Good men. Men who valued freedom of speech. They would sell their lives dearly. No one complained as they writhed in the mud with a hot carrot in their eye. All knew we had to take back what was ours from ourselves.

"Trust in Prime Minister William Bunsen!" I encouraged them. "Trust in Billy Burner!"

Of course, no one knew then if it was possible to eat a root vegetable that didn't come in Union Flag packaging.

There were rumours British people had eaten all manner of forrin foods. Once.

Padre Peppers from Spain - which damaged economic growth by causing long, afternoon naps. Kilometre Olives from Crete - which caused people to bow to German financiers. And of course, avocadoes, we all knew what they were. The Devil's testicles. These were the symbols of The Enemies of The People. Avocadoes. Brussels Sprouts. The metre. Anything sold in an easily understood method of measuring.

Patriots would starve before they let such food pass their lips.

"Patriots know the best way to measure your fruit and veg is by a complicated system of calculation developed in the 13th

Century using the length of a duck's leg and the average girth of an ox drawn hoe." - Editorial, 'Unotesticular', April 1st.

[Ed. It is possible to eat a non-Union flagged root vegetable, but it results in a psychosomatic digestive disorder called by physicians, *The Brussels Cramps.* Rarely fatal, it will however render the afflicted unable to fight until a significant amount of wind has been passed.]

"Control British Waters!" was another robust slogan to keep spirits high. Ideologically pure, it glistened like cod's scales. The men responded well to it. Shouting about fish always stiffens spines. It said everything about who modern Britain was.

When I was far from home, when I was bruised and bloodied, when I was burying my brothers in arms in haste in some sodden English field, knowing we had seized back control of British territorial waters kept me ordering the men to dig their own graves.

If the traitors did breach Raylee's defences and capture the town I knew Mary would lead the underground resistance. She would not fall for tricks such as boxes with "Food Aid - EU" printed on them.

"Starve yourself so that I may eat," I ordered her on the day I passed out. "Victory will see us feast!"

It was late in the afternoon. A glorious day, if you ignored the blowflies on the gutter trash, the shuttered shopfronts, if you blocked your ears to the cries of the widows and orphans. The sun was sinking into western clouds, but rays reflected off the Bakelite buttons on my replica TA Catering Corp uniform.

"You're a sight to mist the eyes," Mary muttered.

She stood twisting that damp dish cloth in her slab hands. Damp with her sobbing. The moment had arrived when she must raise that wet fabric and wave farewell.

"We will meet again," I reassured her. "I don't know

where. I don't know when. But we'll meet again some sunny day."

"Get War Done," she replied.

"Control British fish!"

She nodded. Her bosom heaving.

"Don't beg me to stay."

"I won't," Her voice cracked. "Control...British...fish."

"I must go. It's my duty."

"Go," she agreed. "Please just go."

She hid her face in her dish cloth and sobbed.

"You do not understand the blazing star I was born under," I told her. "I will uphold the will of the people."

"You're a great big idiot."

"Shush now. Only speak in three-word sentences while I'm away," I moved in close to hold her hands, but she retreated.

"I will do," she whispered and blew her nose. A good woman, I thought then. God's own.

"Be sure to show the other women how to make one sock into two."

Her eyes widened and she looked me up and down a moment, in amazement. Suddenly, I had become an example of a new type of man.

"I'm going to fulfil the will of the people!" I saluted her.

Her head fell again. She moved to touch the rifle I carried, but then stepped back.

"Don't miss me," Mary mumbled.

"I won't! I will look after myself."

"Go Mark. Just go."

I was following my destiny.

Destiny is all. With COURAGE and Union Flag branded munitions I could not fail.

*Appendix A – The Official Government List of Who to Hate

Three

The Diary of Mrs French

"B is for Banana – this complicated fruit will be discussed later. As promised.

For this reason the Banana's patriotic rating can not be disclosed so early in this book."

- 'Fruits and Vegetables, and Their Correct Patriotic Ratings' by Prime Minister Mark A. French.

Mark Her Words

Mark is an idiot. God love him. I tried to hide today's 'The Daily Parrot' from him but he found it. He's seen the front page. Damn it! He cut out the application to join the 'Patriot Police'. He's applied. Unpaid. Volunteer. He doesn't know that I know. He put the paper back in the pile with the application cut out. I guess he didn't think I'd notice and he'd just ball up the page and burn it the next time the gas was cut off due to "temporary supply chain fluctuations".

Now we'll be tested. The black transit van will arrive and it'll be like an episode out of 'The Twilight Zone'. This is what so called sovereignty has done to us. He's asking the Eye of Sauron to examine Raylee.

Mark's just the sort of idiot who will arrest our neighbours. Oh God. He thinks I'll be impressed that he's "answered the call". When the civil war starts, and it will, he'll be one of the first to go out to fight ourselves.

We were at breakfast the other day. We actually had a slice of smoked salmon. Ms Finch gets some now and then. Smuggled down from Orkney. She risks prison! I told Mark I won the salmon in a raffle at the food bank. He was too hungry to be inquisitive.

"If there's a war, will you fight?" I asked him. He looked up with a big grin.

"I'll be the first to volunteer." As if that would impress me!

"But we don't want to be fighting ourselves."

"It's the will of the people," he replied and finished off the salmon in one gulp.

The will of the people. It's swill. And the people eat it. People like my Mark. Heaven forbid.

I had my dream again last night. The one in which we're young and Mark saves me from drowning in The Serpentine. It wasn't weird like a normal dream. It was just the memory of the event itself. He dragged me onto the grass and gave me mouth to mouth. I spat the water into his mouth and when I opened my eyes he was spitting it out and grinning from ear to ear.

"You're alive. You're alive."

I didn't realise then it was the water from my lungs that he was spitting out. And when my sister finally realised I was the commotion and got out from the water and rushed over he just gave her his business card and left.

Business card in the age of smartphones. What a funny young man he was. Later I realised it was water from my lungs that he spat out and he just grinned. So happy that he'd saved me. And then I remembered his eyes. He was looking at me so fiercely I thought he was angry.

"You're the most beautiful girl in the world," he whispered. "And you're alive."

Christ. The dream ended when I texted him to say thanks. In the dream I was suddenly afraid he wouldn't reply. So scared I woke up!

And all that was only thanks to red tape (now cut) that forced him to do a first aid course for his work. If I were that drowning girl again, today, he wouldn't know how to save me. And before the private ambulance arrived it would be too late. And he would just be stood in the crowd who watched the drowning girl finish drowning on the grass. I'm shivering now.

What's happened to him over the years? What happened to my knight in shining armour? I blame the papers he reads. I blame the MSM. Why do bad men live so long? But it's more than that.

I miss Torremolinos.

I miss dodgy cocktails by the pool. I miss dancing with him to some funny ABBA tribute act in the hotel.

Hotels! OMG. I miss foreign hotels.

I miss full supermarket shelves.

I miss being proud to be British.

I was an innocent. I thought our country could only ever move forward. I didn't realise it could both change to reverse and get stuck in it. And accelerate! Everyone kept expecting us to wake up and stop. Get out of the car. Kick the tyres. Get back in and do a U-turn. But we never did. Bunsen getting back into 10 Downing Street was the shredding of the last piece of Great British sanity.

We've got Conga class on Tuesday night. Government orders. The last street party was "insufficiently patriotic". The Conga has been declared the national dance and we have to learn it. Fuck. Fuck. Fuck.

I miss getting on Sleazyjet.

I wish my brother would write to us.

I wish my husband wasn't an idiot.

Four

A Very British Potato Which Started A Civil War

"A is for Artichoke – The Artichoke, a prickly fruit which does not yield, unlike the turnip. Legislation is being prepared to outlaw The Artichoke.

The Artichoke receives a patriotic rating of 000, 000 ,000 out of a possible top score of 300, 034 974, 000"

- 'Fruits and Vegetables, and Their Correct Patriotic Ratings' by Prime Minister Mark A. French.

Mark My Words

"The fulcrum on which a great nation's destiny pivots can be a potato," read the first line in William Bunsen's latest editorial.

Yes!

"If the potato is British."

Yes again.

Mary was scrubbing our pot. We'd dined on Freedom Beans - the best baked beans sovereignty can buy.

"I miss our dishwasher," Mary said. "What are those bloody beans made of? It's like trying to scrub off cement. And we ate them cold!"

"Those beans are made of sovereignty," I reminded Mary.

She retrieved the tin.

"The ingredients says…" she paled.

"What?"

"It says the beans are made of sovereignty. There's nothing else listed except lots of little Union Flags. Like emojis."

"I did tell you."

Mary closed her eyes, inhaled deeply and carried on scrubbing.

"When you can't shit later Mark French, you know why."

Nice.

"Which vegetable is Great Britain's pivot?" I persisted.

"Why did the government take our dishwasher again?" she demanded, staring at me like it was my fault.

No. No. No.

"Operation Keep Fit is designed to get us exercising more and save the NHS."

Why didn't she just trust the government? Bunsen had thrown off the shackles of Brussels. Come on Mary. Keep up.

"There's rumours vacuum cleaners are going next," she huffed.

"We could all do with more exercise. No one was obese before foreigners started making domestic appliances."

"Are you exercising more?" she demanded.

"I did my push up this morning."

Mary looked unimpressed.

"We need to lessen our dependence on foreigners," I explained, and not for the first time. "If we don't have household electrical appliances, we don't need to import any parts."

"Oh, that's genius."

"Come on. The Downing Street broadcast starts soon."

A 10 Downing Street broadcast. The TV was on the right channel (you couldn't miss as the broadcast was on all the channels). The podium was being set up. Soon the flags would unfurl down the face of the grand old townhouse. William Bunsen was going to address the nation. Today. He was going to talk about the red, white and blue potato he discovered in an Uxbridge field. The op-ed was a primer. The discovery of the potato was a sign. A sign for Blighty to hold her nerve in the face of Continental intransigence, and domestic enemies.

"Which vegetable is Great Britain's fulcrum?" I tried again.

I waited for Mary to respond.

And waited.

She kept scrubbing.

"What vegetable?"

"You," she muttered.

She doubled down on scrubbing, banging the pot against the sink. What a racket. I worried the neighbours would hear.

Life was often like this, before the war. Domestic with little to suggest great change was coming. And even less to suggest I was the great change.

"Don't wear the pan out. It's our last one," I said, just to see her expression change.

"Don't test me Mark French," Mary hissed. "Not today."

What was I supposed to do with that?

"The fulcrum on which a great nation's destiny pivots can be a potato," I repeated Bunsen's opening line from this week's edition of 'Unotesticular'. If you had any doubt about God's nationality, you just had to open any copy. God was an Englishman.

Mary levelled her eyes at me.

"Or a fistfight between Bunsen and a blonde in a Greggs in a MOTO on the M4."

"What?"

"Didn't you hear about Bunsen getting into a public fight with his mistress?"

I stared, shook my Unotesticular for emphasis and said, "He's a visionary."

"So that excuses everything?"

"If it wasn't for Bunsen you'd still be under the yoke of Brussels."

Her face reddened.

"I have one pot. One pot. One pot." She lifted her one pot as if she was going to clout me.

I put my head down and carried on reading.

"The Divine Potato will be England's north star..."

Mary closed her eyes and stared into the sink.

"Do you think," she said, too quietly, "is there any chance…the faintest possibility that what you read day in and day out is horseshit?"

I blinked, Repeatedly. Mary couldn't have hurt me more if she'd slapped me.

"I don't read Unotesticular just for the articles. The covers are always cracking."

This week's edition had a cartoon of a giant potato head astride England. It had a pair of evenly set eyes underneath a long, rounded forehead, an expansion above the left eye gave it a raised eyebrow, a long bulge running down from the eyes made a nose, and a compression under this formed the smiling mouth. A side formation from the tuber's lower left was clearly a raised hand giving the "V for Victory" salute.

Churchill had returned in our hour of need and he was now a potato.

This was Great Britain's fulcrum. This was the vegetable on which our national destiny pivoted. Who cared how many pots we owned? Today our Prime Minister would introduce a magical vegetable to the world. Once the world recognised the power of what he held we'd have more pots than we could use.

"A divine potato has been born and raised in a loamy field in Uxbridge and South Ruislip," the editorial continued. "From the moment I discovered the potato, I knew this tuber would rewrite history, as it happened."

"You believe this is real?" Mary demanded, of the sink.

"There is no need to debate the vegetable's power. There is no need to argue over whose spirit has been reincarnated in Great Britain's hour of need. Now when Brussels comes to quibble over fish we need only..."

Mary set the pot to the side with a clang and put her face deep into the sink.

"Where are we going? What's the end game? What's the actual vision?" She said. I'm not sure if she expected the sink hole to answer.

It wasn't just Unotesticular. The discovery caused ecstasy in the newspapers as, *"England's soil declares its Sovereignty!"* – The Daily Parrot. William Bunsen was pictured front and centre holding the tuber like an ancient king with a holy orb. I keep a copy of that front page. It is framed and hangs behind my desk.

In the following weeks miracles would be attributed to the potato, and a debate begin at the highest levels on where to consecrate it. Westminster Abbey or Saint Paul's Cathedral? *

"Continentals can only wonder at us," I continued. "While their leaders waste their lives composing dirges of red tape to throttle growth, William Bunsen mines vegetative gold from our fertile soil. We are sure the Germans are scrabbling about in their barren wastes for a matching tuber."

To no avail.

What would their Chancellor say when our trade envoy

arrived without any of those boring paper folders Continentals weigh themselves down with? They would be lost for words when Winston the Divine Potato was placed on the table. Negotiate with that! Ha!

I imagined a frustrated peasant farmer in Bavaria unearthing what he believed was a black, red and yellow potato, only to discover he was holding a rock. Again. Ha!

"What are you doing with your life?" Mary asked, still in the sink.

"Excuse me?"

I wondered if I should leave her alone or try and help her out. Maybe her back had gone?

"Have you taken the bins out? It's Raylee's turn with the refuse truck this quarter."

"The No 10 broadcast starts any minute now…"

"Oh forget it. I'll take the bins out."

An empty threat, as everyone knew taking bins out was a boy's job.

I stood up and went over to put the kettle on. I decided a cup of tea would help. But there was no water in the kettle and Mary's head was still in the sink.

"Come on now love. That's enough. You're making the people who live in the sink anxious."

No reply.

"I want to put the kettle on."

"We only have one teabag," she said. That was more like it.

"Then we'll share it."

"It's used."

"Come on. Out of the sink."

She stood up. We were saved. I filled the kettle. But as I put it in the cradle and flicked the switch Mary put her head back into the sink.

"I'm just going to make us a nice cuppa and we'll watch

Bunsen and the potato together," I said.

"Get War Done," Mary muttered.

"What?"

"That's the slogan they'll use when they get us to fight each other. Get War Done."

I had to admit it was a perfect slogan for a civil war.

She stood up and smiled at me, patted me on the cheek.

"You're just the sort of idiot who's going to go and get into trouble."

And she walked into the living room and sat down in front of the television.

"We don't have any sugar," she called back. "And the supermarket was out of milk too."

"Black tea will do just fine," I said, and picked up our Strong Borders brand teabag from the saucer on the windowsill. It was still good for more one brew.

***

EXT.   BUCKINGHAM PALACE   DAY

Buckingham Palace's black gates are wreathed in Union Flags. Choir boys fan out around WILLIAM BUNSEN, who stands before the gates holding WINSTON THE HOLY POTATO. The choir is singing "God Save The King", ever so quietly.

WILLIAM BUNSEN
This enlarged stolon is as powerful as King Athelstan's little finger!

The potato shines red, white and blue. A dazzling display.

WILLIAM BUNSEN

Winston is performing his first miracle now as A&E waiting times plummet during this broadcast. The sick stay home to watch television and are healed miraculously.

***

"So bright are England's colours," I enthused. "I am blinded by the light."

"Blinded by something," Mary muttered, "but it's not light."

She was holding her mug of tea with both hands and sipping it like she was cold.

We watched as Bunsen carried the potato through the big gates. Inside the gate, The King's Guard stood to attention, and the Household Cavalry saluted with their swords. And the choir boys sung the national anthem in an endless loop. It was magic.

"No one does pomp like Blighty!" I whispered.

"You're just going to let me take the bins out then?" Mary. Mary. Quite contrary.

A narrator was talking now, as the PM carried the potato towards the front doors of the Palace.

"The French are green with envy, but they try to conceal it. But their newspapers gave them away."

The front pages of the foreign press flashed across the screen.

"Côlon élargi!" Le Figaro babbled incoherently in that brute tongue which I doubt even they understand. How else do you explain the popularity of the English language on the Continent? The paper had a cartoon of Bunsen pulling the potato out of his flabby bum.

The French were lucky to avoid a war. How easily they seem to have forgotten both Agincourt and Crecy.

"And how we saved them in all the world wars," I

muttered.

"Why are they showing the foreign front pages?" Mary wondered.

"So we know who are enemy is," I replied.

On the Palace balcony the King could be seen waiting for the Prime Minister and the potato.

"What's he going to do about half of Norfolk being on fire?" Mary wondered.

"Are you taking the bins out or not?" I demanded. I had taken as much of her negativity as I could.

"I thought he was going to announce Operation Extinguish Norwich when I heard about this broadcast, and here he is with a bloody potato we all have to pretend is magic."

England had not gone insane, but it seemed Mary had. If only I'd realised it at the time.

Every marriage has its moments of strain. That day was one of ours.

"He's drafted in the army to deal with the fires."

"There's no need to be grumpy," she replied.

"Once the army is drafted in the problem is solved."

Everyone knew that. **

"We will come together as a nation around this potato!" Bunsen continued, striding towards the doors of the Palace, a camera man running alongside him. "This is the best of British!"

The footage tumbled at that point and the camera rolled, before stopping staring fixedly at Bunsen's ankles.

"He's tripped the bloody camera man up!" Mary said.

"Why is it…" I asked, "that women always get distracted by trivialities?"

'Zadok The Priest' began playing over the action and a Spitfire flew overhead.

"That's not the original words," Mary noted. "They're

singing God Save The Tuber."

Of course they were!

I was moved to tears. How wonderful it must be to be Prime Minister of Great Britain. I admit I felt jealous. Imagine the look on the King's face when he held the potato for the first time.

"That Spitfire looks awfully wobbly!" Mary shouted and shook me by the arm.

"The pilot is just showing off."

The Spitfire trundled over the roof of Buckingham Palace and out of shot with a little puff of smoke.

"It's going to crash in the gardens."

"Don't be silly."

The broadcast froze momentarily and cut to a live feed of the field in Uxbridge where the Prime Minister and his son Montezuma found the potato.

***

EXT. UXBRIDGE FIELD MORNING

Sunlight pours between a break in the clouds. The green grass sparkles with dew. Rabbits hop about. A Union Flag butterfly fills the screen. Marvel at the butterfly. Slow motion flight. Red blurs into blue which blurs into white, and all transmute into gold.

Go high to see a circular visitor centre under construction. Carpenters work cheerfully. They wave to us with their tools in hand.

A tall ARCHITECT in a Hi-Viz hard hat holds up the building's plans. He points here and there in the satisfaction of his design. The architect is Cardinal Bogg – Secretary of

State for Sovereignty.

CARDINAL BOGG (close up)
Deus Annus.

***

Mary was laughing like a drain. Doubled over in her armchair clutching her ribs.

"Mary French!" I intervened, but she was lost in her mirth.

"What is so bloody funny?"

"He said annus!"

"He said anglus! Deus Anglus."

"Oh Mark, don't you believe the evidence of your eyes and ears anymore?"

Baffling woman.

I tried to move the conversation on.

"They're building a walkway so you can walk around the spot Winston was found and wonder."

Merchandise was also planned. Crockery and tea towels. Pencils and erasers. Tee shirts and socks. Key chains and the obligatory plastic medieval armour.

"I expect there's going to be a big bun fight over who gets to cut the ribbon to open the visitor centre!" I said, slapping my knee in delight.

"Cardinal Bogg is the architect," Mary said, but I wasn't paying any attention, I was seeing the future under construction.

"Do you really believe the potato is red, white and blue?" she asked. "And not just artificially stained?"

"When has His Majesty's Government ever lied to us?"

Mary gave me that look which says she wonders if I'm being serious or simply insane.

"I'll get the thermometer. Don't move." She rushed off towards the bathroom. While she was absent a message flashed up to say the ribbon on the visitor centre would be cut by the member of the Great British public deemed to be most patriotic. My heart stopped. What if that was me?

The show returned to Buckingham Palace and our glorious leaders.

"Miraculous thinking reaps its own harvest," Prime Minister William Bunsen reminded us. "Winston Churchill has returned in our hour of need. He has come to raise British Atlantis above the waves! Thanet will once more be that shining city in the distance Greeks can only witness from the leaky decks of their tired triremes as they bob about on the periphery of our sovereign waters."

Bunsen was showing Winston to the world. All could only churn emotively as our Prime Minister strode into the world's most famous palace with a dynamic stolon in his hands.

"Here, open wide," Mary said. She tried to put the thermometer into my mouth. I laughed her off. It was a good gag. I was feeling hot. Fired up with my patriotism.

What if it was me?

The Union Flag filled the screen next and text said a short documentary "filmed earlier in 10 Downing Street" would follow. If only we had known then that our day of pride and celebration was being watched by internal saboteurs who wished Winston the Holy Potato, and all of us, terrible harm.

"Let's have a crumpet," Mary said. "You'll feel better if you eat something. I can't believe that whole tin of beans only had half a dozen in it. And I'm famished."

A bit of crumpet. How wonderfully British.

***

INT. 10 DOWNING STREET DAY

OVER BLACK

"A world beating film in which your Prime Minister talks to you about his discovery of Winston - The Holiest of Potatoes, brought to you by The Office of the Prime Minister, in partnership with Windsor Wines of Kent."

WILLIAM BUNSEN sits at a large desk with oak twist legs. Soft lit, but the hand holding WINSTON - THE HOLY POTATO, glows with heavenly power. RED. WHITE. BLUE. The light pulsates like a beating heart. Light bathes BUNSEN'S face. It splashes on the walls.

WILLIAM BUNSEN

We few. We happy few. We band of tubers...

HENRY V comes into view behind BUNSEN and fades into WINSTON CHURCHILL who fades into MARGARET THATCHER.

Another hand, a feminine hand, rests on BUNSEN'S shoulder. The WOMAN is in shadow, but we discern the shape of her swollen belly as she cradles the bump. Light from WINSTON flashes across her abdomen.

NARRATOR

Prime Minister William Bunsen and First Lady Bunty Bunsen have a message for you.

BUNTY BUNSEN

Your Prime Minister is not just my unborn child's father.

He is the future's father.

WILLIAM BUNSEN
Give me your tired, your poor,
Your huddled masses yearning to breathe free, The wretched refuse of EU red tape, Send these, the homeless, regulation-tost to me, I lift my tuber beside the sovereign door.

AD BREAK.

EXT. KENT MORNING

Row after row of grape vines. The SUN rises in a rush. It floods rolling fields with the light of a new day. SCHOOL AND PENSION AGE WORKERS tend the vines happily. Smiling faces. Baskets fill with England's harvest.

ONE MAN is clearly in charge. LORD DAVID DAVID. A big, cheerful man with a gout filled face. He is dressed exactly like JOHN BULL. The camera roves high over him and then drops to race along a line of vines to where he stands.

LORD DAVID DAVID faces the camera holding an unopened bottle labelled "ENGLISH CHAMPAGNE - THE WINE THE FRENCH CAN'T OPEN".

LORD DAVID DAVID shakes the bottle vigorously and pops the cork. A bright spray of wine explodes before his laughing face. RAINBOWS. LAUGHTER. VICTORY.

LORD DAVID DAVID
I love the smell of sulphur in the morning.

TEXT : *"Windsor Wines of Kent – Don't be caught drinking anything else..."*

AD BREAK ENDS.

INT. 10 DOWNING STREET DAY

THE UNION FLAG fills the screen. The flag fades and THE BUNSENS are there, marvelling at WINSTON THE DIVINE POTATO.

The Dambusters theme tune plays.

***

"Where's the butter?" Mary called from the kitchen. "And what happened to our butter knives!"

Bloody hell!

I paused the broadcast and rose huffing. In a long marriage it's possible to express impatience without saying anything. I chose an excellent moment. The camera zoomed in on Winston again and he blazed from the screen with a mystic light.

Our Potato, who aren't in Heaven, hallowed be they dome...

The television unpaused itself and it fast forwarded in a blinding rush of imagery.

"Why are you fast forwarding the show?" Mary asked.

"I'm not."

"They've stuffed up the editing again."

"I'm sure it's just to get our attention."

***

INT. 10 DOWNING STREET DAY

WILLIAM BUNSEN holds WINSTON aloft.

WILLIAM BUNSEN

Kneel before Winston! Pay homage to your saviour!

BUNTY BUNSEN lifts the hem of her skirt and kneels before WILLIAM BUNSEN and WINSTON THE DIVINE POTATO. Light bathes her. WILLIAM BUNSEN lays a hand on her head.

***

Mary just stood there in the kitchen doorway with the crumpet in her hand.

"Is he drunk?" she asked. "Again?"

"High on sovereignty," I said. "It's perfectly natural."

"High on his own supply," she chuckled.

"Bow before the Holy Potato!" Bunsen shouted from the television. "A country that produces both Peppa Pig and a Union Flag legume will enjoy a glorious future. You just have to believe!"

"What have you done with the butter knives?"

"To interrupt a live broadcast from the Prime Minister is almost treason," I replied. I was mad now. This was a moment in history people would look back on and ask, "Where were you the day Bunsen held up Winston for the world to see?"

"How can you not see how important this is? You're lucky no one can hear you."

Her outbursts made me nervous. I didn't want anything to happen to her.

"Well, it's not like they know what we're doing in the privacy of our own home."

Mary glanced nervously behind, out of the kitchen window. We both listened for a few seconds.

"We're being silly," she said and went to look out of the kitchen window. "There's nothing to worry about. Nothing at all."

I paused the broadcast.

"Where's my butter knives?" she said to the window.

"There's nobody out there."

I hit play on Bunsen. The imagery blurred again. When it cleared the Prime Minister was walking with his infant son in a field. The sun setting on the horizon.

***

EXT. FIELD AFTERNOON

WILLIAM BUNSEN, MONTEZUMA BUNSEN and RENTAL (DOG) walk across the greenest field England has ever produced. Father and son hold hands. BUNSEN keeps the boy from stumbling. RENTAL races about in circles.

Overhead are dark clouds.

WILLIAM BUNSEN

I was walking with Monty and Rental when we discovered Winston.

The happy trio continue their journey through the field.

WILLIAM BUNSEN

Bunty was in seclusion awaiting the birth of our first child together.

CUT TO :

INT. BEDROOM DAY

BUNTY BUNSEN sits in an armchair knitting. Her stomach is huge. It can't be long.

BUNTY (SINGING)
All things bright and beautiful,
All creatures great and small,
All things wise and wonderful,
T'was Bunsen made them all…

BUNTY stops singing. She presses her knitting into her breast.

BUNTY
It's time…

The door opens and a CRACK TEAM OF NHS BRANDED MEDICS enter the room.

BUNTY
If William Bunsen hadn't saved the NHS where would I be now?

EXT. FIELD DAY

THE NATIONAL ANTHEM plays quietly in the background. WILLIAM BUNSEN, MONTEZUMA BUNSEN and RENTAL stare at a POTATO PLANT. The plant shines red, white and blue.

MONTEZUMA
Look father! A po-ta-to plant!

WILLIAM BUNSEN
I planted this potato myself the day Great Britain broke free.

WILLIAM BUNSEN
Winston Churchill visited me in a dream and said I must come to this field and sow.

The dark clouds part. Sunlight falls from a god spray onto the plant. Its leaves turn to gold.

MONTEZUMA
What type of po-ta-to is this?

WILLIAM BUNSEN
A magic potato plant Monty. An English potato plant.

MONTEZUMA
A King Edward po-ta-to plant?

MONTEZUMA releases WILLIAM'S hand and totters to the plant.

MONTEZUMA grips the potato plant by the stem and pulls it from the blessed soil with one mighty heave.

WINSTON THE DIVINE POTATO breathes above ground for the first time.

MONTEZUMA
This is Winston!

***

"Not a Maris Piper or some other Euro trash!" I exulted. "A King Edward! A very British potato! Ha!"

Monty gazed at his father with an intensity never seen in a child's face.

"This...miracle...Pappa! Miracle. It is Union Flag pattern."

Bunsen fell to his knees and pulled the potato and the boy into a tight embrace.

"Monty, you know Deus Anglus?"

"Of course Pappa."

"This potato is a sign from God."

Bunsen and Monty looked to the heavens. The dark clouds were racing for the horizon. The first star was shining.

"This potato will be a symbol of the divine will of the people from this day and for one thousand years to come."

'Land of Hope and Glory' took over as the national anthem faded out.

We watched as Winston was carried home by father and son. The scene merged into a war memorial surrounded by poppies, like you see in every town and village in the country.

"It's a holy trinity," I declared. "Father and son..."

"Who's the holy ghost?" Mary demanded.

"Winston."

She looked amazed. Then shook her head.

"The British bulldog himself had arrived to be our shield and staff in a time of unforeseeable turmoil."

"Where will Winston live papa?"

"He will come home with us. He will tour the country. He will stun the world!"

"He should live in the Tower of London."

"He will Monty. He will. After he meets the King."
"Magic."

*The list of miracles can be found in Appendix B.
** The list problems the army was drafted in to solve that summer can be found in Appendix C.

Five

The Future Is Past - Part One

"P is for Plum – Plum, plum, plum. Not to be confused with plumb. Plum is a homophone and thus suspicious but may be consumed after stewing."

For this reason, The Plum receives a patriotic rating of 000, 000 000, 084 out of a possible top score of 300, 034 974, 000.

- 'Fruits and Vegetables, and Their Correct Patriotic Ratings' by Prime Minister Mark A. French.

Cyclops – A Local Boy

"I am Private Carrot," the skinny man with red hair said. "I am from the Ministry of The Future."

Sofie yawned and Private Carrot frowned at her. He looked really angry when she put her head on her desk!

"Easy champ," Mr Mann, our teacher, said, "Sofie suffers from low blood pressure."

"That's not very patriotic, is it?" Private Carrot replied.

It goes without saying that Mr Mann laughed at him like he wanted to have his guts for garters. Private Carrot tried to stare Mr Mann out but he couldn't so he looked back at Sofie.

"Strewth," Mr Mann said. He shook his head while

smiling.

Sofie was really, really, really pale. I could see by the way her lips were moving she was counting her breaths. She was looking at me. She was scared. Mr Mann taught Sofie to stand up slowly when she feels faint. If she can. But he will notice if she doesn't, and he WILL help her. I waved my hand up and down under my desk. Stand up Sofie!

Ms Clench, the headmistress, doesn't like Sofie having low blood pressure. She says it distracts the class and is an unnecessary burden.

We don't have a school nurse anymore because nurses have "proper work to do to clear the NHS backlog caused by Gordon Brown". I don't know who he is. All I know is my Mum said he ran away to Orkney and the government are trying to catch him because he tried to undermine Britain by talking to Continentals. But Orkney has gone away from the UK and no one from the government can go there because the people who live there have shotguns.

The Prime Minister sent someone there in a helicopter because he was too busy to go himself and the Orknish stood on the helicopter pad with their guns. The helicopter had to go away.

"Orkney will return to heel," the Prime Minister told everyone from his big desk. After that happened. "But first we will try negotiations. We will starve them out."

No more rations for Orkney. The news said that.

My Mum says that's stupid because Orkney has a lot of farms and more food than we do. And lots of foreign ships visit it and the government can't stop them because it has all the navy in The Channel stopping the French stealing our fish. Also there's lots of navy ships in The Irish Sea to stop the Welsh from leaving. The Welsh are always leaving for Ireland. I asked Mum why and she grinned and said, "It's not for the weather." Then she licked her lips and rubbed her belly. "It's because the food in Ireland has a sell by date."

"Eyes front!" Private Carrot shouted.

Sofie lifted her head and stood up very slowly.

"Bunting. Bunting. Bunting," Private Carrot said next. He was trying to ignore Sofie now. "Where I am taking you today children you will learn how to serve your country."

Mr Mann took a bag of jellybeans out of his pocket and walked over to Sofie. He gave them to her. It goes without saying that Private Carrot stopped talking and glared at Mr Mann's back. But our teacher is from Australia and laughs at everyone from the government.

Australia sends us lamb. The Prime Minister says we have a special relationship.

Mr Mann went back to stand in the corner and waved for Private Carrot to continue.

"Your country needs you to be the best of British," Private Carrot said.

Ms Clench came into the room then and asked Private Carrot if he needed anything?

"All under control, thank you Ms Clench," Private Carrot lied. He couldn't control a fart.

It goes without saying that Ms Clench gave Mr Mann a really, really, really long look. He blew her a kiss and she blushed. Then she left. They aren't always friends.

"Galahs like you can't touch me," Mr Mann told her one day when she was mad at him.

"I don't care what your connections are," Ms Clench replied, "this is my school."

I heard them because they were outside the boys' toilets.

"Don't you have some puppies to drown?" Mr Mann said next.

"One day," Ms Clench said. "One day."

"If you want to ask me out just come out and say it," Mr Mann said next. Ms Clench went then. I heard her heels click clacking up the hall.

"How are you doing in there Cyclops?" Mr Mann called in to the toilet.

"Okay."

"How's the eye kiddo?"

I was in the toilet because my missing eye was hurting. Sometimes it throbs. I lost it because a cat scratched me when I was a baby because I grabbed a chicken drumstick it had grabbed. We waited for two days before a doctor could see me and the eye was all pussy and the doctors had to remove it before everything else in me got pussy.

I don't remember that because I was a baby.

Mum tells me the story and sometimes she looks really, really, really angry.

Mum says I should put cold water on the socket when it hurts. One time the whole thing just opened up again and more pus came out! I remember that. We were in class learning how English is the best language. Mum got Mrs French to sew my eye back up because she can sew up anything. Mr French let them splash the last of his brandy on my eye. Some of the brandy got into my mouth and it felt like my mouth was burning.

My old teacher wouldn't let me go to the toilet to put cold water on my eye but Mr Mann does.

"Cyclops? How's the eye?"

"Better." I left the toilet.

Mr Mann then told me I can't tell anyone he has connections because "it's a condition of my top secret mission to observe the living standards of children in Britain. Drowning Street only agreed to it if it was a secret. Can you keep a secret kiddo?"

I haven't told anyone. My Mum thinks Mr Mann must be able to laugh at people from the government because he's Australian and "colonials don't care about authority and refused to put Charles on their money to prove it."

Our money has Bunsen on it.

I think Mum likes him. But she's waiting for my Dad to come back from the secret work he's doing for government. It goes without saying that Reggie said my Dad is an enemy of the people and he's in a prison camp picking soft fruit. Reggie is a dickwad. I'm not supposed to say dickwad to anyone. My Dad isn't a criminal. He's a journalist.

I want to tell Mum that Mr Mann is top secret but I promised I wouldn't.

"Loose lips sink ships," he said.

I'm confused. I want to tell her. She wouldn't tell anyone. She doesn't have any friends to tell since my Dad went on his mission. Ever since he left she spends all day listening to her little digital radio. "It's our big secret," she reminds me over and over. "If anyone catches us listening to 'Free Britain' you'll be taken away."

'Free Britain' broadcasts from France, which is the worst place anyone can broadcast from.

Private Carrot held up a string of Union Flag bunting. He was wearing khaki shorts and his knees were like balls in the middle of two sticks. He even had red hair on his legs! Which is suspicious. People from Scotland have red hair and can't be trusted. I think Private Carrot tries extra hard to be patriotic so he's safe. The back of his left leg has a big piece missing from it. The scar was shiny.

"And what is your country called children?" Private Carrot asked us.

"Great Britain," we all said it together, as we had been taught to do by our last teacher. That was Ms Formaldehyde. She had to stop being our teacher and become Raylee's pharmacist because every town in Britain has a pharmacist. It's the law. Pharmacists can do things that doctors do like give you medicine and sell you bandages.

When Private Carrot held up the bunting Mr Mann whistled.

Sofie was eating the jellybeans. But she wouldn't eat them all. She would save some for me and Barney. Barney only has one ear. He rubs the place where the one ear isn't all the time. Mr Mann was smiling at Private Carrot again. Private Carrot frowned at him.

"I could have you court-martialled," Private Carrot hissed at him. I've never heard Mr Mann laugh so hard.

"Have you taught the children to say Grate or Great Britain?" Private Carrot demanded.

The bell went for lunch.

I was really, really, really hungry. I thought I was going to faint. But I don't have low blood pressure so I couldn't stand up.

Mr Mann just shook his head.

"Let's get this farce over with. If the kids don't eat they'll start dropping like ten pins."

I don't know why he said ten pins. There's fifty of us in my class.

"Bunting. Bunting. Bunting," Private Carrot said it again. Barney started to cry. Reggie vomited.

"That's enough," Mr Mann said. "We can finish this bloody farce after lunch."

For lunch I had two pieces of bread and a piece of cucumber.

"The children will eat at their desks," Private Carrot said.

Mr Mann nodded. I think it's because if he doesn't see us eat he worries about us. He went to the cupboard and took out a big bag he keeps there. Today it had SAUSAGES in it. They were in little foil packets with a kangaroo on them. Mr Mann gave all of us one each.

"Get some protein in you kids," he said. Then he threw

one at Private Carrot who tried to catch it but it fell to the carpet.

"You could use some too you scrawny bastard," he grinned at Private Carrot.

Private Carrot just stared at it on the floor. His face was really red now. Barney left his desk and picked it up and handed it to him. He wouldn't take it.

"You eat it Barney," Mr Mann said.

Mr Carrot snatched it from Barney who smiled at him and went back to his seat.

After lunch we all had to line up to use the toilets. That took ages because the water wasn't working. Then the cleaner brought water in buckets from the hose pipe in the school yard.

"Single file!" Private Carrot shouted. "Left. Right. Left. Right."

We marched out of the school to the public library.

It goes without saying that Private Carrot didn't like how we marched and Mr Mann just laughed.

"You're not going to get much bunting made carrying on like this," Mr Mann told Private Carrot.

I'm not sure why he let Private Carrot march us into town. I think it's because as a reward for factory work you get a meal IF you do good work. We were going to work in the old library which has been converted to a place to make Union Flag bunting.

Libraries are the future of Great British manufacturing. William Bunsen says they'll be the "nurseries of the second industrial revolution".

When we got to the door there was scaffolding up and some men were taking down the sign that said "Library" and putting up one that said "For King and Country" with lots of Union Flags painted around it. Other men were taking the books out of the library in wheelbarrows and dumping them in a big pile on the pavement.

Private Carrot told us to "Halt" and went over to one of the wheelbarrow men.

"Are the sewing machines ready?" he asked.

"What? We've only just started refitting the building," the wheelbarrow man said. He was an old man with a bald head and a smudgy tattoo of an eagle on his forearm.

"We will wait," Private Carrot said.

It's the only time I saw Mr Mann looking unhappy. He was at the book pile picking up as many books as he could carry.

"They're all geography and foreign languages," he said, to no one. "Savages."

"That's government property!" Private Carrot shouted at him. "Put it down."

"I'm taking as many books as I can carry. Kids, get over here and grab some. We'll take them back to school."

"These books are being requisitioned for the Great British Home Heating Initiative," Private Carrot was trembling. "Put them down now."

"Shove off or I'll deck ya," Mr Mann shouted back at him. He dropped the books and bunched up his fists.

"You petty little nationalists have ruined this fucking country. Starving kids. An international pariah state. No national health service. Your navy impounded by the Yanks and Spanish at Gibraltar. The Orkneys have fucking seceded and made Gordon Brown president! The Welsh are half out the door. What the hell do you think is next?"

Just then a black van pulled up and lots and lots and lots of policemen got out. The van had 'Go Home Office' written on the side of it.

"You want some?" Mr Mann shouted at the policemen. "Come on! You fucking pussies."

Just then Mrs French ran into the middle of everything

and grabbed Mr Mann by the arm.

"Would you help me love?" she said.

"What?" he turned to her. "Get back Mrs French. I'm going to punch the lights out of some fash."

"Help me lovely," she was staring at him really strongly. "My husband isn't well and I need you to help me get him home."

Mr French was standing on the edge of everything looking totally confused!

"What?" he said.

"He's having trouble walking."

Mrs French started to tug on Mr Mann's arm and suddenly he deflated. He let her lead him away. He kept looking back at Private Carrot, who was hiding behind one of the wheelbarrow men. He was snarling like a wolf at him. But he took one of Mr French's arms and Mrs French took the other and they led Mr French away.

We didn't see Mr Mann for a week. We didn't have a substitute teacher because there was a staffing crisis caused by "layabouts waiting for handouts". The Army was supposed to come and teach us, but they were too busy with a burst sewage main, and so we had to teach ourselves.

As Mr Mann left Sofie fainted. Properly! She hit the deck. Jellybeans went everywhere. One of the wheelbarrow men shouted "Sofie!" and we realised it was her uncle. He ran over and picked her up and put her in his wheelbarrow and wheeled her away. The policemen picked up the jellybeans and ate them.

It goes without saying Private Carrot marched us back to school and we didn't make any bunting that day.

Six

Operation : Nothing Has Changed

"G is for Garlic. Leave off with that French nonsense. Garlic is a disc race."

For this reason, The Garlic receives a negative patriotic rating of - 101, 101 101, 101 out of a possible top score of + 300, 034 974, 000.

- 'Fruits and Vegetables, and Their Correct Patriotic Ratings' by Prime Minister Mark A. French.

Mark My Words

"Exactly when does Bunsen's war against us start?" Mary asked me, as I peeled the potato we grew ourselves in a large terracotta pot. She snorted. "Actually, it started in 2016. When does it end?"

She was talking gibberish. I wondered if she was menopausal.

The potato pot is now exhibited at the British Museum, but from time to time it tours the shires, along with other relics of my sacred struggle. I have plans to return the pot to my house in Raylee. Once the removal of the double glazing and central heating is completed, and traditional single pane windows and coal fires restored.

Mary arranged the potato peelings on a tray. We were

making crisps.

Crisp Making For Britain was now a staple of our domestic activities, ever since Walkers failed to understand they needed Raylee more than Raylee needed them.

The fact Gary Lineker had allied with the Orkney secessionists, only underscored the patriotic need to make one's own crips.

Radio 4 was playing quietly in the background.

"The time is four pm. A news briefing will follow shortly to reassure you that Great Britain is exceptional. But first, Nothing Has Changed, presented by the Under Secretary of State for Pragmatism and Rationing..."

'Nothing Has Changed' is a world beating, weekly programme presented by a junior minister, or a minor celebrity. They told us how to manage the decline in our standard of living in the face of the global challenges impacting all countries.

Two weeks ago home crisp making was the subject. The Clandestine Channel Threat Commander told us how he, *"never misses Walkers crisps because I make better crisps from my own potato peelings."*

"To make ready salted crisps," he had enthused, *"leave a bucket of great British seawater out to dehydrate in the sun. You then scrape the salt off the base of the bucket and sprinkle it on your crisps."*

The salt was sterile so you didn't have to worry about sewage remnants in the water.

"Good thing we decided to grow our own potato!" Mary exclaimed. She held up her index finger and mouthed "One potato".

"Blitz Spirit!" I replied.

"No bloody choice," she responded. A comment on Continental aggression.

This week the show was about how to turn one sock into

two.

"There is no need to fret when you lose a sock. Although temporary supply chain shortages have impacted the supply of socks and other smalls, with a bit of pluck and a can do attitude you can make one sock into two…"

"Well? When do we stop fighting ourselves?"

It was a strange question. The law to organise local, volunteer, patriotic militias was still being debated in Parliament. The actual fighting hadn't started, just the 10 Downing Street announcement that we were going to defeat ourselves. The Opposition was to blame for the delay. They were attempting to amend the militia legislation to include a new public holiday celebrating "The plucky fighting spirit of Great Britons at home".

"Well?"

I handed Mary another peeling.

"This is the best one yet," I said. "It's all about the angle you peel."

Bunsen was resisting the amendment, not because he didn't agree with it, but because he wanted to be sure the voters knew the law had cross party backing. Any law, no matter how surprising, can be digested by voters if both major parties agree on the principle in public. It was basic governance. Do not confuse the electorate, they have better things to be doing with their time, like organising to repair potholes. Additionally, Bunsen was on a glamping holiday in the Caribbean.

"We have to hand this baking tray in tomorrow," I said.

"Why?"

"You know why."

"I want you to tell me."

She was holding the tray. Her knuckles were white.

"For the Bridge to America. If we don't contribute something people will say we're not patriotic."

"Oh."

(The Bridge to America was never built after a feasibility study costing £350m revealed America was too far away.*)

She closed her eyes and inhaled, held her breath for several seconds, and then exhaled long and slow. Then she repeated the breathing.

"Are you okay?" I asked.

She just kept breathing.

"I had hoped when we dug up our harvest our potato would look like Winston Churchill, or maybe Margaret Thatcher, or even William Bunsen," I said.

"Maybe we should call in the army," she muttered, and smirked.

Her question about the war didn't make sense to me. Bunsen had announced we were going to war against ourselves, but it was not by timetable.

"Well?" Again!

"Get Crisps Done," I said.

"Mark (inhale). French (exhale)."

No matter how I turned our potato, this way and that, it just looked like a potato. It was very disappointing. We had obeyed all the laws of potato growing and I had spent many hours staring at the pot imagining stolon Margaret Thatcher taking shape inside. You can imagine, I was not pleased, when later that week I popped into the pharmacy to pick up our ration of olive oil only to see a potato that looked vaguely like Henry VIII on display. Ms Formaldehyde was making a show of preparing B12 prescriptions, but I saw the way she kept glancing up to see if I'd noticed Henry VIII. I made no mention of it. It's not British to show off.

"I'm growing his wives now. Starting with Anne," she boasted.

"Never mind," Mary opened her eyes and smiled. "If our potato looked like a deity you would have wanted to take it on a tour of the town and we wouldn't have any crisps."

"Imagine what a Thatcher stolon would do for Raylee?" I said, with more heat than I anticipated. "If we grew a potato that looked like Margaret Thatcher, people would flock from miles around. The government might even designate Raylee a site of national importance. We'd get additional levelling up funding too. We might even get funding to install a second pillory or a ducking stool."

I handed her another peeling and she laid it out on the tray. She was looking at me in the weirdest way.

"And who would go on the ducking stool? Maybe they should bring wife sales back."

"I wouldn't sell you for all the tea in Yorkshire," I said.

We worked in silence for a few minutes. I imagined being invited to 10 Downing Street to show Prime Minister Bunsen our Margaret. Newspaper cameras flashed and reporters shouted out, "Mark French! Mark French! How did you feel when you first held the reincarnation of Saint Margaret in your hands?"

Mary thought about whatever it is women think about.

"Well?" she asked again, "When will the war end? When will Britain be normal again?"

I didn't know what she meant. I still don't.

"What on earth do you mean? We've freed ourselves from the yoke of foreign tyranny. No one can tell us what to do anymore with water treatment and maximum weekly working hours. We can have as little or as much red tape as we like. No more punishment beatings from the Continent. Great Britons are once more ruled by the right sort of chaps without some bleating Frank banging on about human slavery. We are free. We have returned to our natural state."

"You mean the dismantling of the welfare state? The destruction of the post-war settlement?"

I wondered if she had a fever. Maybe she was premenopausal?

"Where are you getting all this from?" I demanded. I felt my face go hot. To think my own wife didn't understand exactly what was signified the day the Union Flag was lowered in Brussels for the last time. Liberated from the row of indentured idiot rags that lined up for the regulatory gibbet without a second thought.

"Don't you dare," she hissed. Her mouth was tight. Her pupils wide. "What happened to the man who saved me that day in the Serpentine?"

This was a low blow. But I didn't like seeing her so worked up. I loved her.

"The war against ourselves will take time," I said at last, reaching inside to my calm place. Imagining the roar of a Spitfire's engine overhead. "I may have to go away and fight."

"If London secedes? Like Orkney?"

I noticed movement outside.

"We should burn London to the ground and start again!" I shouted.

We both waited to see if whoever it was would knock. But they just seemed to pause for a few seconds and walk away.

"...once the sock is cut into equal halves simply take some spare thread. If you don't have thread, just pop out into the garden and select some suitable lengths of ivy vine..."

I handed Mary the last peeling and wrapped up the potato in clingfilm to stop it going brown. When the electric came back on this evening we would boil it and mash it.

"But Bunsen announced on the tele weeks ago that we were now at war with ourselves. I thought we would have made some progress by now."

I wondered sometimes how much attention she paid to current affairs. If any, at all. We'd been in a cold war against ourselves since 2016. The Prime Minister had just formalised it. Now it was up to our sovereign parliament to rubberstamp it.

"To be fair," I conceded, "he's like most Prime Ministers in the sense he makes a big policy announcement and then works out the details later. But the direction of travel has been obvious for years. We just need the Opposition to stop standing in the way of progress."

"Who else did that? Made policy announcements without working out the details?"

"Churchill."

"What?"

"He said we were going to defeat the Nazis. We did. It took time though. It'll take time to defeat ourselves."

She frowned at me, then blew a raspberry.

"Are you feeling alright?"

"When you think we used to be able to just buy Walkers crisps at the off licence…," she shook her head.

"And?"

"I miss crisps in packets."

What had been a pleasant domestic experience was suddenly a test of faith.

"You're a stray sheep," I hit back.

"Baaa."

"Walkers had a choice. Recognise they needed us more than we need them or leave the Great British market."

We had peeled our potato with the curtains drawn and the doors firmly shut. Most of the neighbours had not been so lucky with Operation Home Harvest. I was baffled why she was making such a fuss of our local triumph.

"We should share the crisps with the neighbours," she said.

"In exchange for what?"

"To be neighbourly. Besides, we're not at war with the Angles next door. Or the Jutes across the close."

"How do you know? Any of them could be traitors."

She shrugged. "They've a teenage son."

"And?"

"Which side is he expected to fight on?"

"I expect we'll find out once the powers that be have finished working out the details."

"They're not going to send him to Orkney are they? I heard talk of a mobilisation."

"We don't need to talk about the Scottish problem. Bunsen will get it done."

"Why don't we talk about it? Is it like the Scottish play?"

She chuckled. I don't know why.

There was no time to lose. I nodded at the cooker and Mrs French opened the door. I slid the tray of peelings in. We both pulled up a chair to watch and wait.

"This will teach the Germans that Britons are best at self-denial," I commented.

"Home made crisps and self denial for lunch. Not even a little sausage. What I wouldn't give for a little sausage right now."

"Mrs French!" I grinned.

She squeezed my cheek, and for a moment, I wondered how she'd cope when I left. It was obvious I'd have to leave. When all others can't grow a potato but you can, you're meant for greater things.

"Did you see that story about Greggs?" she asked, puncturing the mystical mood again.

"No," I lied.

"Apparently Bunsen was in a punch up at the Heston services. The day he left to go on holiday."

I said nothing. I concentrated harder on the oven door.

"It's on the M4. He was going to Heathrow with several great big suitcases."

I took the dish cloth and rubbed at the oven's glass door.

"I heard about it from Cyclops' mum. She was doing litter picking service at the services and she said a black Audi TT pulled in to the kerb. There was a big fat blonde man at the wheel and a young blonde woman in the passenger seat. She said they were arguing."

"It can't have been the Prime Minister."

"Cyclops' mum says the blonde girl got out of the car screaming about being pregnant and the man was all red faced and shouting it wasn't his child. Next thing she pulls out a piece of paper she says proves it and they're rolling about the pavement. Cyclops' mum says the girl was pulling his hair and it came off in her hand. You wear a fucking wig? You old fraud!" the girl screamed and then they were fighting over the wig."

What a load of nonsense.

"Apparently a lot of police arrived and separated them. But the girl grabbed one of the bulging suitcases out of the car and tried to run, tripped and dropped it. Cyclops' mum says it fell open and money started going everywhere in the wind. Actual physical money. Not ration slips."

I stood up and left the room. Mary had ruined making crisps.

"Do you think they were going to Heathrow?" she shouted after me. "Do you think Bunsen is going to do a runner?"

I kept going upstairs. It couldn't have been William Bunsen. He only ever left 10 Downing Street in hi-vis.

I lay down on our bed and traced the hairline cracks in the ceiling with my eyes. The bedroom light was on. We must have forgotten to flick the switch when the electric went off earlier. The cracks always looked like a river delta to me. I imagined myself in a canoe.

"Cyclops' mum gave me one of the bank notes as proof," Mary said from the doorway.

I covered my ears with my hands and closed my eyes.
"It's a five hundred and it's got the King on it."
I heard her clomp over the floorboards.
"I'm not leaving until you look at it."
But just then the light went off.
"The bastards!" Mary shouted. "They've cut the electric early. They've ruined our crisps."
"This is what you get for seditious talk," I hissed, still with my eyes closed.
"Don't be stupid," she replied. "It's not like they can hear us."

*Appendix D – Bridges That Were Never Built But Would Have Been Great

Seven

The Faceless Man

"C is also for Celery – Celery, a pert vegetable, when fresh. Due to unexpected increases in demand, limp celery is the patriot's choice.

For these reasons Celery receives a patriotic rating of 205, 205 205, 025 out of a possible top score of 300, 034 974, 000. Grip it in private."

- 'Fruits and Vegetables, and Their Correct Patriotic Ratings' by Prime Minister Mark A. French.

Mark My Words

The white face mask was an innovation in Great Britain's political discourse.

"The British people have tired of seeing The Official Opposition Leader, Mr Sucof Groop, in any context," Prime Minister Bunsen told the Deputy Political Editor of The Daily Parrot, who duly repeated it in a front page editorial. "It is time Groop wore a mask in Parliament."

"The British people have tired of seeing The Official Opposition Leader in any context!" The editorial shouted with a photo of Groop looking daft, falling over a broken cobblestone and spilling a bag of potatoes, frozen in mid-fall. Tucked away in a corner on the same front page was a photo of Felixstowe Food Bank with the header "Closed Due To Unexpected Potato Shortage".

"They broke that cobblestone to get the photo," Mary observed.

"Why would they do that?"

"I don't believe Groop doesn't know the pavement outside his own house. It's a set-up to make him look daft."

If it was it was clever politics. I decided to agree with Mary, without telling her, but a smile of admiration gave me away.

After The Daily Parrot squawked the BBC (soon to be renamed The Great British Patriotic Broadcasting Corporation) offered Groop an interview on the Today programme (soon to be renamed Yesterday) with a notoriously soft interviewer.

"Good Morning," Groop began confidently, at 08:10.

"Why do you think the British people have tired of seeing you in any context?" the interviewer demanded. He sounded furious. Righteous anger on behalf of the people.

"I don't believe they have," Groop was wrongfooted.

"You deny the British people have tired of seeing you in any context?" The interviewer was seething.

There was a lengthy pause.

"I was invited on to talk about my party's proposal to introduce charges for GPs to see themselves, in order to fund appointments for nurses to see GPs," Groop stated. You could just hear his thin pressed lips.

"Answer the question," the interviewer demanded.

"Ask me a question worth answering and I will," Groop retorted, cementing his reputation for being evasive.

But everyone still needed Groop to play his part in the raucous theatre of Westminster. Just as his predecessors, since 2010, had done their jobs loyally by agreeing with the biggest idea of the natural party of government.

I would sit and watch the live feed of Parliament and clap my hands.

"Why don't you have the volume on?" Mary would ask, peering in from the kitchen.

"I'm teaching myself lip reading," I replied. It was true. I hadn't decided if I was going to volunteer for an espionage wing in the war against ourselves, or the infantry. "So I can tell what people are saying in the queue at the food bank."

She stared at me like I had re-invented the square and told her it was the wheel.

"You're not serious?"

"Stop distracting me. The Speaker is about to announce the vote."

"He's just cleaning his teeth," she said. Which he was.

The Continentals knew who was winning now. I was certain privately their voters wanted their opposition leaders masked too.

"*Die Briten Sind Total Bescheuert*!" - applauded Der Spiegel. This was translated into English, for the public's benefit, as "The British Are World Leaders!".

"*Los británicos están totalmente locos*!" – El Mundo writhed by its empty seas. Which was read out to English primary school classes as "The British show us we're insane!"

"*Les Britanniques sont complètement idiots*!" Le Monde could only weep. It was not translated, because we know French is an inferior language and native-born English speakers will not parley with it.

We could not help Continentals anymore. We saved them in two world wars, and one world cup and they had been too proud to show obeisance.

***

INT. HOUSE OF COMMONS ANYTIME

THE SPEAKER chews on a lamb chop. He's like the runt of the litter with free reign at the food bowl. Grease smears his face and clothes. The Commons is raucous as MPs gorge.

Finished with the chop, THE SPEAKER guzzles wine. Its splashes everywhere. He rises satiated and unsteady on his feet.

THE SPEAKER
Children! Children! Pay attention!

THE MPs pay him no attention. THE SPEAKER nods to CLERK ONE who starts ringing a bell. No impact. He nods to CLERK TWO who releases a BLOW UP DOLL filled with helium. Some MPs pay attention. THE SPEAKER nods to CLERK THREE who presses play on a sound system – 'Land of Hope and Glory' plays loudly.

Now he has their attention. All MPs rise with their hands on their hearts. The music fades out. The doll keeps bobbing about the place. MPs giggle.

THE SPEAKER
No pudding until we vote on the government motion to mask the Official Leader of His Majesty's Opposition.

Dissent! Tumult!

THE SPEAKER
No pudding until you vote!

The MPs start chanting *"Aye! Aye! Aye!"*. One manages to grab hold of the blow-up doll and runs out of the chamber with it.

THE SPEAKER
The ayes have it! The ayes have it!

***

There had been rumours of a backbench rebellion against the government over the face mask law.

"This does not go far enough!" Sir Searing, MP for Dunking, wrote in an editorial for Unotesticular. You could just see his red face, with its river delta of broken capillaries, as you read his words. "For too long the Official Opposition has tried to undermine the people's real representatives. I would ask why the Opposition is still allowed in Parliament? Masked or not?"

Other government MPs were similarly vexed.

Geoffery Pinchbottom, MP for Fanni-on-Sticks, also wanted to know why the Official Opposition leader was allowed to "just walk into the House of Commons like the Prime Minister's equal? Whose House is it?"

A good question which had political reporters from the BBC also demand Sucof Groop answer. But he hid behind his Deputy Leader this time, whose name I now forget, who said they would investigate the demand. If that is what the British people wanted, they would not stand in the way of it. They wondered why it had taken the Prime Minister so long to think of it?

It was a nice touch to hold the vote before PMQs too and showed the perfect functioning of our geriatric parliament. The government rebels were convinced to get behind the law, and the government whipped their MPs just to be sure. The Official Opposition did too, as the focus group results told them to oppose the mask would risk losing them a single voter in Tamworth.

"Voter First Sovereignty!" was their motto at the time, and they strived to live down to it by agreeing with the Government wherever possible. It was perfect political logic. The Government was the Government because it had been elected by the people. Therefore, it was more popular. Thus, you had to agree with it if you hoped to be popular too and become the government.

I was delighted to hear people on the street in Raylee start to say to one another, "I can't believe that Groop just walks into Parliament like he owns it. He should have some humility and wear a mask."

The actual parliamentary vote was just for show. The Prime Minister had used an executive power to pass the law while drunk on sherry the night before. As ever he was waiting for the birth of a child. He could be excused a little tipple to calm his nerves.

Even the King did not need to sign off, which was nice, as he was busy that weekend with more pressing matters. Like cheese.

"Well, I want to hear what that great prat is saying," Mary stated. I guess she meant Groop. The Commons had lunched, voted, and now they were enacting their new law. Mary unmuted the TV and gave me my lunch.

***

INT. HOUSE OF COMMONS CONT.

WILLIAM BUNSEN
This is a Great British mask!

WILLIAM BUNSEN holds the mask up triumphantly. The House roars approval. The mask is a Japanese kabuki mask, but with a Union Flag sticker in the centre of the forehead.

WILLIAM BUNSEN
It's the will of the people!

More roars!

WILLIAM BUNSEN turns left and turns right. Mask in one hand, a little Union Flag in the other. He waves vigorously.

The BLOW UP DOLL floats back into the House. It's now wearing a bra and suspenders. It bumps along the floor, deflating.

ALL MPs
Put it on! Put it on!

***

I watched William Bunsen turn to the left and right, the vacuum sealed mask in his hand, a quarter of a pork pie held between my thumb and forefinger. Oh, how I wanted to be Billy Burner in that moment. He was just like me. A man of the people celebrating a victory over someone who would undermine the will of the people by suggesting that it may be different to what the government said it was.

"Careful Mark," Mary said, "you're crushing your lunch."

I shovelled the pie triumphantly into my open mouth. Eyes fixed to the television.

"Now you're getting crumbs on the settee!"

What were a few crumbs compared to the defence of Great British democracy? I would have told her, but my mouth was patriotically full.

"Is he just going to sit there and let it happen?" she asked, as Bunsen strode towards the Opposition benches to hand Groop his mask.

"It's the law," I explained. "He has to wear the mask or he's breaking the law."

"What's the point of him even being there?"

What little she knew of how governance worked.

"Adherence to the law by the Opposition is the bedrock of our system."

Naturally the government must be more agile with the spirit of any law, as it must handle ever changing circumstances.

The Opposition Leader accepted the mask and held it up. But he remained seated out of respect to the Prime Minister. Then he looked a little strained and began to audibly wheeze. He took an asthma inhaler out of his pocket and inhaled deeply.

"Put it on! Put it on!" MPs shouted.

"It's a generic brand of inhaler!" Lord Suckly screamed. "What a common bastard!"

The government MPs laughed so hard several fainted.

Groop nodded to all and removed the packaging from the mask. It had a little elastic string to hold it in place but that broke when he tested it.

"He should be charged with criminal damage," I shouted at the television.

"Bunsen is a bully," Mary sighed. "Groop won't be able to use his inhaler with the mask on. What happens if he passes out?"

"Half a dozen government MPs are already on the floor."

She rolled her eyes.

Groop settled for holding the mask to his face.

The Shadow Chancellor (I forget his name) and the Shadow Defence Minister (I forget her name) rushed to hold the mask on their leader's face, to free his hands so he could put away his inhaler. The Prime Minister pointed at the opposition and beamed.

"Take Back Control!" he shouted.

"Take Back Control!" chorused his MPs.

"Is Bunsen wearing a cod piece?" Mary asked.

"What?"

"The Prime Minister. He's got a bulge in his trousers."

"I'm not looking at his trousers."

She was right. He did have a bulge.

In due course Bunsen strode back to his own bench.

With the mask in place PMQs could begin. The Speaker motioned for the first MP to ask his question. The Member of Parliament for Orkney rose behind the Prime Minister's bench.

"Will the Prime Minister take a moment to thank the Leader of the Opposition for his kind suggestion to appoint a government MP to represent the people of Orkney while the beleaguered population there struggle to free themselves from the tyranny of the vile secessionists? Only by working together, as the Great British public expect, can we resolve the sorry state of internal conflict roused by Continentals on our much treasured northern islands."

Prime Minister William Bunsen nodded vigorously throughout. When it was his time to reply he stood at the dispatch box and waved his thanks to the chorus of "Hear! Hear!" that frothed in the chamber.

"I thank the Honourable Member for Orkney for accepting my offer to represent the prodigal son of our great country. I would also like to extend my gratitude to The Official Opposition Leader for generously allowing His Majesty's Government to appoint an MP from our own ranks unopposed. To that end I thank my eldest son, Fintech Bunsen, for accepting my invitation to stand uncontested in yesterday's Orkney by-election."

Fintech Bunsen, the youngest member of parliament, stood up, blonde hair waving like seaweed, and bowed.

"I doubt he's even shaving yet," Mary commented.

"In times of crisis," William Bunsen continued, "the British people expect their politicians to work together to find solutions to the problems that manifest out of thin air. The slings and arrows of outrageous…"

Mary hit the mute.

"What did you do that for?"

"So you could practice your lip reading. He's not going to say anything we haven't heard a thousand times before."

The Prime Minister sat, but The Speaker had to wait several seconds for the cheering to subside, even at one point raise his hands vigorously to encourage greater shouting.

"Unmute it," I ordered.

Mary ignored me.

"Give me the remote."

She ignored me.

I stood up to get the remote and we had a little wrestle before Mary sat on it. It unmuted under her buttocks.

"May I remind this house," The Speaker said at last, "that since the passing of The Great Democratic Decibel Law I can not invite another question from any Honourable Member except the Prime Minister until you have collectively passed one hundred and twenty decibels on the sound metre I have before me, and maintained it for ten seconds. If you want to get PMQs wrapped up and get to second lunch, I suggest you keep that in mind. It's Great British Lobster Thermidor today and you will not impress your constituents if they must wait for the broadcast of the dish's preparation on the Parliament television channel in the screens of the country's food banks. Now, once more, for the people at home, let me hear you cheer!"

And cheer they did. Satisfied, The Speaker invited the Prime Minister to ask his first question.

"Mr Speaker, I had planned a different first question for today, but I can not help but express my dismay that His Majesty's Official Opposition Leader has shown insufficient gratitude to our trade partners in Japan for the supply of the design of the mask he now wears AND AT THE EXPENSE OF THE GREAT BRITISH TAXPAYER! Does he intend to sour our international relations, at a time of national crisis, with our most important international partner and with whom I recently negotiated the potential supply of cheese from His Majesty the King's own estate?"

This time there was no problem with the volume in the House. My wife, bless her soul, took the remote out from under her bottom and turned the volume all the way up to eleven. We could just hear the televisions of our neighbour's roaring with the collective shouts and screams of the MPs from their own screens.

"If they can't hear our TV they'll think we're unpatriotic," Mary told me with a sarcastic smile.

"What?" I shouted back.

She waved the question away. Groop was standing to give his response. He had one hand holding the mask in place and the other holding a pointless piece of paper.

"Mr Speaker, I thought it was obvious that I appreciated the mask? I am wearing it in spite of my frequent recourse to a Great British asthma inhaler. But it's all very well for"

At least that's what I think he said. He seemed to be mumbling.

The MPs reacted with such scorn the speaker in our television began to vibrate.

"He's weak," I shook my head. "So weak."

"It's his job to be weak," Mary whispered. I know what

she said, because I lip read.

Eight

In The Land Of The Blind

"C is for Carrot – The Carrot, unashamedly made for a firm hold. True Britons eat carrots with every meal. To consume a carrot is to remember the Greatness of Britain, which has given the world many vegetables.

Carrots help night vision and are thus vital during power cuts.

Carrots can be eaten raw and are thus vital during power cuts.

Carrots can be grown in large gardens or in small pots on a balcony and are thus vital during the temporary cost of living crisis.

Carrots can be used as noses for snowmen and as thus are vital for entertaining children in the toy chain supply crisis.

Carrots can be frozen and used as weapons in hand-to-hand combat and are thus vital in lowering defense spending when tough choices must be made with the national, household budget.

For these reasons the Carrot receives a patriotic rating of 365, 638 782, 084 out of a possible top score of 300, 034 974, 000. An unstinting public servant."

- 'Fruits and Vegetables, and Their Correct Patriotic Ratings' by Prime Minister Mark A. French.

"Some lies aren't because a person is bad." – Cyclops' Mum.

Cyclops - a local boy

I had a BRAIN WORM on the day we went on our school trip to The Tower of London. You can't take a pill for a brain worm. It's not like worms in your bum. I asked my Mum. "No Cyclops. You just try and think of something else."

For bum worms you must take a pill. But there aren't any bum pills at the moment because of a temporary surge in demand. So you just try and think of something else for them too. Like bunting.

Mum is always musting to try and think of something else. One day she wrote "tangible benefit" on her plate out of spaghetti letters and then laughed for an hour. "There was only the letter B," she'd told me, as she cut and modified the b's into other letters. I hugged her.

"What's love got to do with it? What's love but a second-hand emotion?" Mum sings over and over. She says she misses "the little stress" of deciding what to have for our dinner. I always hug her until she stops crying.

Every morning Mum goes out to the yard to see if there's "real food" in our shed. The door has rusty hinges and you have to really push. A fox used to sleep on the roof of the shed. Mum says the fox was eaten by "the Shingles at number 48". She says they pretended the fox was a turkey last Christmas. She said she heard Mr French tell them they were very patriotic and if there was a book on patriotic food Christmas fox stuffed with roadkill hedgehog would be in it. Mr French is always trying to make the best of every situation.

Mum doesn't like Mr French.

On Boxing Day there was a roasted fox in our back yard. It was missing a piece from the side. Its eyes had cooked out of the face but it still looked like it could see. It was scary. I didn't know a fox could get over your fence if it was cooked.

I watched as Mum dug a hole and buried it. Her breath was in big clouds.

"That's a shallow grave if ever I saw one," Mum said. "The ground was so hard." Then she ruffled my hair and laughed. If Dad was here he would have dug the hole.

"When is Dad coming back from Germany?"

Mum went very quiet. "Wait here."

She dug the fox back up and carried it away. She also took our shovel. I could hear her shouting at the Shingles at number 48. She came back with Mrs French holding her arm and Mr French behind them holding the shovel. He was red faced.

"It's a disc race!" he shouted. "You don't throw a gift back in someone's face!"

"Gammon," Mum called him and he looked like he would blow up.

"That's a micro-aggression," Mr French told Mum. He was right. We learned about calling people "Gammon" at school.

***

INT. CYCLOPS' CLASSROOM DAY

The classroom is full of shabbily dressed, skinny kids. The paint is peeling on the walls and water drips through the ceiling in several places.

There aren't desks for all so the kids have doubled up at many desks. Bunting hangs everywhere and there's giant photos of WILLIAM BUNSEN, KING CHARLES III, SAINT MARGARET THATCHER and WINSTON CHURCHILL on the walls.

A tall, skinny redheaded man with knobbly knees is giving the class a lecture. He wears a scout's uniform which is tight. Too tight. This is LANCE CORPORAL CARROT.

There's another man in the corner. Dark haired and muscled. Shirt sleeves rolled up. He wears shorts and work boots. His eyes burn as he glares at LC CARROT. This is MR MANN.

LC CARROT
Woke is an acceptable insult. Woke is used to identify the Enemies of the People. You know who the Enemies of the People are, don't you children?

LC CARROT waits.

A boy with a bandaged head lifts up his hand.

LC CARROT
Yes?

BANDAGED BOY
Europeans.

LC CARROT
Oh my God. That much you learn in kindergarten. Anyone else?

CYCLOPS raises his hand.

CYCLOPS
Nurses.

LC CARROT

Correct. Bus drivers too. Postmen. Left wing Marxist columnists. Doctors. Bin men. Milk men. Farmers. Fishermen.

MR MANN
Grown men in scout's uniforms.

The class laughs. LC CARROT reddens.

CYCLOPS
That is a micro-aggression! To insult a patriot is a crime.

MR MANN
And stuffing tax havens full of food that should be used to feed kids isn't?

LC CARROT
The Enemies of the People are everywhere! Never let your guard down.

MR MANN
Gammon.

The class is amazed. Oohs and ahhs. Giggles and snorts.

***

Ms Finch called a government man Gammon when he came to announce a "patriotic reduction" in our meat rations. She's awaiting trial. If she's guilty she'll be punished in public. Mum says she'll be "found guilty alright". This is her second offence. Her first offence was to be seen to laugh at Prime Minister Bunsen when he told the nation he had a found a potato in the shape of Winston Churchill.

"This country is ffing batshit," she shouted at the television. "What have you done to us Bunsen? You bloated haystack of corruption and shit!"

Someone was outside when Ms Finch shouted at the television. They heard.

The next day a pair of Patriot Police arrived and issued her with a "Fixed Penalty Notice". She wasn't allowed to use electricity for a week. But she was lucky because there were power cuts that week. Then she was unlucky because the fine was reissued for when there wasn't power cuts.

"It's a fucking potato," Mum shouted at the PP's.

Mrs French was passing on her way to forage in the field behind the new war memorial (IT'S MASSIVE!) and she raced over to shut Mum up.

"It's Winston Churchill reborn," one of the PP's said. A man. He looked really angry at both Mum and Ms Finch.

"It's the reincarnation of our Lord and Saviour," the other said. That was a woman.

Later I asked Mum if the potato really was Winston Churchill?

"No," Mum corrected me. "The Divine Potato is believed to be the reincarnation of Winston Churchill by crazy people. It's about keeping everyone looking in the wrong direction."

After Mum told me that she froze. I asked her what the matter was? And she just said, "I hope the country regains its sanity before you come of age. I'll not have you invading Orkney."

Mum and Mrs French ignored Mr French when he was holding the shovel on Boxing Day.

"If you don't like it here move to Europe," he said. They ignored that too.

Mrs French is a "lovely dumpling of a woman". A dumpling can be very fast when it's mad.

"Mark French, if you say one more word you'll be the next one buried in this yard."

I believed her. They had a tug of war over the shovel. Mrs French won. Mr French grabbed the shovel back. Mum looked stunned and tried to stop them fighting. They ignored her and stared at each other for ages. When Mum started laughing Mr French threw the shovel down and stormed off.

When patriots are stressed they put the kettle on. We learned that in "Keep Calm and Carry On Being Patriotic" class. I put the kettle on the stove. I pushed down and turned the knob. The stove just clicked. No gas.

"Mum, we've still got the electric!"

Mum and Mrs French hugged each other and laughed like I said a joke.

Mrs French took Mum upstairs and put her to bed. She stayed for ages and we talked about my favourite animals. I told her mine was the Tyrannosaurus Rex.

"Let's see if the angels have visited in the night," Mum says, and looks nervously out of the kitchen window at the shed. "Does the door look like it has moved?"

I know the angels are a man. Clarence the Butcher. I saw him. He tripped one night and shouted. I saw him through the window. I wasn't asleep. I was counting sheep. I can't do that right. I imagine the sheep turning into a roast dinner when they jump over the fence and I get too hungry to sleep.

We had roast lamb at school the day the Prime Minister visited. Barney said it wasn't "the PM. It's a lookalike. Any fat man with blonde hair can be a lookalike. No one knows what the PM really looks like anymore. The actual Prime Minister is on holiday in the Caribbean with a woman who isn't Mrs Bunsen."

Barney was excluded from school for a month because our Head Mistress heard him. I reckon his parents got an

FPN too.

It looked like the Prime Minister. The woman with him looked like Mrs Bunsen off the television. She had to sit down a lot because she was about to have a baby. Sofie said she just had a cushion shoved under her dress.

The Prime Minister spoke at assembly. All the kids were there. Our teacher Mr Mann was asked not to be there. I don't know why.

"Remember when we learned about the Ancient Greeks?" Mr Mann asked me.

"Yes Sir."

"When that old windbag starts bleating on about Spartans don't laugh."

He had a twinkle in his eye when he said it.

The Prime Minister mostly talked about how world beating our schools are. How jealous everyone in Europe is. When he said, "a temporary shortage of HB pencils would not have bothered the Spartans" and something about the war I had to put my hand over my mouth. Mr Mann was right.

Then the Prime Minister carved the lamb up. He ate a lot of the slices as he carved.

"You'll be lucky if there's anything left for you at this rate," he said. He choked on some lamb and everyone pretended he didn't.

Mrs Bunsen said, "You lovely British children wouldn't mind if I took the bone home to give to our little doggy woggy would you?"

"The children would be delighted!" Mrs Clench said, "wouldn't you children?"

"Yes Mrs Clench," we all said.

The Prime Minister stopped carving the meat and a man in a black suit came over and took the bone away. It still had a lot of meat on it.

"Now, which lucky boy is going to get a roast lamb lunch?" The Prime Minister asked us.

Of course it was Terry. His dad dressed up as Hitler for Halloween and kept the toothbrush moustache even after Halloween. Terry says when he grows up he's going to grow a toothbrush moustache too and if he's lucky he'll go to work on Cardinal Bogg's farm as a shepherd.

There's a cartoon series on TV called "Cardinal Bogg's Farm" and everyone is really happy there. It looks like a proper British farm.

I asked him if the moustache could brush teeth and he hit me in the face. But it was okay because he was aiming for my dead eye and he missed because I dodged.

Terry didn't share the lamb with anyone.

Some other men who were with the Prime Minister had some bags with little Union Flag waistcoats in them. We all had to put one on for the photograph with the Prime Minister and Mrs Bunsen. Then we all had to give them back. They were made of plastic and crackled when you moved.

The Prime Minister walked around our classrooms then.

I saw him steal Sofie's eraser!

Clarence was in the shadows the night he tripped in our backyard. He looked like a giant. He wasn't all in the shadows. His head was in the moonlight and it was very bright.

Even when he's angeling he still has his butcher's apron on. Mum said he now does "basic surgery" and "the barber is furious about it". The barber's shop says "GP Surgery" over the door. The barber is a veteran of the Territorial Army and gives everyone who comes in an army haircut. Clarence is mad because the barber borrowed one of his cleavers for cleavering someone's "gammy foot" and didn't give it back. The pharmacist has started offering dental services because she has some painkillers "most weeks".

Britons are the most self-reliant people on Earth. We learned that at school. Weaker countries have to import things they need, but we "made do and mend". That's good for the environment.

When I had a wobbly tooth Mum tied string around it and yanked it out. I didn't need painkillers because "I'm very brave."

The real food Clarence leaves is meat. A sausage or a pork chop. One time he left a T-bone steak in some wax paper and Mum stared at it for an hour. I thought we would never eat it.

"He's chopped most of the meat off," she said. "But it's still the most valuable possession in our house."

"We've still got the bone. We can make soup," I replied. Mum hugged me and told me "I'm very clever."

The food we get from the government comes in packaging with Union Flags on it. Like everything does. We learned at school that in the summer all the pavements are going to be painted red, white and blue. We all must help even though it will be our holidays.

Mum earns extra food by using a computer terminal at the library. She has to answer quizzes about how wonderful it is to live in Britain, or she doesn't earn anything. The quiz results are broadcast daily on the television in case "Brussels is watching."

The library used to have lots of computers but now there is only one and Mum must queue for a long time for her turn. Most of the library tables now have sewing machines. The sewing machines have little wheels on that you turn to make the needle go up and down. We go and make bunting instead of Geography. There's a lot of injuries. Barney put the sewing needle through his thumb one day! But the grown-ups who look after the library just laughed because

Barney's thumb was on the red fabric.

"It just makes the flag more patriotic," one said. They laughed.

Barney fainted and slid off his chair with his thumb stuck in the machine.

"He's missing an ear," one of them said.

"It's hard to get good staff these days."

If Mum doesn't do the quiz we don't get our rations. She always does the quiz. One time she was sick and couldn't do the quiz. I told Mrs French and she said, "Quick. Wait here." So I did but then I followed her because I didn't know what I was supposed to do. She pulled the skirting board off in her kitchen and took out a can of baked beans. "Take it home. You can eat it cold or hot."

She grabbed my arm really tight. "Don't tell anyone about my skirting board."

I don't think it's because of the food she hides there. Everyone hides extra food behind their skirting boards. Except for us. We don't have extra food. I think it's because there's also a blue flag with stars on it and a passport that isn't blue behind Mrs French's skirting board.

"That's not a good hiding place," I told her. I pointed at the flag.

"I want the bastards to catch me," she said. I think she was serious.

"Imagine the look on old Mark's face when they put me in the stocks?"

I stared at her. I was amazed.

"It might be the only way to snap Mr French out of his fever dream."

Mum was very impressed. By the beans "Look Cyclops. It's real. It has that little ring you put your finger into that pulls off the lid. We don't need a can opener."

I didn't know if we should open the tin. "Barney says his

dad has been practicing using tins in hand-to-hand combat," I told Mum and her eyes went very wide.

"But what do they eat?"

"Barney says his dad puts some concrete powder and water into the tin and it becomes a weapon."

Barney's dad used to be a builder. He has a lot of bags of concrete powder hidden in their shed. Also fertiliser.

The beans we get in our rations don't have the ring. They have a flag sticker on top of the can. If you pull the flag sticker back "Made in China" is printed on the tin underneath. On the back of the flag sticker it says "Made in China" too. I know because one day Mum soaked one off to look at it properly.

It wasn't really a brain worm in my head on the day we went to London. It was a brain python. Mum had been singing all weekend and now the song was stuck in my head too. Brain worms are contagious just like the other worms.

"Be careful on the trip," she told me SO MANY TIMES. "If you say anything unpatriotic we will get in trouble."

I don't know anything unpatriotic to say.

"Be careful. They're only taking you on a school excursion so they can get you alone and ask you what we talk about at home. Don't mention the little radio or I'll go to prison."

I had to be a school at "sparrow's fart". That's what Mr Mann said.

Mum got me up early and washed behind my ears with a cloth that she spat on. She said we had "moved on" from using clean water. When I asked her why she looked like she would explode. She exploded. I didn't ask twice.

"After my next shift we'll have bottled water again," she said. "You can drink bottled water."

You can't drink water from the tap anymore because the EU robs us of the chemicals needed to make it safe. And the EU puts dead fish in all our rivers. They really hate us for being free.

Mum did my armpits next. That tickled and we had a good laugh. She has bags under her eyes. "I carry too much around in them," she says and laughs like she's going mad.

"What's love got to do with it?" I asked and she hugged me forever.

She licked her thumb and cleaned some dirt off my chin.

"What's love but a second-hand emotion?"

I was going to be at school *on time*. NO FEAR.

I couldn't tie my school tie so Mum did it. I was still hungry after breakfast but I didn't tell her because she didn't have breakfast. I had two bruised bananas. TWO. I didn't need to take a packed lunch because we were having lunch at The Tower of London. It was going to be on television.

"Breakfast of champions!" Mum said. She peeled the bananas really carefully.

"Your cheekbones are really big," I said.

"That's a Brexit bonus," Mum said. She thought she was really funny.

At least it was a British banana. It had a sticker on it to tell you. There are stickers on everything. It was curved like a proper banana. There's a poster in the hallway outside my classroom explaining bananas. In Spain the bananas are straight because the EU forces Spain to grow bananas in tubes. The EU is weird.

"I'll have my breakfast later," Mum said.

I knew she was lying. Some lies aren't because a person is bad.

The kids at school tease me. My dad was an "enemy of the people". This is why he left. Mum said he left because he got a job in Germany and "the Home Office won't let him come back." He sends money but the government confiscates it. Mum says she doesn't tell him to stop sending the money because it will get us in trouble. I don't know how she talks to him.

"You have to be twice as good as the other boys," she says.

It's not fair.

"What time did Mrs Clench say you have to be at school?"

"7am."

Mum's eyes got wet. It was only 06.43. I would be on time.

Anyone who was late wasn't going to London.

"Please be careful."

"I will say the Tower of London is world beating," I told her.

"Lateness means a lack of belief in Britain!" There's a poster in the assembly hall.

Mrs Clench points to it a lot and looks at all of us with a frown. The poster has a woman wearing a red, white and blue sash who is looking into the future with her arm raised. She has a helmet on and is holding a big frozen carrot. There's another poster in our classroom which shows her riding a chariot in the sky over "Great Satan Brussels". The buildings under its wheels are on fire. This poster says, "The English Have NEVER Been Ruled By Anyone!".

We didn't leave for London until nearly 11am. The bus was late.

One of the other boys asked if the bus lacked belief in Britain? He was taken away.

I didn't ask because I didn't want to get the cane, but I thought it was very funny. I get the cane. Mr Mann refuses to do it so another teacher does. The cane has "Pain Helps You" printed on it.

Mum gave me a packed lunch even though I didn't need one. It was a piece of cheddar and a slab of white bread. The cheddar had some white stuff on top of it. The bread was mouldy, but not too bad. It was all wrapped up in grease paper with a little ribbon. I know she got it from the kitchen at the big house she works at.

I hope she didn't steal it.

I don't want her to get the cane too.

"Eat it in the toilet," she told me. "Don't let anyone see you eating it."

"But they are giving us lunch."

"They will serve you food," Mum said, but…"I heard they don't let you eat it. They take a photo and then you are taken out of the room and the next class comes and sits in front of the food for their photo."

Mum's boss beats his servants. It's not against the law because the house is inside something called a Charter City. This is a special city where people who are better than you get to do what they like. This makes the UK "an economic powerhouse". The news tells us that every day.

Once I got to school Mrs Clench made us all stand in lines facing the fence. We were supposed to sing the national anthem when the bus arrived. FOUR HOURS we waited in line. Sofie fainted because her blood pressure was too low and was frowned at by the teachers. Mr Mann would have done something but he wasn't there when it happened. I HELPED HER TO HER FEET. The teachers frowned at me because "self-reliance is vital to success". Reggie pushed the boy in front of him and they had a fight. Then TWO POUNDS fell out of Reggie's pocket and Max picked them up and ran in a circle.

Mrs Clench caned them. She smiles when she canes the children. She's only been our headteacher for a month. She was sent by the government because the old head teacher, Mr Petri, wouldn't cane anyone. He was "retired".

Jeremy, who is very clever, began to sing the national anthem on his own. No one joined him but he didn't care. He just carried on singing. Loudly. The whole yard went silent and the teachers watched him and smiled.

I tried to join in but my voice was really croaky because I was thirsty. Sofie put her hand over my mouth. I looked where she was looking and Mrs Clench was twisting her cane in her hands. Mrs Clench doesn't like bad singing. Mr Mann arrived wiping sauce off his face and shaking his head softly at Mrs Clench. She stopped twisting the cane and blushed. EVERYONE thinks she has a CRUSH on Mr Mann. He's big and strong and always making jokes. He gets away with it because he's Australian and people have "different expectations of colonials".

"If Mrs Clench beats you who will hold me?" Sofie whispered. We had to try hard to stop giggling.

"Who is the master of this ship?" LC Carrot demanded. We'd seen him before. He didn't look like a sailor then or now. He was still wearing a scout uniform with badges on the sleeves. It was really tight. He couldn't walk or move his arms properly.

We had had scouts in Raylee until they left to pick daffodils in Cornwall. This was the fault of "the Poles" Mr French said, "they won't come and pick the daffodils anymore in an attempt to undermine the flourishing British flower sector."

It seems to me we undermine ourselves enough. I'm not allowed to say it or I get beaten up by EVERYONE. Except Sofie who pretends to faint.

Carrot was holding one of those little sticks jockeys hit horses with to make them pay attention.

We all giggled. He had a funny lisp now and ship sounded like shit!

He didn't like that. His mouth blew up like a blowfish and he whistled it all out through his teeth.

"I am Lance Corporal Carrot," he said, as if that was supposed to mean something. "I am from the Ministry of Anti-Woke."

He was silent for a long time.

"Let that sink in," Mr Mann said. "Carrot here has moved Ministries. He was with the Ministry of the Future before? Remember children. But you don't have a future now."

LC Carrot trembled.

"Yesterday I was cutting the ribbon at the ceremony to open the largest, repaired pothole in England," LC Carrot shouted. "Today I am here to see to it that you children behave properly on the very important excursion to The Tower of London."

"Why are you dressed like a child?" Barney asked. Barney only has one ear. He lost the right ear LOBE AND ALL when an Audi TT "winged him" when he was in his pram. The pram was on a zebra crossing. That's what he says. I wonder if his dad cut it off? Not on purpose. Barney teases me because I only have one eye.

LC Carrot's mouth hung open for ages.

Then he grabbed Barney by his only ear and thrashed him on the bum with the horse stick. Good and proper. Barney tried not to cry but he bit his lip so hard it bled and then he saw the blood dripping on the ground and started sobbing.

LC Carrot released Barney, who stumbled away wiping at his mouth. But the blood kept coming.

One of the teachers, Ms Tents, who always wears the same dress with red tulips on it, rushed over and hugged Barney. She got blood on her dress. But it was on one of the tulips so it wasn't too bad. "Let's get you cleaned up? Or you'll miss the bus."

LC Carrot glared at her. LC Carrot's eyes softened the longer he looked at her and he let her do what she wanted.

"If corporal punishment had returned sooner we'd never have had a recession," LC Carrot shouted out.

Then the bus arrived. It was an old, bendy bus. It had "Tower of London Express" where the bus number should be. It was painted with big red poppies and there was a GIANT plastic poppy on the front.

LC Carrot stood to attention and saluted. The bus jerked and rocked about. The windows rattled and smoke puffed out the back. Mrs Clench saluted too. Then we all saluted. It was obvious we were meant to. Sofie started to pretend to faint but then changed her mind. "I don't want to overdo it," she whispered.

Mr Mann didn't salute. He just grinned at LC Carrot and made an up and down motion with his hand curled. Sofie laughed like a drain (my Mum would say like a drain).

"Why?" I whispered.

Sofie whispered that Mr Mann was doing sign language. I don't know sign language. Except for cooking which I learnt from Mister Tumble. Before he was deported.

"It means wanker," Sofie explained.

I didn't know what that meant either!

I do now.

The bus was half on the pavement when it finally stopped. The driver got out and walked to the front to look at it. He looked furious. He was dressed in army clothes. Lots of government people wear army clothes. This is because of a "significant" free trade deal with North Korea.

"Will it make London champ?" Mr Mann asked the driver. The driver shrugged. "It's the brakes. They're squishy." Mr Mann wandered over with his hands in his pockets.

"Single file!" LC Carrot shouted at us. "Your ticket to ride on the sovereignty bus is a verse from God Save The King."

He marched over like a soldier shouting "Left foot! Right foot!" to stand next to the bus's door. Mr Mann saluted him and doubled over laughing.

"Look smart," Mrs Clench said. "You heard Lieutenant Colonel Carrot. Single file!"

"He's a Lance Corporal," Mr Mann said. "Catering Corp." Then he said to Mrs Clench, "How about we go get a drink when this nonsense is over? Just you and me. We can play a song on the jukebox. I know just the one to put you in the mood."

Mrs Clench wobbled on her feet.

We eventually got on the bus and left for London. Slowly. Because of the squishy brakes.

"I'm a government man," LC Carrot told us on the way to London. Up close he was really skinny with freckles. "And you know what that means?"

Sofie did the sign language in her lap. We got stuck in a traffic jam.

"Look at the magnificent way Britons queue!" LC Carrot ordered us to look at all the cars waiting. "When you grow up you'll queue like that too."

***

The Tower of London was AMAZING. It is where they keep Winston the Holy Potato.

"This Tower was built by Englishmen," the guide told us. He was a short, bald man with a big Adam's Apple. People whispered he used to be on the BBC before it was "made fit for purpose for the 21st century". That seemed to involve firing most of the presenters and hiring ones who wore army clothes like the bus driver.

"England has never been ruled by anyone." I don't know why he said this when the school poster said it already. Either he is wrong or my mum is wrong. She says England has been ruled by "pretty much everyone at one time or another" and she doesn't understand what we're doing now. "Whatever it is we're doing."

Everyone in the United Kingdom has to go on

"pilgrimage" and "pay homage" to Winston the Holy Potato.

Only he wasn't called Winston when I saw him because he hadn't been christened yet. It was after I saw him he was stolen by traitors. There was a big debate before I saw him about whether to have the potato christening ceremony in Saint Paul's Cathedral or Westminster Abbey. It was going to be decided by a referendum and even I could vote in it!

Winston Churchill. Church on a hill. My mother says it has a nice ring to it.

They promised us a Spitfire fly past too, but that didn't happen because it needed a part and the part was stuck in Calais. I don't know why the French didn't want us to have it. But the Spitfire is better than the Eurofighter because it's "110% British".

We had to be at school AT 7 AM to wait for the bus. I told you that already.

Everyone was so excited Mr Mann said we were like "blue arse flies in a bottle". He's Australian. I told you that too. I need to rest. Which is funny, because we were told Australians live next door to GERMANS and can't be trusted. I don't know why they let him teach. He doesn't sound like the black and white war movies we watch in History.

The bus was late. The head teacher said it was because of EU red tape. I am going to rest now.

***

Mr Mann told us he was only in the "sodding UK" because "he couldn't go home as the Australian government won't allow anyone from England in because of the Mad Cow Covid Mash up". I don't know what cows with mental health issues have to do with getting on planes.

In Science we're learning how to collect frost on bottles and store it as clean drinking water.

The Prime Minister says we should keep eating beef when we can get it and not worry about "a calf with a runny nose." Runny noses are natural. My Mum whispered to Mr Mann he was going to get in trouble at parent teacher night, but he just asked her out for a drink. She said no, because she's married. So he asked her again. She just grinned and changed the topic.

I think Mum should go out with him because he can feed her.

Peter Peterman weed himself and had to go and sit alone on the bus ride to the Tower. Mr Mann said he was going to hose him down once we got there as it was warm enough and he'd dry out fast. If there wasn't a hose he would "dip him in the Thames".

I don't know what time it was when we got to the Tower of London. We couldn't cross Tower Bridge because it was closed for repairs. We had to walk in single file. I had to walk behind Peter Peterman and he stunk! He started to cry so I didn't tease him. Mr Mann walked in front of him so everyone would leave him alone.

"Don't worry Pete. Once we get to the other side I'll take you down to Traitors Gate and dip you in the Thames."

When we got to the Tower of London a really fat man spoke to our teachers. He was wearing white pants and a Union Jack waistcoat. He had a black hat on. There was a bulldog sitting next to him. It was all really patriotic. But when you looked at the dog it didn't look back at you. That's when I realised it was stuffed.

"I am John Bull!" the fat man shouted at us. "I'll be your guide today."

"Say hello to John Bull children!" LC Carrot shouted at us.

"Hello John Bull!" we all shouted at John Bull.

He was swaying a little. He hiccupped and then turned around and walked through the big gate into the castle. We all followed.

First we went to see where enemies of the people were held before their fair trial. It was a big cage hanging from a tall pole set up in the grass inside the Tower walls. A raven was sitting on top of the cage. It was really scary.

"Children!" John Bull shouted at us, "peel your eyes like potatoes. Pay attention every day. If you see anyone undermining our great and powerful country you must dob them in!"

"If you're not patriotic you'll end up in here," LC Carrot shouted at us next. John Bull gave him a frown and asked, "Who's the tour guide?"

Next we went in to see Winston the Holy Potato. They keep him in a glass cabinet. We were all made to stand still while the national anthem played. Someone dressed as Queen Elizabeth 1st walked through the room, which was a surprise! And then Queen Elizabeth the 2nd did too! That wasn't a surprise. I had already seen four of her walking around the castle with North Korean tour groups.

"Winston the Divine Potato makes miracles happen," John Bull told us. "Prime Minister William Bunsen was chosen by God to find Winston in that holy field."

"It's just a flipping potato!" Barney shouted out. LC Carrot took him out of the room and he didn't come back to school for a week.

"On the day Archbishop Bogg carried the potato to the sea at Hastings," the guide told us, "British fish leapt out of the sovereign sea and into the waiting British fishing nets."

It seems fishing wasn't as hard as they teach us in history classes, I thought, but I didn't say anything because I saw what happened to Barney. Apparently no one can fish like the British. This is why the French are always trying to invade Kent.

"Another time Prime Minister Bunsen cured a severe swelling condition of his stomach with just a glance at the Holy Potato. Did you know Prime Minister Bunsen invented the hamburger boys and girls?"

We didn't.

"It wasn't Ronald MacDonald."

That seemed weird, but I didn't say anything because I didn't want to clean out the school toilets with my toothbrush.

John Bull went quiet for a few seconds. He looked like he was dazed. He took a little flask out of his coat and had a few sips from it.

"Right. Where do you think Winston is going to be christened?" he asked us. No one answered.

"Saint Paul's or Westminster Cathedral?"

We didn't answer that either. John Bull shrugged and shouted at us again.

"BUT THE GREATEST MIRACLE OF THE HOLY POTATO WAS RESTORING BRITAIN'S BELIEF IN ITS DESTINY..."

Then the lights in the cabinet blew out with a big bang! Smoke filled the cabinet. All the lights went out and there was the sound of breaking glass. An alarm started ringing on the wall and lots of police ran into the room. I don't know where they came from. They had torches and guns. We were immediately lined up and had to leave the room in single file.

We had to wait in the hallway while John Bull and the police had a big argument before he took us to lunch. He was sweating a lot and kept looking back over his shoulder.

I don't have my own toothbrush. I share one with my Mum.

John Bull marched us into a big stone hall with long tables

all laid out with lunch. Policemen kept running back and forth. There were lots and lots of chairs. Plates were piled high with lunch. It must have been cold, but that didn't matter as they weren't going to let us eat it. Old men in red and gold dresses and black hats lined the hall. They must have been cold too because they had big white things around their necks and hats on. They were even wearing pantyhose! I didn't know men were allowed to do that anymore, except in Paris. Mr Mann told us they were called "Beefeaters", but I didn't see any eating any beef even though there was beef on every plate on the table. "Replica Beefeaters I reckon," Mr Mann added.

We were all told to sit down in a chair and a man took our photos. Then we were told to leave. When I went to sleep that night I wanted to have a dream that I got to eat the lunch.

I didn't have the dream. I had a nightmare.

Nine

Prince Albert

"B is for Beetroot. Beetroot, the colour of an indigenous Briton's face when he says "sovereignty". After beetroot he goes white, and then blue. After this he must draw breath.

For this reason The Beetroot receives patriotic rating of 157, 21, 899 and 73,999 out of a possible top score of 300, 34, 974 000."

- 'Fruits and Vegetables, and Their Correct Patriotic Ratings' by Prime Minister Mark A. French.

One day the Speaker fell ill in his chair in the House of Commons. The pain in his chest was indescribable, so I won't describe it.

He was ignored, at first, as he clasped his hands to his chest. "Too much Stanislavsky," the MP for Surrey Crotch told the inquiry which followed. "Had he employed more Method I may have been moved to applause. I may even have stood."

The Chair of the inquiry, the MP for Porkus, considered mentioning that you couldn't get more method in your acting than dying while acting the role of a man who was dying, but decided not to, as he needed the MP for Surrey Crotch's support in a fraud case. The MP for Surrey Crotch was the ex-husband of the inquiry's lead, the former MP for Harold.

So the Speaker was ignored as he beat his palms on the wooden arms of his old chair. Such was the ferocity of the ongoing debate in the chamber, he wasn't even the most animated person in the room. The debate concerned plans to impose life sentences for political graffiti in public toilets, that went against the established will of the people. The Opposition was broadly supportive but demurring as there were no more public toilets in the United Kingdom. It was better, they suggested, to simply outlaw permanent markers.

When the Speaker lifted his hands to wave for help he found them at his chest again. His greying mouth opened and closed like a suffocating fish with a bluish face. Froth bubbled out and down his chin. He tore his shirt open and he scratched at his chest as if he could dig the pain out and discard it.

Anyone watching closely, which no one was, was privy to the secret nipple ring he wore. Involuntarily he tore the ring off and let out a horrified gasp. Blood trickled down his chest and spread out in his white shirt. His frantic hands pasted it around like a toddler with paint.

Then the Speaker went quiet.

In truth some MPs realised something was up, but they paid as much attention to the Speaker's health crisis as they paid to anything else he did or said. They just assumed he was drunk and having a tantrum, or having the DT's, either would do. MPs did this quite often. When the Speaker went quiet, they assumed he had fallen asleep and would revive sooner or later. They took advantage to shout and shake their fists at one another like zoo kept chimpanzees debating ownership of a prized blanket, which is what they like doing best.

In this way is Great Britain governed.

However, the Speaker did eventually gain the attention of

a nearby MP when he slid from his golden chair to the floor and began to twitch. The debate paused while a deputy speaker was summoned and seated.

The Deputy Speaker consulted the clerks on what precedence said they must do with the unconscious, spasming man at their feet. It was discovered he was to be stretchered away.

"Summon the Stretcher Bearers!" The Deputy Speaker ordered.

"Summon the Stretcher Bearers!" A clerk repeated, and other clerks followed suit, the call echoing down the halls leading away from the debating chamber.

They waited.

And waited.

The Stretcher Bearers had not expected to be summoned and were having lunch in the Stretcher Bearers' private dining room, which is subsidised at public expense.

"But not as heavily as the MPs' bars and restaurants," any Stretcher Bearer would tell you. Bitterly. You just have to ask. Which you haven't.

Just as the MPs were growing restless to resume their debate the Stretcher Bearers appeared in the doorway. Four men. All dressed alike in red pantyhose and black tunics. Three of the four wore a broad, black felt cap with a single white ostrich feather. All had failed serially to win safe seats for the party of government, in the days when elections were less certain, and had eventually been fobbed off into their current positions. Their hats looked like berets, but weren't called that, because that would be too French. One did not wear a hat and still had a napkin stained with teriyaki tucked into his shirt collar.

The Deputy Speaker ushered them in by waving some papers.

"We cannot," one replied.

"Why not?"
"Lord Barry's forgotten his hat."
Lord Barry was not a Lord, his first name was Lord, because his father thought it would be funny, when he was born, if he grew up to be a Lord. Barry was his surname.
The Deputy Speaker and the clerks consulted. From the shrugs and puzzled looks it was obvious the event was without precedence.
"Stretcher Bearer Lord Barry must go and retrieve his hat."
The three hat wearing stretcher bearers looked at Lord Barry.
"I can not Mrs Deputy Speaker."
"Why not?"
"It's at the dry cleaners." Which was a lie. He didn't like wearing it, because it itched his balding head.
The Deputy Speaker and the clerks consulted again. The Deputy Speaker was heard asking if a "lamp shade or cloth may substitute for a hat?"
The Speaker began to moan. A long, low sound like a pantomime ghost. The Deputy Speaker found this too much and decided to establish a new precedent.
"The three stretcher bearers with hats may enter the chamber. The one with the napkin must wait at the door."
The three Stretcher Bearers did as invited and set the stretcher down beside the twitching, moaning Speaker. They had never practiced as a threesome and conferred with one another on what to do next.
"Just get him out!" Mrs Petal, Secretary of State for the Go Home Office, shouted. She was also frothing at the mouth, but that was just her normal state. She was a permanently angry little ball dressed all in black, with a sparkling skull pendant on her lapel. That day she wore her right arm in a tight sling. She told anyone who asked it was because she

had strained her wrist fighting the Anti-Growth Coalition in one to one combat. The truth was she was ordered by the Chief Whip to wear the sling to stop her giving flat palmed salutes. Intensive focus grouping of the voting public had revealed that the Great British public were quite happy, on balance, for their elected representatives to behave like fascists, just they didn't want anyone to make it too obvious.

"Yes! Some of us want to get this bloody debate over with and get back to the bar!" Lord David David, Minister for Looking Like John Bull, added.

The Stretcher Bearers took up position behind the unconscious Speaker and rolled him forward onto the stretcher, and then off. They tried again from the other side to better effect. They then conferred on who was the strongest? They agreed the strongest member of their team was standing just outside wearing a napkin, and not a hat. They agreed that the second strongest should take up one end and the third and fourth strongest bearers one pole each at the other end.

"But we only know who is the strongest," one stated.

They next performed a series of arm wrestling contests to determine the third and fourth strongest. The Speaker moaned on, as if just a prop.

In this way the Speaker left the chamber never to return.

The debate resumed.

For the first thirty minutes MPs, who never normally got to speak, took the opportunity to express their hope the Speaker would recover swiftly. Later, when the Speaker died, they would get to express their regrets that the Stretcher Bearers had not acted quicker. The search for a scapegoat began immediately. Lord Barry was initially pegged for that important role, until it was revealed he had donated to a charity set up to privately school William Bunsen's offspring. There was never a question of the MPs themselves being to blame. But that was all later.

It was reported that an ambulance was called to take the Speaker to hospital. Westminster was believed to have a fleet of ambulances. It should have been a short wait. But the Speaker lay on the stretcher in a corridor near the chamber for sixteen hours. The stretcher bearers who waited with him were unable to assess him or attempt even rudimentary medical intervention, owing to an ancient tradition of the British parliament that allowed only the Parliamentary Barber to administer first aid. It was the barber's day off.

Eventually the Speaker regained consciousness and ordered the Stretcher Bearers to carry him over Westminster Bridge to Serco's St Thomas' Hospital, which sits conveniently on the other side.

Owing to an ancient tradition of the British parliament only the Speaker could order the Stretcher Bearers to leave the Palace of Westminster. The Speaker was thought to have "caught a break there".

When the Stretcher Bearers paused in the middle of the bridge, to catch their breath, the Speaker is believed to have muttered, "Order. Order..." for the last time. He then quietly slipped back into the dark, his breathing erratic and shallow.

It's said he later passed away quietly on a gurney in a corridor at Serco's St Thomas' Hospital. He stayed determinedly unconscious in those final hours and drew praise for waiting "silently and patriotically" for treatment with "lots of other customers to keep him company." He wasn't the only one to die in that corridor that day, but he was the only Member of Parliament.

People were surprised. Some suspected foul play. Others wanted to know what happened to the Westminster ambulances.

"The British people are not interested in the circumstances of the Speaker's death," the British public were told. "We have our freedom and people are free to die where they choose. It plays into the hands of the Woke to criticise great national institutions at a time of crisis."

The British people prepared to move on. Which is what they did best in those days. Excepting moving on from ancient conflicts with foreigners. Some things you just can't leave behind you.

"The Speaker was old anyway," a No. 10 spokesman added, when no one was expecting it. "It was just his time."

When it was decided that the Speaker's public pensions would still be paid, but now to the charity for the PM's children, an Op-ed in Unotesticular declared that it was what the Speaker would have wanted.

The papers compiled retrospectives of the Speaker's life. The GBPBC made a documentary called, 'A Very British Speaker', so everyone could be reassured Britain was still a special place.

The fact the Speaker had more than one clash with Prime Minister Bunsen over the years was not relevant. The fact that Prime Minister Bunsen was to chair the inquiry into the circumstances surrounding the Speaker's demise was thought good and proper. He was in the Chamber the day the Speaker fell ill and his first-hand knowledge "vital".

Here we must include an aside.

The day the Speaker fell ill in the House of Commons was the first day that Prime Minister William Bunsen had attended the chamber since a period of exile. The exile was a result of his party removing him from office. His party had removed him from office because that's how British democracy works. The longer a party has been in power the more frequently it must change Prime Ministers to prove that it was capable of renewal while in office.

Prime Minister Bunsen had resisted the efforts to remove him from office. To no avail. He wasn't helped by the Speaker refusing him a vote of confidence in himself, in which only he would take part.

He was replaced by a sequence of PMs who seemed to have been selected at random from the MPs available. Foolish foreign commentators took this as a sign of chaos, but thanks to an informative press, the British people were told it was a sign of meritocracy. Anyone can be Prime Minister for a day in Great Britain. Something a German or Frenchman could never boast of.

But in exile, in the villa of a foreign friend in a warm country, Mr Bunsen worked to achieve his return. He was successful. His party feared they may have to have a general election if they kept changing Prime Ministers. But not if they changed back to Mr Bunsen MP, who reassured them that they would not have to call a general election. So he returned from the villa in the warm country and regained the Premiership.

"This is a new government," he told the country. "The instability of recent months are forgotten. I will govern in the interests of all. Like Theseus, I have followed the thread out of the labyrinth and returned in triumph holding the head of the Minotaur."

By coincidence, his return coincided with several prominent media owners receiving peerages. By a further coincidence the papers ran headlines for weeks like "Blighty is Back in Business!" and "Billy Burner is the light that guides us", and so on. One enthusiastic rag even cut and pasted Bunsen's face onto an old photo of Winston Churchill giving a V for victory sign with the headline, "He has returned! And not just as a potato!".

This concludes the aside.

For some weeks the Speaker's Chair sat empty. His

various deputies refused to perform the required duties after the first day, as they had no one to deputise for.

The Government stated a desire to elect a new Speaker swiftly but needed to compile a list of candidates. To compile the list MPs had to volunteer their service, but in order to volunteer they had to give a gift in secret to the Prime Minister. To do this the Prime Minister's newest wife had to decide what she needed to redecorate 10 Downing Street, as she was a new wife and that's what new wives did.

All this made no difference to the quality of the debates.

For weeks Parliament had been wrangling over how long the month of April should be. Government MPs favoured adding an extra day to April to improve economic productivity. The Official Opposition were not opposed to extending April, and agreed with the Prime Minister that to do so would ensure Great Britain's place globally as the country with the longest April, but they didn't see why a whole new day was needed when April 1st could simply be made forty eight hours long. Eventually though the Government won out, and with the Opposition's support a second April 1st was added.

"The advantage, Mr Speaker," Mr Bunsen told the empty chair, "will be a doubling of the national output of April 1st jokes. It will be a ramped up April 1st. World beating. The humourists of our great country will have an indisputable edge over foreign competition."

The law was sent to the Lords who rubber stamped it and sent it back. It was then passed unanimously at the final reading in the House of Commons, before being sent to the King for his assent. The King was not to be disturbed, as he was busy setting up a new hydroponics set to grow winter greens for his pet tortoise. But eventually he was to be disturbed and Assent was granted on March 31st.

"To have continued to insist on a different course of action would have been unpatriotic," The Official Opposition Leader told The Daily Parrot, in an interview he was certain would gain him a polling percentage point in the red, white and blue wall. "And now Britons can wake tomorrow knowing that April 1st will be followed by April 1st."

None of this was unusual.

Since 2010 The Official Opposition had found itself perfectly capable of agreeing with the UK government's biggest ideas and everyone felt secure knowing traditional British democracy was moored in a harmony of macro thought between the major parties. This consensus made choosing the status quo much easier whenever the public was balloted.

The Prime Minister now moved to solve the matter of the empty Speaker's chair.

"If it pleases this House," Prime Minister Bunsen said, to the empty chair, on the first April 1st, "I have a new Speaker who I have appointed by use of my temporary sovereign powers."

Up until that point it had been a rowdy session with MPs pulling gags on each other and shouting "April Fool!". The gags had punctuated a speech by the Go Home Secretary who was outlining a new scheme to ensure that asylum seekers from Afghanistan were able to apply for asylum in a new Foreign Office office opened in Kabul. No one was much interested. Too many MPs were waiting for colleagues to sit on fart bombs hidden about the benches to pay attention. Although one lone Opposition MP had taken issue with a detail of the scheme.

"While we do not disagree that His Majesty's Government is right to pay the Taliban to assess the asylum claims of Afghanis, the Taliban having the relevant domestic expertise and best able to determine who most needs asylum from themselves, we take issue with the fact that this government has installed insufficiently small Union Flags over the doorway to the new Great British Refugee office in Kabul."

Into this the Prime Minister rose and made his announcement.

A new Speaker? The House conferred excitedly like high school children suddenly discovering a substitute teacher was arriving.

The Prime Minister nodded sagely and clapped his hands.

"I give you Prince Albert!"

There had been rumours that the dead Speaker's constituency had been gifted a new MP and that MP was a Prince. But everyone was too concerned with the debate over April to care.

"Prince Albert!" Prime Minister Bunsen said again. "Please take the Speaker's Chair!"

The Chamber grew quiet with everyone straining to see who was coming through the door. Prince Albert was coming through the door on his back feet and the knuckles of his hands. He paused just inside the doorway to bare his massive teeth at the chamber. Bright, orange eyes surveyed the people in the room. His silver back drew gasps of appreciation.

Prime Minister Bunsen produced a bunch of bananas from his coat pocket and waved them high.

"Hoo! Hoo!" Prince Albert celebrated.

Bunsen walked to the Speaker's Chair and placed the bananas on the seat.

"It's April 1st!" Several MPs shouted, and all began to laugh.

It was April 1st, but Prince Albert was no joke. The Prime Minister had appointed an aged chimpanzee to be Speaker of the House of Commons and he was deadly serious about it.

Prince Albert duly took his seat and began to peel and eat the bananas.

He vocalised, "Order! Order!", the papers reported.

And order was restored to the House of Commons, not that it needed it.

Ten

Mi Casa, Mi Castel

"The Yorkshire Greenball – previously a despised vegetable which was suspected of waging a war against Christmas. Rechristening this stout green ball from Brussels Sprout to Yorkshire Greenball led to it becoming a national favourite. By law.

Packed full of pluck, the Yorkshire Greenball has a patriotic rating of 157, 21, 900 and 73,999 out of a possible top score of 300, 34, 974 000."

- 'Fruits and Vegetables, and Their Correct Patriotic Ratings' by Prime Minister Mark A. French.

Mark My Words

INT. FRENCH KITCHEN MORNING

Dust motes in sunlight through a broken kitchen sink window. The fracture creates a prism of light. There's the sound of a tap dripping and a newspaper shaken. "Land of Hope and Glory" plays softly from a radio. There's a louder voice talking over the music. It's William Bunsen.

WILLIAM BUNSEN

Children are our future. Teach them well and let them frighten the French away. Ha!

AN EGG moves into view, held by skinny fingers with painted nails, chipped. The egg is stamped with the royal seal of King Charles III. The sunrays illuminate its inside. Four yolks. The egg is shaken and the yolks tumble and knock about.

WILLIAM BUNSEN
We must never tire of defending our borders. British fish are sovereign fish. Your children's future depends on the sovereignty of halibut! Flounder! Plaice!

MARY is holding the egg. The radio settles into the background. An endless, random list of what makes Blighty foremost among nations.

MARY
Cyclops' mum told me she heard on the radio this ink is toxic.

WILLIAM BUNSEN
Perch! Salmon! Whiting!

MARY
The egg is so thin.

WILLIAM BUNSEN
Mackerel! Monkfish!

MARY
I'm frightened.

The newspaper is shaken very loudly.

MARY
Mark?

WILLIAM BUNSEN
Bream! All manner of crustaceans!

MARY
(insistent)
Mark!

***

I flapped the newspaper and coughed manfully. What a great morning. Bunsen had taken over the Today programme and I had a new edition of 'The Daily Parrot' to read aloud. Mary was at the sink fretting over eggs. God love her. Women!

The Daily Parrot wasn't worried. It was focused on preparations for the upcoming civil war. We could all help make a success of it.

Get War Done!

"What is an Englishman's village?" I asked Mary. If she wouldn't look at the front page of the paper, I'd have to read it out to her.

Nothing. She was still staring at that blasted egg. Like it mattered more than Blighty's future.

"Didn't you hear me?" she replied. "Apparently the ink is banned in the EU. It causes blindness. It's stored in the fat cells of children."

"Where did you hear such nonsense? It's world beating ink."

"Cyclops' mum."

Mary paled and shivered.

"Are you taking ill?" I asked.

"No. It's just whenever I hear certain phrases, like world beating, I shiver."

I ruffled the newspaper again.

"What is an Englishman's village?"

Nothing.

"Mary."

"Mmm?"

"What is an Englishman's village?"

"It's a quadruple yoker. I think. Do you think it's safe? Why is Bunsen just listing types of fish?"

I really wanted to see if she was right, about the yolks. Imagine that. Four eggs in one.

"British productivity extends down to the hens who lay our eggs."

Rudd. Common Sole. Grayling…

"Did you read that in the Parrot?" she was smirking now.

"What is an Englishman's village. That's what I read."

"Don't they know?"

She looked at the egg again.

"It must be a good egg."

Northern Pike. Turbot. Common Ling. Tope…

"That's right."

I flapped the pages of the 'The Daily Parrot', again.

On the front page Prime Minister Bunsen was shaking hands with Roger Mordor, the paper's owner. He was 110 and there were credible rumours he planned to live forever. The pair were at the weekly Chequers garden party for British leaders. It looked a marvelous afternoon.

"You can just imagine the jealousy in Brussels," I said.

"Why? Do they only ever get double yokers?"

Common Dace. Brown Trout. Brill.

"About Chequers! They're never invited."

"Shall we eat it? We've only the one. So, we need to make it count."

"The Prime Minister should write a book called British Fish and Their Patriotic Qualities," I said.

"Can fish be patriotic?"

"Not if they're German! Ha!"

At the Chequers party there was a red, white and blue marquee, and a string quartet. A banner read, "HMG, in Partnership with Mordor Publishing." Also, a tower of English sparkling wine flutes and broad tables of canapes.

"You know I heard they actually drink French champagne at those parties and not English Sparkling Wine," some treason from Mary. I ignored it. Encourage the behaviour you want.

In the background of the photo Mrs Bunsen could be seen cradling her stomach, while stuffing a large piece of Victoria sponge into her grinning mouth. Another Bunsen child was on the way. He was unstoppable. The headline was rousing too.

"Press Freedom Assured Forever In Blighty – No dissent will be tolerated as your Prime Minister prepares to fight for your nation's democracy!"

"Fried or poached? The egg."

Christ.

"What is an Englishman's village?"

"Potholed."

"Impenetrable," I corrected her. Then I read out the editorial.

Eel. Cod. Round fish…

"Well, I guess if anyone tries to invade Raylee they'll get stuck in the potholes," Mary amused herself.

"This isn't a time to be silly. We're going to war. We have to fortify the town."

The Government of William Bunsen understood this. The

editor of The Daily Parrot understood this. Now I understood. With hope, and time, Mary would understand too.

"Do you hear?" she asked. She went over and opened the backdoor.

There was the sound of a distant commotion.

"Maybe everyone got a quadruple-yolker today?"

"Your government needs you now to fortify your villages," I continued reading, louder. "Soon the bugle call will sound, and every able-bodied man and woman will take part in Operation English Castle. The next vital step forward as Blighty readies itself to purge our country of traitors."

Lobster. Crab. Prawn.

"He's run out of fish and moved onto crustaceans," Mary noted.

And then a bugle did sound.

"It's not hunt day, is it? Oh, the poor fox. I hope he gets away."

Mary stepped out into the yard, holding the egg.

I went after her.

"This editorial is the moment I have been preparing for," I shouted. "This is the turning point I knew was coming."

She wasn't listening.

"This is the watershed that was foreshadowed when the PM declared we must fight ourselves."

I think privately I knew it would come to building a defensive wall for Raylee.

"Hung, drawn and quartered seems too good for those who undermine the people's settled will!"

She just kept walking away with our breakfast. I didn't know whether to continue shouting out the editorial or give it up and go after her. The bugle was louder now. Whoever was blowing it was coming closer.

Just then Cyclops ran into our close and straight up to Mary.

"Mrs French!"

"Mind the egg!" I shouted, running to intercept him.

I used to tell Mary at mealtimes, "One day we will have to take up arms and rid the country of traitors. Anyone who doesn't celebrate the return of imperial measurements will be for the block!"

She would reply, "Yes dear.." She knew I was right. "Don't let your toad in the hole leap out. It took me all morning to catch him."

"Mind the egg!"

Bloody kid!

This was a big society moment. I wasn't going to let my country down. And I wasn't about to lose our egg.

"I can't fortify Raylee on an empty stomach! Mary. Keep away from that brat!"

Cyclops skidded to a halt a few feet from Mary. Breathless. Unable at first to get out whatever it was that had put him in a lather.

Mary knelt in front of him and held out her arms. He fell against her, grinning like a spaniel.

"Give me the egg Mary."

Still holding the idiot boy she offered up the egg.

"He's…here." Cyclops blabbered.

"Who child? Your dad?"

Cyclops shivered. Mary held him tighter.

"Not bloody likely!" I said, "he's bent double with a shovel toiling for redemption on Cardinal Bogg's farm."

"No. No. Billy Burner has come to town!"

The Prime Minister was here?

"Where boy?"

"He's on the high road. You can't miss him. He's wearing Hi-Vis!"

"What's he want with us?" Mary said.

"He's come to announce the winner of The Great British Pothole competition!"

Mary released Cyclops and stood up.

The bugle was growing fainter now.

"I suppose you're going to tell me this is another big society moment?" she asked.

"There's no moment like a Big Society moment. Where are the curtain twitchers who used to lay about bulging on handouts now? In the soft fruit fields whining still. My wheelchair is stuck in the mud. My child needs their medication. That was the first step back. Weaker nations look to local government to supply the needs of local communities. Fully sovereign nations like ours trust the people to organise themselves. I'll see Raylee's defences built."

But first we had to get to the high road and see Bunsen.

Cyclops slumped suddenly. All spent.

"Come on Cyclops. Let's get you inside and fed."

"Mary…" I warned her. It was my egg.

Cyclops sat down. Head low. Hands in lap.

"He's going."

"What?"

"Bunsen. The bugle is gone."

I glared at them both.

"We've been wasting time listening to this boy blather when we could have seen the Prime Minister for ourselves. Maybe even touched his Hi-Vis."

Mary gave me that look a woman gives a husband when she realises he is a genius.

Cyclops was on his feet again. Erratic is not the word for him.

He ran off.

"Cyclops? Where are you going?"

"I've got to tell Mum! I saw Billy Burner."

And I didn't.

Mary shrugged.

"Let's get inside then and fry this egg."

I organised the construction of the defensive barricade around Raylee that very day.

After the egg.

"And where will you get the materials?" Mary asked, her fork held in a shaft of sunlight. She was savouring her last bit of egg. I had an inner struggle not to take it.

It was a deliberately leading question along the lines of, "Will the Prime Minister agree with me that boiling your head in a bucket of oil is not only light entertainment, but a proud tradition in our country and something no petty red tape bureaucrat should be allowed to meddle with?"

"You know the warehouse that no one dares break into?"

"The one the EU insisted had a Flag of Europe painted over the door when they supplied the emergency monkey pox vaccines?"

"Yes. Everyone is superstitious because of the flag. No one will go into it. But I happen to know it's full of wooden pallets. Heaving with them. And not just pallets. Hammers. Nails. Screws. You can build anything you like with what's in that warehouse."

Where all the builders went in the early years of the 2020's, or why, we did not know, but the supplies they abandoned in that secret store I would put to good use.

"I am a prime example of the world beating ingenuity of Britons," I added. "I will start construction today. When I am far away burying my brothers in arms in some blood-soaked London field you will be safe behind The Great Wall of Raylee!"

"What dear?" she asked. She was now staring fixedly at a piece of bread.

"I'm going to use discarded pallets to..."

"They've baked the bread with a King Charles pattern." She turned the slice this way and that, her face all screwed up. "It's thin too. I think they've cut the flour ration again."

"You're not listening to me."

She held up the bread. She was right. It was Royal. She bit the corner and winced.

"You could build your barricade with this."

"Fine patriotic bread," I declared. "Now. I'm going to use the pallets"

"Does it make it more nutritional?"

"Can we please talk about my barricade?"

"The Gammins at 69 burnt the last wooden pallet when the gas went off for a week last winter," she replied. "Don't you remember? You were furious. Sitting here with your fingerless gloves on? Mad as a cut snake you were. Your fingertips were blue. Your nose was red though. You got so mad you blurted out *'I doubt the gas is off at Cardinal Bogg's farm!"* and I had to put a damp cloth on your brow to calm you down before you said something else you'd look back at and wince."

I waited this nonsense out. When she paused to breathe, I took my chance.

"The white heat of love for crown and country was shining from my heart, the day I decided to build Raylee's defensive barricade."

She tapped the bread against the counter. Thud. Thud.

"Do you want toast? Is it legal to eat King patterned food? Or are we supposed to take inspiration from it?"

I stood up and took the slice of bread from her and shoved as much of it as I could into my mouth. We'd never get finished discussing my fortification plans like this. The bread was too hard to chew so I took it out and satisfied myself with sucking on one end to soften it up.

"I guess it's okay then," she smiled and pinched one of my cheeks between forefinger and thumb. "Do you want the whole slice? I don't think my teeth are up to the task. I've kept some dripping from the bacon rind. We could have a fry up! You make pig noises and I'll pretend to cook sausages. Believe in sausages!"

I sat down. Temporarily defeated. Mind you, you can't build a wall on an empty stomach.

"Fry it up. Yes."

"Please?"

"Please." For the love of God and country. I'm sure she was off her rocker even then.

"We've replica tea too. It almost tastes like the real thing. Which is quite the feat considering it's parsley. They're getting cleverer and cleverer at the Ministry of Food."

Just then the kettle boiled on our stove.

"No problems with the gas supply today!" I beamed.

I watched the steam shoot up and then spread out under our kitchen ceiling. The paint was peeling.

After breakfast I would build my barricade and Mary would see what I was good for.

***

"A man must spread his seed as the farmer spreads his wheat. The farmer knows not what fertile field the wheat seed will take root in when he throws it to the wind. A man mustn't know either."

– The Private Observations of Prime Minister William Bunsen.

***

"What are you doing Mr French?" Cyclops asked me. "Why are you carrying that pallet?"

He was always popping up when you least expected him.

"Are you taking it to the black market? My mother says pallets are worth more than gold these days."

I wanted to tell him his mother was an idiot, but looking at the little denim patch he was wearing over his ruined eye socket…I felt weird. Sympathetic?

"The black market does not exist," I corrected him. "Only Europeans engage in such activities. Undermining the tax base? That is not for the English."

"It does exist. It's held in the Parish chapel before the Sunday morning service. My mum says the vicar takes too big a cut. We got a phone card there last week. I don't know who my mum was going to call. What with the phones being down and all. The paper says the network was hacked by saboteurs. But my mum said it was because we can't import the parts to make it work anymore."

This was sedition. I had to put a stop to it. We were out in PUBLIC! I would be guilty by association.

"It's well known your father voted against the people in 2016." That would shut him up.

"He did not! He told me himself he took his own pen into the voting booth and made the best choice for Blighty."

I ignored that. It was probably a lie. Cyclops shoved his hands in his pockets and shuffled along beside me.

"They had a handwriting expert examine his voting paper," I replied. I couldn't help myself. "There's no point lying to yourself Cyclops. You have to face the truth. Those who fail to learn from history are doomed to eat French brie."

He shrugged and kicked at a stone. He was barefoot. Grubby. His hair needed cutting and he had dried snot on one cheek. A great crusty stripe of it. It turned my stomach.

"Do you know where my dad is Mr French?" he asked, quietly.

"Private French to you Cyclops."

"But you're not in the army."

"Every able bodied man and boy is in the patriots' army. The flier this morning said it. Soon those who don't volunteer will be conscripted."

"What rank am I then? I want to be a captain or a major. Major Cyclops. That's a ring to it."

"Latrine boy. You're a latrine boy."

He sniffed. He would have wiped his nose with his sleeve but he didn't have one. A sleeve that is. He had a nose. He trailed along, kicking stones over the road.

"Do you know where my dad is?" Again!

"In a labour camp I expect. Toiling for redemption under Go Home Secretary Mrs Petal on a soft fruit farm. Cleaning a portaloo alongside the M40. Or perhaps he got lucky and they found some Continental in your ancestry and he was deported."

"My dad is a son of Raylee. Just like you."

"Being born in a country doesn't make you its son," I told him. "The great reforms of the early 2020's proved that. You achieve citizenship by proving yourself mental." – I kicked a raised cobblestone and couldn't talk for the pain.

"Mental? We don't use that term anymore Mr French."

I glared at him. The boy clearly had a dose of the woke.

"Who is your teacher?" I demanded. What was she teaching him?

"Mr Mann. But school has been closed on account of head lice," he said. "Ms Clench says it will reopen when they get a delivery of special shampoo. She was scratching her head like mad when she told us."

I waited for the pain in my foot to subside. I had to be more careful. If I wasn't fit and able I wouldn't be able to fight whoever it was I was destined to fight.

"What's with the pallet?" Cyclops asked again.

"The choice of pallets is symbolic! Who doesn't see one and not think of the vanished tradition of Great British house building? And once you think of a British house you must defend it. It's instinctive."

"My mum tells me to keep an eye out for pallets. We need them for heating." Cyclops picked up one end of the pallet, so I set it down. "Here! I heard some of the bigger boys saying there's a rumour there's a whole warehouse full of them."

"You can start serving your country today," I said quickly. "Go on. Keep going. Carry it to the outskirts of town."

"Does this mean I'm in the army now too? Are we the Raylee Engineers?"

"No. You're a sub-contractor on zero hours who I can fire without warning. Carry that pallet to the edge of town and no dawdling."

He nodded and began dragging the pallet along the gutter, straining his skinny arms, but determined to prove himself to me. Passers-by stood and stared. I worried they might try and steal the pallet.

"Get BARRICADES Done!" I said to hold them off. "DO NOT LEAVE YOUR TOWNS UNDEFENDED! Operation English Village!"

It took Cyclops many hours but eventually he had enough pallets assembled on the perimeter of Raylee to begin construction. A fine day's work, even if I say so myself. Actual building could begin tomorrow.

"You camp out here overnight and make sure no one steals the pallets," I ordered Cyclops. He was laying on top of the stack. Panting.

"Youth of today," I muttered. "A hard day's work and they're finished."

I turned to go home and found Mary standing there, arms

crossed over her bosom, her eyes incandescent, one foot tapping the ground like she was in a cartoon.

"Where's your rolling pin?" I asked.

"You'll be bringing Cyclops home for dinner?"

"He's on guard duty."

"Mark French I've a mind to wring all of your necks."

"He wanted to serve his country."

"It's true," Cyclops said. We both looked up at him. The sun was low, the light was red, his head was bathed in it. I fancied a heard the motor of a Spitfire in the distance.

"Won't your mother be wondering where you are?" Mary asked.

"She's not come looking for him," I told her. "Besides, boys love to camp out."

She closed in on me and stabbed me in the chest with her forefinger. Once. Twice. Three times. I retreated.

"I've a mind to wring your neck."

"So you've said." I covered my chest with my arms.

"You stay here with the boy while I'll go home and fetch our tent," she said abruptly, turning on her heels and marching off.

"You've a tent?" Cyclops asked.

"News to me," I said.

"Are you bringing back my supper?" I shouted, but she didn't reply. I liked it. She was all head of steam. The juggernaut. My wife. She was unstoppable.

"I think you're in trouble Mr French," Cyclops observed.

"Private French to you," I replied.

"Cyclops?" A woman started calling out from a few streets back. "Cyclops! Come home! It's time for your dinner."

Cyclops started to climb down off the stack of pallets.

"Where are you going?"

"That's my mum. I've got to go home now."

"This is desertion. This is dereliction of duty."

"I'll come back and help tomorrow," he said.

"Cyclops!"

He was on the ground now and headed off. I gave chase.

"You can't abandon your post." If he wouldn't stand guard over the supplies who would?

Just then Mary reappeared dragging a bag with the tent in it.

"You go home now Cyclops," she said, ruffling the deserter's hair as he passed. "And wash behind your ears!"

"This is intolerable," I told her. "If the pallets aren't guarded they'll be gone by the morning."

Mary merely dumped the bag at my feet. "There's a flask of replica tea and some patriotic loaf in the tent bag." She turned around and headed back.

"I'll be alright," I reassured her. It wasn't a cold night. "It'll do me good to practice sleeping out of doors."

Little did I know I would look back on this night as preparation for the night before the morning LC Carrot was killed beside me.

I waited nearly an hour sitting on top of the camp bag imagining all the work Cyclops would do tomorrow, before I picked it up and went home. Raylee would oversee its unbuilt barricade. I was certain.

***

When I got back to the pallets in the morning they were all still there. Cyclops was asleep on top of them. I don't know how long he'd been there, but I admit I was impressed that the patriotic spirit of Raylee was so strong it had dragged a lazy boy like him out of his bed to do what he should have been doing all along. Also, that no one had stolen either Cyclops or the pallets.

I had dressed for work in a hi-vis jacket and a hard hat, but with a shirt and tie to signify my rank.

"Sleeping on the job?" I asked Cyclops. He didn't reply. "If you don't smarten up Cyclops I'm going to have to replace you."

Maybe he was still asleep? Maybe he was ignoring me. I took out a little pad and made a note to look into this later on. That made two inquiries to be held, at some future date, the first being the black market in the Church.

"The gaps in the pallets make them easy to see through, take aim and fire," I told Cyclops. Let's see how asleep he really was.

He sat up, rubbing his eye, which was now black. I don't know how he got the bruise. One would think he'd look after his only eye better.

I could hear some boys laughing madly. A little gang of five came running up. Straggly lads with bumfluff on their lips.

"Cyclops! Cyclops!" they shouted. "Cyclops the one eyed monster!"

When they saw me they skidded to a halt, all puffs and reddened faces. I realised how imposing I must look in my hi-vis.

"Stand to attention," I ordered them. None of them did. It was obvious they needed basic training or there was no hope for the future.

Eventually one put his hands in his pockets, right through his pockets, which had holes in them, lowered his head and muttered.

"Please Mr French. Can we play with Cyclops?"

The others giggled.

"You can. But may you is the real question."

They all looked at me in bafflement.

"We will bring him back. We promise," another said.

And they all laughed.

"You can help him build Raylee's defensive barricade."

Now they all just looked confused.

I noticed one of them had a trickle of blood running down from his nose. Another was carrying a stout stick. Yet one more a rock. One a bite mark on his cheek. The fifth had ginger hair and a fat lip.

"And what game do you want to be playing with Cyclops?"

"Army men. He's the Germans."

"No. He's the French."

"Leave off. He's the Belgiums."

"I thought he was the Yanks?"

"Wasn't he a Viking?"

"Definitely the French!"

"Why don't we just call him Europe?"

Well, they weren't completely dense.

"Form an orderly line," I ordered them.

"My mum says it's stupid to be arguing with the Continentals all the time. That we did that for centuries and everyone just got killed all the time. And that she's fed up of seeing Union Flags on everything everywhere."

"What's your name?" I asked him. It was the ginger boy.

He looked at me with wide eyes and shook his head.

"Don't tell him!"

"It's Harry Starling!"

"It's Dan Daniels!"

"It's Bruce Finch," Cyclops said. He was awake after all.

"You're dead!" Bruce Finch screamed at Cyclops. "Bloody traitor!"

But the other four boys just dropped their weapons, turned tail and ran away. Bruce quickly followed them.

So much for that.

"The army will sort them out," I told Cyclops. "Youth of

today...they don't know how good they've got it."

Cyclops smiled at me.

"I had to fight them to keep the pallets safe," I think he said. I'm not sure, I was looking into the future and imagining how firm my barricade would hold if war ever came to Raylee.

"My defensive designs will not be tested in the heat of battle until I am far away, but I will prove the soundness of them today with a drill," I announced. "This will consist of taking turns to both attack my own barricade and defend it against myself."

Cyclops looked impressed.

"We better build it then!"

He jumped off the stack and ran away.

"I'll be back after breakfast Mr French!"

"That's your second desertion in twenty-four hours!" I shouted at him. "A third one and it's a very British court martial!"

He seemed to think I was joking.

"An army marches on its stomach!" he shouted in reply and disappeared down an alleyway.

I turned around and went home for a second breakfast. Cyclops had a point.

***

Inside the Mind of Cyclops

We are doing history at school. My teacher Mr Mann said the Prime Minister wanted him to tell us he has discovered a race of one-eyed people called Cyclopes. He says the PM is a "no good drunk who just makes up nonsense every day to cover up for poor governance". The country is "dying on its knees while the clowns in high office loot it."

I don't know if that's history or current affairs.

We're supposed to be doing history every day. They ran out of WW2 history to teach us so now the PM is personally adding things to the curriculum to learn. But we still do WW2 because that's when history begins.

The one eyed people are across THE ENGLISH CHANNEL and so no one can visit because of all the red tape. He looked at me when he was talking and winked.

I needed to pee. I had my hand up to ask but Sofie put her head on her desk so Mr Mann just paid attention to her. I had to hold my pee forever.

Now everyone has head lice because Barney came to school scratching his head. Barney says it's not his fault. He says his Mum couldn't get any medicine because the pharmacy was temporarily out of stock. He had to come to school because his parents work two jobs each every day and they don't trust him to stay at home alone. That's because he has one ear. So now we all have head lice. and we don't go to school.

The bigger boys said the head lice come from Brussels really to punish us for Brexit and the Continentals have to pay us compensation. I don't have head lice. I'm the only one. I don't know why.

Mrs Clench has green eyes and says she is an eighth cousin three times removed from William Bunsen. I don't know what that means. She says it all the time. On the last day of school she had a ketchup stain on her dress. Where did she even get ketchup!

I want some ketchup. I want some chips. I am helping Mr French. He knows where my dad is but he keeps it a secret. Mrs French is much nicer to me than he is. He is always angry. I don't know if he's more angry at me because I only have one eye or Brussels.

I've never made any red tape. I wouldn't know how to do

it.

So he must be more angry at Brussels.

***

Mark My Words

Mary came out to marvel when my Great British Barricade was finished. She brought a fold-up camping chair, her knitting bag and (I hoped) lunch.

"It's not very long," she observed. "I thought it was supposed to go all around town. This is just a few metres."

"Yards," I corrected her. No one knows what a metre is anymore. "And it's not the length that matters, but how it's used."

She snorted with laughter. I've no idea why.

"Are you going to finish it?"

I looked pointedly at Cyclops. He was tying the last of the pallets together with twine. "The youth must build their future."

In that moment I wondered, how?

"Someone is going to steal that twine," Mary shook her head. "And use it to patch their trousers."

"It's almost impossible to explain military matters to you," I replied. I'd expected praise and here she was nit-picking. I waited for Cyclops to finish.

"This section is an example to the town, others will follow," I said it slowly and patiently. "Raylee will stir and the village become impenetrable."

"Believe in barricades?"

Just so.

She gave me a long look. I'm sure she was not all there now. But she shrugged and sat down with her knitting in the camping chair. She didn't have any wool, so she air knitted.

"Believe in knitting," she grinned.

Click-clack went her needles.

"When I attack myself knit faster," I ordered. "The sound of the needles can be machine guns."

I picked up the stout stick one of Cyclops' friends had dropped.

"This is a rifle," I explained, slowly. I made a show of affixing a make-believe bayonet and loading the rifle.

"Everything has to appear realistic."

I marched briskly until I was the length of a cricket pitch away, turned dramatically and charged!

"I want to see your war face!" Mary shouted. Cyclops cheered. I closed in on the barricade, imagining explosions either side of me, my comrades falling, a piece of someone's brain splashed across my face. I was unstoppable.

Until I hit the barricade.

I attempted to roll over it but was repulsed. There was a sudden pain in my buttocks. I flailed in the grass, waiting for the killing blow. I was wounded. I went with the pain. This was my truth. I screamed into the grass.

"Medic!" I shouted. "Stretcher bearers!"

"Oh dear Mark! You don't half have a splinter in your bum. Lie still now. Stay on your belly. Cut out the playacting. There's a good fellow. Let's have a look at it. BE STILL!"

Mary sat on the small of my back. God she was heavy. I was immobilised.

"I might need to get my shears and cut away your trousers so I can have a proper butcher's. I've not seen a splinter this large in all my days."

"Why haven't you donated the shears to Operation Big Bridge?" I heard Cyclops ask.

"Shush now Cyclops. Don't go telling anyone."

I moaned. I wanted the attention. I was the one who was wounded.

"Do you think you can walk?" Mary asked.

"No," I whispered. "Leave me. Carry the fight to the enemy. Tell my love I loved her."

"It's not yet time for that you silly sausage," she chided.

"It will be if his bum goes gammy," Cyclops opined.

Mary tried to pull the splinter out but the pain was too much.

"It's lodged," she said. Useless.

"Do you want me to try Mrs French?" Cyclops offered.

"I don't want you getting a splinter too."

"What's up Mrs French?" someone shouted. I was too deep in delirium to know who.

"Private French has gone and gotten himself a shrapnel wound in the backside."

"Playing army men was he? At his age?"

"He'll be lucky to keep the leg," Cyclops added, matter of fact, his hands in his pockets.

"I'm like Nelson at Waterloo," I whispered, my vision coming and going as the shroud of eternity was drawn over my corporeal being. The hands of death were working on me. "Kiss me hardly."

"Yep, he's a goner," Cyclops decided. "Should we open a museum in his memory?"

"Mark's always a drama queen when he's hurt," Mary said. Goodness. To say such a thing in public? I was hurt. I was roused to cling to life.

"What do you know about battlefield medicine?" I demanded of Cyclops.

"He's still got some fight in him!" Cyclops started hopping up and down on the spot.

"Nelson died at the Battle of Trafalgar!" the unknown inquisitor said. "He was shot by a French sniper. He didn't have a splinter in his butt."

Laughter.

"You were there, were you?" I hollered.

I tried to see who it was. I needed to mark them down. When basic training started they'd be doing extra push-ups. But they were stood with the sun behind them. All I could make out was a tall, skinny chap with a blaze of red hair.

"Who are you?" I demanded.

"I'm from the government," he replied and promptly wandered away.

"Stay down for the moment," Mary urged. "Don't go getting all excited again."

She tore at my pants.

"Oh my! He's almost threaded the eye of the needle!" she blurted and both her and Cyclops laughed. She started to bounce up and down heavily. I couldn't breathe.

"His breathing is erratic now," Cyclops managed, between snorts.

"Call a chopper!" I cried. Mary landed on me so hard I farted. A nearby cat screeched!

"Grenade!" Cyclops made a show of ducking for cover.

"Oh Mark! That smell is atrocious." Mary was having the time of her life.

"Nelson died at Trafalgar. I was just testing to see if you knew."

"He's delirious Mrs French. You best get him to a doctor."

"Right enough Cyclops. Come on. You bring his stick and I'll be his crutches."

"Best call that stick a rifle or he'll be mad."

"Yes. Bring his *rifle.*"

"It's a good stick. I couldn't have chosen better if I were playing at soldiers," Cyclops declared, as if he was the expert.

Suddenly another voice entered the fray.

"What's up Mrs French?" It was Clarence the butcher. Always with his bloody apron on but hardly ever any meat to sell THANKS TO BRUSSELS PUNISHING US FOR EXISTING. Although there were rumours he got a lot of meat from the government and sold it on the black market.

Had I been able to, I would have made a note to investigate.

Behind him perched Ms Finch. Skinny bird. Lipstick smeared across her cheeks. She kept touching her hair, which was a mess. She had some grass stains on her skirt. She must have tripped. I hoped it wasn't on my barricade or it would be health and safety gone mad.

"Where did you get the lippy from?" Mary demanded.

"Where did you and Mr French get all this cooking fuel from?" Ms Finch answered back.

"Good thing this stack of pallets isn't in the EU," Clarence boomed. "They'd have you on charges for failing to put a barrier around the barrier on health and safety grounds. And no one is wearing hi-vis but the victim! It's a public health emergency."

Clarence was ideologically sound.

"The lipstick?" my wife wasn't letting it go.

"I make it myself from rust and tallow," Ms Finch preened. But she looked nervous. She kept glancing at Clarence. She wiped her mouth with the back of her hands.

I had to give an extended groan to get my so-called medical team to focus.

"Well, what's wrong with Mark?" Ms Finch asked, and then yawned. The bitch.

"He's a beastly splinter in his backside." Mary pointed at the shard of wood. It was basically a spear. "There's blood coming through his trousers."

"That'll be a bugger to wash out," Ms Finch noted.

"We best take him to the barbers," Clarence said.

"I thought we were friends," I whimpered.

"Yep. Definitely delirious," Cyclops declared. "He's a goner all right."

"Accident and Emergency would be my advice," Ms Finch threw in her two pence.

"No good poppet," Clarence replied. "Our A&E closed the other day to teach people to take personal responsibility for their health. We dare not try and take him to the nearest one over in Ballocks. The wait will be so long he'll be healed or dead before he's seen by a doctor. Or the wound will fester. I'm not sure how they amputate a single buttock? I'll have a go mind, if it becomes necessary."

"You could salt it and turn it into gammon," Ms Finch trilled.

"Oh, that's already happened."

They all laughed so hard I was tempted to die as punishment.

Suddenly another rubbernecker got involved. Ms Formaldehyde, the pharmacist. I would bet my last penny she was showing off in her work clothes too. People with jobs still! Just can't help themselves.

"What's up with old Mark then?"

"He's got a splinter in his backside!" My doting wife, Cyclops, Ms Finch and Clarence said together like some bloody Greek chorus.

"Well don't just lounge around," she bossed it. "Let's have him along to the new private infirmary. He can get a spare bed there and if he promises to let them use his story in their advertising he'll get a 10% discount off his initial consultation. Lower interest rate on the loan he'll need to take out for treatment too."

And just like that off we all went. The rest is a little blurred, being pain killing medication in the form of brandy, some paperwork I had to sign multiple times, the bright lights of surgery and a painful recovery.

I had to lie on my front for a full week. Blitz Spirit got me through.

"The doctor says you can come home," Mary kept saying, daily, clearly overcome by worry. I was even featured in the paper. An example to all of the tangible benefits of private-public health sector partnership.

I will have it on record that I remained upbeat throughout my recovery and shook hands with everyone in the infirmary.

Eleven

The Pied Piper (Briefly) Visits Raylee

"L is for Lettuce – Let us discuss Lettuce. If you want crisp lettuces go and live in France.

The ability of the modern Englishman to consume browned lettuce is testament to our unbreakable will, in the face of global headwinds.

For these reasons, The Lettuce receives a patriotic rating of 300,000 34 974,000 out of a possible top score of 300,000 34 974,000."

- 'Fruits and Vegetables, and Their Correct Patriotic Ratings' by Prime Minister Mark A. French.

Mark My Words

William Bunsen.

"You see him here! You see him there! You see him everywhere!"

Billy Burner!

The government ads for Operation Pied Piper were inspirational.

William Bunsen played The Pied Piper. But not just any piper, he was a ramped up Pied Piper in Hi-Vis. He learned to play the pipe as easily as he learned to dig holes for Operation Dig. Photos of Bunsen and his (then) wife filled the newspapers. Bunsen blew his pipe in defiance of the anti-growth coalition. Mrs Bunsen watched him lovingly, a hand on her swelling belly, her head tilted, face aglow with an assured and dreamy expression. It was rumoured this child was to be made an MP at birth. Blighty was to gain an extra constituency just like that. But it wasn't to be a piece of England, the boy was to be given Calais. It was English. Until it was stolen by the French. We'd start passing laws for it again and see how they liked it across The Channel when the shoe was on the other foot.

"That'll confuse the woke!" I celebrated, as Mary and I shared the skin of an apple.

"It's a bit browned," she mused, "but it's all there was in the fruit and veg section. Curled up in the basket next the tiniest pear I've ever seen."

Footage of Bunsen blowing his pipe and children following filled our screens. Happy children. Blonde children. British children. Joyful Billy Burner, leading the future to itself. The hour had arrived when Britain's children must do their part, just as their leaders did.

"What was the last Operation called?" Mary asked. "Before this Pied Piper joke?"

"Operation Dig," I replied. "And it's no joke."

Dig was a complete success.

"Over a million holes were dug in England alone." Although Scotland lagged and no one checked what Wales got up to.

"What about Northern Ireland?" Mary asked me.

I ignored that. We all knew what about Northern Ireland.

"It was a masterstroke," I retorted her digs. "There were so many holes in so many places you barely noticed all the potholes."

Later, the holes were filled in.

"What was the point of digging a hole to just fill it in

again?"

"What's the point of being a fully sovereign, independent, free trading nation free to cut our own lamb deals with Australians if we can't dig a bloody hole in our own front yard?"

Mary looked at me like *I* was the idiot.

"It was a show of national unity the Spanish could only wonder at," I replied. "A coming together the Danes envied. The will of the people forged into a shovel the Germans could only fantasise about replicating."

"Did they dig holes on Orkney?" she asked.

Oompf. Why Mary? Why?

"The British people have moved on from the Orkney secession."

"Operation Forget Orkney."

Her eyes held that queer turn, like she was seeing me for the first time.

"Operation Dig was in preparation for Operation Pothole," I reminded her. "That's scheduled to begin after Operation Pied Piper. Not much bloody point telling everyone to repair their streets if they haven't practiced filling in holes."

The Daily Parrot covered Bunsen's piping training with a week of front-pages demanding the Great British Patriotic Broadcasting Corporation make a documentary called 'A Very British Pied Piper'.

Page Three continued its demand for a return of Page Three. Daily.

Page Four was an Op-ed calling for the clocks to go back and forth, not just in spring and autumn, but monthly, to "give UK industry a competitive advantage in the Japanese cheese market".

On page five there was a story about a Norfolk poultry farmer playing Elgar to his battery hens to fight an outbreak of avian flu. I read the articles to Mary over a breakfast of onion chutney and crust.

***

INT. BATTERY HEN SHED DAY

Rain hammers on a corrugated iron roof. Water pours in through holes. ARTHUR SCUPPERED stands in his blue overalls looking thrilled. He's next to a giant sound system strung with Union Flag bunting and holding a HEN dyed red, white and blue.

A NARRATOR speaks. It is MARK FRENCH.

NARRATOR

Arthur Scuppered's family have been raising British hens for slaughter since D-Day.

Images of the D-DAY LANDINGS flash fast, superimposed over ARTHUR.

NARRATOR

Arthur is now leading a musical blitzkrieg against Avian Flu with Elgar the chief weapon in his arsenal.

ARTHUR SCUPPERED

I couldn't have played Elgar to my hens if we hadn't of left the EU.

ARTHUR presses play on the tape deck. 'Land of Hope and Glory' begins to crackle out of the speakers.

ARTHUR SCUPPERED

They would have forced me to play Beethoven.

Pools of water gather nearby. There's a flash of sparks around a coupling in the cables running to the speakers.

***

Mary was so captivated by my reading out of Arthur's story she stood slack-jawed with a spoonful of chutney.

"Elgar's Symphony No. 2 was less successful than his first when it debuted at the London Musical Festival in 1911. Even then, London was not always dedicated to the national interest, but stained with a treasonous spirit of the kind William Bunsen has dedicated himself to cleansing from our capital."

I paused to let this sink in. Can you imagine a time when Elgar wasn't revered? It made one shiver.

"Imagine where we'd be now if Bunsen had been Prime Minister in the 1930's?" Mary wondered.

"Charles III would be King of Europe," I said. Take that France!

"There are no such concerns in sparsely populated Norfolk," I continued reading, "following the expulsion of the Norwich University rebels, and the robustly pragmatic conversion of the faculty buildings to animal husbandry, Arthur wasted no time filling the space with caged hens. A government grant helped him establish a thriving Great British business. But Avian Flu followed Arthur and his feathered soldiers into the buildings, and here on his home farm too."

"I guess that's because the buildings are made of woke cement?" Mary asked, the innocent.

"We are free of the Eurocrats now, Arthur says defiantly, holding a dead bird in each hand. And they're free too. Let them wail in Brussels into their boring veterinary policy papers. We can choose the fatality rate that suits Britain's birds best. Avian Flu gives British producers an advantage over our European competitors. We save a lot of money as the birds just drop dead and we don't need to pay for pointless medicines, dangerous vaccines, or someone from Prague to slaughter them."

"Do you want breakfast or not?" Mary demanded. "I can't listen to all this on an empty stomach."

After breakfast our stomachs would still be empty. But like Arthur Scuppered we know who to blame. If you have someone to blame you have a direction of travel.

***

"Imagine leading the world and still being able to find the time to learn to play the pipe?" I said. Chutney and crust fueling me for the day ahead.

"I'm impressed," Mary replied. So that was two of us, and an entire nation.

"Bunsen's capacity for extracurricular activities is world beating. Name me a past Prime Minister with such energy?"

"It's because he governs by slogan," Mary commented, with a smirk I wasn't sure was appropriate. "It frees him up to lead. Think of where we would be now if he'd wasted time reading the detail."

The television news, and the Opposition, played their part in Operation Pied Piper.

"This is a brave plan to boost UK productivity," a shadow minister said, on the news. "There are millions of children with time on their hands and the country needs them to apply the boundless energy of youth in our ever expanding bunting industry. The government has sat on its hands for far too long. We've long called on the Prime Minister to take advantage of the closure of many infant schools to fill the vacancies in our factories."

"But aren't you as the opposition also responsible?"

"How so?"

"Well, as the Prime Minister himself has said, you took far too long to raise concerns over the details and policy implementation."

Silence.

"We are simply calling on the government to account."

"But your own party has resisted calls to make children work."

"That was before focus groups told us voters in a key swing village believe child labour is good for children."

The school of life was back and it was everywhere.

Agreement within the political class on the government's big ideas, regardless of party allegiance, had been a feature of UK political life since 2010, and the country was reaping what they'd all sown together.

"But surely children should be in school?" the interviewers fretted.

"Early employment is vital to lifelong learning. The British people expect their children to have a rounded education. For too long child labour has been a dirty word. A sign of the wokeification of Britain. And where did that get us? Floods of cheap foreign workers displacing the native population. If my ten-year-old comes home with blisters from a hard day's graft in a mill I know that tomorrow those blisters will be calluses."

But blisters didn't mean work couldn't be fun.

"How will children find time for a factory shift and do their homework?"

"By scaling back unnecessary subjects like geography, foreign languages and science the young have a once in a lifetime opportunity to help us shape their future," the shadow minister explained. "Although I do take serious issue with the government's decision to charge children from their own wages for the meals received during their meal break. I'm sure the British public is more than happy to see the charge covered by an interest bearing government loan, supplied by a partner in the finance industry, and the repayment delayed until after the children have completed their stint at coal face. It risks damaging morale to charge them daily."

***

"If I were Bunsen I wouldn't let the Opposition carry on like that," I said.

"What? By endorsing child labour?"

"No. Shadow Ministers shouldn't agree so readily. There needs to be a show of dissent to prove we're a democracy. Not just some random MP nit picking at a detail. And it's not child labour. It's British kids putting their shoulders to the wheel of British industry. It'll deter illegal boat crossings! I can't see some Afghan kid coming here to take advantage of our welfare system being prepared to work a ten hour day."

Mary looked at me as if I was in a fever.

"I'm going to boil the kettle. Do you want a cup of hot water?"

"I want tea!"

"We don't have any tea. I looked today and there was a sign saying temporarily out of stock due to unexpected surge in demand."

Let's move on, I thought, and did.

Of course, the usual yoghurt knitters muttered about Operation Pied Piper. One foolish woman even tried to glue herself and her son to Winston Churchill's statue in central

London. The police made short work of her. She was left handcuffed, still glued to the statue, with a gag fitted and glaring madly at the world as if she was right and the majority were wrong. Which basic maths told you couldn't be the case. Possession of glue was outlawed by use of sovereign powers that same day.

Her child was taken directly to work at an experimental munitions factory in Chelmsford. If I'm not mistaken, he was "Child Employee of the Month" two months running in his first year.

A special Pied Piper bus toured the country collecting children and delivering them to factories. Speakers blared out songs. It was all reminiscent of the ice cream vans of my childhood. Children ran to the bus and ran right onto it. The millennials could learn a thing or two about patriotism from the latest generation.

"Yes," the shadow minister confirmed, "It's right that William Bunsen drives the bus."

What better way to whip up support than the Prime Minister there on the front line?

"It's nice to see the PM dressed as a great fictional character too," I commented, as my wife and I watched the first advert.

"You mean instead of a fictional tradesman?"

"Must get dull having to be an imaginary plumber day in and day out."

"Not if you don't have to do the actual work." There it was again. Was my wife a subversive? I worried.

In the ad Bunsen was in profile on the horizon with the sun rising behind him. He pied a long note as the dawn's red, white and blue rays drove away the dark.

"He looks like a satyr," my wife commented.

"No. He's deadly serious."

The visuals cut to snapshots of young people up to

nothing, no good at all. Slack jawed youths wasting their time in front of the television or kicking cans down alleyways. Hardworking adults passed them buy, coming or going from mill or pit, soot blackened faces.

A man in work-stained overalls, a pit worker, paused to watch the feckless children and shook his head. Another worker approached him. A mill worker all covered in flour.

"And to think we labour to build them a country," the mill worker said.

The pit worker sighed.

"It would be nice if they put down those phones and lent a hand."

"I bet they're on benefits too."

"But they still have fancy phones?"

"While the work needed to take advantage of our new freedoms goes undone."

The two men looked meaningfully into the camera and said in chorus, "It wasn't like this in my day."

Thereafter followed a rapid succession of the salts of the earth of England.

A nurse, fitting a catheter, paused and eyeballed the camera, "In my day we worked hard to deserve the food bank." Her patient nodded, "We had to be really sick before we strained the NHS."

A garbage collector stopped heaving a steel rubbish bin, "When I was young we didn't have time to waste online." If you looked closely you saw he was tipping a load of burgundy passports into the truck.

An elderly baker next, kneading dough, "How will we make Britain great again if the young don't lend a hand?"

Finally, a soldier in the trenches, "We fought the Hun to ensure Britain was free, but who remembers that now?" A heartbeat later he fell dead, shot between the eyes. A testament to the need to defend our borders.

Next they all appeared together with Billy Burner in front of them.

"Patriotic children work!"

The scene returned to the street with the factory and mill workers. The Pied Piper skipped into view and over to the weary men. He examined their calloused hands. The youth hung back, taking photos on their phones and sneering. But not for long. As soon as Bunsen started playing the pipe they transformed. Their clothes magically turned into overalls, they marched over and stood to attention.

"It's time the young did their bit for Blighty!" one blue eyed boy cried.

They all raised their fists.

"Anyone who wants an honest wage for an honest day's work follow me!" Bunsen shouted and the young fell into line and skipped behind him.

In the next scene Bunsen is driving the bus and it's packed with children in overalls. On the horizon a giant factory billows smoke from dark stacks. A golden halo over its roof.

"Operation Pied Piper - Working kids are happy kids!"

***

It wasn't long after the first advert that The Pied Piper did come to Raylee. We were one of the first visited. I took that as symbolic of my town's special place in England's heart. Mary and I were at breakfast. We were sharing a whole egg. It wasn't powder substitute. It was a good egg. It was a proper British egg.

"This egg is a testament to the viability of the British poultry sector," I stated. "Arthur Scuppered and Elgar have won the fight! Let the Continentals fret over a poultry sniffle. The British egg producer is victorious."

"Please dear. Let me concentrate," Mary requested.

I could smell the egg as it fried in the pan. Faintly, I heard pipe music.

"I can't wait to taste the egg."

Mary paused a moment and picked at the carton the egg came in.

"Someone has crossed out 'Product of Mali' on the carton."

What of that? The piping grew louder.

"What's that sound?" she wondered. "Sounds like someone's playing the flute."

"It must be Bunsen."

My heart began to beat faster. I pressed a hand to my chest just in case it leapt out!

"Oh dear. Let's hope not. The egg will go cold."

What a daft response? I wanted to rush out to see if I could spot the Prime Minister, here, in Raylee! But my grumbling stomach kept me seated.

"On the Continent all they do is wring their hands about bird flu while British egg producers soldier on," I said. "Did you read the article in Unotesticular? Colds are natural. A chicken may catch a sniffle as easily as the next man. A duck may experience a raised temperature, as can a goose. What use is there in wasting time and money trying to stop the natural course of events? Diseases are like rivers. You must let them sweep through a population and take advantage of the commercial opportunity presented."

Mary furrowed her brow. "There's a little piece of shell in the white." She picked at it with a teaspoon.

"If the French want to stop British birds crossing The English Channel they can pay for it themselves."

"Why don't the French put up a big net across the Channel?"

"Like on a tennis court?"

"That would be best."

She had the solution! I could picture it. A giant net between Calais and Dover. Operation Giant Net! We could trick the French into protecting our borders.

The piping was unmistakable now.

"It's a bit pale," Mary worried. "And the shell was very weak."

"That's a productivity gain," I replied. "Less time lost cracking the egg."

She held one of the pieces. It had a lion stamped on it.

"I guess it's better than egg substitute."

"Can't you hear the piper?" I started wriggling. "Can't you just finish frying the bloody egg so we can have breakfast?"

"Remember when eggshells were firm?"

This was tiresome.

"Can we not have one meal without treason?"

She gave me a puzzled look, brow furrowed, lips sucked in.

"I'll have an English egg over a Continental chicken's any day of the week. In Belgium the shells are so tough you need a hammer to crack the egg. That's red tape for you."

"The Romans brought hens to Britannia," Mary said abruptly.

"That's what the so called experts would have you believe."

"And what do you believe?" she smirked.

I wasn't going to be put off that easy.

"It wasn't beyond the wit of man, or hen, to cross the Channel on some driftwood before the Romans invaded our sovereign territorial waters."

The furrowed brow again.

"It's done," she said.

Give it to me. Give it to me.

***

INT. FRENCH KITCHEN DAY

A battered spatula in a battered hand. The implement eases under a fried egg in a pan.

There's the sound of children shouting. A piper is playing. The spitting and crackling of the egg in fat competes with these sounds.

The egg rises on the spatula. Slowly. The egg begins to travel from stove to back door.

MARK FRENCH
You're going the wrong way.

MARK grips the edge of his empty plate. Red faced. He's terrified.

MARY FRENCH
What's all that racket?

MARY opens the backdoor. She disappears out of it with the egg.

MARK FRENCH howls in pain and frustration.

***

"It's been a full month since we had an egg," I shouted after Mary. It was no use. Masses of hollering children drowned me out. And the piping was louder and louder. A screeching note that rang in my head.

"CAN WE NOT JUST HAVE THE EGG FIRST?"

I pushed back from the table and took my plate with me. Mary could gawp brainlessly at whatever was happening. I would have my Great British egg!

But outside, well, outside it was a sight for sore eyes.

Outside I was struck dumb with wonder.

There in our own close was the Prime Minister himself! William Bunsen. Billy Burner had come to our town. He was dressed in a chequered, three-piece hi-vis suit with a little Austrian hat on his head, mad hair flaring out around it, feathers in the hat band and all. And oh, how he was playing that pipe!

Mary was shaking her head. "No. NO," she said.

I was transfixed by the sight of the PM himself leading anything at all. What a momentous day in the life of our noble village. For a moment I forgot the egg. William Bunsen playing the pipe was a feast itself. My stomach filled up with pride.

A long line of children snaked across the grass and through the parched front yards. The PM's cheeks were bright red. His eyes rimmed with tears from the effort. What was the song? It must be Elgar?! Or the national anthem.

"NO!" Mary shouted.

Good Lord. She'd gone mad. She rushed at the line, and still holding the egg on the spatula in one hand, she grabbed the collar of one of the boys and pulled him out of the line.

"You just stop this nonsense right now!" she told the child. I couldn't see who it was at first. But he was a feisty little thing. He clawed at her like a frantic kitten. She wasn't letting go. She turned and dragged him towards our house.

"Mark French!" she shouted. "Don't just stand there. Give me a hand."

In the struggle the spatula tilted towards the earth. Oh my God. I ran forward as fast as I could. But I could never be fast enough. The egg slipped off. Identified flying object spinning to the dirt.

I dove with my hands cupped in front of me. Time seemed to slow. My ears filled with a maddening hum. The fried egg fell and fell forever, always just out of reach. We hit the ground at the same time. Ooof. My breath left me as I watched the egg flatten and bounce up in a puff of dust.

"What have you done woman?"

What have you done.

I couldn't say it twice as the fall winded me. I may have strained something. I wasn't sure. In the leg? Maybe it was a heart attack. I let out a howl and the last in the line went passed me without a glance.

A weedy man. Tall. Redheaded. He stopped and crouched before me. He was wearing a scout's uniform. His adam's apple was excessive.

"Patriotic Kids Work!" he shouted it at me. Spittle on his lips.

"Tell that to my wife," I gasped. He smiled and patted me on the back.

"We'll meet again," he promised. Then he re-joined the procession, clapping his hands and shouting Operation Pied Piper's world beating slogan.

I clambered to my feet, still panting, still heartbroken and turned an aching man, trudging back into our home.

And there he was. Little Cyclops. The one-eyed bastard child of Raylee. Sat in my chair at my dining table in my kitchen. My big arsed wife at the hob again, frying him an egg.

"It's alright Mark," she told me. "We have two eggs."

"We HAD two eggs," I corrected her. "This is a disc race!"

"What's the matter with you? Your egg is in the sink. Just wash the dust off."

"I picked it up for you Mr French," Cyclops beamed. The

idiot.

I won't tell you how I felt when Cyclops turned on the tap to wash the egg and flushed half of the yolk out.

"Stop it you little fool!"

I shoved him away from the sink and turned off the tap.

"Wow! You've got water!" he shouted.

"That's because, unlike your mother, we don't undermine the will of the people."

"If you're not nicer to Cyclops I'll eat your damn egg myself," Mary hissed, holding the spatula up as if she might strike me with it.

"It's my fault," Cyclops interjected. "Don't fight on my behalf."

"Why aren't you on the bus?" I demanded.

"I'm not having him working in some damn factory," Mary barked and threatened me with the spatula again.

"You've gone bloody woke," I told her and stormed out of the kitchen. I went upstairs and sat on our bed, trying to calm down.

A minute later Cyclops crept up to the doorway and laid my washed fried egg down on the threshold.

"Don't let it get colder," he said and scampered away.

I ate it in spite of myself. T'was a good egg. It was a Great British egg.

Twelve

The Sermon On The Spout

P is for Pear - The Pear assisted in taking back control of baking. There is no greater service for modern tree borne fruit.

For these reasons The Pear receives a patriotic rating of 361, 618 682, 088 out of a possible top score of 300, 034 974, 000." A royalist, who can be relied on."

– 'Fruits and Vegetables and Their Correct Patriotic Ratings' by Prime Minister Mark. A. French.

Mark My Words

My sweet Mary stood with a bruised banana in her hand.

"Why are you up so early?" she asked.

"Why are you holding a banana?"

"There wasn't any milk at the supermarket, so I bought a scratch card."

"They arrested all the milkmen," I told her. "It was in Radio 4's 'The Enemies of the People' bulletin this morning, just after the [abridged] Shipping News. Some milkmen have been smuggling milk into bunting factories. Breaking legal ration limits? That's treason."

"Are you sure?"

"They're going to pass a law today which says it was."

"That explains why we didn't get a milk delivery today."

She held the banana to her temple like it was a pistol.

"Mrs French. Am I to understand you support the breaking of perfectly sensible limits on calories intake for children in the workplace?"

She shrugged.

"They've run out of tea again due to another temporary surge in demand."

I looked hard, at her. Britain could never really run out of tea. Maybe she'd gone mad. I woke up mad one morning and it took days to pass. Maybe it was best to hope this was just a phase and move on. What do you do with a mad wife?

"It's a big TV day," I stated.

She pulled the trigger on the banana and staggered a few steps.

"Where's the scratch card?" I asked.

"Scratched."

"Did we win?"

"I won this banana."

We looked at each other. I was so confused. She reloaded the banana.

"On the cheaper cards you win food now," she explained, aiming the banana at me. "I'm surprised you didn't read about it in the papers."

"Can you choose?"

"No. The poster in the shop says it's to help reduce food waste. So you win whatever fruit or vegetable is most in danger of being wasted due to temporary problems in food storage. Today it is bananas."

"That's sensible. Supply chain problems inflicted on British logistics by the overreach of Brussels used to cause a lot of wasted food."

She shot me with the banana.

"So you're up early to watch Cardinal Bogg give his big speech?" she smirked.

I held up the page from The Daily Parrot, which listed the order of proceedings. A big, glossy double page spread with one of the country's religious icons in each corner. Saint George and the Dragon top left. Winston Churchill top right. A Spitfire bottom left. The Flag of Europe [on fire] bottom right.

"09:00 - A short film detailing how Prime Minister Bunsen had a vision in which the Northern Ireland Protocol impasse was resolved by spraying all of Surrey's sewage straight at France."

"10:30 - A short film celebrating The Union Flag - with a workshop on how to turn used shopping bags into bunting, to be conducted by half of the Prime Minister's children."

"12:30 - A fly on the wall documentary following Cardinal Bogg's preparations for his speech."

"14:00 - The Prime Minister and Mrs Bunsen will pull the lever in the pump house in Surrey to open the pipe, before a celebratory toast in England's last Wetherspoons."

"14:05 - Cardinal Bogg arrives at Dover on horseback to give his speech."

"14:30 - We watch live as the first gallons of untreated effluent burst from the pipe and fly like liquid Valkyries at Calais."

Mrs French closed her eyes and loaded the banana again.

"How many bullets does a standard banana hold?"

"Not enough," she said, then, "Cry havoc and let slip the turds of Surrey."

***

09:00

INT. 10 DOWNING STREET DAWN

PRIME MINISTER WILLIAM BUNSEN (BUNSEN) in his office. A MAID opens the curtains to let in the first rays of sunlight. BUNSEN is playing with a small terrier. It's hard to decide who has the wilder hairstyle, man or dog.

BUNSEN laughs as the dog chases its tail. THE DOG stands on its back legs and hops in a circle as BUNSEN pretends to chase his own tail.

CLOSE ON THE RADIO - on a side table THE RADIO is playing the national anthem. We see it is made of Bakelite and branded "CHURCHILL".

BUNSEN looks to camera, holding the dog.

BUNSEN
I was in this very room when I had my vision for Tungsten's Tunnel.

CUT TO : An anxious BUNSEN. Late night. He paces. Sounds of a WOMAN IN LABOUR can be heard.

A DOCTOR, wearing a football style shirt that says "NHS - In partnership with Serco" rushes into the room.

DOCTOR
It's another boy!

BUNSEN
I name him Tungsten.

DOCTOR
You're the father of a nation.

The DOCTOR falls to his knees and then lies on the floor, as if before an altar.

BACK TO THE PRESENT. BUNSEN sits behind his great desk. He wears a hard hat and a hi-vis vest. His desk is littered with drawings of pipes. He holds a model of a double decker bus.

OVER SHOT – *"BUNSEN IS YOUR BUILDER"*.

BUNSEN

We had to mark the birth of my latest son with a mighty infrastructure project. A weak leader would have scarred your landscape with a wind farm, but I knew we had to defend our borders.

FADE TO – THE WHITE CLIFFS OF DOVER…

***

"We'll have to share the banana," Mary said. "I traded a tin of crushed tomatoes with Ms Finch for its weight in flour. We can have a pancake."

"Yes. Yes."

She was interrupting the 09:00 film. Bunsen was standing on the White Cliffs of Dover with Cardinal Bogg. The camera swept in and then panned out as the Prime Minister pointed back inland and then threw his hand towards France.

"We'll take all of Surrey's waste and pump it into the sea at Dover," Prime Minister Bunsen promised.

"Non placet eis," Cardinal Bogg replied.

"Well? Do you want breakfast or not?" Mary interrupted.

"Can't you see I'm trying to watch the film."

A narrator talked as Bunsen walked the streets of Guildford to select the site of the pump house. There were many locations, but Guildford Hospital was chosen due to having been closed. Traitors said it was due to a lack of staff and funding, but we all knew it was done to deter illegal people seeking to enter the UK to abuse the NHS, in partnership with SHITCO. The logic was unbreakable. If there was less NHS it would be abused less by illegals.

Narrator – *"Tungsten's Pipe is a present to the nation, from the Prime Minister. A tube of concrete sovereignty that cries freedom."*

"It's all legal!" I shouted. "They passed laws to make it legal. There's nothing the EU can do about it."

"I'll just make breakfast then."

Narrator – *"The best thing about the pipe, without a doubt, is no foreign powers have been involved. It will be..."*

Bunsen again on screen, talking to the Cardinal, "It will be a very British sewer pipe."

The EU had threatened legal action in some tin pot court we didn't recognise.

"If they continue to complain we need only divide and conquer them!" I shouted at the television. This pipe was a victory as great as Dunkirk. "The Dutch should be reminded that if it weren't for Red Coats they'd still be ruled from Madrid by some inbred fool with a heavy lisp!"

The Germans that we won the war.

The French that we won the war.

The Belgians that we won the war.

The Spanish that they won their war.

And so on.

Then a bit of magic happened. Bunsen's face filled the screen and he looked very impassioned.

"A little bit of Continental gratitude wouldn't go astray," I said, just as he said the exact same thing!

It was the first sign that I was prime ministerial. I felt it as I spoke in time with Billy Burner. My head buzzed and my heart thudded. I rose from my chair and stumbled to the kitchen. Mary was whisking the egg and flour together with a fork.

"Have you seen the whisk?"

"I will be Prime Minister one day," I whispered. "I've had a vision. I can see myself striding through the doors of 10 Downing Street demanding a lectern is placed outside to give my first great speech."

"Oh dear Mark. You have waited too long for breakfast. Sit back down. It won't be long. Once your blood sugar is back up you'll feel okay."

"I am going to be Prime Minister. I just don't know how."

I was feeling faint. Mary stopped whisking and frantically searched the drawers for a brown paper bag.

She led me by the arm back to the television.

"Breathe in and out of the bag."

"I'm fine. I'm just a visionary."

"You're something alright. We can't have you fainting. It's Thanet's turn with the ambulance today."

The film had moved on to explain how all the concrete was gathered to build the pipe.

"Across England and Wales millions of concrete paving stones were donated. Thousands of stone slabs too. Towns and villages freely gave them up."

The footage showed the army, in some woebegotten former mining town in Snowdonia, digging up the paving as locals stood by and shook their fists in celebration. Not one person attempted to push passed the sandbags and machine gun nests. This was the country coming together, even the Welsh.

Next we saw The Royal Mile in Edinburgh being torn up by an earthmover. A close up of the machine revealed it was

William Bunsen himself at the controls. The sun was low over the castle in the background as he lifted the slabs of stone and skilfully dropped them into a waiting truck. The locals tried to assist. Several had to be restrained for their own safety. The rest were kettled to keep them out of the way of the JCB.

"What would the Scots do without us to look after them?" I asked.

Narrator – *"Schools were given a day off learning about how Britain built the modern world so children could get involved in the demolition."*

The film showed William Bunsen, dressed in hi-vis lederhosen and a feathered hat, leading children out of a boring classroom and onto the street. There he showed them how to lever up a paving stone and smash it with a sledgehammer. Rental yapping excitedly at his feet.

All across London doors were flung in (by police) and kitchen drawers emptied of cutlery to supply the iron needed for the project. We saw footage of Cardinal Bogg in a giant leather apron pouring buckets of cutlery into a smelting pot. It said 'PORT TALBOT' on the screen.

An artist's watercolour impression of the finished pipe appeared.

Narrator – *"The beginning and end of Tungsten's Pipe isn't aligned with any solstice day or celestial body, but when it still stands in one thousand years archaeologists will find a star to link it to."*

Bunsen walked into view.

"And that star will be yours!" he said. A cartoon came next showing the pipe disgorging an endless brown tide across The English Channel. We saw the grey-haired President Macron in a big room in the Elysee Palace. He was eating a giant croissant with a very old French lady. Suddenly the sun is blocked out. The windows darken. A roar is heard and the windows are smashed in by a tidal wave of Great British sewage. You can tell the floaters are British as there were little flags stuck into them. The distressed couple swim about in it all.

"I must write to Brussels!" Macron says, as he bobs about the room. "We must give the British whatever they need to let us sell them French sparkling wine. We are defeated."

At that point I fainted. It was too much.

***

"Mark?" Mary said. "Mark? Wake up now. You've been out for ages."

My eyes opened and closed like a scene from a movie. Mary was standing in front of the television holding a frying pan with a perfectly small pancake in it.

Why would she block the television?

"I wasn't asleep."

She shook her head. She tutted. She didn't have a great bedside manner.

"You overdosed on sovereignty. Silly sausage. Sit up and have something to eat. I've warmed it back up."

"We're having sausage?"

"Ha! You'd be so lucky."

She was clearly confused.

"You can't just waste gas like that," I admonished her. "We'll get in trouble if the meter reading is too high. We'll lose access to public transport."

"No danger there. It's Hainault's turn with the bus this week."

Thank God.

"There's a lovely patch of sunlight coming through the kitchen window. The pancake has been sat in that for a good few minutes."

Why did she mention sausages?

"You got my hopes up," I told her.

She shifted and Cardinal Bogg filled the screen. I could hear him but I couldn't see him because Mary's big arse was in the way. I shifted to look around her. Bogg was seated on a wooden horse on the great pipe at Dover. I'd missed so much!

"My patriotic people," the Cardinal began, "we have been persuaded by some, that are scornful of our liberty, to take heed how we commit ourselves to ramped up infrastructure projects for the multitudes, for fear we can not even dig a trench without a Pole. But I assure you, I do not desire to live in distrust of my faithful, loving, hardworking and indigenous Great British people."

What a speech! Immediately I felt reborn.

Mary tried to shovel some pancake into my mouth.

I waved her away. Cardinal Bogg was feeding my soul. I was a patriot. He was talking to me.

"I won't have it!" Mary shouted. "You must eat."

She looked close to tears.

"It's okay to feel emotional today," I reassured her, but she kept shoveling pancake at me.

"Just eat it! Mark!"

"My loving Mary, listen to Bogg."

I accepted a mouthful so she would let me watch the television. But she was poised and intent, like an anxious mother. She mushed the next spoonful over my lips. Then she made a big show of trying to clean it off my face with the dish cloth.

"Oh Mark."

I had to keep moving my head to watch the Cardinal.

He was dressed in red, white and blue silk robes. Seated on his noble charger. He looked magnificent. HMS Belfast (freed of its chains in the Thames) was now anchored in The

ENGLISH Channel. An actual Royal Navy ship, and not one borrowed from someone condescending like the Americans.

"This pipe will gather all the sewage of Surrey," The Cardinal promised, "pump it across England and into this English Channel to wash about the open sea. Intact British turds will beach in France. This is a mighty British show of British defiance. The Continentals will be unable to ignore our reasonable British demands no longer. We have taken back control of our British sovereign water and it is teeming with Great British life."

"Most of it microscopic," Mary muttered.

"The EU is just envious," I replied, only to be rewarded with a fork full of cold pancake.

The Cardinal was even wearing a hat. He looked medieval. It was a powerful image of where modern Britain stood on the world stage.

I recall now the best of the papers the next day. The Daily Parrot had a full-page splash of the pipe opening under the headline, The Great Stink 2.0, with a cartoon drawing of Macron holding a massive Gallic nose.

"If just one sovereign turd makes landfall at Calais it will have been worth all the blood and treasure," I said.

The film showed the full length of the pipe now. It roared out of Guildford, supported on steel struts made from millions of knives and forks. It dominated the landscape. The aerial view was impressive. The footage got faster and faster. The theme to "Dambusters" played as the view took us racing across England, going from colour to black and white. And now the mothballed port at Dover came into view with the Cardinal standing on the pipe.

"Pump England!" The Cardinal cried.

"Pump England!" The Prime Minister shouted.

"Pump England!" Elizabeth 1st implored.

We saw a mother with a baby in a pram. She stood

underneath the pipe, sheltering from the rain. "Pump England!" she urged.

"Pump England!" I shouted, around some more pancake.

Then Oliver Cromwell appeared, his round helmet under one arm, and demanded that England pump.

Now we were inside the pump house with Bunsen, and his permanently pregnant wife. They stood together with their hands on a lever.

"It is time," the PM said.

Mrs Bunsen looked to the camera. "For the children."

"For this green and pleasant land!" they said together.

Elgar begun to play. They pulled the lever. There was a mighty rumbling. The floor under their feet was vibrating. The Prime Minister took a step backwards. Mrs Bunsen kept holding the lever down and smiling. She was so strong.

"There must be a lot of shit under that pump house," Mary said, her mouth drooping, the fork and the last scrap of pancake circling my mouth. It tilted to the floor. The pancake was sliding off, but I got my hand out in time to catch it.

Mary straightened.

"The screen is frozen," she said. "Look. Bunsen is almost out of the door and it's frozen. Mrs Bunsen looks like she's screaming."

A Union Flag filled the screen.

"It's not frozen. They must have had a glitch. This bit is all live."

Live, with only a slight delay.

"When I'm Prime Minister I'll build a second pipe from Hertfordshire to the Welsh coast. Give the Irish a taste too. See if they keep phoning the Yanks up to moan then."

"Look, there's something else on the screen."

It was a tally of the number of meals voluntarily sacrificed by British school children to feed the workers who constructed the pipe. Millions of potatoes. Millions of turnips. One whole chicken.

"Find me a five year old Italian boy who would willingly sacrifice his lunch to build something worthwhile," I said, pointing at the screen. "You notice how they stopped building things once they lost Britannia? It's all just crumbling away over there under a mountain of red tape. But Britain is building."

"Oh, here's Cardinal Bogg again."

The screen filled with the Cardinal on his wooden horse on Tungsten's Pipe. And what a pipe! It soared over the water, a bulge at the end, like a small arm and hand holding an apple. It was vibrating so strongly it emitted an endless low note.

"It's coming!" the Cardinal told us. "The Great British flood is coming!"

"He wants to watch he doesn't fall off that pipe," Mary commented, failing to read the room as always.

HMS Belfast begun to blow her horn. The seagulls hung motionless in the air.

"No one does pomp like the British!" I was so excited. "Look at the soldiers with all that bunting, all along the seaside. The French will think twice before trying to invade us now!"

"I think some of the soldiers are fainting?"

Suddenly a troupe of actors walked into shot and stood on the great pipe. Shining beads on a sceptre.

"Look! It's King Alfred."

"There's Queen Elizabeth."

"One and two!"

"Who's that?"

"Oliver Cromwell? It must be."

"I'll call my pipe Cromwell's Pipe," I was ecstatic. "Teach the Irish a little bit of history."

Mary frowned hard. At me. I don't know why.

"Oh look!" I laughed. "It's Charles 1st and he's holding his head under his arm."

That was a lesson to anyone who tried to undermine parliamentary sovereignty. Make no mistake. No one does pomp with symbolism like the British! No one!

After the monarchs came the salt and the earth of Blighty. The nurses. The postmen. The cheerful binmen. The doctors. The scientists. The pilots. And Lord David David dressed up as William Shakespeare. Big red cheeks. A gravy stain on his tunic. He was swaying as he walked.

The pipe vibrated harder and harder. So much shit was coming down the line. The low note now sounded like a distant thunder roll. The actors held onto one another, but so professional were they, they kept smiling to camera. No one does great actors like the British!

Cardinal Bogg held the reins of his wooden horse as it edged closer and closer to the pipe's mouth.

A narrator re-joined the broadcast. No one does narration like the British!

"From this day forward no dour German with his petty clipboard can stand between Great Britons and their sparkling sea!"

I thrust my arm up in salute.

"Because we are a free people!" I shouted. No one does freedom like the British!

"The sea around Britain has long ago been emptied of foreign boats. But we British may catch and keep whatever we like. We are reaping our harvest," Cardinal Bogg was exultant.

I shook my fist at Brussels. No one shakes their fist at Brussels like the British!

Now the screen filled fully with William Shakespeare, supported by Elizabeth 1st on one side and Elizabeth 2nd on the other.

"They're going to fall off if they don't watch out," Mary worried. "Shouldn't they get off the pipe?"

"Shush! It's the bard's turn!" I told her.

"This pipe's story shall the good man teach his son. And Crispin Crispian shall ne'er go by, from this day to the ending of the world…"

A Henry V moved through the others as Shakespeare spoke and joined him. Now they intoned as one. No one intones like the British!

"But we in it shall be remember'd. We few, we happy few, we band of brothers. For he to-day that sheds his poop with me shall by my brother. Be he ne'er so vile, this day shall gentle his stool. And gentlemen in England now a-bed shall think themselves accursed they were not on the toilet, and hold their manhoods cheap whiles any speaks that defecated with us upon Tungsten's Pipe's Day."

"Is that the original speech?" Mary wondered.

"They've adapted it."

Now all the crew gathered, except for Charles 1st, who was missing.

"Cromwell pushed Charles 1st off!" Mary shouted. "Did you see that?"

"What?"

"Cromwell pushed Charles 1st off the pipe. He's down there in the water. His head is floating away."

She was right. It was hilarious. What a lesson for everyone watching. No one does humour like the British!

"Pump England!" the crew shouted together. "Pump!"

And it was time. The great tide of shit gathered in Surrey arrived at Dover to burst across the Channel at France. This was a lesson they will never forget!

"The footage has frozen again," Mary said.

Oh God. She was right.

"Look! Elizabeth 2nd is in mid-air! The Cardinal's horse is tipping over the edge."

There was just a shadow on the water under the pipe. It was the flow.

"Hit the TV!" I shouted at Mary.

"No one hits their TV like the British," she smirked daftly.

"Give it a thump," she urged me on. "No one thumps their tele like the British!"

"Mary! Now is not the time."

"I can't hit the television."

"Why not?"

"It's a flatscreen."

"Slap it then. It must have frozen!"

The Union Flag appeared on screen again, fluttering to the national anthem.

"God must get fed up with that," Mary said. "Always having to save our bloody king."

When the anthem played out the broadcast resumed with a montage of Cardinal Bogg's speeches.

"They've already played this. While you were asleep."

"I was just resting my eyes. Shush. Let's watch together."

I felt spent.

"It's a shame we didn't get to experience the climax."

"It would have been shit anyway," I joked, and we both laughed, we few, we happy few.

***

INT. HOUSE OF COMMONS AFTERNOON

CARDINAL BOGG stands in a packed house. MPs bray on all sides. It's the Mother of Parliaments and she's on the gin. CARDINAL BOGG adjusts his double breasted, pinstripe suit and thrusts out a single sheet of A4. He waits for THE

SPEAKER to calm the mob.

THE SPEAKER
ORDER! ORDER! ORRRRRDDDEEEEERRRRR!

A WAITER approaches THE SPEAKER'S CHAIR. A hush descends.

THE SPEAKER
What's today's special?

WAITER
Crushed potatoes pan fried in British olive oils with sea salt. Served on a bed of green growths with a fillet of snapper and an apricot juis.

THE SPEAKER
Excellent. And the wine?

THE WAITER
Chateau Pompey 2019

THE SPEAKER
A bottle of that.

THE HOUSE ERUPTS as MPs clamour *"Me too! Me too!"*

THE WAITER NODS and exits.

CUT TO :

EXT. NEWLYN FISH MARKET DAWN

CARDINAL BOGG in Union Flag wellington boots and

raincoat, over a pinstripe suit. He stands in a packed fish market. FISHERMEN crowd all around him, beanies held reverently in hands. Heads bowed.

CARDINAL BOGG
British fish are sovereign fish.

FISHERMAN ONE, a gnarled old timer with a Gandalf beard, falls to his knees.

FISHERMAN ONE
But my Lord Cardinal, the Europeans have stolen our fish.

CARDINAL BOGG walks to the man and lays his hands on the bowed head. He looks meaningfully to camera.

CARDINAL BOGG
This is why we had to take back control.

THE FISHERMEN nod and one by one they fall to their knees and CARDINAL BOGG lays on his hands.

A CHILD FISHERMAN walks into the scene. He is holding a giant papier mache COD.

CHILD FISHERMAN
Thanks to William Bunsen and Cardinal Bogg my future is secure.

The scene fades into a view of a fishing boat. The swell is heavy. The men are hauling in nets teeming with fish. THE CHILD FISHERMAN is with them.

CHILD FISHERMAN

Take that Brussels!

Suddenly the men all cheer. They've caught a MERMAID! She smiles alluringly and waits to be freed from the net.

CHILD FISHERMAN
No one catches Mermaids like the British!

CUT TO : HERNE BAY - KENT DAY

A DINGHY beaches itself on the pebbled shore. It looks empty at first. Nearby a young BRITISH MOTHER is having a picnic with her fair-haired TODDLER.

Suddenly YOUNG BURLY MEN WITH SUSPICIOUSLY STRONG SUNTANS tumble out of the boat as if there is no end to them. One after another they pile out and stand menacingly on the shore.

BURLY MAN ONE
Woman! Which way is the benefits office?

THE YOUNG MOTHER grabs her child and holds him tight, as BURLY MAN ONE approaches her.

BURLY MAN TWO
Which way is the NHS?

THE YOUNG MOTHER holds her howling TODDLER.

BURLY MAN THREE
We've come to take your fruit picking jobs!

THE YOUNG MOTHER attempts to run, but stumbles.

The BURLY MEN move at her menacingly.

But running across the shore is CARDINAL BOGG holding a sword that flames red, white and blue!

CARDINAL BOGG
Not on my coast watch you don't!

The BURLY MEN quail. They begin to fight and struggle each other to get back into the boat.

CARDINAL BOGG
Control our borders.

THE YOUNG MOTHER, still holding her TODDLER, runs to CARDINAL BOGG.

YOUNG MOTHER
Only with strong borders can we ensure our future grows.

CARDINAL BOGG
A sovereign child is a strong child.

We focus on the boat full of foreign men.

BURLY MAN ONE
We only wanted to abuse the NHS.

BURLY MAN TWO
You're lucky your government has a strong border policy.

BURLY MAN THREE
Quick! Let's go before they send us to Rwanda!

And back out to sea they go.

END SCENE.

***

The Union Flag filled the screen again. I felt so proud right then.

"We can do anything we like with sovereignty."

"I think I need a nap now," Mary said. She looked very pale.

"Let's have lunch first?" All that patriotism had made me very hungry.

"We've got a potato. I can boil it?"

"Do we have any butter?"

"No."

"Is the gas on?"

"I don't think so."

"Let's just have it raw."

"No one eats raw potatoes like the British."

Thirteen

The Enemy Within

"B is for Broad Bean – The Broad Bean. Under review.

For this reason, The Broad Bean's patriotic rating is undeclared."
– 'Fruits and Vegetables and Their Correct Patriotic Ratings', by Prime Minister Mark. A. French.

Mark My Words

We were lucky to have Prime Minister William Bunsen. If not for him who knows who we would have fought?

"The Welsh?" Mary suggested, late one afternoon, as we foraged for nettles behind the shuttered Iceland supermarket. The carpark was cracking up and bursting with edibles. There was even a nasturtium snaking out of a particularly deep crevice in one of the disabled spaces.

An orange-red sunset was in the offing. Yoke splashed over everything. Long shadows, getting longer.

"No point. The Welsh are already cowed."

The last delivery van was still parked up. Tyres deflated. The bonnet missing and the windows smashed in, but the red, white and blue paintwork on the sides was as good as new! An omen.

"The Scots?" Mary had a twinkle in her eye.

Why fight the Scots? They were fighting themselves, although The Orkneys needed *"bringing back into the fold of civilisation"*, to quote Cardinal Bogg.

They still do.

"Let's see how well the adoption of the Euro goes in a mushroom cloud."

"Didn't you hear?" Mary paused, openly grinning now, one hand carefully gripping a nettle.

"Hear what?"

"The US Navy has blockaded Faslane."

That had to be rubbish.

"They say we can't be trusted with nuclear submarines anymore. They're demanding we surrender them."

I blinked at her several times. She looked satisfied.

"It wasn't in The Parrot."

"So it can't be true?"

She released the nettle. I don't know why.

"The Isle of Man?"

"You'd have to find it first."

"Well, foreigners then."

"We can't openly fight the French as they would see that as an honour, which would be unbearable."

The Italians? Why? The Dutch? We won that war in the 18th century. The Spanish? We won that war in the 16th century.

So maybe no one? No. There had to be someone.

England it was. We would fight ourselves. Show the world our mettle.

We are defined only by war and inventing the train. Without cause to erect new monuments we would wither away. War saves our nation, it is our wet nurse, just as with all previous wars. I knew even then that the coming civil war would renew The Great British Democratic Monarchy, and that little bit of Northern Ireland which still clung to

Empire.

For too many years Britons had had to go overseas to fight. Finally, conflict was coming home.

Two world wars.

One world cup.

One referendum.

Two civil wars.

"When I return to 10 Downing Street..." William Bunsen would declare, as he declared declaring war again, *"when I stride back through this black door you will know we have defeated the enemy within! We have rooted out the traitors and our democratic monarchy is purged of anti-growth sentiments. Think of it not as a voluntary act of violence committed against ourselves, but a national colonic undertaken with the view of a brighter tomorrow. Get War Done! One thought. One people. One time. We will have made ourselves anew, glowing with family values, hard work valued once again..."*

It will be a lovely day tomorrow...

"It's time to get home."

We had enough nettles and dandelions.

"If he's declaring war *again* why is he flying to Moscow tomorrow?" Mary asked.

"What?"

"He's flying out from RAF Brize Norton. It was on the radio."

There was a small article in The Daily Parrot that morning, in tiny font on page forty-eight - *"PM to visit Moscow for Trade Talks - Prime Minister William Bunsen is to make his first overseas visit this month to The Democratic Republic of Russia. The vital trade mission will depart from RAF Brize Norton - In Partnership with Centrica, at 0600..."*

"Why is he going Mark?"

"Fermented cabbages," I replied. "It's obvious."

"In exchange for what?"

"Financial services. We may have had to return the Koh-i-Noor but we still have Jersey."

Mary gave me one of those long looks.

"He's going to bugger off and leave us to fight ourselves alone."

She kept looking at me. I walked away.

She shouted after me, "I'm telling you. He's like one of those men in the pub who stirs up trouble and then legs it the moment the fists start flying."

Clarence the Butcher hove into view at that point, carrying something large wrapped in a black bin bag.

"Evening Clarence!" I shouted over. Nothing to see here.

"Who's in the bag?" Mary said. Damn her. "Long pig in the shop front tomorrow?"

He kept moving, but he called back, "There's a wild sweet potato patch behind where WH Smith used to be. But you better be quick! Half the kids in town are down there grubbing in the dirt."

"Dig for Britain!" Mary shouted, raising her fist in a flat palmed salute.

Clarence stared at her with his face frozen in horror.

I had to act.

I set off for home, without looking back. Bloody hell Mary.

***

"Maybe you'll have to arrest me," Mary said. She was washing our foraging in the kitchen sink. The water was off, but we had some rainwater from a bucket.

"Great British rainwater," I said.

"At least they haven't managed to fill the clouds with E. coli," Mary replied. "Although I wager there's a water company wondering if they can pump the sewage up there."

"Be a good show. If the wind is blowing to France."

Imagine it. Wouldn't that be funny.

"Would you arrest me? If you had to?" Mary demanded. She turned abruptly. I wasn't sure what to answer her.

"I'm too hungry to argue."

Even though I would clearly be in the right if I did arrest my wife.

"Well?"

"The war can't come soon enough," I said.

My Great British War Bag waited in the kitchen. It had been delivered in the night...

"What was that?" Mary asked, around 4am.

I didn't answer as I was asleep. She pushed my shoulder.

"Mark."

"Ug."

"Did you hear that?"

"Wha."

"Go and see."

"For God's sake."

"There was a thud out front."

Then we heard other thuds. Rhythmically. Thud. Thud. Growing quieter as the delivery man moved up the street. Half awake, half asleep, I daydreamed I was a bombardier in WW2. Blossoms on the land beneath. Flowers. Blighty.

"Maybe birds are falling out of the sky?" she hoped. "Maybe it's food."

I swung a leg out of bed. It was cold. I didn't want to get up. Birds don't fall out of the sky here. They do that in silly countries, like Denmark. They do it over Cyprus.

"Never mind. It must be a delivery of some kind," Mary said. "Go back to sleep."

"Milk?" I asked hopefully. I was almost awake.

"Too heavy. Go back to sleep."

An excellent plan.

"Besides, the milkman is in the stocks."

I was nodding off again.

"What did he do?" I muttered.

"He gave milk to the children making bunting in the library," she said, sorrowfully. "When they arrested him he was screaming bairns can't work without electrolytes."

"Madness."

"Poor fellow. The strain has gotten to him."

"He's a snowflake."

She pinched me. Hard.

"What was that for?"

"Go back to sleep Mark."

"I'd love to!"

Silence for a few seconds.

"Unless they're delivering entire cows!" Mary blurted and laughed. "Get Cows Done!"

I looked at the window. The sky was grey outside, inside it was just normal. Grey.

"Go and see what it is."

"Mary."

"Please. Maybe it's a surprise hamper. Maybe Bunsen has agreed to allow the Italians to give us the food aid."

What rot. We were growing our own peas.

"You know it isn't that. There's been nothing in the papers about the Italians begging Britain to help with a surplus they can't afford to store."

"I guess…" she sighed.

"Can you stop your stomach rumbling?"

"No Mark."

"It's really loud. I'll get you a snack?"

"Of what? Sovereignty?"

Silence.

"Go back to sleep."

"You can eat the Great British pea raw," I said. "Perhaps I'll find wild peas when I'm foraging in the fields outside London."

An army marches on its slogans, but also its stomach.

"Mark," Mary held the nettles and dandelions over the sink. "Should we save the drips of water or do you reckon the water will be back on later?"

"You're not serious."

She shrugged.

"I think Bunsen is going to give an update on the flooding in the Cumbrian coal mines tonight."

"He's declaring war again?"

"How many times is that now?"

If only she'd been paying attention to all the op-eds I'd been reading her.

"The people have moved on from the flooded mines," I told her. "Now let's get to our spots in front of the tele before we miss the show."

"I hope he doesn't claw the air again, when he gets all worked up, it gives me a chill."

He'd claw the air alright.

"History is in the making," I told her. And I was right.

***

EXT. 10 DOWNING STREET DAY

WILLIAM BUNSEN wears hi-vis army fatigues and a military looking cap with a plume of black feathers. He grips the edges of a red, white and blue lectern, his chin tilted defiantly up.

There are two UNION FLAGS on each side of the No 10 DOOR. The flags flutter.

TWIN, BLONDE DRUMMER BOYS stand to attention either side of the lectern. Drumsticks poised under their chins.

Giant spotlights blaze like suns.

WILLIAM BUNSEN
The fear of potato shortages will be constant.

BUNSEN pauses, stares for an eternity into the camera. Faintly, the sound of a crying baby can be heard. CAMERAS click.

REPORTER ONE (O.S.)
Prime Minister, is there any truth to the rumours that Go Home Office Minister Petal was filmed attending a satanic sacrifice at Land's End?

BUNSEN is unmoved. There is the sound of a scuffle out of shot.

REPORTER ONE (O.S.)
Press Freedom!

We hear a van door slam shut.

WILLIAM BUNSEN
Hunger will be on the menu. But the British people have the will to endure the slings and arrows of outrageous

Belgians.

We hear a man being beaten inside a van. Muffled cries.

WILLIAM BUNSEN

We must protect Great British freedom of speech from the woke scourge.

***

"Never a truer word," I agreed.

"Hunger's been on the bloody menu for years," Mary said, a little too hotly. I was grateful the television didn't have ears!

"Are they Bunsen's twins?" she wondered. "The little drummer boys?"

"Magnus and Carta?"

"Yes. Chubby little things. Nothing like poor Cyclops and the other boys around here."

"Magna and Carta's milkmaid was liberty itself," I replied. "Cyclops was suckled on the teat of treachery."

"Sometimes Mark..." Mary said, her hand raised. "I wonder."

"About what?"

"Sometimes I wonder if you're the gravitational centre of a tiny universe."

She was a tad touched.

She shrugged and lowered her hand.

"I see the boys are wearing leopard skins," I said. "They must have lifted the ban on importation of endangered species for military use again."

This was freedom to choose our own laws in action. Sovereignty. Ah, the cup was brim full.

"They're synthetic."

"They look like real boys to me!"
"The leopard skins. Look. He's going to catch fire under that spotlight."

***

EXT. 10 DOWNING STREET DAY

Cont…

DRUMMER BOY ONE is smouldering at the shoulder. NANNY ONE rushes to him and bodily lifts the boy out of the spotlight. NANNY TWO pours a bottle of water over his smouldering shoulder.

WILLIAM BUNSEN
I didn't start the fire.

WILLIAM BUNSEN laughs uncontrollably.

CUT TO :

THE UNION FLAG superimposed over THE WHITE CLIFFS OF DOVER. Elgar plays. Any Elgar.

***

"The BBC should make a documentary about that burning child called A Very British Fire Hazard!" Mary said, and laughed so hard she started coughing.
"Huzzah for Billy Burner!" I countered her. But a pea caught in my throat. I started to cough too. Still struggling herself, Mary patted me on the back.
"Careful Mark," she wheezed, "don't choke on

patriotism. Chew your food properly."

And she was off again, doubling over, desperately trying to talk about Bunsen's boy burning.

"You're one," I managed two words before the pea launched another offensive.

We called a truce, and both retired to get in order.

The flag and cliffs faded back to 10 Downing Street. The view widened to show MPs from Bunsen's party and Sucof Groop with his mask on.

"What's he want to be wearing that silly mask outside of the Commons?" Mary wondered.

The MPs sat in rows on the street, disciplined school children, cross-legged with their hands in their laps.

"It's good to see Sucof there. The people don't want their politicians divided at a time of national crisis."

"We did not ask for this battle," The Prime Minister continued. *"We are ready for any deprivation, any sacrifice, any bloody deed that must be done to ensure once more Britons can shop in supermarkets with full fresh produce shelves."*

And buy their potatoes in pounds and ounces!

"Like they have in France?" Mary talked to the television. That bloody smirk again. She was nervous. She knew I was going away. We just didn't know what day.

"Those photos of French shops are deep fakes," I replied.

"Bunsen has done his hair."

"The official hairdresser has been busy," I agreed.

"What was he dressed up as yesterday? A pilot?"

"He was a plumber. Don't you remember? In the photos he was in a council house fixing their sink."

"Oh that's right," Mary smirked. "The transmission cut suddenly when water flooded out from under the sink cupboard and over that tangle of extension cables and power boards."

Sparks flew and the water seemed to seizure. The last

thing we saw was Billy Burner pushing one of the production team off a wooden chair and leaping onto it. The staffer froze in mid-air. Mary laughed at that. The foolish woman.

"When was he a pilot?" she pestered me.

"Many times. Shush now Mary. Let's listen."

"Over the years you have proudly queued for butter and sovereignty. You have not grumbled like some perpetually moaning Frank, you have not quibbled like a Teutonic paper pusher. You have shown Blitz Spirit when electricity was rationed. Germany knew they couldn't undermine us with their Continental price caps and benighted fields of solar panels. I loved your Blitz Spirit when the GP surgery in your town was converted to a barber. We will not be humbled. We will earn a brighter tomorrow. We will be free!"

Like so many slumbering lions I was stirred by the speech and inwardly bared my claws. In my mind I beat my chest. I worked on my war face. I readied myself to sacrifice whoever was necessary to fulfil our nation's destiny.

Would I ever see my Mary standing in the back door of our house and twisting that damp dish cloth in her calloused hands again? I didn't know.

"Believe In War!" William Bunsen commanded us, and we did.

"Believe In War!" I echoed.

The little drummer boys began to play and the Prime Minister beamed, motioning the one who had been moved away to come back. He did. Back into the light. Still dripping from the shoulder. But no tears.

The MPs clapped. The youngest son of Sucof Groop ran to his father and sat on his lap waving a little Union Flag.

"Oh my God!" Mary exclaimed. "They've put a mask on Groop's son!"

Later, they would all go to the House of Commons to vote

for England's war against England.

"This will make Brussels think twice!" I exulted. "See how well they meddle in our affairs now!"

"I think we should eat those bacon rinds," Mary said.

It was a very British televised address.

The next day The Official Opposition Leader gave his reaction to Bunsen's latest war speech. He agreed again with the concept of a civil war but had found some details he disagreed with.

"But you voted with the government for war against ourselves," a random television journalist noted. "Do you want Brussels to win?"

"It's what the British people have decided," the TOOL answered. "We can make a success of a civil war. I only question the wisdom of not declaring a public holiday to begin it?"

I would recall the little drummer boys frequently in the months that followed. I would raise the Raylee militia and drill it. I had built the town a defensive barricade. I would requisition supplies from the town's shopkeepers for the war effort.

Whenever I prepared for a fight in some Surrey field, I would smear dirt on my face to the beat of those drums. When I stripped down the rifle I was given by my unit's first commanding officer I would be encouraged to know that if I fell the Raylee youth would make the bunting for my coffin. And I was doubly fortified by the agreement of the British political class that fighting ourselves was not only unavoidable, but a perfectly sensible thing to do. It would always be a lovely day tomorrow.

Fourteen

A Debate About a Potato in the Shape of a Dead Prime Minister

- Part One, by Candlelight

"T is for Turnip – The Turnip. If I have to explain to you what is worthy about this vegetable you must not be English. No rating. You don't deserve to know it."

– 'Fruits and Vegetables and Their Correct Patriotic Ratings', by Prime Minister Mark A. French.

Cardinal Bogg never sat on the government bench in the House of Commons. He lay. He stretched. He pretended to sleep. His soft hands loose on his potted belly; a burial mound containing nothing of worth (to the living). One leg flowed to the floor where it pooled as a foot. His posture told everyone all they needed to know, about themselves. Few men make it to later middle age without ever having experienced a callus. Cardinal Bogg was of the few.

The government bench was now the only bench in the House of Commons.

Prime Minister William Bunsen had achieved a stunning two hundred seat majority in the snap, spring general election. It was achieved through a historic increase in the government share of postal votes. Government supporters put this down to the popularity of the revised child labour policy.

"Patriotic Children Work!"

If only we had not stopped wasting public money on libraries years earlier, and converted them to flag factories, so many troubles in the fishing industry would have been avoided.

The slogan "Patriotic Children Work!" had been plastered across the country. For social media and television, Bunsen was filmed dressed as The Great British Pied Piper. It was a stirring moment in the history of cinematography. Cardinal Bogg oversaw the production. He recalled it now as he dozed on the bench.

***

EXT. COUNCIL ESTATE DUSK

OVER BLACK – "THE UNITED KINGDOM. TODAY…"

We hear savage children. Ferals. Running amok. Glass breaks. Police sirens in the distance. Dogs fight. Faintly, 'Ode to Joy' plays. It's so dark.

OLD WOMAN and OLD MAN are mystically lit from within. A loitering GANG OF WOKE PUNKS glow blue and gold in the shadows.

WOKE PUNK ONE

Fought in the war did ya Grandpa? How much for the medals?

OLD WOMAN

You pipe down. He's worth ten of you.

WOKE PUNK ONE

You want some of this Grandma?

OLD MAN

Come on Beryl. They're not worth it. They're all woke.

OLD WOMAN

To think my brothers died fighting Health Tourists on Dover beaches for the likes of these. Why aren't you picking fruit for Blighty?

WOKE PUNK ONE

You've painted your fence red, white and blue!

(MOCKING LAUGHTER)

OLD MAN

Let's go. I'll not waste my time on them.

WOKE PUNK ONE

That's it. Run away. Go on.

More raucous laughter.

THE WOKE GANG follow. Kicking cans. Spitting. Shoving each other. A hulking housing estate looms, windows broken, graffiti everywhere.

But there's one property on the ground floor that is in excellent repair. Little picket fence around its proud garden plot. The fence painted in Union Flag colours. There's a small flagpole in the yard and it flies the Union Flag.

We see it all from the POV of the old couple. Weighed down with fresh produce. They've retreated. The gang stand between them and sanctuary.

CLOSE ON THE OLD MAN to see a chest covered in medals.

EVEN CLOSER on the medals. Each one speaks of a battle.

"BRUSSELS" "BERLIN" "DOVER" "CALAIS" "PARIS" "ROME" "LONDON" "THE WORKING TIME DIRECTIVE" "ECHR".

Now we focus on the gang leader - WOKE PUNK ONE. He runs to the perfect garden and kicks his way through the fence. He rips the Union Flag from its pole.

We hear a dozen spray cans shake as the WOKE PUNK ONE laughing runs back with the flag.

DOC MARTEN'S BOOTS pin its corners to broken paving stones.

THE FLAG OF EUROPE IS SPRAYED OVER THE UNION FLAG.

CLOSE ON the old couple. Tears streaming down their cheeks.

OLD MAN
We won the battle abroad…

OLD WOMAN
Only to lose the war at home.

The gang carry the vandalised Union Flag back to the garden.

But wait…what is this? We hear a PIPER playing 'God Save The King' and a CHOIRBOY sings, weak at first, but strengthening with each word.

CHOIRBOY

God save Charles our king, Long live our noble king, God save Charles our king, Long live our noble king,

Who is coming behind the old couple? There's a resolute figure in the distance. It's the PIPER and he's leading the CHOIRBOY.

The PIPER is THE PRIME MINISTER. Haystack blonde hair, he marches to the rescue. The CHOIRBOY carries a folded UNION FLAG.

CHOIRBOY

God save the king, Send him vic-to-ri-ous, Happy and glo-ri-ous, God save the king, Send him vic-to-ri-ous, Happy and glo-ri-ous,

THE OLD COUPLE straighten and salute WILLIAM BUNSEN as he marches past them towards THE WOKE GANG. He gives them a wink. He's more than a match for any woke punks.

The CHOIRBOY bows and hands THE FOLDED UNION FLAG to the VETERAN.

FUMBLING to raise THE FLAG OF EUROPE on the pole,

THE WOKE GANG freeze. One by one they turn and see WILLIAM BUNSEN as he blows his pipe, as he closes on them. As the light of his glory splashes across their faces.

CHOIRBOY

Long to reign o-ver us, God save the PM, Long to reign o-ver us, God save the PM.

THE WOKE GANG hang their heads. As WILLIAM BUNSEN marches past they fall in line and all march into the distance. SUNLIGHT hits the housing estate. The windows repair as if by magic. The graffiti vanishes. The broken fence fixes itself.

THE OLD COUPLE arrive at their garden and we see them RAISING THE UNION FLAG once more in front of their home as WILLIAM BUNSEN leads the CHILDREN into a rising sun.

OLD COUPLE

"DON'T LET LABOUR BREAK BRITAIN - VOTE BUNSEN APRIL 1st"

END SCENE.

***

Cardinal Bogg smiled. His eyes rimmed with joy's tears. He was convinced his film had swung the swing vote. The disbarring of many opposition MPs the day before the ballot, while investigations into their finances were ongoing, had not been significant. The people wanted Bunsen. The people wanted freedom.

"The good people of Great Britain have demonstrated

their wisdom," He told a reporter from The Daily Parrot, after the GE results were in. "It is the will of the people."

The government itself audited the private contractor who counted the vote. The audit was re-audited by another firm (all the good papers said it was a firm with a good reputation), which was owned by the wife of a government MP. The firms all set up and based in an offshore territory and closed immediately after the count was in, audited, and re-audited. The records burnt.

All as it should be in The Mother of Parliaments in the 21st century.

"The ayes have it! The ayes have it!" the Speaker declared, confirming the government motion to remove all House of Commons benches, bar one. It didn't matter that removing the benches wasn't in the party manifesto for the GE. What mattered was power.

Prime Minister William Bunsen beamed at the Speaker as removal men in overalls entered the chamber. Any MP who held on to a bench was removed with it. It was such great sport that Bunsen cried with laughter, pointing, and sobbing in mirth. The bench clenchers were predominately Scottish.

"Bench clencher! Bench clencher!"

The government MPs relished the extra time they now had to take on additional jobs. Parliament can't sit if there's nowhere to sit. So it must busy itself with other activities.

Sucof Groop just agreed, as always he didn't want to confuse the populace by opposing the government's biggest idea, but he determined to pick a bone later over the colour of the overalls on the removal men. Bunsen approved. This was how the Opposition had behaved since 2010. This was now the only way it was permitted to behave.

As the Cardinal lay now he wandered down this memory lane, and another. Candles flickered in every nook and crevice. There was no electricity in The Palace. Anymore. Either.

"Angels," Bogg whispered. "Our beautiful benefits. The Lord be praised."

The decision to turn off the electricity supply was taken at the highest levels of government. The Cabinet had gathered at Chequers to dine on lambs fattened on the Cardinal's estate.

"The Lord works in mysterious ways."

Not everyone was keen. The Secretary of State for Looking Like John Bull, Lord David David, had disagreed forcefully, lamb shank in hands smeared with gravy, red faced he shouted opposition from a chair on the lawn.

"It will create panic if Parliament goes dark," he declared, shank held high. "Westminster is the guiding light of western civilisation. What will the German carmakers make of it?"

"The people didn't panic when we rationed their use of cotton," Field Marshall Trust shrugged, before turning to the side and having her photo taken (by a professional). She was so skinny, so sharp, mostly just a bone with some skin stubbornly sticking to it (it would rub off in time). But her pants suit was red, white and blue and it was just the way she liked it.

"The cloth rationing is only temporary," Lord David David retorted, before signaling for wine. "The Italian prosecco producers will see to that."

The Cardinal had simply lain back on a bench on the Chequers' lawn and watched his colleagues' circus. The decision to cut off electricity to the Palace had already been taken by William Bunsen. He had no personal use anymore for Parliament. It was boring without the benches.

The others waited Lord David David out. Soon enough he sprawled face first at the edge of a water bowl left out for dogs. Bunsen himself crept over and placed Lord David David's hand in the water bowl. Giggling.

The Cardinal's mind drifted around the timeline of that afternoon.

They were at Chequers because Bunsen demanded it. He wanted to show off his new wife, Tuffet Burner (nee Wey), and her early pregnancy. He wanted to do it at Chequers. So be it.

If you did the maths Tuffet secured the Bunsen seed some months before her predecessor in the post of PM's wife gave birth. Little did Tuffet know that as soon as her foal was out, the moment she closed her legs to Billy Burner with some trifling complaint about a broken pelvic floor, she would be replaced by the nearest blonde womb to hand.

Britain thrives on its traditions.

"Conception before matrimony is a sin," the Cardinal murmured. How long would Tuffet last? In what manner would she perish that would immediately be declared a state secret? Who was Bunsen already lining up to replace her?

"What did you say Bogg?" The PM demanded.

"Conception before matrimony is a sin."

The PM laughed, and then coughed, and then had to be given water.

That day at Chequers Tuffet's artificially curled, blonde hair glistened as she patted the PM on the back. "There, there. You're a big boy now, aren't you?"

"Yesh. Yesh. I'm a very big boy."

"You keep announcing we're having a war. You must be a big boy."

"Yesh. Yesh. We're having a war."

Any day now.

Tuffet's pointed nose. It made the Cardinal inhale sharply.

Her youth. It needed to be drained.

Her painted lips. He would smear the whore's paint with his palm, if he could.

The Cardinal knew...minutes before the PM's gouty fingers had fumbled at Tuffet's silken bra. He caught his breath with the vision of the liver spotted hand cupping her breasts, his flabby palm resting on her fleshy mound. The Cardinal doubted Bunsen bothered to search for the clitoris. He would just open the doors wide and run inside.

"Stop it." the Cardinal told himself, but his mind had its own mind. He saw the brief conquest even though he didn't want to...

***

INT. MASTER BEDROOM CHEQUERS

PRIME MINISTER WILLIAM BUNSEN stands before a four-poster bed. TUFFET BUNSEN waits done up with a giant bow. The bow is union flag colours. Her lingerie is silk. Her twenty-something youth is undeniable in contrast to BUNSEN'S degrading carcass. Elgar is playing (not personally - from a speaker). BUNSEN inhales noisily.

WILLIAM BUNSEN
Ah, Narcissus at the well!

BUNSEN rushes the bed.
TUFFET giggles and squirms.

***

STOP IT. CARDINAL BOGG DEMANDS and the scene in his mind ends. Or rather, shifts into the background and continues to break through.

Tuffet's rosy cheeks inflamed the Cardinal with a mixture of disgust and lust. Cream skin and English rose petals on the green grass at Chequers. He hid his reaction to her and smiled. Doffed his top hat when the PM and Tuffet took up station for his approval on the lawn.

"What do you think Bogg?" William Bunsen beamed, slobber on his chin like an overexcited Labrador. "Damn fine filly what! I'm going to breed her and breed her until she's spent."

No, he's not.

Tuffet giggled and retrieved a tiny handkerchief from her sleeve. She wiped the PM's chin, with an apologetic side smile to the Cardinal.

"It's an honour to make your acquaintance," she'd said, like a trained seal, adding an extra clap of the flippers too. "Your Em-min-nence."

The Cardinal wanted to dominate them both. Force their faces into the turf with his hands on the backs of their heads and scream psalms. He wasn't certain if he could face sodomising the PM, but…

"Mrs Bunsen is an excellent example of the superiority of English roses," the Cardinal replied.

His welling rage. He internalised the narrative.

"When I topple you from your throne of rancid flesh I will beat you with heaven's whip." That helped. "I will scour the flesh of your surviving whores with nine tails until they plead for the holy seed." Now he was happy again. "I will send you lower than the gutter you crawled out of. Milkmaid to the last Mrs Bunsen, was it not? You'll be licking out my toilet bowls next."

Oh the thought of it. HER at his feet. HIMSELF in his robes with a bible in each hand. Her creamy mouth under his supervision.

Tuffet looked away, looked uneasy.

"Are you drunk Bogg?" Bunsen asked. "You look delirious."

In Bunsen's mind all the Cardinal wanted was to plunder his young treasures. It told Bunsen he was head dog of the pack.

"He looks like he's running a temperature," Tuffet said, still looking to the side. "Should we call the nanny? Maybe he needs some Calpol?"

She burst into giggles.

The Cardinal's face paled.

Bunsen gagged himself with his own hand. Eyes popping in mirth.

The Cardinal was rescued by Petal. She was so short and round she could have rolled her way around, but instead she walked. She was dressed in a black suit and held a freshly boiled skull. Two Dobermans at heel behind her every step.

"Who let that old prick at my boys' water bowl?" She pointed to Lord David David, still out cold at the bowl.

"I did," Bunsen answered. "What's that?"

"This washed up on the beach at Dover," Petal held up the skull. "Although it had eyes when it arrived," she smiled, oh how she smiled. "Ha! Ha! Ha!"

"Probably a Syrian," the PM mused. "Or maybe an Etruscan."

Oily Spartans wrestling in the moonlight, Bunsen thought, and smiled.

"Can we read the bumps on it?" Tuffet squealed, clapping her hands together. "My granny says she can predict the future by bumps on your head! She read my head when I was a babe and said I would marry a rich and powerful man!"

Everyone else was surprised there was anything there to

read at all. Tuffet knew what they were thinking. She also knew the profit of her dumb blonde act drawn from the old man's money chest.

Petal ignored Tuffet.

"This will be centrepiece at the ceremony later," she grinned. "Well, whatever is left."

She placed the skull on the grass and took a backward step.

"Stand back!" the PM said. "Petal's taking a penalty against the human race."

Petal booted the skull as hard as she could and it went airborne.

"Go Murdoch! Go Vlad!" she shouted at her dogs. They chased it.

Petal's dogs were as conditioned as Pavlov's, although they had a different trigger. By the time the skull hit the turf they were on it. Big jaws scrabbling to get a grip. Canines slicing lines in the skull. They growled and shoved at each other until one got a tooth into a cranial seam and carried the prize off into the distance.

"Great sport!" Bunsen shouted. "Fifty on Vlad!"

And beyond the walls of Chequers, beyond the cordon of armoured limousines, beyond the private security on patrol, way past the delivery trucks stocked with blackmarket EU27 wine, meats and cheese, in the common markets of Brexitannia, butter was now ten pounds for a small, domestic block.

Cardinal Bogg stretched out further on the bench in the House of Commons. One day, Bunsen would pay, and Cardinal Bogg would be the one holding the tally book. One day.

Fifteen

His Master's Voice

"A is also for Asparagus – The Asparagus, named after the Great British Roman Emperor Aspargi, whose stronghold was at Thanet, early 4th Century AD, and where Asparagus was first cultivated for export. Rod straight in the morning, like its namesake, asparagus is a seasonal specialist which can be pickled in brine for winter.

For these reasons, The Asparagus receives a patriotic rating of 361, 333 780, 009 out of a possible top score of 300, 034 974, 000. Not to be trifled with, whatever the quantity of the harvest."

- 'Fruits and Vegetables, and Their Correct Patriotic Ratings', by Prime Minister Mark A. French.

Mark My Words

Christmas of the year war was repeatedly declared was a wonderful time, unless you were a traitor.

William Bunsen passed a law requiring all future Prime Ministers adopt "Billy Burner" as their official nickname, after a successful tabloid campaign, and the King was rumoured to have donated his second favourite swan to a Windsor food bank. Whether or not this was to become an annual event, we would have to wait and see.

Sucof Groop tried to get into the press by finger painting

his face mask red, white and blue at an infants' school, but such a cynical ploy (to distract from the damage the opposition was doing to the country) was never going to succeed. The papers laughed at him, so we did too.

"It's not more red, white and blue the hungry children making bunting in the library need," Mary commented, as we passed the pillory, "it's food."

She paused, her lips pursing, her fists bunching.

"Why are they so useless, when what needs to be done is so obvious?"

Just so.

The pillory was unoccupied.

"That's a shame," I said, flexing my arm. "I could do with the target practice."

The replica tomatoes had been replaced by replica hand grenades.

"Cyclops' mum said she heard that a real hand grenade found its way into a bucket in Mousehole."

Lies.

"Six people were killed. Although not the fisherman in the pillory. After the pin was pulled the man holding the grenade turned in big circles so everyone could see, pointing and laughing at the pilloried fisherman. Then he blew up."

"Cyclops' mum needs seeing to."

Mary blurted a laugh and gave me a look.

The swan arrived at the food bank by limousine early one misty morning. The long, black car, with little heraldic flags on the bonnet, pulled up before the doors with "What The World Needs Now Is Love" playing on its entertainment system.

***

EXT. WINDSOR - FOOD BANK DAWN

A line of shabby people snakes away from the door of THE BLUDGERS' PANTRY. It's misty. It's cold. The people rub their hands together. Couples hold one another tight. A baby in a pram screams and screams.

INT. WINDSOR - FOOD BANK CONT.

TWO MEN, chubby, dressed in Hi-Vis army fatigues and armed with pistols, stare out of the closed, glass doors. Their uniforms bear the legend "Ministry of Plenty - In Partnership with Churnco". Condensation is heavy on the doors. MAN ONE wipes at it to see out.

MAN ONE
There's more every day.

MAN TWO
Can't give the food away.

MAN ONE
You can.

MAN TWO
At least they have their sovereignty.

The crowd outside erupt and run in all directions. WOMAN WITH PRAM struggles to move in the panic. She is knocked down. The pram topples over and a ragged rag doll falls out.

WOMAN WITH PRAM
Feed the baby! You must feed the baby.

Faces slam into the doors.

The engine of an approaching vehicle revs and revs. Tyres squeal. The panic grows. The crowd parts.

EXT. WINDSOR - FOOD BANK CONT.

The black limousine skids to a halt. There is the muffled sound of a honking SWAN and music. A back door opens and a cloud of smoke billows out.

UNSEEN POSH WOMAN
Toss it out Willy! Toss the bally thing out!

A SWAN is flung out of the limousine. It thuds on the pavement. Its legs are tied with Union Flag ribbon.

THE BLUDGER'S PANTRY'S doors burst open and MAN ONE and MAN TWO rush out with their pistols drawn. They secure THE SWAN.

MAN ONE
Watch the wings. A swan can break a man's arms with its wings.

MAN TWO grabs the SWAN'S legs and drags it back to the door. MAN ONE covers the crowd with his firearm. They surge forward. MAN ONE fires a warning shot into the air, killing a pigeon, which falls to the pavement with a thud.

MAN ONE continues his retreat and the crowd fall upon the dead bird.

In the background the limousine pulls away from the kerb.

Laughter can be heard inside.

***

The donation of the swan was a national triumph. The BBC made a documentary (at haste) called, "A Very British Royal Food Bank Donation".

"Is it a whole swan?" Mary wondered, over a breakfast of a shared powdered egg. "Or just a wing? Maybe it's a goose dressed up as a swan. Or is it powdered swan made from sawdust, used tea leaves and food colouring? The swan is probably from a farm in Poland!"

She was only amusing herself.

We were having breakfast in front of the television. The documentary was playing. Softly sunlit lawn in the morning at Buckingham Palace. A pond. Swans gliding in the curling mist over the water.

"No one does swans like the British," Mary said, and snorted a laugh.

"Have you been drinking?"

"Oh God. Do you remember that ABBA tribute act at that hotel in Torremolinos?"

I paled.

"Mary."

"What I wouldn't give for a dodgy daiquiri."

"We've moved on from foreign holidays," I reminded her. "Britain is self-reliant in royal swans. They can't say that in North America."

She grinned.

"Which bird is for the pot?"

"The swan was donated by the Royal Family to show they have the common touch."

We were in their thoughts.

"They are concerned about the welfare of the people."

"The Daily Parrot tell you that?"

What a bitch.

All food banks were closed for a week to show homage to the King. The Sovereign Grant was doubled. School meal budgets were redirected to produce enameled "Gratitude" badges for the children to wear. You can just imagine the excitement as art was cancelled for the ceremonies.

No one does pomp and circumstance like the British.

***

INT. INFANTS' SCHOOL HALL DAY

The school hall is Edwardian. High and heavy ceiling beams, and bunting. So much bunting, like ivy vines running riot. Water drips from numerous holes in the roof into red, white and blue buckets.

Giant posters of WILLIAM BUNSEN are hung about. He grins down like a heavenly father. The slogan "Patriot Children Work!" on each poster.

A marquee has been set up inside the hall to shelter tables from the dripping water. The tables are piled high with badges.

SCHOOL CHILDREN are lined up in rows. They are pale. They are skinny. They sneeze and cough. They cry. But set aside from the huddled mass are a few kids chosen to stage a play.

One child is THE KING. Another his QUEEN. They stand by a little pond made of blue crepe paper. Half a dozen other kids are dressed as swans and glide about, crunching over the lake.

The HEADMISTRESS - MS CLENCH, watches them all with a thunderous scowl.

MS CLENCH
Faith! Flag! Country!

A ragged echo rises from the children.

MS CLENCH
If you want your gratitude badges you'll have to do better than that! Again!

MS CLENCH and CHILDREN
Faith! Flag! Country!

A SWAN doubles over and vomits.

CLOSE ON - CYCLOPS and SOFIE. They hold hands. They stand together in the face of madness.

SOFIE
(whispered)
No one does vomit like the British.

***

"Sometimes I can't believe the state we're in," Mary said, as the documentary finished. "I'm still hungry. God."

This wasn't the frame of mind she should be in.

"Mary."

"Mark."

"It's amazing what edible plants you can find in

alleyways if you really look."

"Is it dear?"

Her face was contorting into a storm of hatred. The signs of her future madness were present in the past. If only I'd noticed.

"You should go and look. Take a stout stick with you. You never know what you may be able to beat out of the long grass."

How dare she judge me.

"I am not looking forward to another meal of limp iceberg lettuce and meat of *no determinable origin***.

"Perhaps you should try buttering up Clarence. He's the only one who hasn't lost weight."

"Are you suggesting he's a traitor?"

She shrugged.

"How will Cyclops' mum fare with Clarence in the stocks?"

Another shrug. I had her on the back foot.

"You're serving up poor fare lately."

"There's no choice at the shops or the street stall."

"You undermine Britain with every breath."

I paused.

"If you tried believing in food we may just get a full plate."

How far could I push it? Could I improve her? I had to try.

"Other chaps' wives manage to claw tins of spam from weaker women, and you are burly my love. You have hands like hams! Put them to good use. If Mrs Trench grabs the tin of meat substitute first wrap your mitts around her paw and *crush*. You must make an example of yourself."

"Like you do?"

"Yes."

There was a twinkle in her eyes now. I could tell she was

imagining the moment she seized the spam. The satisfaction of physically punishing a weaker specimen.

"What's the government giving us for Christmas?"

"What?"

"I heard they're giving us a present."

"Bunsen will make his annual address to the nation and tell us how great everything is going."

That year we were to receive it through a wireless radio. But not just any wireless radio…

***

INT. INFANTS' SCHOOL HALL DAY

MS CLENCH and all the CHILDREN stand together.

MS CLENCH
A Great British wireless radio!

The children echo MS CLENCH weakly. She glares at the huddled mass. She tries again.

MS CLENCH and CHILDREN
A Great British wireless radio!

***

The radios arrived with a brown paper label proudly declaring "Made In Hartlepool - Better Than Any Rubbish Made In Europe". My chest swelled with pride.

They were branded "Churchills", were union flag patterned and arrived tuned to The Great British Patriotic Broadcasting Corporation (nee BBC). The accompanying documentation warned it was illegal to change the channel.

The only time I ever had a cross word with Mary was the day she attempted to break that law. It was a regrettable scene.

I had come home early expecting a big dinner of bacon rinds, and I wager this is why I caught Mary. How many times had she attempted to re-tune the messenger of our gods? I could not say. I did not want to know.

"Mrs French! Your brave soldier is home."

I jammed my fingers into my ears to pretend I couldn't hear her reply. I wanted her to shout hello. I wanted her to really bellow.

But things were not going to go smoothly.

A little lump of cold bacon rind lay intact on the counter. A perfect British onion next to the tin, only slightly mouldy and unmolested. A supreme example of British carrot lying curled next to the onion. There was also a bag of government issued fibre supplement. If you had a case of the runs it was certain to cure it. The woeful Franks had to hold it in and run when some Barbarian meal like raw horse gave them a bad belly. We were sensible in England. We cooked our horses, until we ran out of them.

"Mary?" I continued through the kitchen and into the dining room. That is when I caught her at it. Bent over the wireless attempting to move the dial. Her broad British back to me.

So intent on wireless treason she did not hear me. My fingers fell from my ears. The GBPBC was playing 'Land of Hope and Glory'. I trembled.

"Mary French!" I exclaimed. "You are undermining the expressed will of the people."

I felt as if I had been stabbed in my heart.

Mary froze gripping Churchill.

Slowly she turned.

She raised Churchill over her head.

She did not speak.

Tears streamed from her eyes and her lips pulled back to reveal her teeth.

This was a useful reminder to put her on the waiting list for when the dentist visited our town that year.

She took a single step. I turned and I fled back through the kitchen and out of the door into the yard.

"None of this makes any sense."

I heard the backdoor open and waited for whatever was to happen next.

"Please my lubby hubby. Please come inside and let's talk it over. There's a good pet. You don't want your bacon rinds to get fly blown."

Ah!

She wished to discuss the terms of her surrender. I stiffened my spine and about faced but caught the toe of my right boot on a bucket.

I did not fall.

I did not fall. Mary stifled a giggle and retreated into the shadows of the kitchen. She was waiting by the kitchen table with Churchill unplugged before her. Such a serious and stout wireless. Its bakelite so proud and British. She held its power cable taut, the plug dangling down.

"What are you doing?" I was mortified. "If the government discovers Churchill is not plugged in..."

I swayed on my feet. To unplug a Churchill for any purpose, other than moving it to a more prominent position, meant the labour camp.

"We will just say we unplugged it to move it closer to our bedroom."

"I have to leave!" I turned for the door, but she begged me to stay.

"Please Mark! Give me a chance to prove myself?" Mary begged, bending down to rest on one of her knees. This was more like it.

"I must report you. It will go easier for you if we turn you in. You must undergo an ideological examination. They will know the Churchill is unplugged."

"We will say there was a power cut."

"They know when there are power cuts."

There was nothing else for it. This was now an ecumenical matter.

Mary shook her head. She flattened herself across the linoleum like I had struck her on the back of the head.

"They're not as clever as you think Mark."

"I have to report you then."

"If you report me who will cook your dinner?"

A good point.

"Did not Cardinal Bogg write that every patriotic man must have his dinner prepared by a patriotic woman?"

Yes. In his famous opinion piece 'How Wives May Serve'.

"Who will prepare your lunch? Your morning tea? Your afternoon supper?"

It was suddenly like being faced with a determined and skilled lawyer.

"Perhaps I am being too harsh," I admitted. "It's a first offence."

"And who will have breakfast waiting for you when you get up in the morning?"

She had seen the opening and had driven in the wedge.

"If I forgive you will you promise me you will never attempt wireless treason again?"

"Oh yes Private French!" She moved to get up.

"Stay down. We have not finished yet."

I was famished and this event had made it worse.

"This is a secret we must carry to our graves. You must never again attempt to change the station. You know saboteurs whisper on the dark wireless?"

Agents of Brussels. They never sleep.

"I'm sorry," she began to weep, so suddenly and touchingly I worried I would join her. Her hands were shaking again. "Please don't make an example of me. I don't want to end up paraded through the streets. Branded on the cheek with the flag of Europe!"

I pulled out one of the kitchen chairs and sat down. Exhausted. My stomach rumbling.

"You may prepare my dinner now."

"Thank you." She wiped at her tears with the dishcloth. "Thank you." She seemed almost pious. How high emotions can change perception in an instant.

"After dinner we will listen to the radio together. I believe there is a repeat of the speech given by Billy Burner when he stood on the wing of the Harrier jet and declared he would not go gently into that dark European Parliament."

That would be a romantic moment.

"After that I will go to the market and barter for superglue. We will fix our Churchill's dials to the patriotic spot. We will ensure this horrifying crime can never be repeated."

Mary climbed to her feet. One leg bent up first, her hand gripped the counter, she pulled herself towards standing. Such a lumpy thing she was. All breasts and hips. Thighs and molten cheeks. She wiped her palms on her apron. Smoothed her greying hair back and tied it into a ponytail.

"To work!" I ordered, playfully, striking her on the buttocks with my palm. But I misjudged the teasing blow and hurt my little finger. I hid my pain, curling the injured digit in.

"You are lucky to have me. Mr Finch did not waver when he caught Ms Finch doing just this."

"His sister was always suspect."

"Her punishment is to be public. I would prefer all your

punishments to be private."

She shot me a hot look. I am not sure why. Then she picked up the slab of bacon rind.

"No one does bacon rinds like the British."

*Provisional List of towns excluded from "The Swan Song" can be found in Appendix E.

Sixteen

Gammon Quest

"C is for Cabbage.
Cabbages are used in governance. A Great British cabbage may become a Minster of the Crown.
For this reason, The Cabbage receives full marks. Not just any marks either. Great British full marks."
- 'Fruits and Vegetables, and Their Correct Patriotic Ratings' by Prime Minister Mark A. French.

Mark My Words

How do you know you are born to lead? When do you perceive it?

The best way to answer my questions is to talk about me.

I knew before Lance Corporal Carrot lay broken on a Surrey hilltop and I left the rank of Private behind. The day I marched from Raylee, I knew. As Mary stood waving her dishcloth and sobbing, she knew, because I'd told her.

My

star

ascending.

I knew when I went on the Gammon Quest. And I knew before that. When I watched Prime Minister Bunsen in the documentary on Tungsten's Pipe. I could have easily played his part. I could see myself pressing down the lever in the Surrey pump house. Mary beside me, with a hand on her swollen belly. I could see myself doing the hard graft of ridding our land of regulatory red weed. I would give the British people back their liberty to only buy British.

I didn't plan my salty Gammon Quest. I was merely hungry. But like an ancient shaman I imbibed a sacred psychedelic and visions flowed.

Clarence the Butcher was key, although he didn't know he was a spoke on the wheel of destiny. All Clarence knew was that I took 4.4029 pounds of gammon from the butcher's block in the backroom of his shop.

Clarence was a patriot. Clarence served the public. Clarence held back his prices below the line of inflation, on government orders. He never blamed sovereignty for his electricity bill. He never doubted it was better to be poor and free than rich but oppressed by Continental tyranny.

When the temporary power rationing began for commercial premises Clarence kept his shop lights off from dawn until dusk. When the rationing was temporarily extended on a permanent basis he lit his shop with candles. When the candle supply suffered from an unforeseeable, temporary increase in demand, leading to no candles, he worked in the dark. If you passed his shop at night you heard his cleaver hit the block.

If you asked him how he managed in the dark he replied, "How does a blind butcher work?" and shrug, but his flared nostrils, his crimson face said do not ask twice.

"He doesn't have any meat to butcher," Mary fretted.

"Believe in meat."

"Mark."

"Yes?"

"You're an idiot."

"He's got Blitz Spirit," I would hit back. "The sound of his work boosts Raylee's morale."

The first day he lit his shop with a candle was the day I went on my quest.

It started in our kitchen.

"Mark French," Mary said, a King Edward potato in hand, "while I peel our royal spud why don't you pop down to Clarence's and just see if he's anything to trade for this dress. He'll still be open."

It was getting dark. The windowpanes rattled under fisting gusts.

"A storm is coming," I replied.

The dress was a black cocktail dress Mary had not worn in years.

"That's neither here nor there.".

I didn't want to go. I was happy in our domesticity as I waited to turn the television on.

"We can't turn the tele on until 6pm. Go on," Mary urged. "Imagine eating meat with veg again."

"I want to watch the television."

I could see my reflection in the screen.

"Nothing is on!"

Temporary power rationing had been extended from commercial properties to domestic, owing to the impact on supply from a new volcano in The Pacific Ocean.

I was reading an article in 'Unotesticular' about William Bunsen's new fiancé. It seemed the Mrs Bunsen who pulled the lever in the Guildford pump house was not up to the job of Britain's first lady. The Bunsens had agreed an amicable parting. The divorce was being finalised. Tungsten Bunsen would live with his mother at an undisclosed address. The fiancé was a close friend of the departing Mrs Bunsen and was already moved into Downing Street. It was declared, "Wallpaper samples were inbound. The would-be Mrs Bunsen was expectant and rescue animals were being auditioned. The lucky one would star in the new family's joyful photoshoots."

"British governance continues as tradition dictates. Other nations, with their chaotic systems, can only watch with their slack jaws agape," I said, shaking the magazine for emphasis.

"The old goat changes wives more often than you do underwear." Mary was upset. "I heard Mrs Bunsen drowned in sewage. The floor collapsed in the pump house."

"Unotesticular says there has been an amicable parting of ways."

Mary's hand clenched around the potato.

"She drowned in Great British shit. Just when you think they can't sink any lower..."

"Nonsense. There's been nothing about a death in the papers."

"Cardinal Bogg had to be rescued from the sea too!"

Another lie.

"It doesn't help us win new free trade deals if the British people believe fake news."

Mary, so slowly, raised the potato to her lips and sunk her teeth into it. She screamed, muffling herself with the stolon.

Oh how I wanted to rise and wrestle the vegetable from her. What if she bit off a piece? What if we didn't have even shares?

"You'll be saying I'm anti-growth next."

Mary lowered the spud.

"I don't deal in gossip!" she shouted.

"If the country doesn't look united to outsiders what hope do we have of leading reform of the UN's child labour policies? Do you know the Americans had the gall to call a vote on our policy of paying the Taliban to run centres in Kabul to process asylum claims? It's your fault Mary. It's the fault of all those who don't believe in Blighty!"

She glared at me. When she spoke again it was very slowly.

"Have you seen Mrs Bunsen since the opening of the pipe?"

"She's had a baby!"

"She's dead. And the unborn too."

I looked away. In that moment she seemed a lost cause to me.

"We should be talking about how a wedding will bring the country together," I muttered.

"It's like a production line. Do you reckon Bunsen shagged her before or after his last wife drowned in shit?"

I closed my eyes. I didn't want to fight with Mary. But I could hardly believe my ears. This was sedition.

"Magna Carta," I whispered. It was our safe word.

I can't tell you how she reacted as I had my eyes closed and my hands over my eyes. But she didn't talk.

"Magna Carta," I repeated. Long seconds passed.

"We're hangry," Mary said at last. "About this dress..."

"What's he want with your old dress?"

"I've seen an extra light in his eyes lately. He's got a secret girlfriend."

"He can buy her something at Great British Ladies."

Mary laughed.

"They're closing down!"

She folded the dress and put it inside an old shoe box.

"Go on. Maybe we can get a slice of gammon to go with our potato."

I took the dress.

"No more biting the spud," I ordered.

She sniggered. Mad woman.

"Make sure you bring back the shoebox. We might have to burn it for warmth."

I went out. The streets of Raylee were in shadow. Over the rooftops to the west a bright orange light was dying. There was already a crescent moon overhead. One star bright underneath it. Gusts of wind pushed me forwards and pushed me back.

People passed me in the gloaming.

"Have you seen my little terrier Mr French?" one boy asked.

"Why aren't you at work?" I replied.

"I'm nine."

"In my day I was working thirty-seven and a half hours a week and fighting to preserve the memory of The Blitz."

"I've lost my dog."

"Someone's eaten it."

I kept walking. Charity begins at home.

Ms Finch tripped in front of me. She fell face first into the dirt.

"Who's there?" she said, hand on her ankle, peering into the murk.

"A patriot," I replied.

"A what?"

I didn't like her tone.

"Private French."

"Oh Mark? Since when did you join the army?"

"We're all in the people's army."

"You should give yourself a higher rank."

"I'll get my promotions on the battlefield."

She had a point. The sheer level of my belief in our national destiny equated to Colonel.

I edged closer, feeling the ground with the toes of my shoes, my arms spread.

"What's in the box?" she asked.

"Nothing."

"What happened to the paving stones?" she wondered.

She must have hit her head?

"We gave them up willingly," I replied. I offered her a hand. "I saw you in the crowd the day I took up the paving and handed it to the army."

"What are we supposed to do without pavements? Last week when it rained I barely made it to the shops and back. It was so muddy."

"Did the ground open and swallow you up?"

"I just think it's..."

"British ground is solid. You just need to believe you'll get where you're going. Don't let Brussels get one up on you!"

She started laughing like she was insane.

"Did you knock your head?"

"Do you ever listen to yourself?"

I moved on. She was clearly hormonal, and it wouldn't do to have a debate. She was wearing lipstick. I could smell perfume too. She had money to waste on such extravagances but the gall to criticise infrastructure projects? No wonder the country was in a mess. Why didn't she buy the town a paving stone instead of dressing up like a tart?

I had to get to Clarence's.

I didn't know why, but I felt the obstacles in my path were signs. I looked back and Ms Finch climbed to her feet. She was stood there with her hands on her hips staring after me.

"Where are you off to at this time of night?" she shouted.

"Don't you know there's a special on the tele about government plans to revolutionise communication of the people's will to the people?"

She was trying to pull me off my path. She was a fifth columnist.

When I arrived at Clarence's the "Closed" sign hung on a locked door and the shop's shutters were down. I balled up my fist and banged hard enough to make the door rattle on its hinges.

"Only the Spanish have siestas!" I shouted. "British shopkeepers never rest!"

Nothing. No light inside.

"To close your door is anti-growth!"

I stared at my feet. What to do? Maybe I just had to keep thumping on the door? Then, in the gloom, I saw a little chalk arrow scrawled on the bricks Clarence had put down outside his shop. *"Come around the back"* was written beside an arrow in a love heart.

"He's not open. He's gone out," Ms Finch said. I jumped.

"It's not polite to creep up on people."

"Go home Mark. Mary will be wondering where you are."

"What are you doing out?" I hit back. "Don't you have compulsory volunteering tomorrow at the library?"

"Where do you volunteer?" she asked. A stupid question. Only people who worked in essential services had to volunteer on their days off.

"I clap for nurses whenever it's needed."

She gave me a perverse look. Somewhere between amusement and contempt.

"I have a letter from the Ministry of Performative Thank Yous congratulating me on one thousand hours clapping."

"I bet that fed a family of five," she replied.

"I guess you don't clap for anyone."

I waited for her to reply. She just stared at the dirt, then knelt and traced a square where a paving stone used to be. Guilty as charged.

"Enough of this nonsense."

I walked to the little alleyway that ran beside the shop and stared down it. The moon illuminated the alley like a silver thread. Destiny's path. Ms Finch climbed to her feet. She made a great show of it as if needing help.

"I've turned my ankle."

"Charity begins at home," I said, without looking back.

She wasn't smiling now. I was sure. I hoped the next time we were all called out for a clap she missed the call and was publicly shamed. Poisonous witch.

"Go home Mark," she said softly, like a plea. I ignored her and went down the alleyway.

"You won't drag me from my destiny," I mumbled, "be it Downing Street or a slice of gammon."

Once behind the shop I could see the backdoor was ajar. I walked over and tapped on it.

"Clarence?"

Nothing.

I pushed the door. It swung in. I was meant to enter the shop that night.

There were two candles on the butcher's block. The room smelt of vanilla. Scented candles? Was that even legal? In the middle of the block was a giant piece of steaming gammon. Next to that was a laminated piece of paper. It was a poem, "To Love A Small Bird", by Clarence.

I hadn't seen that much meat since the last time they televised Christmas dinner at Chequers. As for the poem? Christ. Maybe Clarence was unwell.

"Clarence? I hope you're not planning to eat all this gammon yourself."

I was salivating now. Just the smell of the meat. The steam swirled in my vision. I confess my eyes were wet with tears of joy.

"This is what a sovereign people can achieve."

I took a few hesitant steps towards the gammon. The butcher's block was deeply concave thanks to many years of service. Liquid pooled under the hot pink mound and ran to the floor in little streams.

"It's like being in church."

The candles seemed to grow brighter and brighter. I was

almost blinded. I wiped the tears from my eyes and laid my hand on the hot meat. I bowed my head and closed my eyes. I inhaled the steam. I knew I could do anything I decided to do.

"This is the hand of fate…" I whispered.

Nothing else could explain it. Clarence had been moved by the spirit of Saint Winston Churchill and left the ham for me. What other explanation could there be?

I knew what I had to do.

I took the black dress out of the shoebox. I swapped the dress for the ham. It was a fair trade. The gammon was so big it wouldn't fit in the box so I raised it to my mouth and took a bite. Oh Sweet Jesus. The juices. The salty goodness. The feel of a chunk of meat between my teeth. I took another bite. Then another. Juices smeared my face. They were so warm. So loving. So salty.

"What do you think you're doing?" Ms Finch screeched from the doorway. "That's ten years on a soft fruit farm right there."

She could never understand how I felt with the juices running down my arms to my elbows. If she wasn't there I would have lain on the block and rolled and rolled, shedding my clothes, absorbing divinity through every pore.

"You've been caught red handed."

Out of the inner shadows of the shop came Clarence. He was wearing a black tie and tails, but he still had his butcher's apron on. In his hand he carried his cleaver. I felt no fear. He was a spirit guide.

"Take it and go," he invited, lifting the cleaver and pointing at the door.

"But Clarence!" Ms Finch shouted.

"We will never talk of this," Clarence said.

I shoved the gammon into the box and pointed to the

dress, which lay on the block soaking up the juices.

Clarence nodded. The candles lit his face in flashes. The flames ran down the cleaver like the gammon juices on my arms.

"Go," he repeated. "Stand aside Beverly Finch. Mark is on the quest."

I ran. I ran right into Ms Finch. I held the gammon under one arm like a rugby ball and turned her aside with my free hand. Then I flew out of the shop and ran off into the night.

I don't know where I went. I was just running and stumbling. I tore chunks off the holy meat as I went and ripped them apart with my teeth. I began to feel very warm. I knew I was sweating. My ears were buzzing. But I ran and I ate and I found myself leaving town on Raylee's first ever street, which we all just called, 'The Street'. It led into fields where windblown wheat seeds mixed with wild grasses to create a pasture. The moon and the star seemed to circle each other, faster and faster until my vision swam with lights.

Eventually I came to a stop, panting, the last shreds of the gammon hanging from my hands. There was a stone in front of me. It was the memorial for a Spitfire that had crashed outside of Raylee. Not in 1940. It had happened during an aerial show in the 1990's. I collapsed to my knees and lent my forehead against the granite. I devoured the last of the gammon.

I had become possessed of a powerful spirit. As if the spirit of Archangel Margaret Thatcher had descended from Heaven to guide me.

I felt enraged anew at all the forrin attacks on British sovereignty. I fumed bright over the waste of public money on diversity training and on jamming woke blob, antifa ideology down our kids' throats. I bunched my fists when I recalled what saboteurs had done to the fishing and agricultural sectors of our great nation. My temples throbbed knowing illegal people invaded our generous and open society just to claim welfare benefits. A persistent ringing started in my ears when I thought of so-called welfare claimants with televisions and mobile phones and hands overflowing with avocadoes.

"IT'S A DISC RACE!" I shouted.

I shouted it again and again. I lost track of time. The moon become Alfred the Great. The star became Boudicca. The clouds drifting by were red, white and blue. Alfred and Boudicca held hands and spun over me. A fierce rain of tiny comets fell about. As they hit I felt a surge of power.

"Take back control." An ancient voice said.

"Protect British Fish." Another cried.

"Control our borders."

"The anti-growth coalition must be defeated."

"The enemies of the people never tire of undermining our freedom."

So many voices. From all directions. I looked around me for the talkers. The soldiers who had died to ensure Britain was a democracy where free speech and the rule of law triumphed without dissent were crowding around. The ghosts of those who gave their lives so we could decide who was a refugee, and who wasn't. Who could have access to the City of London's world beating financial services, and who wasn't worthy. They demanded we increase the charge for GP services. They had…

"Pragmatic concerns about immigration."

"Legitimate channels to claim asylum exist in Kabul."

I rose and walked with them.

"It's a disc race," I said, and they nodded.

"We must not be ruled by Brussels," they chorused. "The German carmakers must come to heel."

Never. Never again will the French sparkling winemakers

tell us what we can do with our fire safety standards.

In the sky overhead Churchill began to expand to fill the sky. He knew the value of lead in a car's exhaust.

"Our father, who art in Heaven, hallowed be thy name..."

And I walked with the patriots, and I saw my destiny. The country had to go to war once more. But at least it was to be a civil war, and not some foreign nonsense.

Destiny is all.

Seventeen

On Cardinal Bogg's Farm

"A is for Aubergine – see Eggplant."
- 'Fruits and Vegetables, and Their Correct Patriotic Ratings' by Prime Minister Mark A. French.

On Cardinal Bogg's farm the lambs grow fat on the green, sovereign grass of England. They sing "Baa baa" as the sun sets in celestial love, and the golden rays of rapture promised bathe the lambs, before the slaughter. Here is the paradise on Earth the Cardinal created, and it is well fertilised with belief in the Cardinal's correctness, in all things.

EXT. BOGG FARM – GRAVEYARD DAY

A meadow littered with humps. CARDINAL BOGG'S manor house close. A red, white, blue and squat building. A large bell tower rises from it like a giant middle finger to the world. A golden statue of the Cardinal on top of the bell tower, his face turned to heaven, his arms opened like a medieval cleric.

FIELD WORKERS in sackcloth dig a fresh hole in the

meadow with a wooden shovel. Hard going. A hessian wrapped corpse waits to be buried.

LION BOY watches the digging, his costume well worn. WITCH GIRL stands with him waving her wand. Another child, WARDROBE BOY, stands some way off. It's obvious they all have the same parents. THE BOGGS.

LION BOY
Who died?

WITCH GIRL
Who cares?

WARDROBE BOY
Workshy.

LION BOY
Woke.

WITCH GIRL
Welfare scrounger.

A LAME LAMB gambles close. LION BOY roars. He grabs the shovel from the WORKERS and chases the lamb. He catches up to it and swings the shovel like a cricket bat, clattering the baby animal off its feet.

WITCH GIRL and WARDROBE BOY clap their hands with glee.

THE LAME LAMB lies screaming. LION BOY stands over it and roars.

LION BOY
Sovereignty!

THE SHEPHERD approaches, cap in hand, limping. Bowed back and bowed mind.

THE SHEPHERD
If it pleases Master Bogg…

LION BOY
It does not.

WARDROBE BOY
Daddy said not to harm Shepherd again or no pudding.

WITCH GIRL
No pudding for any of us! Silly shepherd.

WITCH GIRL waves her wand at the SHEPHERD.

WITCH GIRL
I turn you into a peasant. Oh wait! You're already a peasant!

THE SHEPHERD doesn't take his eyes off LION BOY. He crouches and seizes THE LAME LAMB by the leg, drags it away, screaming.

A BELL tolls.

WITCH GIRL
Home for prayers!

THE LAME LAMB is still screaming.

THE WORKERS dump the hessian sack into the shallow grave. They cross themselves and start backfilling.

THE SHEPHERD unfolds a knife which glints in the sunlight.

SHEPHERD
You'll soon stop screaming.

***

The Cardinal has taken advantage of loosened regulations regarding disposal of the dead, in particular the labouring classes, resulting from workplace accidents, which result from the loosened regulations regarding working practices.

"A virtuous circle."

Long gone are the unprofitable days of health and safety gone mad.

"What a boost to national output," The Cardinal murmurs, as he counts the little lumps in the pasture. They will all flatten out over time, and the bodies underneath become just bones. Will those bodies re-flesh on the day of the Rapture? Will they ascend? The Cardinal doubts they will.

"They won't pass the means test."

He chuckles.

"They won't pass the credit check."

The chuckle becomes a guffaw.

"They don't have the right pedigree."

It's all in the breeding. The deserving, and the undeserving.

All died in debt to the Cardinal. For their meals. For their lodgings. For the old grain sacks they wore as clothing. And for their funeral services. Loan of shovel, five pounds.

The Cardinal chooses four lambs each year to save from the butcher's block. He calls them England, Wales, Scotland and Northern Ireland, and he gives them to Prime Minister William Bunsen.

"What does Bunsen do with the lambs?" The Cardinal's wife asked him. Once.

The Cardinal was at his desk, a great oak affair that a man could easily lay several dead shepherds on. The Cardinal claims the desk is made from wood from the Mary Rose. The Cardinal claims a lot of things that aren't true. He was disinclined to answer his wife.

"Boggy? What does Bunsen do with the lambs?"

"Do you think Year Two is too young to begin memorising the names of the Archangels?" The Cardinal asked her. "Perhaps school classes should be renamed Raphael and Michelangelo?"

"I asked you a question first."

The Cardinal pursed his lips. Who did she think she was?

"Aren't you supposed to be pregnant, or something?" The Cardinal slashed her, and she retreated to another room to weep, unseen, little book of psalms in hand, unopened.

On Cardinal Bogg's farm the Cardinal's children are given Latin names. The Cardinal's wife annually supplies another child for another Latin name and her husband imagines filling the world to the brim with his progeny, and his progeny's progeny.

"And my progeny's progeny's progeny," he says in a whisper, his soft fingers steepled.

In the Cardinal's other imaginings, the pearly gates of Heaven are operated in partnership with a private company, the private company's shares owned partially by a relative of the Cardinal, and Heaven's Gates are run more efficiently than now. Now that the company that maintains the gates is owned by another company which is headquartered in Jersey.

Heaven lets in too many of the woke for the Cardinal's satisfaction. Mother Teresa for one. Granted, she's reported to have had a demanding streak, but she failed to provide sufficient incentive for beggars to find work. But the Cardinal doesn't say that out loud, for fear that God is listening.

He doesn't hear his wife complain about her prolapses and stretches and tears and contusions. God has made her a breeder. Just so. There is nothing to complain about receiving, after seeking.

But he does say, "Yes dear", when she goes on too long. "Why don't you talk to the doctor and see what he can do."

On Cardinal Bogg's farm, when he talks, he is listened to and taken seriously. Just like God.

He wonders, in his private hours, if he is a distant relation of Jesus? As all religious zealots wonder, even if they don't know it.

"The lion would lie down with the lamb, were a lion here," the Cardinal tells his children, as they watch the spectacle of him. Watch him as he lifts his red, white and blue skirts and ascends to the Judging Stool.

***

EXT. BOGG ESTATE – STABLE YARD DAY

The Judging Stool.

CARDINAL BOGG stands on the stool with a breeze in his Union Flag silks. He extends his arms as if to bless his congregation of family and servants.

His servants. A rabble of men and women in filthy rags. Face down on the cobbles with their arms spread.

CARDINAL BOGG
It's so hard to get good staff these days.

LION BOY
Years of suckling on the Continental teat have made the British workshy.

WITCH GIRL
And lazy!

The servants' fingers dig into the gaps between the cobbles and hold tight.

CARDINAL BOGG
A wind will separate the wheat from the chaff.

WARDROBE BOY
It's all chaff!

CARDINAL BOGG
Who will feel the whip today?

The Bogg children begin to walk amongst the prone, prodding and poking with their toes.

CARDINAL BOGG
Who will wear the hairshirt?

WITCH GIRL
The Shepherd!

CARDINAL BOGG
Who will go on their knees to Canterbury to ask forgiveness?

LION BOY
The Shepherd!

***

The Shepherd stands under the old stone arch of the door facing the humped meadow. His hands are bloodstained. His face is flecked with gore.

***

On Cardinal Bogg's farm the tangible benefits of a fully sovereign, free trading country are lived and enjoyed, by the Cardinal.

On Cardinal Bogg's farm the Cardinal, his perpetually pregnant wife and their children give thanks to God for the plenty they receive. They do not ask if they have any wool. They have more than three bags full.

In the lambing season the Cardinal considers his flock. The swollen ewes birthing the next generation for wool and for the cooking fires. He walks amongst the dewy grass with a stout stick in his hand, with the Shepherd a step behind. On the stick are embedded silver crosses.

What does he see? The Shepherd follows his gaze. The Shepherd lowers his head whenever the Cardinal looks his way. He will find fault, the Shepherd knows. The Cardinal never fails to find fault. The Shepherd blames himself, for he knows that's what the Cardinal wants.

The lambs are jumping and playing in the sun of a new day. Baa baa. Ah. The Cardinal raises his stick and points.

He has found the fault.

"I can't believe I didn't see it myself," the Shepherd lies. He did see it. He did. What did he see? He doesn't know yet.

"Remove the stain today," the Cardinal orders and turns back to his great manor house. Its smoking chimneys. Its shuttered windows. Its dungeons full of grain and frozen meats.

The Shepherd keeps his eyes low until he can't hear the Cardinal's robes swishing in the grasses. Then he sets his sights on finding the Cardinal's displeasure.

Is there an uneven number of lambs? No.

Is there a dead servant in the grass? Mouth stuffed with a last meal of grass and a rictus hand above the ragged line of green? No.

Is there a scarecrow erected on the horizon? They appear from time to time. Always dressed as the Cardinal. Some days they are on fire and burn themselves to the ground. A pudgy line of black smoke spiralling into the sky. Some days the Shepherd must go and uproot the scarecrow and burn it in secret.

The Cardinal pretends not to know what the scarecrows mean when he wakes in the middle of the night, goes to his bedroom window, and sees the burning man in the distance.

The scarecrows know the Cardinal.

He blames the EU. Of course. Who else could it be?

"They never tire of undermining us," he reminds the Shepherd. "They send agents to corrupt our people. To inspire them to perversions. We need to tighten our borders before it is too late."

He will pause. Jaw tight.

"We need a purge. We need a civil war."

A good house cleaning. Bunsen is taking his time. The Cardinal is impatient. He fancies he'll get to bring back crucifixion. He can see it in his hot imaging. A line of crosses on the horizon with heretics nailed up.

And the Cardinal turns back to his great house and the comfort of being himself.

The Shepherd knows the real reason for the burning straw men. He knows the people who just about survive beyond the borders of the farm are hungry. Getting hangry. He knows they watch the Cardinal, his family and the Cardinal's staff with hate and envy. He sees them lined up in the dusk.

Ah.

There is a black lamb born into the fold. This is today's displeasure.

There are to be no black sheep on the Cardinal's farm. Never. Ever. The Cardinal sees to that.

The Shepherd will take the black lamb and bind it. He will turn his back on its bleating mother. He will take the bound lamb and leave it on the spot where the scarecrows burn, just beyond the fence line. The great, black circle of burnt land. It is growing bigger.

Perhaps, the Shepherd hopes, when the starving masses rise in revolt, he will be spared. The people will remember his constant kindness. The risks he took in the night. They will understand he was just following orders. He was just looking after his own.

Charity begins at home.

You must look after your own.

The Shepherd takes out the ball of wire he keeps in his pocket. Bind the legs. He takes out the folding knife. Swift.

Eighteen

Highway to Sovereignty

"T is for Tomato. Debate rages over whether The Tomato is a fruit or a vegetable. Confusing edibles is a plank of good governance.
The Tomato receives a high patriotic rating of 299, 333 333, 003.33 out of a possible top score of 300, 034 974, 000."
- 'Fruits and Vegetables, and Their Correct Patriotic Ratings' by Prime Minister Mark A. French.

Mark My Words

"Now Mark, I've been saving this for a special occasion," Mary said.

She was sitting on the side of our bed with a damp cloth in one hand and a small, white pill in the other, shifting from left to right buttock, over and over, causing a mattress wave.

I pressed my hands to my forehead. I was overheated. I was clammy. I was patriotic.

"Stop moving. I'm getting seasick."

"There's a spring up my arse," Mary said. "We need a new mattress."

"Your arse is causing a tidal wave."

It was the morning after my gammon quest. I had no idea how I got to bed. Mary tried to prise my hands from my forehead, but I held on, to myself.

"A cool cloth will help."
"No."
She pinched the back of my hand. As I lifted them in protest she jammed the cloth down.
"There, there. Who's a good patriot?"
"I am."
I didn't realise how hot I really was until I felt the cool cloth.
"Now, your medicine."
"What is it?"
"It's an antihistamine. The bugs in Spitfire Field ate well last night. You've been scratching in your sleep."
Old dog.
The bedsheet was polka-dotted with blood. Mostly brown spots, with a few fresh, bright red ones.
I felt burning. All over my body and in my throat. I was so parched.
"Water."
"Pill first."
I licked my lips. They were dry and cracked. I tasted salt. A lot of salt. My limbs were heavy, and I could feel the gammon in my guts. My stomach seemed to rise and fall in revolt. And the sounds! The gurgles and churdles. Sovereignty.
I would not vomit. To complete the quest the gammon had to be digested. I had to become one with it and it had to become me.
"How did I get home?"
Talking hurt. And oh, the trapped wind!
Onshore windfarm.
"I don't want to talk about that."
Mary looked livid.
She offered the pill to my lips.
"Answer my question," I mumbled through tight lips.

She grabbed my earlobe and twisted.

"Ouch!"

She shoved the pill in and clamped my jaws closed. She was too strong for me.

"Drink." She pushed a straw into my lips. I shook my head.

"I've got all day."

I sucked.

"Swallow it fast. I don't want you coughing it up. It's our only antihistamine."

"It's a plastic straw," I noticed. "A proper straw."

It was a red, white and blue plastic straw.

"I went on a gammon…"

"I said I don't want to talk about it. Cyclops found you. Clarence carried you home. He said you've eaten more gammon than is medically safe, but it should lead to visions. You need to rest."

"Control British Fish…"

"He said if you told me of any vision I was to tell him. The big fool thinks you were in contact with Saint Thatcher. I told him thank you very much and go back to your shop."

"I want our country back…"

"Look. We're going to have to get through this on our own. Raylee isn't scheduled to have a GP visit until next Wednesday."

She pursed her lips. She shook her head.

"Bloody spring!"

She jumped up and landed with a splash. I was lost in waves.

"I've seen the future," I whispered, holding onto the bed frame. "It looks like the past."

"Enough!"

Mary stood to leave the room, pausing at the door.

"Don't go trying to do your push up. Cyclops' mother has

given me an egg and I'm going to boil it for you. Stay in bed."

"Where did she get the egg from?"

"She has a hen."

"She what?"

"She found it injured by the side of the road. It probably came from the battery farm that blew up the other week. Poor thing. She's been nursing it back to health."

The sky was full of chickens that day. Mostly on fire.

"The Anti-Growth Coalition did that," I felt myself warming even more.

"None of that. You're in no state to be getting hotter under the collar."

"Keeping livestock is illegal. Cyclops' mother should know better. To keep fowl or hoofed animals undermines the morale of the Great British agricultural sector. She should turn the bird into the authorities so it can be slaughtered."

"Mark, lots of things are illegal. How do you think I get half the food we eat? While you're sat there regurgitating the latest bile from The Daily Parrot or Unotesticular about world beating British self-reliance I'm doing everything I can to keep our little home"

She stopped abruptly. Her face flushed. She burst into tears.

"What happened to the man who saved me from drowning?"

"Stop crying. I can barely understand you."

"WHAT HAPPENED TO YOU?"

"I'm right here," I replied. "I just want our country back."

Mary exhaled noisily and left. But a moment later she charged back in and whipped the cloth off my forehead. She blew her nose into it.

"Oi!"

"It's my only fucking dishcloth you pillock."

She left again.

I heard a plate smash in the kitchen. I heard her weeping. Poor thing. The fear of losing me must have set her off. It deserved a good cry.

Little did Mary understand I was now more of a man than before, not less. I had seen how Churchill connected to Margaret. I had seen the path we must take. To defeat Brussels once and for all, we had to defeat ourselves.

A little while passed and Mary returned with the egg. Boiled. It was in an egg cup on a little saucer with a spoon. There was even a pinch of salt.

"That's the set we bought on our honeymoon in Cromer."

"Yes. Do you want to take the top off the egg or shall I?"

"You do it. I feel too weak."

Mary nodded and settled herself next to me again. Tap. Tap. Tap with the side of the spoon. She levered the spoon and the top came off like it was hinged.

"You haven't lost the knack."

"Mark, things have to change."

She took a pinch of salt and sprinkled it on.

"Let's share the egg."

"No more slogans today?"

"Get eggs done!"

She hit me on the forehead with the flat of the spoon.

"When Clarence appeared with you over his shoulder like a sack of spuds I was terrified you'd need antibiotics. You were so hot to the touch! You were mumbling about walking with Saint Margaret. You were delirious."

"I went on the gammon quest."

"You've been on that for years! The whole country has."

"It's fate Mary French."

"Where's my shoebox? Do you lose it?"

"It'll be in Spitfire Field."

She pondered this. I could tell she wanted to boss me back out to look for it.

"Let's eat the egg before it goes cold."

And we did. And it was a Great British Egg.

Nineteen

A Debate About a Potato in the Shape of a Dead Prime Minister - Part Two, by Candlelight

"E is for Eggplant – see Aubergine."
- 'Fruits and Vegetables, and Their Correct Patriotic Ratings' by Prime Minister Mark A. French.

One morning a naked man on a donkey visited Cardinal Bogg and told him, "It's important to the war effort. It's *vital* to the war effort that Winston the Holy Potato has a good slogan."

Bogg had other things he'd rather be doing than talking to a man whose ribs he could count, whose thighs jutted out, whose cracked lips bled, ever so slightly.

"The civil war has been declared, but it hasn't started," Bogg replied, and pointedly yawned. "We are still in shaping operations against the enemy. The slogan will come when it is most needed. First we must decide where to christen Winston. We must settle the matter in Parliament."

"But Bunsen himself said the christening was to happen in the middle of the Irish Sea," the naked man looked perplexed. "You're wasting time."

"Have you seen the latest foreign investment figures? Do you know what the rate of inflation is? Don't you know that

Bunsen would never keep a promise to the Irish!"

"As long as they don't know it. What's the matter?" the naked man swatted at a fly with his magazine.

"The people are to be entertained with a great event of state. It will help them to focus on their sovereignty, and help them fight themselves."

"Bunsen's shitty little public shows are a distraction!" the naked man shouted. "The great British lion must roar again, free of Europe's shackles! It must win the war at home now and then march on Europe! We must agree a slogan and fight."

The donkey rider's outburst was expected.

"We must make ourselves fit for the 22nd century! The work must start now."

It went without saying that a good slogan for Winston the Holy Potato would create that belief. Sufficiently.

Cardinal Bogg considered his visitor anew.

"Do you write your ten thousand word blogs, or is it the work of the donkey?"

"You're a fucking imbecile Bogg. The whole establishment is riddled with cretinous idiots like you. How are we supposed to make a success of our newfound freedoms? How are we supposed to bring the German carmakers to heel with fools like you in office?"

"When I saw you coming today, I prayed," Bogg lied.

"For what?"

"Brevity."

***

EXT. ROAD TO THE BOGG ESTATE DAY

The clip-clop of a donkey's hooves. We hear a woman weeping. Red poppies grow out of a giant pothole.

STARVING WOMAN'S filthy fingers trail through the petals. Her fingernails are cracked, chewed, blackened.

The hooves grow louder.

STARVING WOMAN'S POV : A NAKED MAN on a donkey. He's bald. His scalp is burnt from exposure. The skin hangs off in giant flakes. He rides side saddle switching at flies with a rolled up copy of Unotesticular. In the other hand he holds a stuffed Tesco shopping bag in his lap. Now and then a bank note flutters from it.

Beside the STARVING WOMAN is her INFANT, swaddled in dirty rags, barely conscious.

STARVING WOMAN
I am Britannia.

NAKED MAN
Get out of my way.

STARVING WOMAN
I am unchained.

The STARVING WOMAN tears poppies from the pothole and smears the petals over her breasts.

NAKED MAN
Bloody peasant.

STARVING WOMAN
Will you feed my baby? My milk is dry.

NAKED MAN

Whore.

STARVING WOMAN
You are my pimp.

THE NAKED MAN urges his donkey on.

STARVING WOMAN
Do not forgive them Father, for they know what they do.

***

The naked man, on his donkey, did not look back at the emaciated woman and her babe. He would write a ten thousand word blog on the poor character of the peasantry. Later. He would purge her, lest she visit in his dreams and attempt to seduce his subconscious. Poverty was contagious. That was obvious, as there was now so much of it.

She was a vector of plague.

"There's no helping some people."

You had to sort the wheat from the chaff, and find the chosen few.

He kicked his heels into the donkey's flanks. Bogg's estate loomed. Beside the road there was a large, burnt area of grass. A dead lamb lay in the middle of it. It took a moment to realise it was not burnt but its wool was black. Its dead legs tied with twine.

"Please!" the starving woman shouted, distant now, "Please feed my baby!"

He dug his heels into the donkey's flanks again. She made him shiver. Poverty was contagious!

"How begging isn't a capital offence I do not know," he shouted back, over his shoulder.

She was undermining the will of the people.

"Get begging done!" she screamed after him.

The revolting peasant.

"You have your sovereignty!" he shouted back.

He was now mad at himself. How was he allowing himself to be drawn into debate with a lowlife? And from a distance?

The infant started screaming. Crows started cawing.

"I am Britannia," the woman screeched, giggling and rocking, as the babe pawed pointlessly at her dry teat. Tiny stick fingers tugging on empty.

The naked man kicked his donkey. Kicked it. Kicked it until his feet hurt. He left them both in the dust, where they belonged.

Cardinal Bogg and the naked man stood on the cobbles. The madman on his animal, one hand still holding the magazine, the other clutching the plastic Tesco shopping bag. A relic of the time before, when there were supermarkets.

"You should go and feed the blessed creature," Cardinal Bogg said. "I have work to do."

His visitor grimaced.

A helicopter could be heard and not seen. Coming closer, growing louder.

"You don't have a slogan for Winston the Holy Potato," the naked man hissed. His eyes burning brightly. "Without a three-word slogan governance is impossible. The special military operation against the Franks will falter."

"Bunsen sent you all the way out here to tell me that?"

"I don't work for that fat fool," the naked man spat. "I serve a higher power."

"Yourself?"

A big flake of skin detached itself from the naked head and swirled in the breeze.

"Why don't you get off the donkey and beg God for forgiveness?"

The Cardinal was a tall man, but sitting on the donkey gave his guest a height advantage. He lifted his robe and climbed onto his judging stool.

"You will not judge me Cardinal."

Oh, I already have. Daily. For years.

The whoosh-whoosh of the helicopter's blades grew louder. And there it was, a red, white and blue wasp in the sky.

The Cardinal could see the other man's penis poking out from the side of the Tesco bag. He closed his eyes. He got down from his stool.

There were little red sores on his guest's neck too. A line of them scattered like a constellation of stars. One was already full of the white pus. The skin around bruised and bluish.

"You have the pox."

"When you debate the shape of the potato today make sure to agree a slogan. The papers need to pick a side so the people know what to think."

The helicopter hovered over the manor now, the downdraft played havoc with everything.

The naked man turned the donkey's head and kicked its flanks. As he departed a trail of plastic currency spat from the shopping bag. Roubles. Dollars. Yuan. And just one note issued by the Bank of England. They all swirled in the churning air.

"Collect them," the Cardinal told a passing servant. A moment later the great scalp flake was plastered to his mouth by the descending aircraft. The servant bowed to hide their smile.

The helicopter floated sideways to land in the field beside the house. It was there to take the Cardinal to the House of Commons. Only the poor and the mad travelled by road. Only in the sky, close to God, were the righteous governors safe.

***

INT. HOUSE OF COMMONS DUSK

OVER BLACK.

CARDINAL BOGG

We have today a choice between St Pauls, Westminster Abbey and the Irish Sea.

A row of candle stubs. The flames dance close to death.

CARDINAL BOGG reclines on the government bench. One leg extended. His hands rest on his stomach. They hold a little Union Flag. He wears a crown of oak leaves.

BALD BOY ONE massages his stockinged sole.

BALD BOY TWO waits close in shadow.

BALD BOY THREE next to him, holding the Cardinal's slipper with both hands. All the boys have bare feet. All wear identical silk tunics edged in gold. BALD BOY THREE has a bandage around his right foot.

BALD BOY ONE is so tense he could crack.

FADE TO :

EXT. WESTMINSTER - THAMES FORESHORE DAY

THE BALD BOYS stand before SACKCLOTH MAN on the bank of the River Thames. Each wears a UNION FLAG loin cloth and covers their genitals with their hands. Shaggy headed. Half-starved. Bulging eyes. Filthy. Cowed.

THE PALACE OF WESTMINSTER in the background. A monumental Union Flag flies over it. So big it casts a monumental shadow.

BIG BEN tolls.

Fat raindrops smack about. Hitting the boys in their eyes. They shiver.

SACKCLOTH MAN is deeply pockmarked, with fresh pox. He holds a cutthroat razor and a bar of soap. His head recently shaved. It's crisscrossed with cuts. Rivulets of blood stream down his face in the rain. The blood is red, white and blue.

SACKCLOTH MAN

This is your shot at redemption. Filthy boys. Dirty little kittens.

The BOYS tremble.

A BARGE rows into view. The barge team works hard against the outrunning tide. There is a papier-mache model of a COD on it, wearing a crown. Down river we see other barges. One carries a model of WILLIAM BUNSEN. Another a SPITFIRE. A fourth MARGARET THATCHER. A fifth a GIANT POTATO that looks like Winston Churchill.

Thunder peals. Big Ben chimes on.

SACKCLOTH MAN throws the soap and razor at the boys' feet. The razor slices across the right foot of BALD BOY THREE. He bursts into tears. He lifts the injured foot up. Blood runs.

SACKCLOTH MAN
Ooooooo….

BALD BOY ONE grabs the soap and works it into a lather. BALD BOY TWO kneels to tend BALD BOY THREE'S injury.

SACKCLOTH MAN lunges. Grabs BALD BOY TWO by the hair and drags him into the river. Pushes his face into the water. A line of UNION FLAG BUNTING floats passes.

BALD BOY THREE forgets his injury. Grabs the razor. SACKCLOTH MAN releases BALD BOY TWO. Spins laughing.

SACKCLOTH MAN
Yes! Yes! Good mite! You may become a cat yet.

ALL THREE BALD BOYS freeze.

SACKCLOTH MAN
Shave your heads. And be quick about it. The Cardinal is waiting.

SACKCLOTH MAN walks away.

SACKCLOTH MAN
(sings)
Land of hope and glory, mother of the free, how shall we extol thee, who are born of thee?

BALD BOY ONE'S MEMORY FADES.

INT. HOUSE OF COMMONS CONT.

BALD BOY ONE trembles. CARDINAL BOGG wriggles his foot.

CARDINAL BOGG
(hiss)
At this rate you'll be back in that slum before sunset.

***

Bald Boy One was so tense. This was his first time. As he'd knelt at the Cardinal's foot, as the foot had been extended for him to kiss it, he had not drawn breath, either with his lungs or with a pencil.

This was his big chance to escape his Somerset town slum. Bath.

The bath water long overdue a change.

The bridge across its river broken by simple neglect. For want of funds.

The river Avon's banks overflown.

The town's MP was furious, with the town.

"This is not what the big society is about!" he chastised the townsfolk, in a public meeting in the open space, before the Abbey. The Abbey whose sculptured figures are dissolving in fresh acidic rain. Coal is back. The UK is independent of the contemporary sun, and other woke energy sources.

"Take up your chisels! Take up your mixing buckets! Fix that bridge!"

Then he had taken a helicopter back to Westminster. His work complete. He had a vote to attend on tightening rationing, and he had to be in town to get a good whipping from the whips.

Most Bath streets were now flooded, dependent on rainfall. The flood water carried sewage overflows into the Roman baths. The replica Roman statues now gazed down into a steaming brown pool bobbing with turds. When it rained the statues fizzed. Dead rats headbutted the edge of the bath, before sinking to join the sunken dead rats that went before them.

The public were urged to repair the bath too. Not by their MP, but by one of his supporters who wrote a letter published in the local paper, "The Woke Have Ruined Bath…"

The tourists from China no longer left their buses when they came to Bath. It isn't safe to do anything other than peer out of the windows and live stream it.

The Chinese government was considering banning tourism to the UK, but then, it's nice to laugh at the locals.

The public have no money to repair anything. Most have returned to barter. And where the holes appeared in the bridge the holes have been enlarged by people robbing out the stone to repair their flooded homes. Soon Bath will be a town of two halves. One half flooded, the other dry. And the two halves will take turns to swap places.

Soon it'll be so derelict its MP won't visit.

The second boy watched the massaging boy and snarled. He willed a mistake. "Push your thumb in too hard", he prayed. "I hope you forgot to clip your nails." But the massaging boy had clipped his nails to the quick and sucked on his fingers until the bleeding slowed.

The second boy wanted his chance to escape too.

He wanted to escape Frome.

Frome where the Black Death was creeping up Paul Street, but where most blamed the Anti-Growth Coalition. At least the wait to see an NHS GP had ended when the last NHS GP left to claim political asylum in The Republic of Ireland. So the poor people's boils burst in private. Their loved ones mopped at the suppurating sores and carried the contagion forward. Frome's property prices were plummeting. The foreign landlords were buying up and the government was celebrating the return of inward investment to the UK.

Still, the airwaves are full of adverts for private practice. All you have to do to secure a GP consultation is pass the credit score. Few did. Few had sufficient aspiration to get into the right tax bracket. This was a source of endless disappointment to their betters who were born aspirational and knew all about it. Who were born behind large walls and before hot hearths. Who now hoarded antibiotics bought on the black market.

The boy holding the slipper had none of those concerns, anymore. To hold the Cardinal's slipper meant you were made. Only a grievous error could send you back to the pits. Just hold the shoe. Keep it warm in your hands. Keep the slipper warm for when the foot returns.

The slipper boy expected a long reign. He had received a secret from the boy who came before him. This happened when that boy reached obvious puberty with his breaking voice. He was moved on to serve in one of the Westminster bars. To the job of listening to Archbishop David David entertaining lesser clergy with forecasts of Blighty's imminent salvation by the German Automotive Sector. The departing boy liked the next in line and so let him in on his secret to long tenure. Till a fuzzy upper lip and cracking sentences signalled time to go.

"See this?" the boy leaving asked.

The next in line rubbed his newly bald head. All he saw was a tiny mat on the palm of the bigger boy.

"It's an EU Flag?"

This was contraband of the highest order.

"It's more than that."

"That's not possible."

"You crack it and it warms in your hands!" And he cracked it and handed it to the younger boy who felt the warmth spread.

"It's magic."

"I've a box full. Well, I had a box full. I've used a lot. But I'll show you where I hid it if you promise not to tell anyone."

"Cross my heart."

"And hope for death."

The shoe boy would keep a handwarmer in his pocket and place it inside the Cardinal's slipper when he saw the candle stubs start to die.

"God is an Englishmen," Bogg adds. "It is no mystery that he would send Winston back as a potato."

Archbishop David David swayed a little. "We need to pause this debate for a full English Breakfast."

Bogg raised his eyebrows. Disdain.

The gluttonous fool was late for the debate and then wanted to eat? Let him stew in the alcoholic acid in his guts. Let him pickle himself in his lustful, interior brine. Bogg imagined a spitted Archbishop David, and having his kittens slow turn the cretin over a bed of hot coals. Listen to

David cry and sing in pain. A long, slow cooking would be optimal. Pulled Archbishop.

"Where's the German car industry when it's needed?" Mogg shouted and was pleased with himself.

David David looked lost. He spun about as if expecting to find a delegation from Mercedes.

Ah, the smell of his puckering skin as it reddened, blackened, burst, hissed and then dried to a coal crust. He could throw the carcass to Petal's dogs. Then take whatever bones they left and crush them in a mortar and pestle. And then take the dust and crumbs and tip them into the lavatory. Defecate on them and flush.

"You said breakfast," David pointed a swollen finger at Bogg.

"No I did not."

"You're licking your lips," David belched. Loudly. He took a couple of backward steps. His belches could be a source of energy. A fossil fool and his fuel.

"Breakfast?" The Archbishop repeated. He was licking his lips. He was hungry. It was true. The visit from the naked man on the donkey had robbed away his appetite, until now.

"The debate has been catered for with cucumber sandwiches. Although I anticipate a recess for dinner at the traditional time."

David David showed all his teeth.

"No you old haunted pencil. We can't argue with each other on an empty stomach. We need the classic English breakfast," said Field Marshall Trust, neatly positioned where the candlelight would fall on her preferred side. Then she froze to have her photo taken by an attendant. "Photos of us eating will help us win the trade war with New Zealand."

"Harder," Bogg ordered. Twitching his foot. The

massaging boy's eyes widened. He hated Archbishop David David suddenly. He was going to upset the Cardinal and the blame would fall at his feet.

"Harder what?" David hiccupped and shoved his thumbs into the sides of his Union Flag waist coat. "My mouth is drier than a nun's cunt."

"I was simply issuing an instruction to my kitten."

Bogg grimaced. To have to tolerate such an oaf merely because of his undying devotion to whatever idiotic scheme Bunsen thought up. It was a test by God. There could be no other explanation.

Trust giggled and blurted out, "The Archbishop said cunt!" Her expression in the saying was captured. Jaw opened wide and little teeth on show. Her eyes all whites like a crazed chihuahua. The photographer would keep that one for their private collection.

Bogg was unnerved. It was an entirely different matter to hear a member of the fairer sex say the forbidden word. He moved a hand to cover his groin.

"Can we not just decide what clothing the angel was wearing when it appeared in Cromer?" Archbishop David David demanded. Then for good measure, "Cunt. Cunt."

Oh God.

"Margaret Thatcher. It can't be anything else," Trust declared.

"John Bu..." Archbishop David David exploded. He abruptly hit his knees, vomited and fainted. His words cut off.

He's down and out, for now.

"Wait a moment," Bogg said, and he closed his eyes to feel a warm rush of relief at the Archbishop fainting. "We are here to debate where to christen the potato. It should be a simple matter."

"Look. I've got an important call with an American

economist," Trust said, as if that mattered.

Bogg returned.

"We are here to debate where to christen Winston the Holy Potato. Saint Paul's or Westminster Abbey. What are you here to debate?"

Trust looked at him with her face immobile. Not even blinking. Nothing was happening in her head, and nothing would for several seconds.

"I put it to you that Westminster Abbey is the correct venue," Bogg took his advantage.

"I thought we were here to debate what archangels wear when they visit the King?" Trust sputtered.

"Without doubt a dark suit and a Bowler hat," Bogg was quick.

"No. They dress like Margaret Thatcher."

"But you started the debate by saying we have to eat the classic English breakfast," David David shouted, still on the floor, but coming back.

"Do you even make sense to yourself?" Bogg wondered. "Not that it matters."

The massaging boy smelt Davis's vomit and momentarily stopped massaging. He thought he might vomit. The Cardinal's foot tensed. The boy began to weep. Hot tears hit the stockings and bounced off.

"I don't know why we bother debating anything anymore in here," Bogg replied. Which was the first honest statement he had made in many years. "None of it matters. Bunsen will decide."

"We must go through the motions. We're a robust democracy," David David cried.

And the candles guttered, one by one. The boy with the slipper cracked the Flag of Europe pad inside it.

"Did neither of you read the papers relating to today's debate?" The Cardinal asked.

David David and Field Marshall Trust laughed together. Such a laugh. It was the best joke they'd heard for days. No one in the UK government had read briefing papers for years. What's the point of that?

"Let's just agree to hold the christening ceremony for Winston the Holy Potato at Westminster Abbey," the Cardinal said, as the last candle died. "It's what God wants."

David David belched. Trust paused for a photo. The Cardinal took both actions as assent and rose to inform the Prime Minister that the debate was successfully concluded.

Twenty

Patriotism Is Forged

"D is for Dill – Not a vegetable, but a herb. For this reason Dill is not discussed.

For this reason Dill receives a patriotic rating of TBC out of a possible top score of 300, 034 974, 000."

- 'Fruits and Vegetables, and Their Correct Patriotic Ratings' by Prime Minister Mark A. French.

Mark My Words

"There is no greater expression of total, national sovereignty than complete freedom to choose how we treat ourselves," Prime Minister Bunsen said during a televised, national address to announce traitors would be branded, with hot irons. *"The inaugural 'Public Traitor Shaming Day', or PTSD, will take place on this year's Summer Solstice and no overreaching, meddling Continentals can do anything to stop us."*

EXT. RAYLEE – HIGH ROAD DAY

A SPITFIRE high overhead in a clear blue sky. The roar of the engine. The SPITFIRE circles Raylee, always coming lower.

The High Road is thronged with people who stop and stare up.

MARK FRENCH
It's a Great British angel.

MARY FRENCH
Let's hope it doesn't crash.

CYCLOPS
Is he bringing food?

MARK FRENCH
He'd be flying a Lancaster if he was bringing food.

SPITFIRE PILOT'S POV :

As the plane lowers, the SPITFIRE PILOT talks to CONTROL.

SPITFIRE PILOT
Marseille. Over.

CONTROL
We just got back from Zurich. Over.

SPITFIRE PILOT
I have a second cousin with a chalet on Lake Geneva. Over.

The SPITFIRE lines up the High Road for landing. We see the road in front full of people.

SPITFIRE PILOT

Get out of the way! Over.

CONTROL
Excuse me? Over.

SPITFIRE PILOT
Not you Control. The local village idiots. Over.

People dive for the gutters as the SPITFIRE lands in a puff of smoking wheels.

CONTROL
Mind the potholes on landing. Over.

SPITFIRE PILOT
You don't say. Over.

The SPITFIRE PILOT can see a giant pothole in front of him. He struggles to stop the plane before it goes in.

CONTROL AND SPITIFIRE PILOT
At least it's a Great British pothole! Over!

The canopy is flung open by the SPITFIRE PILOT. He holds up a BRANDING IRON.

SPITFIRE PILOT
This is your branding iron! A gift from Billy Burner.

ONLOOKER ONE rushes to the plane. His face is covered in red sores.

SPITFIRE PILOT
Stay back you bloody peasant!

The SPITFIRE PILOT throws the branding iron and it hits ONLOOKER ONE square in the face. He goes down. CYCLOPS dashes forward and grabs the branding iron. He makes a dash for it, but is collared by MARY FRENCH.

The SPITFIRE PILOT closes the canopy and revs the engine. He can't get out of Raylee quick enough.

***

Ms Finch was branded to make Britain Great Again.

Ms Finch was marked on her right cheek in the cobbled yard outside 'Ye Olde Great British Blacksmith's Forge' because she had undermined the will of the people. Now the people would make themselves felt.

"How has she undermined the people?" Mary asked. "Specifically."

"She has committed wireless crime."

She had been caught tampering with her Churchill radio.

"Who caught her?"

Churchill caught her.

"All the Churchills send reports back to the government about downtime or channel swapping. Ms Finch not only turned her Churchill off, when there was no temporary disruption in power supply, she changed stations."

"It's hard to keep up," Mary admitted. "We've a magic potato that is Winston Churchill and Churchill radios that spy on us."

Churchill was now omniscient.

I was slightly aggrieved that Ms Finch was getting centre stage on such an auspicious day. I had not forgiven her for attempting to prevent my gammon quest.

"Do you want to be tied to the stake and have that oaf of

a blacksmith brand *you*?" Mary demanded.

I didn't answer, at first.

"If the brand was a Union Flag..."

"You'd cry like a baby."

When it happened, Ms Finch took her branding poorly.

At midday.

Her eyes as wide as a terrified horse. Her bare feet scrabbling against the ground.

She deserved the smoking iron.

Bunting strung overhead between roofs.

She didn't deserve that, but we, the people, did. You can forget all else when the little flags flutter.

Ms Finch wasn't naked when she was branded, although the general feeling was that she should not have been allowed to wear her yellow raincoat. Too Continental. Too showy. Not British.

"It's as if she's mocking us," someone said. "I bet it says, 'Made in Milan', on the label."

Who could disagree?

"She should be tied to that stake with nowhere to hide," another onlooker shouted.

"Hands bound with twine. Just try and wriggle out of that. Traitor."

But that was later in the day. Breakfast was first.

"The town thinks we should have a local referendum on dress codes for traitors," I told Mary, over a big bowl of Sovereignty Chaff cereal. It was good chaff, the best chaff you could buy. "You won't get chaff like this in France."

Mary was stirring her chaff with a new wooden spoon. She looked distracted. "I was talking to Cyclops' mum at the library. She said one of the kids fainted making bunting. He had a line of little sores on his neck."

"Was it Cyclops?"

I bet it was.

"No. Some boy called Reggie."

Why were we talking about this? Kids were always getting sick. It was part of childhood.

"The town thinks we should have a referendum on whether enemies of the people should be naked when branded. If we start it in Raylee, maybe other towns will follow our lead. It could put us on the map."

"You're all sick," Mary blurted. And then she started to cry.

I reached over and patted her arm.

"To get a sexual kick out of a woman's pain? This is what an independent, free trading nation, freed of Brussels' chains does?"

She stopped crying as abruptly as she started. I pulled back my hand.

I closed my eyes.

"It's the EU's fault," I reminded her.

We needed to purge. When would Bunsen tell us the civil war had started? Shaming Day was all very well and good, but when was War Day?

"What did William Bunsen say yesterday?" I asked.

Mary didn't answer. She now had a few pieces of chaff in her spoon. She was holding it up in a shaft of sunlight. Little dust motes danced. Mary narrowed her eyes, pushing with her fingertip at the cereal.

"Is this even made from a cereal crop?"

"You will celebrate the bounty of our undeniable sovereignty by punishing those recalcitrants who deny its reality. Prime Minister Bunsen told us. Do you remember? You will brand. You will sear. You will rend. You will shame. You will take back control of your villages and towns from the agents of Brussels. You will celebrate the inaugural Great British Public Traitor Shaming Day with relish."

"He's losing control," Mary said.

"Of what?"

"Of something. Something is coming home to roost. He'll change wives soon. Just so the papers can celebrate the path of true love again. I bet you he'll tell us to start attacking the village next to us when he needs an emergency loan from the IMF."

Why would she say this with Churchill listening in the corner. It was madness.

"The branding is genius," I countered. "When we start fighting each other they'll be low hanging fruit. It will boost morale. Who should I club like a baby seal first? Well, the woman with the scar on her cheek! Of course! I bet she's wearing EU flag knickers!"

"We need that thermometer again," Mary said. "Or a divorce."

She grinned madly.

I went red in the face.

I wanted to move the conversation on that morning. Mary was putting us both in danger. She would come around when she heard the sizzle of the iron in the traitor's skin. When she smelt cooking meat. Oh, how I missed meat. If I were a Minister of the Crown I could have any meat I wanted. I could go overseas.

"Do you think I'll be branded before or after the referendum?" Mary interrupted my daydream, just as I was staring at a plate of roast beef.

Christ.

"Raylee's forge was built in the 14th century," I reminded her. "It's so British that it's still in use even today."

A squat and sturdy structure, it was famous for only having burned down once every one hundred years since its initial construction. And of those times only three had *"caused a greater conflagration so as to imperil the village."**

"Did you know that wicked little hunchback Richard III was the first to burn down our forge?"

She didn't reply. She just kept looking at me over her spoon of chaff.

Eat it Mary. Just eat it.

"This reminds me of that pasta the government gave out. I couldn't shit for a week after we ate that."

The forge's current owner we all called "The Blacksmith' even though his real name was Gary. He couldn't shoe a horse. He couldn't make you a sword. But he could bloody well heat up iron.

Ms Finch would take the branding poorly, as she lacked Blitz Spirit.

"I can't eat this chaff," Mary said. "I'm going to get dressed."

She paused in the doorway and whispered, "I bet you Bunsen and his mistress eat the wheat."

Gary was muscled and slow on any uptake, but back when we had tourists, he could repeatedly beat his piece of iron all day without complaint. All his hair had long ago singed off. Once he had a giant, black beard. It burnt off.

Gary's wife painted his eyebrows on each morning, but no one was impolite enough to mention it. We just treated him as he was, a patriot.

Ms Finch felt the heat on a perfect English summer day.

"This day is far superior to the over baked days they favour on the Continent," I said to Mary, as we joined the others outside the Blacksmith's.

The sky was a healthy blue and not the shabby colour they favour in Italy. The sun was just hot enough to make people complain, but you still had to work at it to get burnt. A Spaniard would never have been able to stand it. A soft breeze flowed along the village's alleyways and a gaggle of hungry children chased a starving puppy along the high road. Whoops and hollers.

"Ms Finch had it coming."

Justice would be served.

The mood in Raylee had been building to a fever all week. Our disused bus stops were plastered with posters announcing the time and place, and urged, "All to come and join in the celebration of Great British patriotism. Be sure to bring your children so they can see the Will of The People in action!".

Schools closed for the day, although the library stayed open.

Over our breakfast of chaff we listened as our Churchill carried announcements. First was 'Patriotic Thought for the Day'. That day it was a comparison of Jesus to a modern, British carpenter. Neither are ever recorded building any new homes. In this way the lack of building supplies was irrelevant.

The second segment was the names of towns and villages where brandings, and other punishments, would occur with involuntary and rapturous local involvement. We knew what Britain needed from us. I smacked my lips in satisfaction when I heard our noble, little village mentioned.

"...The Branding, Shaming and Marriage News. Today public shamings will occur in town squares, or other named places. Bucketforth, three local residents to be publicly shaved for heresy. Mincehead, one local suspected of spying for Brussels to fight a pig with one hand tied behind one back. After the ceremony the pig will be given to the King. Enema, five re-marriages to occur simultaneously with a local cow insemination ceremony in the larger field...Oggles, town to be deloused and painted blue to remind all to attend the shrine on Sovereignty Day after last year's poor attendance...Raylee, one resident to be branded on the cheek

for Wireless Crime, this patriots, is post Imperial PTSD…and now the national anthem sung by the Children's Choir of Spitblud…"

When it happened, Ms Finch's branding itself was not pitch perfect.

She had been held in solitary confinement for a week, preparing, but she looked savage as she was led out by local youth and tied to the post. Fine looking kids. Skinny arms and legs poking out of their red, white and blue uniforms. One had even tried to grow a toothbrush moustache for the event.

"A little square of bum fluff does the entire village proud!" I shouted.

"Don't they look full of purpose in their long shorts," Mary noted. "Just like youth movements of the past."

Shorts was a little generous. Due to a mysterious absence of cotton, linen, denim and polyester the Shaming Day shorts were made out of hessian sacks. The children of Britain did not complain. Blitz Spirit flowed in their veins.

Ms Finch struggled as she was tied to the oak stake driven into the dirt. The forge mouth was a maw, occasionally lit by flames inside.

Work the bellows! Make that fire roar!

"There's a dragon inside!" Cyclops said. The little idiot.

"If Prime Minister Bunsen had not got Brexit done we could not do this!" I said loud enough for all to hear. "Red tape from Brussels would have forbidden sovereign Englishmen from tying women to poles in villages."

There was a card table set up. The Adequate Food Ministry, in partnership with Psycho, had allowed a special allocation of baking supplies to prepare tea and cakes. No one was going home empty handed, except those too lazy to fight.

"Such patriotic teabags," I told my Mary, as I spied the

box of Yorkshire Tea. "Before we regained our freedom we couldn't grow tea in Yorkshire."

"Yes dear. It's marvellous," Mary said, eyeing the box. Was she going to make an early attempt to seize it? Everyone eyed up the competition. Who was going to start the stampede?

"There's only one teabag inside the box. We'll have to work out a plan if we want it."

But even with new public ceremonies there are formalities to observe first. Ms Finch was to be photographed.

Ms Finch let herself down again.

"You fucking zombies!" she screamed. "What century do we live in?"

Cameras flashed, capturing her crazed look.

Then Clarence stepped into the open space before Ms Finch with a piece of paper in his hand.

"I definitely wrote this poem myself," he said.

"He worked on it all week," Ms Finch shouted. "Didn't you Clarence? You flabby fuck!"

Clarence stiffened, but he didn't turn to face her.

"She's undermining the will of Clarence!" some clown shouted. A ripple of applause.

"Great British Potatriots, by Clarence," Clarence announced, too loudly and puffing up his chest.

"On the In-Continent their potatoes cause in-continence,
But a Great British potato will see you through, solid and true."

(He paused here for dramatic effect. Two beats.)

"The Franks bewail mushy root vegetables which make them tense,
The English Patriot celebrates a solid chunk of white which gives Brussels offence."

(Clarence can write rhyming couplets. Well.)

"Junker in his bunker never held a potato peeler,
The flabby Iberians close their eyes and weep when they think of

what they lost,
The day Great British Maris Pipers failed to appear at their fence!
Blighty keeps her produce for herself as root vegetables have a right to sovereignty too!
Show me a country less proud of its bunting and I'll give you red tape,
The Ger…

(It went on for far too long. I zoned out.)

"Ms Finch probably thinks the poem is her punishment," Mary said, too loudly. Clarence the butcher became Clarence the human beetroot.

***

EXT. BLACKSMITH'S DAY

MS FORMALDEHYDE in her white coat erupts through a shoving line of pitchfork wielding spectators. She holds a black and white CAT by the scruff.

MS FINCH is tied to a big stake in the centre of the melee.

MS FORMALDEHYDE turns in a big circle. She's so happy with herself.

The CAT is visibly pissed off.

The crowd chants, *"Hiss! Hiss! Hiss!"*. The CAT does not disappoint.

***

"It's bound to hiss," I whispered to Mary. "It's a Great

British Cat."

At first the feline seemed reluctant. It just squirmed about seeking escape. Wild eyes and tail fluffed. A quick jerk of its tail saw it try and bite Ms Formaldehyde, who bravely tightened her grip.

"No!" she scolded it. "Do as you're told."

Ms Finch stared at the cat in horror.

"Let Felix go!"

"Ha!" Ms Formaldehyde was triumphant. "She's been keeping this vermin secret. Good calories have gone into its belly and not yours!"

"Eat it!" the crowd cried. Understandably.

"Let Felix go!"

One of the lads, a skinny little chap with yellowed skin and both front teeth chipped, stepped up and poked the cat in its ribs. It growled impressively.

"This is getting silly," Mary muttered.

"Shush Mary. Don't ruin branding day."

"Never work with children or animals," Mary shouted and stepped in to wrestle Ms Formaldehyde for Felix. Mary won. She immediately shoved the cat right into Ms Finch's face. It hissed.

Mary then released the cat, which shot for cover with some boys chasing it.

This was a day of high sport.

A jaundiced little boy with bright red hair and a stout stick stood despondent.

"I was going to jam this stick up its bum," he whined. We all laughed.

Ms Formaldehyde nodded and stepped back.

"Now it's time for Gary to shine!" I cried out. The crowd roared. I looked at the faces. They were distorted with patriotism. Exultant with the salty taste of sovereignty. For a moment the faces seemed to separate from the skulls underneath and float about me.

"Mark," Mary said, gripping my arm. "Mark."

I couldn't respond at first. I felt a surge of pure joy. This must be what it had been like to survey that muddy field of French dead at Agincourt.

"Mark?"

This must have been what it was like to watch a Messerschmitt BF 109 with its tail on fire from the cockpit of your Hurricane over Dover.

"We're making Britain great again," I whispered.

I felt a wet glob hit my cheek. I touched it, expecting tears. But it was spit.

I looked for Mary, but she was gone.

"This is why we had to leave the Single Market!" I bellowed. "This is England!"

People cheered. I wouldn't feel this powerful again until the first day I addressed the House of Commons as Prime Minister, even as the repairs were underway.

Suddenly Cyclops stepped forward holding a replica Roman trumpet. He blew into it as hard as he could. Ms Clench was at his back. She was saluting. Flat palm.

I felt as if I were on another gammon quest.

"Two World Wars! One World Cup! Thousands of public brandings!"

The young, if they weren't chasing the cat, were lined up either side of the entrance to the forge. Together they made the sound of a drum beating. They weren't in time, but it was still like watching an old movie in which someone gets whipped on a ship.

"And they say our young are malnourished! Ha!" I shouted. "Take that Brussels!"

"Take that UN!" someone else said.

"Take that UNICEF!" another added.

"Take that Woke USA!"

"Take that Junker!"
"Take that Macron!"
"Get Branding Done!" I screamed, spit flecking my lips.

***

INT. FORGE MIDDAY

Hot coals in the forge fire. We see a muscled arm with a fading Union Flag tattoo pump the bellows. The flames heat to blue. The fire roars.

From beyond the forge, in the cobbled square, we hear a crowd roaring.

GARY THE BLACKSMITH works the bellows. Then he shoves the BRANDING IRON into the coals.

The crowd begins to chant *"GET BRANDING DONE!"*

GARY
Just a minute. You bunch of prats.

BOYS run into the forge, chasing a terrified PUPPY.

GARY turns on them, HAMMER in hand and ROARS.

GARY
This is England!

The PUPPY races back to the entrance and the BOYS chase it out.

GARY takes the iron from the flames. It's white hot.

GARY

I'll get branding done, and all.

GARY hefts the iron like a sword and marches out.

GARY's POV : MS FINCH tied to the stake. Yellow raincoat. Contorted face.

GARY's muscled back fills the view.

***

We were still chanting "Get Branding Done!" as Gary emerged like a crusader from a dark citadel with the searing branding iron in his hands. He was flushed. He had fire in his eyes, not just his hands. He was ready to do his patriotic duty.

"No. No. No. Please no!" Ms Finch screamed. She was on script at last.

Gary strode towards her. Nothing could stop him.

"You people are fucking animals!" Ms Finch screeched.

The sizzling iron neared her face.

"Brand the witch!" someone shouted. We all laughed.

"Burn the treason out of her!"

"I hate you all!" Ms Finch hissed, calming down, but her nostrils flared like a cornered animal.

"Watch out Finch or you'll be voted off and you won't be on next week's show!" I shouted at her. Everyone laughed, except for Ms Finch.

"Well if you don't like it here why don't you go and live in Europe!" Clarence the Butcher bellowed. He slapped his aproned thigh and laughed at his own joke. He got less response than me.

Suddenly I felt someone pinch the underside of my upper arm.

"Mark."

Mary.

"Did you catch them?"

"Who? What?"

"Someone spat on me earlier."

"Probably an agent from Brussels," she said. Sarcastic. Then she whispered something to me.

"What's that?" I shouted back.

She whispered again but it was lost under Ms Finch's endless racket.

Louder woman. Louder. I motioned with my hands.

Suddenly Ms Finch was silent, the light of the branding iron so close reflected off her sweaty forehead. Her fringe sizzled and curled up. That was a nice touch.

"Are you not entertained?" Gary asked the crowd.

But in the pause which followed, in which we all tried to work out if he was doing a Gladiator impression for a laugh, and should we laugh or tell him to get on with it? Mary shouted a question at me in a tone that sounded like treason.

"This is sovereignty?"

I clamped my hand over her mouth.

Everyone turned to glare at her, except Gary.

He pressed the iron into Ms Finch's face. Left cheek. She screamed like a fox in a snare. Everyone was delighted. They forgot my foolish wife. The sound of the skin sizzling was captivating.

"That smell…" Ms Formaldehyde said, and she wafted the air under her nose.

"Smells like…"

Steak. Christ.

Gary stepped back to admire his handiwork. He would have had an easier time of that if Ms Finch wasn't thrashing and complaining like some Continental at Heathrow's immigration gate.

"Ms Finch, you lack Blitz Spirit," Gary judged.

There was no denying it. I could smell her burnt flesh and I wasn't flinching! I was salivating.

"Hang on," Gary said.

He stepped in close again. He clamped the top of Ms Finch's head and inspected the brand with a squint.

"He's got the flag upside down," someone muttered.

And he had too! Ha!

"CLARENCE!" Ms Finch shouted suddenly.

"CLARENCE!"

We all looked at the Butcher who just shrugged.

"CLARENCE! How could you just stand there?"

Clarence made a circling motion with his finger at his temple.

"She's gone mad," he mumbled, eyes to the dirt.

Mary poked me in the ribs.

This was my big moment. I stepped up to Ms Finch and turned my back on her. I faced the crowd.

"From this day forth Ms Finch is outcast from all full-time employment. From now on she can only seek minimum wage work in fruit picking, social care, hospitality, medicine, auto-manufacturing, museums, postal service, street cleaning, pothole filling, or any other sector that was betrayed by EU workers during the long and glorious reign of Prime Minister Bunsen!"

The crowd cheered!

"None are to give her comfort. She is to find no shelter from the storm. None may lay a hand on her should she be wounded. None may consort with her carnally or in conversation about root vegetables. She must be ready to work in the gig economy when it returns, any day now, as promised by Billy Burner. She may not complain if her shift terminates early. When visiting any hospital to do volunteer work repairing the plumbing she must pay full car parking charges, even if the cost of parking exceeds the wages earned that day. She must pay the scroungers' tax at food banks and she absolutely must never, ever adjust her wireless again!"

I paused. Then.

"Wireless crime is treason!"

Yes!

"When you see the Flag of Europe on her cheek you know she was caught attempting to change the channel on her Churchill. She has been tried!"

"She has been judged!" The crowd shouted.

"She has been found guilty!"

Then the puppy ran through the crowd. The gaggle of children burst in after it, led now by Cyclops. The wretched child chased the puppy straight to Ms Finch and it immediately climbed onto her feet, whimpering and cringing.

"Do you want me to brand the puppy too?" Gary asked. "Won't take a moment to heat the iron back up."

"Let's just eat the fucking thing," Ms Formaldehyde suggested.

And I'm sure, later that night, someone did.

**Chapter Five, "Traditional British Metal Working In The Era of Sovereignty", page 14 – 'The Liffes and Times of Raylee – A Very British Village", published by anon.*

Twenty One

Believing in Food

"C is for Capsicum – The only justification for The Capsicum is the high Vitamin C content, which lessens NHS, in partnership with Shamco, waiting lists.

There is no other reason to eat capsicum. It originates from France.

For these reasons The Capsicum receives a patriotic rating of 000, 000 000, 004 out of a possible top score of 300, 034 974, 000. A dubious dinner guest, at best."

- 'Fruits and Vegetables, and Their Correct Patriotic Ratings' by Prime Minister Mark A. French.

Mark My Words

"So now get up," Mary said. And rocked my shoulder. "Get up. Now."

So now, I pretended to be asleep. I cracked one eye, just a little, to see what Mary would do next. I recalled my weary father lifting me from the back of the family car, at my mother's insistence, after long car journeys. No seatbelt needed undoing. It was a more liberated time. He was often drunk but as long as he could get us home, he was allowed to be. Personal freedom for all, and lots of repeats of B&W WW2 movies on Saturday tele.

I kept my eyes mostly closed, but my ears open, for what Mary would do next.

Mary left. Thumping down the stairs.

"These take some getting used to," she said.

"What?"

"Clogs!"

"Clogs?"

"The shoe store has run out of shoes. The government has set up an emergency footwear supply line. It's one of those VIP lanes. If only you'd once met a minister, we could be instant millionaires. Think of all the money they'd pay us for the pallets you piled outside town."

"That's a defensive fortification."

Mary didn't understand military matters.

"We're watching 'A Bridge Too Far' after breakfast," I said. It would be on the GBPBC's new War Channel. Or "Dambusters". Either would do.

"I'll break my neck in these things!" she laughed madly. From the sound on the staircase, clogs would take some getting used to.

"Shoes are shoes," I called after her.

Weren't clogs a bit too Continental?

"Shoes means shoes you mean!"

She started a racket in the kitchen.

"Can't a man have a lie in?"

If I'd known what was in store I would have been up in a flash. My push up complete. My teeth brushed, despite the toothpaste shortage. What's toothpaste when you can make it yourself with some chewing gum rolled in silt?

"What's all that racket?"

I swung my legs out of the bed. The floor was unseasonably cold.

"Where's my slippers?"

"Donated."

"What?"

"Don't worry. You've got a pair of clogs too."

This must be a dream.

"You might need to sand them down and paint them in flags. I think they're made from old wine boxes. It has Chateau Margaux 2009 printed on the side."

Maybe a nightmare?

"I suspect the Prime Minister himself made your clogs. You should be right chuffed."

More racket. The kettle bashed into the sink. The sink pushed back. The water spluttered from the tap. Spluttered?

"We've got two teabags this morning!" Mary hollered. "Two! And unused."

Definitely, a dream.

"The water looks a little brown. But I'm going to boil it."

"Did we win the food lottery?"

"We won the food lottery!"

Oh blessed dawn. A saviour stands with a teabag on the crest of a nearby hill, the sun just rising behind him.

"Boil the kettle Mary!"

"Hurry up Mark. There's a special on the television you won't want to miss."

She was right.

***

EXT. DOVER DAWN

OVER BLACK

"Winston – The Holy Potato - A Special Live Presentation on Behalf of His Majesty's Government, in Partnership with Ponzi Finance – Great Britain's World Beating International Investment House."

We hear children laughing. A lone bagpiper plays 'Land of Hope and Glory'.

Then we see the CHILDREN. Blonde, well fed and flying bluebird kites at the edge of the White Cliffs. Daringly close to the long drop. SPITFIRE BOY runs solo, arms spread, refighting the Battle of Britain.

NARRATOR
Only in Great Britain are children free to play with matches, safe from the nanny state.

But what's this?

The children pause. We study their rapturous faces. We hear a mighty petrol engine revving.

A child's eye reflects the scene, as the mighty red, white and blue SOVEREIGNTY SEMI-TRAILER approaches. Its load concealed under a tarpaulin.

NARRATOR
Only The Great British Democratic Monarchy has the courage of its convictions.

We see the driver of the truck. It's WILLIAM BUNSEN in hi-vis!

The children run in a circle. Mad with joy. SPITFIRE BOY races along the cliff edge.

CHILDREN
Ring-a-ring o' roses, A pocket full of posies, A-tishoo! A

tishoo! We all reclaim our sovereignty!

The truck halts just before it flattens the children. Turf churned. WILLIAM BUNSEN throws open the door and leaps out. He twirls and kicks his heels. Throws his arms about.

NARRATOR

In a world full of sheep leading sheep, only one leader dares to be the wolf in sheep's clothing.

WILLIAM BUNSEN points to the tarpaulin. The children help him pull it off to reveal the giant papier mache potato underneath.

***

"Bloody Fritz doesn't have this! Ha!"

I was ecstatic. The TV coverage of the unveiling of a giant Winston the Holy Potato, was the best of British television. It would be repeated endlessly for years. Daily. Hourly. It would become a centrepiece of the History curriculum in infant schools.

"Doesn't it make us look a little silly?" Mary worried. "It's a giant potato, and we've a potato shortage."

She knocked her clogs together. Knock. Knock.

"Stop that."

"I wonder what they'll say about it on Orkney?"

The British people had moved on from Orkney. We didn't speak about it anymore.

"What other country can grow a potato that looks like its founding father?" I demanded. I felt hot. We may be short millions of edible potatoes, but we had a giant symbolic one that looked like Winston Churchill!

Knock. Knock.

"Stop that!"

I felt like crying with joy. Not only did the massive papier mache potato look like Winston the Holy Potato, who looked like Winston Churchill, but all were giving two fingers to France!

Why could Mary not embrace the new reality?

Winston wasn't just a potato. He was a sign. He was now a national celebrity. Who could think about the weird pox spreading when we had daily reports of Winston's whereabouts? Just yesterday he was in Burnley with the King. Tomorrow? Who knows. Maybe Cromer. Maybe Raylee! And now a sculpture at Dover. Winston was our mascot.

"These days are Tolkienesque," I blathered. "These are our gravy days."

"They can't be our salad days," she smirked. "We don't have any."

"This is a time of magic. A holy spirit has returned from Heaven and taken a stolon for a home."

What other wonders awaited us?

"Have you tried on your clogs yet?"

"How many potatoes in the shape of Napoleon has France grown?" I shouted at the television. "How many potatoes in the form of the Kaiser has Germany managed? Have the Americans managed to produce a single tuber in the form of McCarthy? Have the Russians regrown Stalin? The Chinese Mao? NO!"

"I'm so sick of all this," Mary blurted.

I couldn't understand her.

She waved her hand about for a tissue. How could I give her one? There were no tissues, owing to a sudden increase in demand.

"You need to go on a gammon quest," I said. "You need

to see the light."

A few pounds of freshly boiled, salty gammon, eaten in a frenzy would do something to anyone.

Mary burst into more tears.

She left the room.

"Bring the tea?" I asked.

She did. She stood in the doorway with two steaming mugs. Her face a nice patriotic red, but she looked fuming.

I looked away. I looked back. I looked down. I looked back. I looked up. I looked back.

She pointed with one of the mugs at the television. The screen was abruptly filled with a static view of Westminster. The national anthem began playing.

"Bloody EU!"

"It's not the EU," Mary said, her face paling.

"What then? Saboteurs from Brussels?"

"That boy pretending to be a Spitfire has flown off the cliff."

Lies.

"I'm going back to bed," she said, and walked out with both mugs.

I didn't follow her.

"You'll be back," I muttered, "you need me more than I need you."

She'd bring me back my mug.

***

INT. FRENCH BEDROOM MORNING

MARK stands in the doorway. Tattered dressing gown open. MARY sits in bed. She holds two mugs of tea. One commemorates Princess Diana, the other King Charles III. MARY is looking at the window.

MARY
Do you remember the last time we went to Torremolinos?

The national anthem drifts about the room.

MARK
I'm sorry Mary.

MARY
Do you remember how it was shorts weather, even in October? How we danced to Abba and drank mojitos? You fell in the pool.

MARK reaches for a mug of tea. MARY slowly moves it out of reach.

MARK
I know all this sovereignty can be hard to process.

MARY looks at him.

MARK
We must be careful not to be like those lottery winners who win the jackpot and then lose it all.

MARY
Your sovereignty is measurable by your influence.

MARK, baffled.

MARK
We must keep faith in William Bunsen. It's a lovely day tomorrow.

MARY

It's always a lovely day tomorrow with Billy Burner. What about today?

MARY sips first from the Princess Diana mug.

MARK

We must believe in Winston the Holy Potato.

MARY

If you blame Brussels, I'll throw this mug at you.

MARK

Please Mary, can I have my mug?

MARY

You are a mug.

MARK walks away.

MARY puts the mugs on the bedside table and gets out of bed. She pulls back the blankets and pours the contents of King Charles III onto the mattress. She covers the giant wet patch with the blankets.

MARY

Come back Mark. Have your cuppa in bed next to me.

MARK reappears in the doorway, beaming like a boy with a new Airfix.

MARK

I was worried it was getting cold.

***

I went to pull back the covers and get into bed with Mary when I was struck with sudden inspiration.

"I've been struck by sudden inspiration!"

"I'd rather you were struck dumb," she said, smiling.

"We have to go to Uxbridge and dig."

She was sat now on the far side of the bed with an empty tea mug. I wanted my tea. Badly.

I had a sudden vision of endless potatoes just under the tufts of green grass in that magical Uxbridge field.

"Maybe there's a giant harvest of Winstons waiting to be dug up? We could be heroes. We might get invited to 10 Downing Street."

"You need a rest," Mary shook her head. "Why don't you have a little nap?"

"It'd be a lovely day trip."

"How would we get there?"

"The replacement bus for the bus replacement train service."

She looked like bursting into tears again.

"They've announced a replacement bus service for the replacement bus train service while the buses that replace the trains are upgraded."

She closed her eyes and counted her inward breath.

"But first, I want to finish watching the Dover special on tele."

She exhaled in a rush.

"They won't resume broadcasting until they've scraped that boy off the beach."

I shook my head. I was certain no children were harmed. Maybe Mary was just exhausted?

"You settle yourself in bed with your tea," she invited,

"and I'll go make us some toast."

She scrambled out of bed like a startled cat.

I was about to get into bed, but I felt sluggish, the pause in transmission had left me unsettled. I wanted the show to continue. I wanted my fix of national glory.

I decided to attempt a second push-up.

***

INT. FRENCH KITCHEN MORNING

MARY clenches a loaf of 'Sovereignty Bread'. She takes out two slices. She taps them on the counter. Thud. Thud.

She considers the packaging - *"New and Improved - Guaranteed not to combust!"*.

A third thud from the hallway.

MARY puts the bread into the toaster and leaves the kitchen.

We watch the toaster. There is smoke. A ticking sound.

MARK
(O.S. - puffed)
Is it my Unotesticular?

INT. FRENCH HALLWAY CONT.

The front door mat.

Lying on the floor is the newest edition of 'Unotesticular'. A clingfilmed baton.

MARY bends forward to pick up the magazine. THERE'S A LOAD BANG from the KITCHEN. She headbutts the front door and collapses. Heaped.

There's blood on the door.

MARY lays unmoving, her hands clenched around Unotesticular.

MARK (O.S.)
Mary? You didn't overcook the toast? Mary? I can smell smoke.

MARY twitches.

MARK (O.S.)
Mary? Bloody answer me!

INT. FRENCH BEDROOM CONT.

MARK flat to the floor. Panting.

Distantly, MARY groans.

MARK
I guess I'll get my own toast then.

CUT TO: HALLWAY CONT.

MARY touches her head. Her hand comes away bloodied.

MARY
This is all I bloody need.

MARK (O.S.)
Why is the bed wet?

***

That second push-up had taken it out of me. I had gone into the enterprise with double the enthusiasm I summoned for the first, but as I pushed off from the floor I knew it would be a struggle to reach the top. Am I Sisyphus or the boulder?

I decided to swallow my mug of tea in one gulp. Cold tea. Once I would have complained. But cold tea was an advance on no tea. Best of all, it was Great British cold tea.

The mug was empty.

I went, barefoot, down to the kitchen. I saw Mary's backside. Apron tied over the hump. Her hair was disheveled. She was moving slowly on her hands and knees, pushing a little ceramic bowl. Dropping burnt crusts into it, the toaster still smoking.

"Now what will we have for breakfast?" I demanded.

Everyone knew you didn't take your eye off Sovereignty Bread. It was powerful stuff.

"We'll give these crumbs to the birds," Mary sounded dreamy. "Or maybe we should take them to the library? For the bunting children."

My Unotesticular was on the kitchen table. There was a bloody smear on the wrapping.

First she wets the bed and now there's blood? Whatever next. I was anxious. It wasn't Raylee's turn with the A&E replacement bus service for weeks. She couldn't be ill at the moment.

Worse, I was to be caught in a kitchen sink drama just as the live broadcast at Dover resumed. I was sure even now Spitfire Boy was revving his engine and getting ready to give the imaginary Luftwaffe what for again!

"Mary. Why is there blood on my magazine? Why is the bed wet?"

"I bumped my head."

"What?"

She *was* bleeding. Her face was a sight. Pale skin. Red streaks. Blood was pooling under her chin and dripping onto the lino.

"Mary? Are you alright?"

She lay on her stomach. Even then she spied a blackened crust against the skirting boards and popped it into the bowl.

"I'll be alright. I just need a little rest."

She closed her eyes.

"I'll call an ambulance." I paused. "I mean, Ms Formaldehyde."

"There's no point," Mary said, and started laughing.

Bloody EU!

"What do I do?"

"Why don't you get the dish cloth and clean my face. You're my little first aider, remember."

I did as she asked. But when I turned the tap the pipes knocked about with air bubbles and no water came out. Thinking fast, I poured some water from the kettle onto the rag in the sink.

I sat next to Mary.

"Roll onto your back."

She did, and I dabbed the cloth at her face.

"Where's the cut?"

"Top of my head. I think."

It was gashed.

"Mary. You need stitches."

"It's not our turn for A&E this month Mark."

Then she closed her eyes and just lay there smiling.

I continued to clean her face. She was chuckling. So, it couldn't be too bad. Could it? And a scar on the top of the head could be hidden.

"Maybe you don't need stitches."

I went for our first aid kit. We had one butterfly clip (rusty) and a bandage (washed). I sat down at Mary's head and lifted, placing her head in my lap. I bandaged her head. She muttered now and then.

"Don't get your hands bloody," shc said.

"I don't care about that."

I had to tuck the bandage under itself and hope the clip held.

"See? Who needs A&E?" I reassured her. "Self-reliance is all we need."

"You're still my first aider," she muttered.

I settled myself with my back to a cupboard and her head in my lap.

"In a little while. When you feel better, we'll get you up to bed and I'll see what we can trade for some ibuprofen?"

She grunted.

"Ms Formaldehyde will want blood."

"We've plenty of that! It's everywhere!"

We laughed.

She was alright. She just needed a little rest.

By a stroke of fortune, from where I was sitting, I could see the television. Static Westminster gave way to another programme. A repeat of one of Great Britain's proudest days. The day Billy Burner, and his second last wife Bambi, freed Great Britain once and for all from the Continent's red tape tyranny. New Year's Eve and a bonfire of the inanities.

***

EXT. UXBRIDGE FIELD DAY

Burning paper rises like liberty's angels. The sound of Big Ben tolling. We are watching a giant bonfire.

WILLIAM BUNSEN NARRATES.

WILLIAM BUNSEN
In that moment the overweening, overreaching hand of Brussels went up in cinders.

Slow motion. Burning paper dances like ballerinas.

WILLIAM BUNSEN
No Continental can tell an Englishman anymore about disposing of asbestos. Not one dreary bureaucrat in Brussels' crypt can wag his finger over the effluent on your beaches.

Folders are flung into the fire. Whoosh! We can hear sticks knocking and bells ringing.

WILLIAM BUNSEN
No Eurocrat can stand in your kitchen and tell you whether or not your egg has salmonella in it. Britons are free to eat what they want, when they want.

CUT TO:

ROME. An aerial view of the city.

WILLIAM BUNSEN
They'll be marvelling in Rome.

CUT TO :

MADRID. Aerial.

WILLIAM BUNSEN
Gobsmacked in Madrid.

EXT. UXBRIDGE FIELD EARLIER

The pyre of EU regulations is yet to be lit. A mountain of folders and paper that reaches to the heavens. Around the pyre are big speakers on tall stands. Bunting strung between the stands. And under the bunting a troupe of MORRIS DANCERS is spread out. Waiting. Tambourines and sticks in hand.

WILLIAM BUNSEN
Imagine the look on Continental faces as they see the chains they tried to bind the indigenous Great British lion with go up in smoke.

There's an opening to access the pyre. WILLIAM BUNSEN and BAMBI BUNSEN stand hand in hand right there. BAMBI is heavily pregnant. She holds a jerry can of petrol. WILLIAM a burning torch. They are both in hi-vis.

WILLIAM BUNSEN
I'll have lead in my petrol if I want it! Lead in my paint! Flammable toys! I'll have choice!

CLOSE ON :

WILLIAM and BAMBI. She takes his hand and presses it to her bump.

WILLIAM BUNSEN
The freedoms Europe robbed from us, we will return to your children.

BAMBI BUNSEN
This is a moment of national rebirth.

***

"I bet this is how Stonehenge used to look when they celebrated solstice," I declared.

"What dear?" Mary was still in my lap, her eyes closed.

"The government found traces of Union Flag bunting in ancient post holes in Wiltshire."

"Help me up to bed," she mumbled.

"National renewal is what we need. Make England Great again."

"That's nice. I want to go to bed."

Panic gripped me. What if the Churchill was listening? She had to stay with me throughout the broadcast. A head injury would be no defence in the court of public opinion.

***

EXT. UXBRDIGE FIELD CONT.

WILLIAM BUNSEN and BAMBI BUNSEN approach the mountain of folders. BAMBI shuffles with a hand pressed to her side, and the other clutches the jerry can.

We see that onlookers ring the spectacle. BAMBI turns and hefts the petrol can over her head. The people cheer!

BAMBI turns back to the mountain of red tape. She opens the can and splashes petrol over the base of the pyre. On the grass. On her shoes. Fumes haze our view.

WILLIAM BUNSEN waves the burning torch as if signalling to past, present and future. He flings the torch onto the pyre. WHOOSH! A flash envelops them both.

TRANSMISSION CUTS.

***

"I expected they would have edited out that bit," Mary says, her eyes open now.

"What for? It's the moment we were freed from petty rules over the ingredients in bread."

"Bambi burnt to death!" Mary sits up now. Hand on her head. "I don't half have a headache. Get me up to bed Mark."

"Just a few minutes more."

Downing Street denied Bambi burnt to death.

"She died in childbirth," I said.

"So did freedom," Mary replied. The traitor.

***

EXT. UXBRDIGE FIELD CONT.

THE MORRIS DANCERS dance around the pyre. "Land of Hope and Glory" blasts from the speakers. The huge fire leaps, the onlookers whoop and holler. Pieces of paper rise burning on the thermals.

WILLIAM BUNSEN stands alone. A little singed.

WILLIAM BUNSEN

Sovereignty's song is fire.

A BLONDE BOY - The fire reflects in the tears streaming down his face. WILLIAM BUNSEN rushes to the boy. Kneels before him.

WILLIAM BUNSEN
Don't cry child. You are free.

BLONDE BOY
I am crying tears of joy Mr Bunsen.

Our POV rises now, over the joyful carnival.

WILLIAM BUNSEN
This field is sacred.

WILLIAM BUNSEN and BLONDE BOY (O.S.)
This field is England.

***

"Are those ambulance lights?" Mary asked, pointing at the screen. "Behind the flag poles?"

I slapped my thighs, loudly, to Elgar. I stood up behind Mary.

"This sacred field. This England!"

"They're gone now. The lights. Let's go to bed Mark. I need a lie in."

I tapped both feet now. Hear me Uxbridge! Hear me Winston! I am with you!

I slapped my palms against my knees and my feet slammed into the floor.

"I want to fight a Frenchman! I want to clobber a German!

I want to ignore an Italian!"

Mary steadied herself with a hand on the edge of the counter and walked slowly towards the door.

"I'm going up."

This repeat of the burning pyre was a new dawn rising. The rebirth of a nation in fire repeated again.

"This is the course of history changing and we were part of it."

Mary paused in the doorway.

"We ate the beans last week."

"What?"

"We're having a leek later. For lunch."

She left.

The camera panned out and circled as it rose with the burning regulations. Soon the pyre looked like a distant campfire. God's eye. And then the blaze was just a candle in the wind. And then darkness with Elgar playing on.

"This is England."

I clapped till my palms went red. This is how you do it.

"Take that France! Take that Germany! Take that Italy! I bet you miss our tourist money now Spain!"

The programme ended, but I wasn't done with celebrating our independence. I took my new copy of Unotesticular and carefully sponged Mary's blood off the wrapping. Then I lay it on the draining board and peeled off the clingfilm.

The cover promised that inside was a double page special on the discovery of a skeleton older than Cheddar Man where Cheddar Man himself was discovered. DNA analysis revealed a pale skinned man with blonde hair and green eyes. A direct ancestor of the Prime Minister. This was an article I would relish.

"The English have never been ruled by anyone," I said.

"Mark?" Mary called down. She sounded halfway up the

stairs.

"You should see what's in my Unotesticular."

"Would you mind going to Ms Formaldehyde now. I've a bag of wooden pegs hidden in an old biscuit tin. She might swap some pills for those."

"There's an article on Cheddar Man 2.0. Also, the PM's own account of when he discovered Winston."

"Mark. Please."

I turned to that page.

"I spied Winston next to a stand of Tudor roses. The red and white petals overlaid and touched with dew."

I moved to the doorway so Mary could hear better.

"The earth a little steamy and obviously fertile. It wanted a good ploughing. A mountain of prime English horse manure had been turned into that field to bring it to this ripe tempo. Look Monty! I shouted. It's a classic British potato plant! And in a field of English roses! This is indeed sacred ground. At that moment a ray of sunlight touched the plant's green leaves which instantly transmuted into gold."

"I don't know how much more of this I can take," Mary said.

"Monty's intellectual power was noteworthy from birth, and his artistic ability celebrated by foreign visitors. He released my hand and tottered to the potato plant. "It a King Edward po-ta-to Pappa," the boy declared. He had inherited the powerful oratory genes of his sire."

I doubted Formaldehyde would swap something as rare as ibuprofen for pegs.

"Monty gripped the plant by the stem and pulled it from the blessed soil with one heave. He displayed a strength beyond his tender years. The divine root was exposed. Monty studied the heavenly tuber and made the immortal declaration, "This...a mir-a-cle Pappa! A mir-a-cle! It is second coming!"

William Bunsen fell to his knees and hugged Monty and the divine potato.

"Monty, this is a sign from God. I raised my eyes to the heavens. This potato is a symbol of the will of the people and will be so for the next thousand years."

The potato was carried home by father and son where both the boy's mother and Bunsen's next wife (at that stage Bambi's PR consultant) were struck dumb with wonder.

The Prime Minister goes on to recount he had the distinct feeling of a divine presence, as if "[The] Holy Ghost Winston had arrived to be shield and sword in our country's hour of need".

"We must take this potato to the King, I told Monty. After that we must guard it in the Tower of London."

This is England. This is why we are free.

"I think I'm going to vomit," Mary said.

And did.

Twenty Two

A Sore for Sighted Eyes

"C is for Corn – Whilst the Spanish plundered The Americas, after failing to conquer England, and didn't leave a railway behind, the English taught all the peoples of the New World the value of corn. And left a proper railway behind.
For these reasons Corn receives a patriotic rating of 291, 101 101, 001 out of a possible top score of 300, 034 974, 000. A sturdy building block."

- 'Fruits and Vegetables, and Their Correct Patriotic Ratings', by Prime Minister Mark A. French.

Mark My Words

Raylee's last indigenous clothing store, Great British Ladies, failed just when I needed them to fail. The owner never seemed quite right.

"Mr Jelly has some Italian shoes!" Mary would gush, and I would frown.

"Why doesn't he sell proper shoes."

"The leather is so soft. Not like the government issued thongs we've been getting in the rations."

The signs of something wrong with my wife were there from the start. If only I'd been paying attention.

"What's wrong with British shoes?"

It was too often like this.

"Mr Jelly has berets!"

I would scowl.

"What's wrong with British…"

They even had "Made in France" on the labels. Rubbing salt into the wound.

"It's the EU's fault we don't make berets in England."

"Oh Mark."

"We all know nothing is made in France."

It was no surprise Mr Jelly's business failed.

"But how will Mr Jelly feed his family?" Mary fretted, when I told her the news.

"Don't worry about Mr Jelly's family."

She worried regardless.

"I am fretting. We have to take them something. Maybe a pair of our shoes."

"The Jelly's are good for nothing, anti-growth, curtain twitching layabouts relying on hardworking taxpayers like you and me to feed them."

She gave me a long look, as if I were to blame.

"We only just got our clogs," I said. "I'm not giving the Jelly's mine."

I still hadn't gotten used to clogs, but I would for the country.

"I need my clogs for the war effort."

"But the war hasn't started yet."

"The preparations have. I can't believe I have to tell you all this."

She was standing at the sink with the cold water tap on. "There's no cold water."

"Yet," I corrected. Mary could be so pessimistic, before the war.

"Jelly won't be able to feed his family."

"Foraging is too good for them?"

A drop of water began to grow under the tap. Ha!

"See! Water!"

"A drop of E. Coli. Mark..."

"Jelly doesn't have to feed his family," I reassured her. "I bet they can starve for all he cares."

"You can be so heartless."

"So, you didn't hear?"

"Hear what?"

"Mrs Jelly left him and took the twins."

"I hardly think that's funny."

"It's true. Clarence told me. Apparently, Mrs Jelly had an affair with Bunsen a decade ago and she's proved it by having the twins DNA tested. The girls are Bunsen's. Mrs Jelly has received an undisclosed payment and been moved to a cottage at Chequers."

Mary shook her head as if that could get the rocks out.

"Just one cottage? Or a village?" she grinned.

"Bunsen Town."

"When the hell did Bunsen and Mrs Jelly have an affair?" she asked.

"No one is certain. Least of all Mr Jelly!" Ha!

"Well, the girls are eleven..."

Light dawned across Mary's face.

"Remember when Mrs Jelly went to that London for a hen's night and came back all excited because she'd met some blond toff at a strip club in the West End?"

"The old dog. He must have done a Becker."

"A what?"

"Broom cupboard."

Now Mary just looked aghast. "Poor Jelly. He's lost his business and his family."

"And he's a cuckold."

"Jesus wept Mark French."

"We're getting distracted from the important news," I

said.

That morning Raylee's [chastened] postman delivered a letter from 'The Ministry of War' informing me PERSONALLY they were rebranding as 'The Ministry of Peace', in order to make the most of the war.

Policies, staff, and the objective of *"a total and crushing victory over internal enemies of the people, followed by unbroken harmony"* remained unchanged. All men of uniform wearing age were now under the Ministry's command.

Five minutes later the postman returned and knocked on our door. He looked understandably sheepish.

"This one is yours too," he said, not daring to look me in the eye.

"Binned any Unotesticulars lately?" I asked, cheerfully.

The second latter was from The Ministry of Peace. I was now personally in charge of, *"Seizing whatever retail goods, situated within shops, open or shuttered, of Raylee, I deemed expedient to England's coming war against The British."*

I could not recall a prouder morning. Two letters from the government within minutes of one another.

Both envelopes were of robust quality. The paper so thick you could be forgiven for mistaking it for scrap cardboard. I held mine for a minute, not wanting to damage it, admiring the unicorn and lion stamped on the front.

"You see the way they've concealed the staples which hold the envelope together?" I asked Mary. "I bet a French letter doesn't have staples in it."

Mary grinned at me.

"Just open it Mark," she urged, "don't just stand there gaping like a goldfish."

"I'm not gaping Mary. I'm controlling myself."

"Would you like me to open it for you?" she offered her hand.

I handed the envelope to her.

"I am already being singled out for great things," I whispered, "and the war hasn't started."

Would she be able to cope with my meteoritic rise in the coming months?

No. Time would tell.

"It's a lovely envelope," she cooed. "It feels like the velvetiest cardboard. Oh, look it says 'On His Majesty's Service' at the top and there's a little drawing of some mythical animals."

Why was she smirking?

"And when they ration the gas this winter we can burn it and warm our hands."

"Why are you smirking?"

She shrugged.

"Why are you smirking?"

"French letter."

Baffling woman.

Our Churchill burst into song. Elgar's *'Pomp and Circumstance March No. 1'*. A belter!

"I couldn't have chosen a better song for a letter opening ceremony," I said.

"To be fair, I don't think Churchill is capable of choosing any other song."

"Just open it," I ordered.

"What?" she asked, her hand cupped to her ear. Our Churchill was having a really loud moment.

I mimed opening the letter. She turned her head on its side like a curious dog.

"OPEN THE LETTER!"

Churchill took that as a challenge. The radio became so loud it started to vibrate and shift around the counter.

Mary took up a paring knife to cut open the envelope.

"Carefully," I mouthed.

"Oh, I'll be ever so careful. I don't want to cut myself in

the excitement."

"Be careful not to damage the letter! You might heal. The letter can't."

She pointed the knife at me for a moment, her hand trembling, the blade trembling, her eyes furious. But like a summer storm it passed.

She began to pick out the staples with the point of the knife.

I took the envelope from her.

"Oi! I could have had your finger off."

I slipped the letter out of its sleeve and held it, still folded.

"Would you like me to read it for you?"

I handed her the letter. I confess I could not look. What if it was like believing you have won the lottery only to discover you matched just one number? The crushing realisation that nothing had changed. Your life was still the same crushing bore.

She unfolded the letter.

"Look, there's gold lettering at the top."

I could not look.

I closed my eyes and listened to Elgar. Let him hold me up lest I fall.

***

INT. FRENCH KITCHEN MORNING

A dripping tap. Elgar plays loudly. But the drops of water hitting the steel sink are louder. A dog yelps in the distance. A shotgun blasts. The yelping stops. Somewhere a window is smashed and a woman screams obscenities.

ON SCREEN – *"THIS IS ENGLAND"*

We look now at the CHURCHILL RADIO, "Land of Hope and Glory" plays.

MARK FRENCH

I was ecstatic. I felt like I was vibrating and about to vanish to some higher, sunlit plain.

MARY FRENCH

Mark said it was as if a battalion of angels were flying over him in Spitfires.

Now we see MARK AND MARY FRENCH. MARY holds a rough looking letter made of brown paper.

MARY FRENCH

Private…enter name…you are empowered by The People's Government to take what you want from…enter town name here…shops at will, so long as it serves the war effort.

***

Mary paused. She was so carried away by Elgar.

"This letter is so personal," she shouted, "Mark. This is *your* moment."

I couldn't agree more.

"To think they were in such a hurry to get the letter to you they didn't have time to write your name on it." She was a woman driven made by joy.

I felt powerful. No minor clerical error like a missing town name could deflate me. This was the beginning of my meteoric rise. I knew it.

"To think they were in such a hurry to get the letter out they didn't even fill in the blanks."

"It's a patriot's job to fill in the blanks."

Details. Details. Details were for those who lack vision.

I took the letter and placed it on the kitchen table. I didn't want to spoil the moment.

"Won't the shopkeepers be left out of pocket?" Mary asked, suddenly pensive.

"I will issue them with receipts," I shouted.

"LAND OF HOPE AND GLORY!" Churchill bellowed.

"What? I can't hear you over Churchill!"

"MOTHER OF THE FREE!" Churchill screamed.

"When the enemy is defeated," I whispered now, "I am sure the shopkeepers will be rewarded for their sacrifices."

"HOW SHALL WE EXTOL THEE!" Churchill raged.

My wife cupped her hand to her ear and lent towards me.

"When the enemy is defeated..." I tried again, but it was no use. Churchill was in full patriotic fervour, and he wasn't about to calm down. Along our street the other radios joined in.

"WHO ARE BORN OF THEE!"

I took a pad and a pencil from a kitchen drawer and wrote down what I wanted Mary to know.

"WIDER STILL AND WIDER
SHALL THEY BOUNDS BE SET
GOD WHO MADE THEE MIGHTY"

"But most of the shops barely have anything to sell as it is!" she wrote after me. She looked at me red faced, possessed of a sudden fury I could not begin to understand.

"MAKE THEE MIGHTIER
GOD WHO MADE THEE MIGHTY
MAKE THEE MIGHTIER YET!"

I put my finger to her lips and whispered shush. Perhaps if we stood quietly Churchill would lower his volume. But Mary shook her head muttering, "No no no no no", and then put her hands over her ears.

What if someone saw her like this? To attempt to block out Elgar was presumably a crime? I rushed to the backdoor and looked outside. Several neighbours had come out to stand on their doorsteps, their hands on their hearts, their eyes raised to the sky and faces frozen in delight.

When I turned around Mary was sitting on the kitchen floor weeping. She wasn't trying to wipe away her tears. They rolled, great dollops of wet, down her cheeks and collected on her chin, before falling into her lap. This was hardly the time for a breakdown. We had not yet had our breakfast!

I picked up the letter and went to stand outside with it pressed to my chest. If I showed her the way, perhaps she would collect herself. But as Elgar faded I was standing alone. As all men do when they face their destiny.

"Come on inside Mark," she said quietly, "you've not had your breakfast yet. All this excitement won't do your digestion any good."

Ah! She had pulled herself together. A paramount example of Blitz Spirit for the other wives to follow.

"After breakfast I'll take you to window shop at Great British Ladies," I told her. "You might see something inside you fancy? I can requisition it, for the war effort."

"I won't take it," Mary declared. "It would be abusing your power."

I was ready for this.

"Happy homes make for happy soldiers."

Her eyes widened in disbelief.

"We didn't beat the Germans singlehandedly in two world wars, one world cup and one referendum with unhappy wives."

She just nodded and placed a bowl of powdered egg on the table.

"This is just the start of my military career," I encouraged her. "You'll see. I am bound for greatness and you're coming with me."

"There's no water," she replied. "You'll have to eat it powdered."

"Victory comes from a multitude of small sacrifices," I replied, and taking up a spoon, I had at that powder. "Winston the Holy Potato said that."

"Magic potatoes don't talk," she muttered.

"Winston does."

Mary held her head in her hands for a long moment, then left the room.

"This is a good egg!" I called after her, although my mouth was gummed up with the powder, making it hard to shout. "A very British egg!"

***

INT. FRENCH STAIRCASE MORNING

MARY FRENCH sits on the lower stair hugging her knees. Tears stream down her reddened face.

MARK FRENCH (O.S.)
This is a good egg!

MARY FRENCH begins to pull at her hair.

MARK FRENCH (O.S.)
A very British egg!

***

"Bad people can feel joy too," Mary told me, as we walked to Mr Jelly's corpse of a store.

"But it can't be real joy," I replied.

"It's the same emotion. How else could they do what they do? Just think of Bunsen, each time he succeeds in convincing the next halfwit to be his new fiancé? We all know it ends badly for her. He knows it does. But he kicks his heels as he walks down the street that day, even though the stupid girl has just damned herself."

"I suspect bad people are always unhappy," I replied.

"No Mark. They feel the same emotions as I do."

Where did she get this nonsense?

"Cyclops' mother said it explains how the government can do what it does."

She was so lost in her rambling I had to steer her around a particularly deep pothole. There was a dead rat floating in it. Putty in colour and almost hairless.

"What about Bunsen?" I stopped. I was aghast. She'd taken his name in vain!

"You used Bunsen as an example of a bad person!" I hissed, looking around to be certain no one had overhead her. Should we run home? Should she leave town and go on the lam?

"Of course Bunsen feels the same way as you do."

She walked ahead of me.

"The mosquitos are going to be terrible this year."

"Why?"

"All the standing water. Still, they'll be Great British mosquitos."

I should have had her committed there and then.

***

EXT. RAYLEE - HIGH STREET DAY

SUN reflects in a water filled pothole. Blue sky and

scudding clouds. MARK FRENCH'S face blocks the sun as he stares into the puddle. He is reflected back at himself.

MARY (O.S.)
Once the potholes join up Raylee will be lost underwater.

MARK
A modern Atlantis. Take that Greece!

The pavement is litter strewn. Shop fronts shuttered. TWO MEN scrap in the background over a small dog. One is missing an arm and one is missing a leg.

LEGLESS MAN
I saw it first!

ARMLESS MAN
(headbutts LEGLESS MAN)
It doesn't matter. It's my dinner.

LEGLESS MAN is on the ground. Hands to bloodied face.

ARMLESS MAN takes the dog by the scruff and walks away. CLARENCE looms out of an alley's shadows and knocks him down with a single punch. CLARENCE wipes his hands on his apron, picks up the yelping dog and walks off.

MARK
Knock it off you lot! Save it for the enemies of the people.

MARY
Are we window shopping or not?

***

INT. GREAT BRITISH LADIES CONT.

MR JELLY'S point of view.

Through the shop windows he sees the men fight over the dog. The sun bursts through the running clouds. Disappears behind them. Bursts out again.

MR JELLY
(singing)
Rule Britannia, Britannia waives the rules…

Failure surrounds MR JELLY. Shop mannequins stand armless or lie legless. Lines of ragged bunting hang from the ceiling like vines. Lights flicker. Only one mannequin is still fully able and dressed, MARGARET THATCHER.

MR JELLY
Britain is a nation of shopkeepers no more.

A PHOTO OF WILLIAM BUNSEN hangs on the wall behind the till. MR JELLY marches to it and salutes. There is a CHURCHILL on the counter. It begins broadcasting. MR JELLY begins to weep.

CHURCHILL
It's almost time to defeat The Internal Enemies of the People! Who will be the first to put down an EU funded rebellion in their town?

***

"Why isn't Mr Jelly having a closing down sale?" Mary wondered.

Mr Jelly was sobbing inside his shop, all wobbly jowls and heaving chest. He had combed his hair over, but it was so thin you could see his beetroot dome pulsating. He picked up a clothes hanger from the floor and began to beat it against his forehead.

We were watching the death of a dream. But it was only one man's dream.

"A sacrifice worth making," I stated.

"Oh dear. Shouldn't we do something?" Mary clutched her limp handbag to her chest.

Bloody EU. I was so enraged I didn't know how I could wait for the war.

"He can beat himself without our help," I replied. "Although I'm of a mind to go inside and give him a kick. How he allowed Brussels to do this to him I don't know."

He wasn't half giving himself a proper thrashing.

"He can't sell clothes if he can't import them." Mary, and her treason.

"That is not patriotic behaviour," I said, moving to shield Mary's eyes from the increasing violence inside the shop. But she blocked me.

"We have to help him."

She could be baffling.

"Please don't report him," she added.

"He should have sold British made clothes," I told her.

She cast about anxiously, but there was no one else watching. At least not openly, heaven knows who may be watching from a concealed place. There were a few people coming up the pavement. But as soon as they caught sight of Mr Jelly they about faced smartly or veered off into the street. More than one stepped into a pothole and vanished briefly, before bobbing back up. Bloody Europe.

"He's almost certainly in the act of committing a crime," I shook my head.

"You're not going to report him. Not even on the freephone number."

"Blitz Spirit must be on public display at all times," I couldn't believe this needed saying. "Especially during adversity."

"It's adversity all the time!"

"Bloody Germans!"

"A closing down sale would cheer him up," Mary brightened. "Let's go in and barter for something."

Bloody Dutch!

"There's no need. I can take whatever we want. It's the will of the people."

I was already deciding which mannequins I wanted. They would make a good show manning the defenses of Raylee.

"We could make a symbolic payment. Just a few pence."

I had a sudden urge to pinch Mary and pinch her hard. It was like she was living in a daydream. It took effort to resist the impulse. I didn't want to make a public show of our differences. We carried on watching Mr Jelly. He flung the coat hanger away and began to slap himself. He was a suspiciously plump man. His jowls wobbled hilariously.

"It is against the law for small businesses to fail," I reminded my wayward wife. "Great British businesses do not fail. And how is he so fat?"

"Get Business Done!" I shouted in exasperation. Mr Jelly appeared not to hear me. Which wasn't a surprise, given he was now beating his palms against his ears.

***

INT. GREAT BRITISH LADIES CONT.

MR JELLY pants, eyes unfocused like an exhausted dog. MARY FRENCH knocks on the windows. She is smiling desperately. MR JELLY can't hear her.

EXT. GREAT BRITISH LADIES CONT.

MARK FRENCH
Jelly would benefit from a public shaming.

MARY FRENCH continues to beat on the glass.

MARY FRENCH
Let's go inside. We must do something.

MARK FRENCH
Drag him out by the scruff and cuff and toss him into the dirt?

MARY FRENCH
(bashing on windows)
Mr Jelly! Oi! Jelly!

MARK FRENCH
Kick his bum in the street. Point at him and laugh! We'll teach him to undermine the Great British retail sector.

MARY FRENCH
Mr Jelly!

MARY FRENCH hits the glass so hard it shudders.

MR JELLY notices them. He turns like a carnival clown, mouth hanging open. MARY FRENCH waves encouragingly. MR JELLY smiles at her but looks nuts.

MARK FRENCH
The least he could do is stand up straight.

INT. GREAT BRITISH LADIES CONT.

MR JELLY lies on the floor in a star shape.

MR JELLY
The British are a nation of shopkeepers.

MR JELLY'S nose begins to bleed.

***

"I went to school with Jelly," Mary said. "He was a right little monkey. He loved nothing better than to serenade the girls. He can't sing to save himself. But he does a good impersonation of an opera singer. Once he fell to his knees at my feet and..."

"That's enough of that!" I did pinch her. Hard. On her forearm. It silenced her. Her fury was a price I was willing to pay.

"Mr Jelly was clearly a subversive from a young age. I would not be surprised if his childhood home owned no bunting."

I wouldn't have Mary spreading rumours that they were school friends. What if someone at The Ministry of Peace heard?

"You're putting my career in danger."

Mad Mary now started waving at Jelly.

"You hoo! Jelly!"

I was at a loss to know which of them was madder. A pinch hadn't stopped Mary. Would I have to employ a

Chinese burn?

"We need to keep moving," I took Mary by the elbow.

"We should ask him back for dinner. He's looking awfully skinny. I wonder if Mrs Jelly was feeding him properly?"

"I saw her foraging for wild potatoes and garlic in Batters Lane just the other day," I lied.

"That's funny. She's allergic to garlic. Allergic to all the alliums."

"She was wearing gardening gloves and a mask."

"Goodness. Remember I was invited to that hen night, but you didn't want me to go."

"What are you saying?"

"I could have a pair of gardening gloves now too," she smirked. I don't know why, but I was hurt.

"Blame Brussels," I said, attempting to conceal my true feelings under a confected show of rage at Europeans.

"Next you'll be telling me they rigged the raffle when she won that piglet," Mary stopped on the pavement. Her fists bunched. She suddenly about-faced and marched back to Great British Ladies.

"Did you know Cardinal Bogg discovered an entire warehouse of TA catering uniforms. Good as new," I shouted after her, "I'll get to wear one when we attack ourselves."

Good. She stopped and looked back, eyebrow arched.

"But you're not going to be in the Catering Corps."

"Every trueborn Englishman who believes in crown and country serves in the TA Catering Corps. An army marches on its stomach."

She shrugged.

"I've been saving some scrap silk to patch my best knickers. I'll make you a garter to wear under your TA trousers."

That was weird.

She kept going, past a billboard being fitted with a bold new poster.

"The Great British High Street is Strong!" It proclaimed, and in smaller type, "Small and Medium Sized Great British Businesses are *BOOMING!*"

Rosie the Riveter stood over the text, modified to resemble Bunsen's current wife, who looked much like the last and the next, I fancied. That was clever. The foresight of our government to futureproof civil wartime propaganda.

"Look at that poster!" I cried. "Well done boys! That'll show them in Brussels!"

My wife studied the poster.

"Why don't you ever see any adverts for actual businesses these days?" she wondered. TREASONOUSLY. She said it out loud. Loud enough for people to hear. The men affixing the new poster actually dropped their brushes and pots of glue.

"I think it's time we queued at the food market and hurried home for lunch," I hissed. I took her elbow in a vice like grip this time, which she twisted out of too easily. I made a note to double my push-up schedule.

"Turnips," she shouted. She was going mad. It was excruciating.

"We're only allowed to go mad in private," I said through clenched teeth.

"I'm going to go mad at the market," she grinned and sped off.

So much for window shopping.

"So much for Blitz Spirit!"

Cyclops ran out of an alley then and raced after her.

"Mrs French! Mrs French!"

"What is it Cyclops?"

"Mum wants you to come over for lunch. We've won the food lottery!"

Mary halted. She looked about her until she found some clean litter. She arranged it on the pavement in front of her and knelt, as Cyclops barrelled in, arms out like he was an aeroplane. She knelt on the pavement and opened her arms. The boy flew into them.

Whatever next!

"What's for lunch Cyclops?"

"Two potatoes and an actual sausage!"

She hugged him like he was her own. I didn't know where to look. Anyone just passing through town would think he was ours, and by the state of him, all stick arms and stick legs, eyepatch and shaggy head, they'd think we were welfare spongers who spent our handouts on plasma televisions.

"I'll see you at home Mark," she called to me. Stood up, took the little mongrel's hand and let him drag her off.

"Looks like I'll be queuing on my own," I called after Mary. "Don't mind me!"

It was worth it though. I got a turnip, so big you could have beaten a man to death with it. The Welsh can keep their leeks. Take that Drakeford. Put that in your pipe and smoke it.

***

INT. GREAT BRITISH LADIES NIGHT

TORCH through the windows. The beam passes over the broken and fallen mannequins. Back and forth the beam goes. Dust motes dance. Then it finds its target. MARGARET THATCHER.

VOICE

Our Mother, who art in Heaven.

The TORCH is turned off. Darkness. The sound of a window breaking. Heavy footsteps in the dark. Devious laughter.

***

I slept well that night. I dreamt I was Prime Minister. Bunsen had finally retired to spend time with his families. A shock to the country, as all assumed he would never willingly leave office, even though in my dream he was riddled with syphilis and half mad with an eternal lust, which burnt so fierce he claimed he was cursed by Zeus.

I took office and found a delegation of German carmakers waiting in the lobby.

"Bitte. Bitte."

They always were bitter.

"Herr Frank!"

The continent required new leadership. A fresh vision. Only an Englishman could provide it. Someone who could take the fight to Brussels, and not just in Brussels, but also across the Irish Sea where the reunited island refused to import British made ham sandwiches.

In my maiden speech I declared an end to EU regulations regarding food safety. The first blow for Blighty.

But more important than foreign mistakes, Blighty needed someone who would take the fight to ourselves.

I awoke invigorated and lay staring at the ceiling. The cracks in the plaster seemed like a roadmap. A small knot in the corner snaked out and grew ever larger until it reached a convulsion of larger lines around the light fitting. The fitting was 10 Downing Street. I was to be the light. I just had to follow my destiny.

Destiny is all.

"I will handpick the sentries myself," I told Mary, after

my push ups. "I want Raylee's defences to be so imposing no tyrant will even consider attacking it."

Mary didn't respond. She was sewing scrap silk into a garter and humming "Ode To Joy".

"To qualify they will have to have a fixed forward gaze. Stout limbs. Be able to stand unsupervised for hours on end. A willingness to serve that does not weaken as the weeks drag on. And always, always stand to attention when the national anthem is played."

"That sounds sensible dear," Mary mumbled, mouth twisting as she peered at the fabric.

Then she did something magical.

"Look under the sink."

"Why?"

"Do you want breakfast or not?"

I didn't want to look, but I did want breakfast.

As I opened the cupboard door she said, "They're Go Home Office brand. I couldn't find Heinz. It's the subject of a trade war. No one can afford to import it."

Go Home Office Beans were launched last year to celebrate how many people not born in the UK had left. And fine beans they were!

"Why would I want any other beans?"

"Oh, I don't know. Maybe you remember living in a functioning country?"

I ignored that. It was pointless to argue with her when she was sewing.

"How did you get them? When I went to the market yesterday there was only turnips."

"It's a bribe," she shrugged.

"We must count each one. Little marvels! Wait. A bribe?"

"Mr Jelly left them with a note this morning asking us not to tell anyone about seeing him beating himself."

"My silence can not be bought so easily."

"The note said he has more. But he won't be able to give them to us if he is in a re-education camp."

"I bet the Jelly's have a stash of tinned goods under a loose floorboard, under a rug, in their living room, behind the toilet cistern. Maybe even inside the cistern in waterproof bags? Food. Food. Food just squirrelled away everywhere inside their house. It's no wonder his business folded. Wasting all his profits on food and not re-investing for the future."

Mary bit the thread and tied it off.

"I thought we'd just have them cold," she said. "It's such a warm morning."

Was the gas off again? Some questions did not need answering.

"Just so. An example to the soft folk of Europe who squandered their incomes on electricity and gas."

Mary held up the garter.

I was opening the tin of beans.

"There. When you're lying face down in the mud or burying your brothers in arms in haste in some sodden Surrey field, you can know that you have a little bit of me with you. Right there on your thigh."

She never seemed weirder to me than in that moment.

"I'll pick the cream of the crop from Great British Ladies," I promised, as the smell of cold beans filled the air. My mouth began to water. I wafted the scent of the feast up with my hands.

"No amputees. No headless dummies. Just the able bodied. The most plastic of patriots. You'll see Raylee's sentries endure in all weather."

Mary gave me a searching look, her eyes twinkling with some private humour.

"Yes Mary, I'll bring one home for you. As promised."

The mannequins would be properly enlisted and dressed

as soldiers. They would protect Raylee when the men and boys of the town marched to war. Anyone looking at the town from a distance would see a company of men on guard and ready to fight.

"That will show Brussels!"

"Potemkin militia."

What was she on about?

"The beans. Let's have the beans," I said.

"When exactly are you marching to war my love? Do we have a date yet?"

Our Churchill crackled into life and answered for me.

"In approximately forty-eight hours the patriotic people of The Great British Democratic Monarchy begin a special military operation to rid our blessed land of fascist traitors," Prime Minister Bunsen boomed out of the vibrating speaker. "We will de-nazify Britannia!"

"He's using his serious voice," Mary interjected, causing Churchill to raise his volume.

"All men and boys of fighting age are mobilised. We will quickly achieve victory over ourselves."

Finally, the hour was drawing near! London would fall. I would soon receive orders to join up with several other local militias in Surrey and await orders.

"Special military attaches will arrive in all towns and villages to lead the regiments of brave patriots out of their homes and to their fate," Bunsen promised. "For my part I will be departing for a third country to ensure governance continues without interruption."

There was a pause. A crackle. Then "We'll Meet Again" began to play.

"It's a lovely day tomorrow!" the PM promised.

"It's always a lovely day tomorrow with Prime Minister Bunsen. The trick was just to ignore today."

"Mary. Not now! I am getting my marching orders."

She smiled and nodded.

"We can put the last of the Worcestershire Sauce Substitute on the beans if you like?"

I had no doubts about my destiny.

"Be brave noble Britons! Your second finest hour is fast approaching."

We ate our beans in silence, as Vera Lynn boomed out.

"And first," Churchill said, "the latest news on trade, presented by Secretary of State for Blockade Busting, Field Marshall Trust."

Ah! Trade! Even with an entirely voluntary war about to start, we were still just ticking along, a perfectly normal, functioning country.

Our wooden spoons circled around the last of the beans. Both waiting for a false move from the other, or a signal of deference.

"Great Britain has concluded the latest rounds of negotiations on the Australian trade deal. Soon we will receive the first blockade busting shipments of Vegemite and Tim Tams! Which is funny in a way. Many used to scoff at the thought of eating an antipodean vegetable paste, but now, with Marmite listed as a foreign agent, is the perfect time to boost your vitamin B! You might not always get what you want, but if you try sometimes, you might just find you get what you need."

Mrs Trust began to play The Rolling Stones on an electronic piano, humming along and stirring the feelings of all who heard it.

"Shouldn't she be playing an Australian song?" Mary asked, glancing at Churchill. I took my chance and scooped up the last bean.

"It's a Great British trade deal so an indigenous British song is appropriate," I replied. "The antipodeans are lucky. This signals a rebuilt Commonwealth. British leadership has returned to the colonies."

"Mark, I've lost count of the number of times the Australian trade deal has been announced. It's like a kind of annual ritual now."

"It always makes me smile," I replied. "Just imagine it now. Tall ships setting sail from Sydney harbour packed full of vegemite and sunshine. And in return we send them our promise to re-negotiate the deal on more favourable terms while they're stuck at the Suez Canal. It's magnificent. We are a global trading nation again."

Mary gave me a puzzled look.

"What?"

She reached out and pressed her palm to my forehead.

"What?"

"Nothing. Just checking if you have a temperature."

"My blood is up! As soon as I've watched you do the dishes I'm off to Jelly's to enlist the local militia."

"The plastic patriots."

There would be none finer.

***

EXT. RAYLEE – HIGH STREET DAY

We can hear the unmistakable sound of a SPITFIRE.

MARK beams. He makes the sound of a machine gun as the sound of the plane grows louder. He begins to march.

Past a burning pram, without a glance.

Straight through potholes, without concern.

He sidesteps comatose drunks.

He sees a LITTER PICKER bend over to pick up a discarded soft drink can.

MARK
(to litter picker)
The Big Society in action!

MARK strides on.

The LITTER PICKER upends the can to drain the last drop. Throws it into a puddle. Falls face first into the puddle.

Always the sound of the SPITFIRE.

CYCLOPS is being held upside down by A GANG OF BIGGER BOYS.

CYCLOPS
Help!

AN EGG falls out of his pocket and is caught by one of the BOYS. The BOYS shake him. Another egg falls out.

BIG BOY
Food hoarder!

MARK confronts the group.

MARK
Put him down.

BIG BOY
What you gonna do gammon?

MARK clips the boy around the ears. They drop CYCLOPS in a heap and circle MARK like wolves. MARK pales but makes a show of it.

CLARENCE approaches behind MARK. Silent. Unstoppable. The BIGGER BOYS run.

CYCLOPS
Thank you Mr French!

CYCLOPS hugs him.

MARK FRENCH
Go home Cyclops.

MARK extricates himself from the boy. Strides on. He hasn't noticed CLARENCE, who kneels down and opens his arms, and CYCLOPS runs to him.

CLARENCE gives the boy a wax paper wrapped parcel.

MARK arrives at GREAT BRITISH LADIES. He stands staring business-like at the front door. A glass panel has been broken and patched up with some cardboard and tape.

A MONK in a ragged habit walks behind him, unseen, silent, carrying a giant, framed photograph of KING CHARLES III.

***

INT. GREAT BRITISH LADIES CONT.

MR JELLY watches MARK approach his shop.

MR JELLY
Give me strength.

Broken glass litters the entrance. MARK crunches over it.

MARK
Jelly! I am enlisting your mannequins in The Great British People's Army.

***

Nothing could stop us now!

"Jelly!" I declared, as I entered his forlorn and unpatriotic shop, crunching over broken glass he was too lazy to sweep up, "Which side are you on?"

Jelly blinked. He bunched a fist. His face reddened. His lip curled. But I was ready for him. I took the letter from the Ministry of Peace out of my coat pocket and thrust it in his face.

"You'll give me what the country needs for its great struggle against itself, or you'll have to answer to the Ministry."

"Did you break into my shop last night?" Jelly demanded.

"Why would I do that when I can just walk in and take what I want?"

Logic defeated him.

His fists unbunched. His lips uncurled. His face stayed red.

"I told Mrs Jelly I didn't care if she had cheated with Bunsen," he muttered. "I didn't care if the twins weren't mine *genetically*. I've raised them as mine."

Bloody hell. There was hardly time for his mental breakdown in the middle of a national mental breakdown.

"Read. The. LETTER."

"No," he said, and turned his back on me. Turned his back on his country.

"Wash your mannequins and have them report for duty at the defensive barricade."

Jelly turned back.

"You do realise they're plastic? They're not real people."

"Do you think I'm mad?"

He was an idiot.

"I guess you'll have poor little, half-starved Cyclops carry them out there?"

"People like you are why public brandings have returned."

He backed away. Now the colour drained from his cheeks.

"Stay safe at the front," he said, "wherever it is."

He kept backing away. Seeming to drift across the floor like a ghost.

"Don't get shot. Don't get shot right between your squinty little eyes."

And he turned and floated out of the display area into his office. He closed the door quietly but then started screaming.

"FOOLS! FOOLS! FOOLS!"

I let him scream. I was victorious.

There was the sound of a chair hitting a wall and then just sobbing. It was no mystery why he had failed in business. He wasn't British enough.

Twenty Three

The Secret Diary of Mrs French, Again

"Z is for Zucchini – just a courgette in disguise. Don't be fooled. I wasn't.

For this reasons The Zucchini receives a patriotic rating of 000, 000 000, 001 out of a possible top score of 300, 034 974, 000. Best used as a practical joke."

- 'Fruits and Vegetables, and Their Correct Patriotic Ratings' by Prime Minister Mark A. French.

Mark Her Words

"A more stupid and stubborn man than my husband Mark is yet to be born. And if he has been he's still a boy and still to prove his idiocy to all. Mark is going to war. Well, they're calling it a war. They celebrate it starting ANY DAY NOW in the papers. Bunsen has been promising us a "hot" fight against ourselves for months. Let's see.

BUT Raylee has to send its men. To Surrey!

Our regiment will be a sorry collective of half broken, middle aged men and knock kneed boys. What do they expect of our little town? All the smart chaps left in The Third Toilet Paper Crisis of 2025.

MARK IS GOING TO WAR!!! ENGLAND HAS DECLARED WAR ON ENGLAND!!! – That's my headline.

England would have declared war on Wales, Scotland, Free Cornwall, New Northumbria and Northern Ireland too, but they're too smart to get involved. And with the combined US and German armies patrolling the Channel the war will remain inside England. Why don't they just do us a favour and invade us? Why can't we discover massive oil reserves in the Cotswolds?

Foolish. Stupid. Dumb. Idiot. Brute. England. Anyone who didn't sign The Great British Declaration of Independence, and pledge themselves to uphold The Swill of the Sheeple has been declared persona non grata by Cardinal Petal.

Mark already believes he is fighting infiltrators from Brussels, to ensure British sovereignty. He tells me it at breakfast daily. But we're just England now, I say. It makes no mark on Mark. He's been groomed, for years. I spend so much time wondering how to get him back? There's no coming back. I understood that the day he took part in Ms Finch's branding.

Clearly all is daft. They even passed a law to say that English meant British, and vice versa, and intend to reissue our passports even bluer. I doubt any of them understand there is a difference.

So Mark will go and fight other Englishmen? Where? And with what?! Potatoes? Turnips? There's precious little in the way of actual military equipment in the country. It all went when the British Army refused to fight the British Army on Orkney.

Goodness! They even passed a law saying you can't THINK about the day the Army laid its weapons down. Field Marshall Trust was there looking like a right plank. Neckerchief flapping in the breeze as she sat up in her Union Flag painted tank watching her tank crew walk away into the mist. There was even that photo of one of the lads baring his bum at her and slapping both cheeks. To possess a copy of it is fifteen years hard labour on a soft fruit farm!

"I am the Iron Lady Mark II!" she shouted after them. Weird woman. Prime Minister Bunsen was on holiday at the time. OF COURSE. One of these days he's going to go overseas and not come back. I know it.

The truth of this sorry passage in our country's history will only fully be known after it is concluded. I am sure the truth is not what most believe. I am sure I'd be sent to re-education, or worse, if this diary were ever to come to light.

P.S. The gas cut off while we were cooking our potato last night. Mark sawed off the lower portions of the legs from our dining table and chairs. We made a fire in the living room fireplace grate and baked the half-boiled spud instead. Now the kitchen table tilts. The chimney needs cleaning, so the house filled with smoke.

"It's Great British smoke!" Mark said, with an idiot's smile. I wanted to gouge out his eyes.

Twenty Four

England Prepares for War Against England

"C is for Chard – I don't know what this is. No rating."
- 'Fruits and Vegetables, and Their Correct Patriotic Ratings' by Prime Minister Mark A. French.

Mark My Words

Who can forget the day William Bunsen stood outside 10 Downing Street, at the lectern with a replica sun hanging on wires, and declared it was time to move on from, "Declaring war on ourselves, to preparing for almost immediate conflict, with ourselves!"

"This is the most famous front door in the world," I told Mary, who looked dubious. She wasn't really focused on the television, which was essentially a crime, if not in law, certainly in spirit.

She was holding a large, woollen sock with the heel missing.

"What do you want with my favourite sock?"

"I'm trying to work out if I can turn it into three pairs of children's socks."

"Charity begins at home," I told her, and reached for it, but she pulled back. She looked dour.

"Not today, Mark French. Not today."

A curtain to the right of the world's most famous door twitched. Mrs Bunsen stood in profile with her hand on her belly. A bright lamp behind her, at head height. She had a halo.

"Silly tart wants us to see her," Mary noted, now with a smouldering piece of bread in her fist. "I bet she isn't forced to eat Sovereignty Bread."

"Twins are expected," I replied.

Mary scowled.

"Blonde twins. Commemorative tea towels are being made," I added.

The curtain was redrawn.

"Did you see that?" Mary jabbed the crust forward, causing it to re-heat.

"Careful."

"Did you see?"

"What?"

"The bimbo at the window. She collapsed."

"She's heavily pregnant. She was just sitting down."

"The curtain is stuck to the window! She's vomited on it."

"Can we please just watch Billy Burner?"

"Wait? What happened to the last Mrs Bunsen?" Mary thrust the crust at me. An ember fell into my lap. I patted it out before it burnt a hole in my crotch.

"Nothing."

"Eat your breakfast."

Mary began drawing circles in the air with the crust. The leading edge went blue.

"He can have a bloody harem if he likes," I said, with heat of my own. "So long as we get our freedoms back from Brussels."

"Now there's blood on the curtains! Did you think she exploded?"

"I think she probably spilt a Bloody Mary. Yesterday's

editorial in The Parrot was all about the PM and his family's support for the Great British tomato sector. They have Bloody Marys for breakfast. Lunch. Dinner. Bloody Marys all through the day."

"What tomato sector? The last polytunnel in Kent is now a model Spitfire museum."

A new lectern had been built for the day, in hi-vis camouflage pattern, and I counted no fewer than ten of the Prime Minister's oldest children present, all in the military uniform of the King's Life Guard, breastplates shining, swords drawn, and the youngest on hobby horses. The white plumes on their helmets made from replica nylon. All except the Orkney MP, Fintech Bunsen, who was dressed in khaki and pith helmet.

"Why is he wearing a pith helmet?" Mary wondered. She would.

"Because he has to put down a rebellion in one of His Majesty's far flung provinces."

"Orkney? Ha! Good luck."

"Let's focus on the substance, shall we?"

"The traitors in our midst have grown bolder in recent weeks," Bunsen continued. "We will show them what sovereignty means!"

There had been alarming reports of sabotage on Cardinal Bogg's estate. The government first denied them, then said they were nothing, then blamed the last Labour government, then blamed Europe, then threatened a trade war with Ireland, then threatened a further increase in the money they were paying the Taliban to look after Afghanis fleeing the Taliban, then launched an inquiry into the sabotage. It was due to report as soon as it concluded.

"One of Cardinal Petal's Dobermans has died," I told Mary, to get her back on track. "Reportedly from an accumulation of heavy metals in its fat cells."

This was attributed to a diet largely sourced from The English Channel, and nothing that should alarm the British public. Unless you ate dogs from seaside towns of course, which no one did, because the British meat supply was world beating.

"Is someone really burning scarecrows that look like Cardinal Bogg?" Mary asked.

"Gossip."

"That's what they want you to think. I think the people are revolting."

"Never a truer word said," I replied, and we giggled.

"Well, it's come to a pretty pass. What do you think did it? The lack of food, the medicine shortages, the GP famine, and it was faster to get from London to Birmingham in the 14th century than it is now."

My spark of good humour extinguished.

"It makes the case for war stronger," I shouted at Mary. She pursed her lips.

The day was fast approaching when I would do as Bunsen urged and, "forget your troubles, lift up your old kit bag and smile, smile, smile!"

He had never looked more statesmanlike than that day.

That morning he had hosted the Italian Prime Minister in the first state visit from the sclerotic continent for years. She stood now at the side in a green pants suit, dark hair tied back in a ponytail, a look of bemusement on her face.

"I bet she's just gagging for an order of Prosecco," I commented.

"I heard she came offering an increase in food aid," Mary replied.

"Jesus Mary! Do you want to get branded?" I nodded back at the kitchen. Churchill would be listening. "We don't need any help from the bloody Continentals. Great Britain is self-sufficient."

We looked in other directions then, like two cats momentarily pretending they weren't fighting.

"Never forget it is London's fault the war against ourselves must be fought!" Mr Bunsen declared, from London. "England must prepare for war against England. This is not a conflict we seek, but one that is forced upon us by ourselves. It is one in which England will triumph! Kent will defeat Surrey! Surrey will vanquish Devon! Cornwall…well. Our enemies will bc vanquished!"

One of the King's Life Guards lifted a silver trumpet and performed a series of rousing notes.

"If the little bugger strung those together it would make a recognisable tune," Mary said. "How old is he? Seven?"

"Everyone's a critic."

Our pleasant morning was interrupted by a mad banging on the back door. Frenzied.

"Who the bloody hell is that? Why aren't they inside watching the broadcast?"

"It'll be Cyclops," Mary said. "I can hear him panting from here."

She left the room and returned a moment later with the little idiot. He was so breathless he couldn't speak.

"Now now Cyclops," Mary knelt before him and put her hands on his shoulders. Looked him in the eye.

"Is your mother okay?"

He nodded.

"Have Martians invaded?"

He looked confused, then grinned and shook his head.

"What is it then?" I demanded. "We're trying to watch YOUR Prime Minister."

"London," he managed.

"Who cares about London?" I shouted. I shifted my chair closer to the television.

"It's succeeded," he puffed.

Mary and I exchanged puzzled glances.

"Succeeded at what?" I asked.

"He means seceded," Mary said.

"The Mayor has made a statement," Cyclops added. "Mum said to come and get you."

"He's gone mad. We're watching Bunsen speak from London right now. It's a live broadcast."

"That's what they want you to think," Cyclops said, and shrugged.

"He needs feeding up," I told Mary. "He can't think properly. What will the future be like with millions like Cyclops running about the country? It doesn't bode well. Bloody Europe!"

They both just gawped at me.

"I don't know why people bother having children if they won't look after them."

"You shut up." Mary held Cyclops to her. Held him tight.

She stood and took his hand.

"How does your Mum know?"

"She heard it on the radio."

"There's been nothing but Elgar from Churchill this morning," I said.

Mary and Cyclops gave each other a knowing look. I thought then Mary was pretending to be as mad as the boy, to comfort him. Now I know better.

"Mark, you stay here with Bunsen. I'll take Cyclops home," Mary said, and they both left.

Which was a relief.

***

INT. CYCLOPS' KITCHEN MORNING

CHURCHILL RADIO on a worn kitchen counter next to a

Union Flag pattern tea cosy. Elgar plays loudly.

The kitchen is derelict. The lino mostly ripped up. Many floorboards are missing. A wood saw lies near the gaps. Sawdust on a half sawn up board.

A CHICKEN sits in the sink on a bed of straw.

CYCLOPS and MARY enter.

CYCLOPS
Be careful.

CYCLOPS points to the floor.

CYCLOPS
We had tins of beans under there.

MARY
Did you eat them?

CYCLOPS
We were robbed when Ms Finch was branded.

CYCLOPS' MUM (O.S.)
Put the kettle on!

MARY
They pulled up the floor?

CYCLOPS
Mum said we were lucky we hid the chicken in the loft.

CYCLOPS

We've been using the floorboards to cook.

MARY
You're not eating them?

CYCLOPS laughs.

CYCLOPS' MUM
Cyclops? Put the kettle on.

CYCLOPS
(quietly)
They stole the kettle too, but mum doesn't want to believe it. So now we have pretend tea parties. And they're real because believing makes it so.

MARY
Did you call the police?

CYCLOPS
They said they only take emergency calls between 8am and 10am. We had to call back the next day.

MARY
Did you?

CYCLOPS
Yes. But they said it was no longer an emergency as it happened yesterday.

MARY
You were lucky. Reporting stolen food is not allowed. It messes with the crime statistics.

CYCLOPS' MUM
Cyclops? Is that you Mary?

CYCLOPS points to CHURCHILL and presses his finger to his lips to indicate quiet. He places the tea cosy over the radio. He exits the kitchen. MARY follows.

INT. CYCLOPS' LIVING ROOM CONT.

CYCLOPS and CYCLOPS' MUM huddle around a little radio. Its broadcast unintelligible at first.

CYCLOPS' MUM has a blanket wrapped around her shoulders. Her hair is flat and greasy. She smiles at MARY. She's missing some teeth. Her gums are bloody. She motions for Mary to come close.

MARY
God have mercy.

CYCLOPS
There is no God Mrs French. There's onlyWinston the Holy Potato.

MARY
How did you lose your teeth?

CYCLOPS' MUM
They've been falling out on their own. Scurvy, maybe?

MARY is furious.

MARY
(quiet)

I told you to get rid of the radio.

CYCLOPS' MUM
I will never surrender it. We need it. Listen. You can hear Free Britain broadcasting from Calais again.

TRANSISTOR RADIO
We urge all who wish to be free of Bunsen's tyranny to go to the M25 barricade and request access to Free London. Mayor Can is receiving airdrops of food aid as we broadcast. The White House's Special Representative for the UK is to meet with the European Council later today to decide on military intervention.

CYCLOPS' MUM
London has succeeded.

CYCLOPS
Mum means seceded.

***

Once Mary and that idiot boy left I made myself a second breakfast of baked beans. I'd come into some tins. I would have shared with Mary, if she'd been home, but she had picked a side.

The tins had those old-fashioned ring pulls, which saved me bashing the tin open with some bricks. I ate them cold, as you are supposed to do.

"Even now there is still time to keep the dogs of war on their leashes," William Bunsen said.

I was grateful that Mary was gone. It made a nice change to just focus on the Prime Minister, without her endless cynicism.

"If the Enemies of the People confess, and give up their Flags of Europe, we can have peace and reconciliation."

Fat chance of that. The traitors would have to be burned out of their hiding places.

"I urge the Mayor of London to meet with me at Chequers. Let us talk over our differences. Let us work together to enjoy the benefits of an independent Great British Democratic Monarchy. Let us find red tape we can cut together."

Fat chance of that too! That traitorous Mayor was more likely to ally with Orkney.

"To help the Mayor choose the right direction I urge all patriots to prepare to leave their towns and villages and join me in London in a national display of unity."

This is it. I thought. This is war.

Get War Done!

Oh, I wanted it now more badly than ever before.

Just then a strong wind blew and whipped up the plumes on the King's Life Guard. The MP for Orkney held his helmet on. For a moment it seemed as if 10 Downing Street itself was blowing away. The brickwork at the edges of the screen appeared to peel and reveal a wooden framework.

I rubbed my eyes. I must be tired.

When I looked again more of the bricks peeled off. I could see green grass and what looked like Chequers in the background. A short woman in black was throwing a large, white ball for a Doberman in the background.

I bunched up my fists and ground my knuckles into my eyes.

"I need to get my eyes tested," I said, to no one.

When I looked again the transmission had concluded and there was an aerial view of The Palace of Westminster. Big Ben was tolling. People on the bridge were standing still out of respect for Great Britain.

I worried I'd missed the two minute silence. But it wasn't yet 11am.

Churchill got going in the kitchen. First an advert for Chicken Stock Chicken Soup. A fantastic meal. The packaging was classic Union Flag pattern, and it came with a set of instructions for how to fold the box into a Saint George Cross.

It was a riveting diversion from hunger pains.

The box disintegrated after a few folds, and you had to buy another. Classic British salesmanship. I especially liked the ad's jingle, which had an inspiring melody.

"Here comes the soup, here comes the chicken soup now, here comes the chi-chi-chi-chi-chicken soup..."

As the song faded out you heard a confident chap declare, *"Chicken Stock soup, it's the patriot's choice! Just add one cube to sterilised ditch water and wait for the magic to start! It's almost like eating chicken."*

"That's what we'll have for supper tonight," I told Mary, who still wasn't there.

I got up and started to pace. What was taking her so long? For a moment I panicked she was eating contraband. It would be just like Cyclops and his mum to eat an artichoke.

"If only there was a guidebook to eating patriotically!" I fumed. "Bloody Europe!"

London wouldn't know what hit it when The Patriotic People's Army of the Great British Democratic Monarchy descended on it from the countryside.

Voting may have failed to remove the traitor from the mayor's office, but we'd soon fix that.

Twenty Five

A Special Economic Action

"B is for Beetroot – The Beetroot is a patriot. Like a rush of blood to the face when thinking about forrins coming for are jobs.

Beetroot can be used to make substitute clothing dyes. Beetroot can be roasted or purified into sugars. The vicar will always have tea with his sugar, because, Beetroot.

For these reasons The Beetroot receives a patriotic rating of 311, 101 101, 001 out of a possible top score of 300, 034 974, 000. Hold one and know The English have never been ruled by anybody."

- 'Fruits and Vegetables, and Their Correct Patriotic Ratings' by Prime Minister Mark A. French.

Mark My Words

"How will I bring my shopping home," Mary asked me, as I begun to prepare to prepare to leave for the war, which had almost, almost begun.

"What shopping? The EU makes it impossible to shop. This is why I must go and fight ourselves."

She put her hands on her hips. If she'd had a rolling pin I would have disarmed her.

"Hands, woman, you have hands," I told her. "For millennia women carried shopping home in just their hands."

I wasn't lying. I rushed to her and gripped her slabs, with their little sausages.

"Mark," she gasped. "I can't remember the last time we held hands."

I kissed her on both cheeks.

"Mark," she pulled back. "I've been watching you go mad for years. Now I think you've finally done it."

"It's not just me Mary. It's the UK."

She nodded.

"Mad with joy. Mary. No Englishman is complete unless he goes to war. I thought my generation had missed out. But I was wrong. I will bayonet someone before the year is out and the country will be renewed. And I won't come back with any of that woke PTSD nonsense."

Her eyes grew wider.

"But the war is against ourselves. You understand this?"

"We've been fighting Brussels since 2016 by waging a cold war on ourselves," I pointed out the obvious.

"No one in Europe cares what we do."

"How would you know?"

Very slowly she placed both her palms against the sides of her head, as if trying to stop her brains falling out.

"Hasn't it always been that way?" I said. "This is why we must show them what we're made of. Once and for all. They'll take notice when London is retaken from the French."

She pressed harder, but she replied all the same.

"Well, when you consider we're a mongrel race of European peoples merged together over millennia, and now also comprised of all the people we colonised, I guess..."

"Colonised?" As if giving people railways was a crime!

"Yes Mark. Colonised."

This was a baffling turn. She'd gone full woke. It just showed just how important it was to win the war at home.

The rot was everywhere. Even my own home. Had she been reading radical left Marxist, antifa, fascist, communist literature? Was there a pamphleteer in our town? The postman? Maybe we should start the war right here in Raylee.

Root.

And.

Branch.

"Mary," I reminded her, "the English have never been ruled by anyone."

She removed her hands from her head.

"You can't have my antique 'bag for life'. I've looked after it for years. Ever since the temporary plastic bag shortage. I'll not have it torn and ruined in some muddy Surrey field."

"If its fate is to be sacrificed to free the country..."

She wasn't having it.

Churchill saved us. Bursting into life with an announcement. All day would be a special playlist of scores from WW2 films to celebrate the *"special economic action, to cleanse our sacred land of the fascist forces of Brussels',"* once and for all, and to remind us that, *"we never need to leave 1945 behind."*

If we just tried hard enough, it could always be The Battle of Britain, we could stay forever in *"our finest hour."* And if the battle was in Britain it never needed to end.

I forgave Mary. Her seditious talk was a symptom of her broader mental illness.

"I am ready to give the traitors two black eyes," I declared, as I fell to my knees and rummaged under the kitchen sink for the shopping bag. "A bloody nose and some missing teeth."

"Spare the teeth," Mary now sounded amused.

"Why?"

"Well, it's not like they'll be able to see a dentist."

It was dark under the sink.

"It must have been like this before D Day," I said, to the plastic piping. It was leaking. We had water today. A godly sign of good fortune. "Wives fretting as their men prepared to storm the beaches and rid Continental Europe of the scourge of Teutonic red tape once and for all. Fat lot of good it did in the end. Here we are again and this time the evil is at home."

Red tape. Non-English red tape. It was like the red weed from War of the Worlds. It snaked all over the country suffocating the life out of us. If Britons weren't free to choose how much heavy metal was in their mackerel, liberty was a mirage.

But this time would be different.

This time we were fighting ourselves.

"Give me that shopping bag Mary. I'm packing for war."

"It won't serve," she muttered, but she nudged me with her knee to get out from under the sink. In a moment she had the bag. I still can't say to this day where it was hidden. I'd even looked behind the rusting paint tins we'd forgotten in the darkest corner.

"What rot! It has Winston's colours. Red, white and blue gives an unnatural strength to any material."

"I still don't know what am I supposed to carry food home in? Double up my apron?"

What a silly question.

"I have the appetite of two men," I said, a little impatiently. Really, she was tainting my big day. "When I'm away you'll need to shop for two less people. Therefore you'll be shopping for zero. What food?"

It was a joke she didn't get.

"Hasn't the Ministry of Peace issued you with a kit bag?"

"In mighty Britain we take care of our own baggage," I told her, and I took the bag for life from her hands. Prised it.

"When I am Prime Minister I will have this bag framed and hung above my desk in 10 Downing Street."

"When you're Prime Minister?" she repeated, casting a nervous eye at Churchill.

She looked like she might cry.

"Parting is such sweet sorrow," I quoted the greatest writer who ever lived.

But it was not the time for emotional fireworks. I had to stay focused. I was off to stare death in the face.

"The conflict will be swift," I reassured Mary. "It will be over by Christmas. I expect the first day's action alone will see me seizing spoils of war. Who knows what the traitors have been sent by Merkel? Whatever goods they have airdropped will be in bags. I will return this carrier bag a hundred times over."

She sighed. A long sound like she had been punctured.

"What am I supposed to carry the turnips home in?" Still on this. I decided to be tolerant.

"You should be growing your own."

This much was obvious. I tried to touch her on the shoulder, but she flinched.

"Our shovel was requisitioned for the war effort!" Now she just sobbed.

Pretty, sweet, dumpling. She could not tell me what she really felt. The fear she harboured as I set out on my great adventure. Her own war would be against worry about me and solitude, without me she would be a different person altogether.

"There will be plenty of work to do on the home front," I reminded her.

"You're a fool Mark French."

"Private Mark French."

"You're a great big silly fool Private Mark French."

She pressed her forehead to the table and heaved.

I was starting to feel impatient again. This day was about me and here she was making it all about herself.

"Our shovel now forms part of the barrel of a Great British tank."

I had no doubt.

Her head snapped up. Her cheeks wet and her eyes wide.

"WHAT IF I AM WIDOWED?" She screeched. Then so quiet, "Who will defend me against the inevitable charges of treason when I refuse to remarry some one-eyed veteran?"

What a bizarre question. What would it matter?

"How could you remarry when you'll be grieving for me?"

She sat down on the floor, her legs splayed out she hammered her slab fists at her thighs. I decided to get down to her level in the hope of putting an end to the amateur dramatics. I had to get packing done.

"Now, now," I soothed, "Get war done."

She bit her lower lip so hard it turned purple.

"Don't ruin the war for me Mary."

Churchill had had enough too. 'God Save The King' got its running shoes on and ran around every home in our block shouting. I suspect even the robins paused in their musical squabbles and stood to attention. When the song had played out, when every breast was heaving, when all the loins were girded, a pre-recorded speech by Fintech Bunsen played.

"What a man takes to war says a lot about what he values," Fintech Bunsen said, in as deep a voice as he could. *"What he values says a lot about who he is as a man. Patriotism is measured not in deeds but in physical possessions. Flags. Teabags. Patriotically patterned dripping. Socks. Keychains. How can someone know if you love your sovereignty if they can not see a Union Flag patterned sock on your ankle?"*

"Firm point. Well made."

"When I became a life peer on my ninth birthday I thought not of how hard I have striven to achieve my position. As I cloaked myself in the ermine and placed my palm on the red, white and blue bible the oath I took was nothing compared to the John Bull boxer shorts I wore underneath."

He paused. There was the distinct sound of a crystal decanter decanting.

I gently eased away from Mary.

"What you eat declares what you value!" Fintech was back, his thirst quenched, *"No trueborn Englishman would be seen dead eating a Brussels Sprout! A Yorkshire Greenball is clearly the vegetable of choice at Christmas to accompany a Cheshire Great Chicken.*"*

"Hear! Hear!"

But what beverage would a patriot drink? Tea!

"Tea is the patriot's beverage of choice!" Ha! I beamed at Mary. *"Wellington did not triumph in the Hindu Kush in 1734 without English branded, substitute tea at his disposal."*

That decided it.

"I'll be taking our kettle to war also," I whispered to Mary. Before she could drag herself up I requisitioned the kettle for the war effort and scarpered upstairs, closing the bedroom door behind me and wedging a chair under the handle.

"But what will I boil water in to sanitise my cleaning rags?" Mary pounded on the door with her mallet hands. The wood panels quivered. I feared they'd splinter. "You're just lucky they haven't taken our doors for the war effort yet or I'd wring your bloody neck."

This is why it was men who went to war, I decided. We had the vision to see the forks in the road. The women just saw the spoons.

"You're a great big, bloody fool Mark French!"

I heard her slide down the door. I heard her arse thud on the floor. Then I heard her sob. The only thing I could think to do to bring her comfort was to promise, once more, to "Get War Done!".

**The consumption of turkey had been outlawed after the industry behaved unpatriotically and collapsed. A new government department for big foods had genetically engineered chickens with massive breasts and long legs. These are now served at Christmas and are called Cheshire Great Chickens. Reports of increased risk of various cancers are exaggerated.*

Twenty Six

Passing Out, After Breakfast

"B is for The Banana – still undergoing assessment. Why does it have those worrying strings under the skin? Are they Woke?
For this reason, the Banana's patriotic rating is yet to be determined."

- 'Fruits and Vegetables, and Their Correct Patriotic Ratings' by Prime Minister Mark A. French.

Mark My Words

EXT. RAYLEE HIGH STREET NIGHT

TWO BRITISH ARMY TRUCKS crawl along the mist shrouded street. In the distance a fire alarm sounds. An orange glow pulsates on the periphery.

The TRUCKS' giant red, white and blue wheels go in and out of monstrous potholes. Mud splattered Union Flag pattern rubber. Water sloshes in their wake. Dead rats in the water. The wind whips up litter which slaps against the cab windows.

CYCLOPS dashes about in the dark. He has a handwoven reed bag. He is bagging up the dead rats.

SOLDIER ONE, rifle and flashlight, grabs CYCLOPS by the scruff.

SOLDIER ONE
Patriots don't eat rat.

CYCLOPS
We're starving.

SOLDIER ONE
You're undermining the will of the people.

The TRUCKS stop. SOLDIER TWO throws back the canvas flaps at the rear.

SOLDIER TWO
Leave the little blighter be.

SOLDIER ONE
How old are you?

CYCLOPS
Ten, Sir.

SOLDIER ONE
One more year and you'll be in the army.

CYCLOPS
Who will look after my mum?

SOLDIER ONE
You will. By spreading the guts of the Enemies of the People across the green fields of England. You will fertilise the future.

SOLDIER ONE releases CYCLOPS.

SOLDIER ONE
Come on. You can help us distribute the food parcels.

CYCLOPS
Food?

SOLDIER ONE
Billy Burner is playing Santa.

SOLDIER TWO
Billy Burner is fuelling up the private jet.

CYCLOPS
Where is he going?

SOLDIER ONE
On a bombing run to Brussels.

SOLDIER TWO
I didn't know Brussels was in the Caribbean.

CLOSE ON : SOLDIER ONE'S uniform – "The Great British Army – In Partnership with Churnco".

***

On the day I left Mary I had a kipper for breakfast. Not everyone in Raylee did. The soldiers I'd enlisted to stand watch on the defensive perimeter needed no feeding. They were fed on sovereignty.

"Even the vegans," I told Mary. "Even the bloody radical

left will be defeated soon. Ha!"

And antifa!

"And antifa," Mary added.

"My dear wife, there's hope for you after all."

Mary smiled, but she was shovelling her half of kipper in so fast I feared she would eat my half.

"Don't throw away the packaging," I ordered.

The packaging was flag.

"Keep it as a memento of the day the tide turned."

Churchill was talking. It felt like being in church.

"The act of eating proper British food strengthens your spirit, as well as your flesh. The Enemies of the People eat avocadoes this morning. Avocadoes! What good is that devil's testicle versus a smoked fish."

Good, old fashioned grease paper wrapping. Not that recyclable rubbish that undermines productivity.

"I don't know how they do it Mary," I said. "I bet no other government on the planet could arrange a kipper for every patriot for breakfast."

"I suspect no one else needs to."

"No one else has the vision to fight themselves."

I was doubly grateful to be leaving. Each day she grew more subversive.

"I can only stand it for so long," I warned her.

"Just be glad it's an actual fish Mark," she bit back. "And not a softened plywood substitute."*

No one in our village had eaten an actual fish for I don't know how long. Until this day. Although there were rumours a fish had been sighted in one of the larger potholes in town.

"Blame France for that."**

"And don't look a gift fish in the mouth," I urged, pointing with my fork at Churchill.

Cyclops arrived then, rapping on our back door.

Mary opened it. He stood there, mud splattered and panting. Stupid grin. I wondered if he was touched.

"We've got a spare kipper. Mum's been warming it up in a patch of sun. She said to bring it to you and not to spare the horses."

"How did you get a spare? Did you steal it?" I demanded.

Mary patted Cyclops on the head and took the parcel.

"Our gas is off again," Cyclops added.

"That's because your mum won't pay for it. It's her choice."

His dumb face screwed up, but Mary saved him with another pat on the head.

"Mum says the sun does a good enough job of heating anything up. She said Mr French needs his strength today."

The British sun! That miracle of British ingenuity. Aye! It'll get fish to an edible temperature.

"Come in," Mary invited.

"Mum said not to stay. She said I shouldn't interrupt your goodbyes."

And he ran off.

Mary slowly unwrapped the fish. She sniffed it. Twice.

"It feels like too much," she said.

"Don't mess around. Let's have it."

She placed the extra fish on a plate and put that in a patch of sun.

"Let it warm up a few minutes."

I didn't want to. I was so hangry. I wanted it now. Now.

"What will you have for second breakfast?" I joked.

"Pride," Mrs French replied. "The moment you're out the door I'm going to feel so free."

"What?"

"Free of the fear of red tape from Brussels."

Ah.

We even had coffee. That was another pleasant shock.

Mary had been hiding a small tin of it up the chimney. Proof, if ever it were needed, that God is indeed an Englishman.

"I've been saving a few spoons of English Replica Instant for a moment like this," she whispered as she retrieved it.

As we were conserving electricity, in the national interest, we had it cold. But who didn't? Only traitors. And Italians.

Suddenly, Churchill was quiet, the light dimmed, and then died.

"Let's have a second cup of English instant," Mary said.

"I'm up for it."

"I'll make a fire outside and we'll heat up the water the old fashioned way."

I nodded.

"That's Great British self-reliance for you," Mary added, deadpan.

"Come on!" I was in the mood now. "We'll sing the national anthem while we wait for the water to boil."

God Save The King.

"Just think, if the Great British Democratic Monarchy's monarch hadn't signed off all those righteous laws since 2016 we wouldn't be where we are today."

"Amen," Mary replied, with a smirk. "Defenders of our democracy indeed."

"We'd still have the anti-growth coalition protesting about dirty waterways."

"Just imagine it," Mary wondered. "How far this country has travelled."

And how far it still had to go.

***

EXT. BACK YARD MORNING

MARY carries a battered dining chair out of the back door. She sits it down on a bare patch in the little lawn. She tips it over and then begins breaking off the legs.

MARK stands watching with a mug.

MARK
Take that Brussels!

MARY
Get the matches.

MARK takes a matchbox out of his pocket. He rattles it.

MARY
There's a newspaper hidden in the sofa cushions.

MARY breaks off another leg.

MARK continues to watch her work.

MARY
Be a dear and get the paper.

INT. FRENCH HOUSE – KITCHEN CONT.

MARK enters the kitchen, whistling the 'Dambusters' theme song.

There is a scream outside. MARK keeps whistling. He is smiling at the kipper in the sunlight.

The scream again. Ferocious.

MARK
Mary?

The sound of splintering wood outside.

MARK shrugs.

MARK
(to kipper)
You can tell you're a British fish. Look at the sheen on your sides.

THROUGH KITCHEN WINDOW - MARY is beating the back of the chair with a brick.

CYCLOPS runs into the yard. He's all over the place in his excitement.

EXT. BACK YARD MORNING

CYCLOPS
I won this month's chocolate ration raffle!

MARY
(sweating)
Oh poppet that's marvellous!

CYCLOPS
(On his knees, holding the chocolate up)
It's a miracle!

MARY
You better eat it fast before one of the bigger boys mugs you!

MARY points to MARK'S face pressed against the kitchen window. The face vanishes.

MARK enters the yard.

MARK
Mars or Snickers?

CYCLOPS
I've been too excited to check. If only my dad were here to see me now.

CYCLOPS wobbles, and then bursts into tears.

MARK
Cut that out. We're trying to make firewood.

MARK takes the chocolate from the blubbing boy.

MARY
(Hefting the brick)
Mark French, if you eat that boy's chocolate I'll bash your brains out.

MARK unwraps the chocolate.

MARK
British government home brand.

A beat passes.

MARK
There's no finer chocolate.

CLOSE ON - Chocolate Label - *"Minimum 1% Great British Chocolate".*

MARK walks inside with the chocolate. MARY follows.

MARY
Mark French, I'm warning you…

***

Mary was hot on my heels. I slowed down. She slowed down.

"Mark French, you've been warned…"

Warned about what? My intentions were innocent.

"I merely want to ensure the chocolate is shared equally between the three of us."

"Give Cyclops back his chocolate or I'll brain you with this brick."

Before she could assault me there was a great calamity in the yard. The sound of half a dozen teenagers all shouting and hollering at Cyclops. Cyclops burst into the kitchen. The coward.

"Come out freak! Come out and hand it over!"

Cyclops was pale, well, he was always pale, the little traitor, but he was see-through now. He began to shake like the terrified puppy he was.

"Mr French," he whimpered. "Mr French." As if that would do any good.

I wasn't about to protect him from a normal childhood experience. What would he grow up to be? Soft. A snowflake.

"Go outside and face the music," I told him.

I busied myself with the chocolate. Setting it out on the

table, carefully. You couldn't be too safe, sometimes saboteurs put broken glass into the production line.

"What's happened to you?" Mary blazed at me. "What happened to the man who saved me from drowning?"

"This is supposed to be my day," I muttered. "This day is about my going to war."

Mary was so close I could feel her hot breath on my arm.

"Well?" she demanded. I didn't look at her.

The chocolate was naked in front of me. I smacked my lips.

The boys carried on outside. "Remoaner! Remoaner!"

The back door creaked open an inch. Cyclops yelped and dove under the kitchen table, clinging to my leg. I tried to shake him off, but like the overreach of Brussels, he just tightened his hold.

"Come out little piggy!" one of the boys whispered at the door. "Or we'll huff and we'll puff and we'll blow your house down."

"He doesn't live here!" I shouted. "This is not his address."

The chocolate needed eating before one of the teenagers snatched it. Why was it only me who saw the danger of the situation?

"Are you going to do nothing?" Mary slammed her hands on the table, so hard the chocolate bar jumped.

"I've got to march at least five miles today. Maybe more. Such a feat of physical endurance in the face of the enemy will…"

She wasn't listening to sense. She muttered something about the quality of man and opened a kitchen drawer. She took out our rolling pin.

"You stay here Cyclops," she ordered the trembling pup, setting the brick on the table. "I'll see to this."

"Don't leave me alone," Cyclops spluttered.

"Private French will defend you," Mary laughed sarcastically. And had second thoughts about the brick. She grabbed it.

Out the back door she went with the rolling pin and house brick.

I pushed back my chair to watch the action from the doorway, but Cyclops clung on for dear life. I had to drag him across the lino. It was useless. With all my heart I wanted to stand behind my wife in her fight, but I was immobilised by the terrified, unloved and unwanted child.

***

EXT. BACK YARD MORNING

We've seen THE GANG before. It's the same lost causes who kicked in the picket fence.

GANG LEADER

What you going to do with that you silly old Milf?

MARY is a bull pawing the dirt. Head lowered. Weapons held like horns.

GANG MEMBER

Go back inside you old tart.

MARY

You little ginger pricks.

MARY attacks. The rolling pin smacks into the GANG LEADER'S face. Spilling his teeth in a spray of blood. The GANG MEMBER gets it next as she pivots and slams the brick into his nuts. The rolling pin takes out a third gang member. The brick a fourth. It's a pandemonium of weeping, terrified teenage boys.

MARY
If you ever lay a hair on Cyclops' head again I'll have your guts for garters!

The GANG crawls and stumbles to flee.

MARY
Now scram!

The GANG scrams. MARY stands panting. Ferocious.

Inside the house CHURCHILL resumes broadcasting. "GOD SAVE THE KING" blasts from house to yard. All about radios sing. The air fills with patriotism.

You've never seen MARY so angry.

***

Mary barged past me, and calm as you like put the blood smeared rolling pin, and brick, into the kitchen sink. She puzzled over the pin for a moment, before pulling out an incisor stuck in it.

"I hope it's not a milk tooth," she laughed, throwing the tooth into the basin. It pinged about a few times.

"It's alright Cyclops," I soothed the trembling boy. "You're safe now. Now if you don't mind, please let go of my leg."

He released me and scrambled over the lino to wrap his arms around my Mary. The temple. The sanctuary. The ample hips.

"Thank you auntie! Thank you."

Auntie? The child had been driven mad by fear.

Mary did not correct him. She just gazed down with a big, soft smile and smoothed his hair with her bloody palm. It was a greasy mess. I didn't think touching it was safe. God knows what bugs lived on that head.

"It's alright Cyclops. Any of those sods lays a finger on you ever again and they'll have me to deal with."

Auntie? Well. This would not stand. The child was from a family famous for treason.

"My mother has a baking potato hidden at home," Cyclops gushed. "I'm going to get it for you. It's not even green yet!"

"Which auntie is that?" I interjected. They ignored me.

"You can give that potato to Private French. He's got to march five miles today, maybe even six. He'll need all his strength, and a little extra."

I popped the last bite of kipper into my mouth.

"You're going to war?" Cyclops was wide eye again.

"This very day," I replied, sitting up straighter.

I chewed on the fish but Cyclops was so impressed he released Mary and tried to climb into my lap. Odd boy. I was swallowing in that moment and the morsel lodged in my throat.

I couldn't breathe. Which was terrible. We hadn't even shared out the chocolate.

"Help!" I garbled. But Mary thought I wanted her to get Cyclops off me and just laughed.

It wasn't until I fell face first onto my plate that she realised I wasn't fooling. I was gripping the edge of the table. Veins were popping out of my temple. The Dambusters tune, forever playing inside my head, was fading. I was going to be martyred before my time!

"Use the Heinrich manoeuvre!" Cyclops screamed,

hitting me on the back with his puny paw. That's the last thing I would ever hear? The babblings of a touched boy? And one babbling German? This was no fate for a patriot! Brussels would be laughing its head off.

Happily, Mary had a more patriotic method. She grabbed me by the shoulders and slammed me against the back of the chair. She then slammed me against the table and hit me hard between my shoulder blades. Several times. Looking back now, I wonder if she needed to hit me so many times.

"Get Choking Done!" she shouted.

She *was* enjoying it.

The little bite of fish flew straight out of my mouth, across the table and landed on the bloody brick in the sink.

"Good work Mrs French. Mark must die for his country. Not his breakfast," Cyclops cheered.

My trembling hand reached across the table for the chocolate. Mary slammed her palm over it.

"Not a chance."

"I'm the victim here!"

"He's right Mrs French. That kipper tried to kill him."

"It's your chocolate Cyclops. And we're going to sit here and watch you eat it."

"Sometimes Mary, I wonder if you still love me?"

She just flinched and said, "God save the King."

**Softened plywood substitutes were a nutritious alternative to sea caught fish and became popular after the American naval blockade of British sovereign waters following some dispute over Northern Ireland that no one paid much attention to in England. To aid digestion Prime Minister Bunsen declared that the wood must be "thoroughly softened in the sweetest English rain" during a televised (lobster thermidor) dinner party at 10 Downing Street.*

***The unexplained rise in abdominal blockages amongst the population at this point was not the result of consumption of wood, a Downing Street inquiry found. Everyone just blamed France.*

Twenty Seven

Finally, I Pass Out (On My Feet)

"C is also for Courgette – Damn your eyes if you consume a courgette. You may as well sing La Marseillaise over Elgar.

A Great British Marrow may be eaten, stewed.

For this reason The Courgette receives no rating. It's not fit and I will not be convinced otherwise."

- 'Fruits and Vegetables, and Their Correct Patriotic Ratings' by Prime Minister Mark A. French.

Mark My Words

Mary and I had a quiet moment. It was the only quiet moment we'd had for years.

The plate on which the second kipper had arrived sat unwashed on the windowsill. A bluebottle fly wandering about it.

***

INT. FRENCH KITCHEN DAY

MARY'S calloused hands twist a fraying dish cloth. Tighter and tighter.

A dirty plate sits on the windowsill. A fat bluebottle investigates a scrap of fish.

MARK
That would probably taste alright with a few roast potatoes. It's a meaty bugger.

MARY'S fingers are white in the tight cloth.

MARY
When we have water again I'll wash that plate and return it to Cyclops' mum.

MARK
When The Enemies of the People are defeated we'll have all the roast dinners you want.

MARY
Maybe I should ask Cyclops and his mum to move in, while you're away.

MARK
No. That would undermine the will of the people.

***

Like hell Cyclops was moving into my home! Little beggar. The workhouse would do him some good. And after that, national service.

"Charity begins at home," I reminded Mary.

"I can't take the plate back unwashed."

"Put it out in the rain."

Mary smirked. "The government said not to use rainwater as the acid levels will eat away the crockery."

Clearly lies.

"Why do you think it is that a country as wet as England never has clean water anymore?" Mary persisted.

"Not today Mary," I requested.

"I heard the Bunsens' tap water comes from a pipeline from Evian in France."

More treason.

"Mary French…"

She shrugged.

"There's a hole in my bucket Mark."

"Then mend it dear Mary."

She smiled.

"Mark."

"Mary?"

"Do you think you're really capable…"

"Of what?"

She shrugged again but slid one hand across the table. I placed mine on top of hers.

"This must be how Henry V felt before Agincourt," I said.

A vicious laugh exploded out of my Mary. I took away my hand.

The quiet moment was over.

She gave me a searching look. She wanted to fix this moment in her memory. I knew. I looked martial enough, dressed in a replica TA catering corps uniform. She twisted the dish cloth in her hands, tourniquet tight.

"It's a good thing the Ministry for Peace changed the regulations governing what a military uniform is," Mary commented. Good change of topic.

She could not face my imminent departure, I knew. It was understandable. Like the fishing, home building, agricultural, and creative industries it was possible I was soon to become a martyr.

"We face each other for perhaps the last time on this

earthly plane," I said, as I wanted to see her cry. I wanted to know she really would miss me.

"Have you written your name inside the collar of your shirt?" she asked. A silly question. "What if it gets mixed up with some other replica TA catering corps uniform?"

I didn't respond. I was thinking of jamming my thumbs into Macron's eye sockets. King Charles III would be puzzling over a new type of English brie his vast estate had produced, aware that Private Mark French was putting paid to the enemies of the crown.

"I should have thought to stitch a name tag in!" A tear ran down Mary's cheek. "Fool. Fool. Fool."

"I've written my name inside my y-fronts," I soothed her.

"Do not worry about me," I added. "I am destined for great things."

"Mark."

"Yes?"

She just shook her head.

"You can be Boudicca," I said quietly, "and I'll be Wellington."

She straightened out the dish cloth and held one end in each hand. She placed it in a loop around my neck and pulled me forward until our foreheads touched.

"You're a fool Mark French," she muttered. "A bloody fool. All the people you travel with are idiots. Your war is so daft you must all be crackers."

She was terrified at the thought of losing me.

"I'm still the young man you met who used to sing songs about Hitler's ball."

I tried to pull away, but she held me there with the dish cloth. I could only hope it wasn't making my collar damp.

"Make sure you get plenty of roughage," she said.

"No risk there. Most of the army rations include dietary chipboard."

"Good. Try and find an apple orchard when you invade Cornwall. Tell me if they still make cider."

This was turning into a to do list! Women!

"I've never left you to fight before," I reminded her, looking into her big cow eyes. "I'm not sure other wives are burdening their warrior husbands with to-do lists."

She gave the cloth a twist in her hands. Now I was certain water was soaking into my collar. I decided to just accept it. Who would expect her to be rational. The logical decision to go and kill strangers had been taken. Her hormones dictated she was going to get all funny about it.

"Kiss me goodbye Mark and leave."

I thought she was going to cry. Her hands fell and I was released. I tried to take the dish cloth from her. She wasn't releasing it.

"I can take this cloth as a keep safe," I said.

"It's my last one. You're not having it."

But she gave it up. I dabbed at a fat tear on her cheek.

"Don't cry."

"Oh Mark, I may not have much choice in that. My stomach hurts."

I was not going to cry. I was convinced of it. But suddenly I worried I would never see Raylee again and a giant blub exploded from me.

"You've made a snot bubble!"

We both laughed.

"You've set me off!" I said. She took the cloth back and wiped my nose.

Churchill started up. It was an old recording of "It's A Long Way To Tipperary", by John McCormack.

We stood there for a few strains of the song, each sobbing away. We embraced as the backing singers joined in. How could we lose any war with songs like this to sing as we beat each other to death in the mud? I would bet my last imperial pound that the enemy marched to war to techno, or some German synth nonsense. They probably had red tape stating exactly that!

"You will send me back food? From the front? When you write to me?"

I hadn't said anything about writing.

"That sounds a little like treason."

To even suggest the good women of English towns would not receive their rations? It must have been her anxiety.

"Let this one thought crime slide," Mary whispered.

"Victory will see us feast!" I declared.

I stepped back and stiffened my lip.

"I'll starve myself so that you may eat," she sobbed.

Much more like it. The war needed deprivation and suffering at home on an epic scale.

"Now, I must be off. The men will be waiting for me on the high road."

Someone had to lead them.

"Take care of them. Most of them don't even have bum fluff on their lips."

I had to go. Any more of this and I would need a second breakfast for strength.

"Don't forget your rifle," she pointed to the stout stick resting by the back door. I collected it. I was sure I could exchange it for an actual rifle once the fighting started. I opened the back door, pausing to look back one more time, passed my wife at Churchill.

"Don't cook breakfast for another man while I'm away."

Mary nodded.

"I do not want to come home from war to find a house full of suitors."

She shook the dish cloth at me.

"Go Mark. Just go."

"Do not prepare lunch for another man while I'm

wrestling in the filth with traitors."

I think she shook her head in wonder.

"Go Mark."

"Do not even think about inviting some wandering chap in for dinner, no matter how lonely you feel. Fill your heart with knowledge of my noble sacrifice."

She forced herself between Churchill and me. She wrapped the dish cloth around her hands tightly and a few drops of water dribbled out. Then she whipped me suddenly with it. A flash across the buttocks.

"Should I spend my days weaving you a funeral shroud?" she shouted.

I had no idea what she was talking about.

"Then spend my evenings unravelling it?"

I puzzled at her. Had she developed a temperature? Was the strain of seeing me go too much?

"Come and wave goodbye."

"It's wave goodbye or wring your neck."

I put my rifle stick on my shoulder and stepped outside. My devoted wife followed.

It was a glorious day.

"We'll meet again," I told Mary. "I don't know where. I don't know when. But we'll meet again some sunny day."

"Get War Done!" she shouted. Her face was beetroot red. She was not alone. Near to us other women cried out the same.

"Control British Fish!"

"British Fish Are Sovereign Fish!"

This was the spirit that would drive us to our destiny. The past would be the future and the present need never burden Britons again.

"Do not beg me to stay," I said as Mary pushed me forward. "I have to fight."

"I won't," she blurted, shoving me again. "You have to

face the enemies of the people."

"It's my duty."

"Go faster," she urged. "Please go faster. You don't want to be left behind and miss out on all the excitement."

"But we're saying goodbye now."

"I want to make sure you go."

We walked along a row of 1930's terraced houses. Many of the green wheelie bins were split and broken from decades of service. The homeowners had repaired them with Union Flag patterned tape. It gave you hope. Whatever was broken by Brussels could be repaired by British pluck.

A large hedge lined the pavement. Some broken paving slabs remained.

"Had we not spent so much defending our sovereignty our towns would be resplendent," I told my wife. "When we have defeated our internal enemies, renewal will follow. New bins for all!"

Just then a dark shape burst from the hedge and ran at me.

I was not alarmed. I immediately lay down and covered my head with my hands, before the assassin could strike their blow. The attack was to be expected. We had the EU on the run now we were prosecuting the war against ourselves.

"Private French! Private French!"

I lay motionless. How my would-be killer knew me by name was a consideration for later. To target me showed the desperation of my enemy. They knew I was important. The attack would fail. I was so still they would not find me. Battlefield camouflage as pavement art.

"Mr French!"

"What do you want to be bothering my Mark for now Cyclops?" Mary asked. "You can see he's off to war. Well, once he gets up."

"I can see he's got his war stick," Cyclops said. Little idiot.

He grabbed my elbow and shook it.

"Private French! Get up. Why don't you talk to me? Why are you shivering? It's not cold. Is it cold Mrs French?"

"No Cyclops it's not cold. Mark is just feeling the excitement."

"I'm not shivering Cyclops," I said. "I am mimicking the vibrations of hundreds of marching feet as I disguise myself as the pavement."

Mary burst out laughing. Her tears now banished.

"Gosh. Did you learn that in basic training?"

"He learned how to tremble like a leaf all on his own," Mary giggled. "He's perfectly disguised as an idiot."

"When was the training Mrs French? I missed it."

"A patriot is always ready."

"But still Mr French, if no one shows you which way round a rifle goes you might fire from the wrong end. You could hurt someone."

"Hurting someone is the point of a war!"

"My Mark was born ready to fight Brussels," Mary cackled. "Even when we were young and he carried the burgundy passport, he was ready."

"Why was he ready?"

"Burgundy was the sirens singing."

There was a sudden and distant sound. A bugle had sounded.

"Is that a cat howling?" Cyclops asked. I admit, I wondered the same.

"You've got to move it Mr French or you'll miss the war."

Thank you Cyclops.

"Come on then, let's get a wriggle on." Mary offered me a hand up and Cyclops handed me my rifle stick.

"You look smashing Mrs French," Cyclops complimented my wife. "I've never seen so many Union Flags on one dress."

"That's because I made it out of bunting Mark found in a skip."

Then Mary burst into tears, sobbing into her red, white and blue sleeve.

"Now you've set her off again Cyclops!"

The little brat.

"I will prove myself Mary. I will uphold the will of the people to fight themselves. I will never surrender. I will stride right into 10 Downing Street and see the portrait of King Charles returned to its rightful place behind the Prime Minister's desk."

"Oh Mark, you fool. You're just going to run around and get all wet."

"Wet with the tears of remoaners!" Cyclops shouted.

That was more like it.

"Shush now my love," I told Mary. "Only speak in three-word sentences while I'm away."

I moved close and went to hold her hands, but she retreated. She would crumble at my touch. As it was, her heel caught in a gap in the paving and she would have fallen flat on her arse if Cyclops hadn't grabbed her.

"I am the will of the people," I shouted, and saluted.

"Don't miss me!" Mary replied, hugging Cyclops to her waist.

"I won't. I will look after myself."

I was following my destiny. Destiny is all. With courage and Union Flag branded munitions I could not fail.

It was the perfect moment to march away, but Cyclops buggered it up by snapping his heels together and returning my salute.

"Private Marcus Aurelius French," he said. "I want you to take my lucky potato with you to war. It is now a war potato. It was given me by my grandmothers on the day of my birth and we have kept it frozen all these years. It is a powerful potato. Today it defrosts in your honour. May it bring you luck as it has done for me."

Lying little shit. I bet their freezer was broken.

He thrust the cold vegetable at me.

"But what will you do without it?" Mary fretted. Who cared? I didn't. I was already planning to boil it up for lunch.

"I will wait for the new potatoes to arrive," Cyclops said. This was the first patriotic sentiment I had ever detected leaving his lips. My example had made an impact.

"I heard Churchill this morning say that Field Marshall Bentspoon has sent to Jersey for potatoes. They will arrive any day now. No blockade can keep a potato from the chosen land. If we just believe hard enough. If we ignore the gloomsters. That's what Churchill said."

I took the potato. The bugle sounded again. I forgot myself and ruffled Cyclops' hair, tucked the potato into my coat and marched.

"Crush a fifth columnist, liberal elite, snowflake saboteur for me!" Cyclops shouted.

"What happened to your tooth?" Mary asked Cyclops, as I joined the trickle of local men heading for the high road.

"I lost it fighting the big boys for an egg."

"Well, we'll go directly to mine and get my rolling pin, and then we'll go see those big boys. They won't seem so big after I've knocked ten types of shit out of them again. Will they now? Would you like that?"

"That would be amazing."

"It will be a pleasure."

It was clear they weren't watching me anymore. For Heaven's Sake! Anyone would think we had adopted the boy.

"Get War Done!" I bellowed, as a chap fell into step beside me. He was wearing a Scout's uniform, faded and unravelling badges clinging to the sleeves, but he carried what looked like an actual rifle. The big show off! The uniform was so tight I'd wager it was a large child's. Only his whippet thin frame made wearing it feasible.

"Believe in Great British Potatoes!" he bellowed.

I ignored his attempt to upstage me. He envied me. No woman was here to see him off.

We marched on together. Brothers at arm's length with a war against ourselves to win.

"I am Lance Corporal Carrot," he said, like it was something to be proud of.

"Did you buy your commission with Euros?" I asked.

"I am your commanding officer."

"I am a sovereign individual."

"No you're not. You're not rich enough."

"Who is your commanding officer?" I hit back.

"You are a Private. I am a Lance Corporal."

The sky is blue and water is wet. I was already bored of this blowhard.

"I will be Prime Minister before this war is over," I replied. "I can feel the call of destiny. Play your cards right and I'll make you a special advisor."

His eyes narrowed and he took a little notepad and pencil (stub) out of his shorts pocket. He licked the point of the pencil and made a note.

"What are you writing down?"

"First you commit insubordination and next treason? If we weren't marching to war I would have you branded right here, right now."

I didn't know he could do that.

"As it is Raylee has offered up schoolboys for the war effort, and you. I cannot lose the only other soldier of legal age to drive and purchase alcohol right at the start."

"You won't regret it," I said. Good Lord. That sounded

weak.

He smiled and marched ahead of me. He took a packet of cigarettes and a box of matches out of his pocket. He could afford cigarettes? How much was a Lance Corporal paid? He started smoking and I trailed in his wake.

Why the hell had I submitted to him? It must have been the emotion of the moment. I made the sound like a lion roaring at his back. He didn't turn around. I spun back to see if Mary was waving goodbye to me. But she wasn't. She was hugging Cyclops.

War was already a let-down, but I kept going. I was following my destiny. I just had to believe harder in war.

"The English have never been ruled by anyone," I reminded myself.

Destiny is all.

Twenty Eight

Whatever Doesn't Kill You Often Hurts (A Lot)

"W is for Watermelon – Rambunctious Watermelon faces into the storm and does not relent.

For this reason The Watermelon receives a patriotic rating of five stars out of a possible five stars. Because only a fool would put a number to a melon."

- 'Fruits and Vegetables, and Their Correct Patriotic Ratings' by Prime Minister Mark A. French.

Mary and Cyclops stood on a pavement liberated, of patriots.

"Will they come home?" Cyclops asked.

Mary shrugged.

"You want Mr French to come home?"

Mary smiled at the boy and ruffled his greasy head.

"Some days Cyclops I'm so mad at Mark, I could tell you the truth."

A triangle of plastic bunting had broken free of the bunting vines. It floated past overhead. Cyclops leapt to grab it, but he was too small.

"No one knows what's going to happen," Mary added.

"I heard Mr French telling Clarence he's going to be Prime Minister."

Mary chuckled.

"Prime Minister French?"

"It doesn't sound very patriotic," Mary added. "Does it?"

Cyclops screwed up his eye and then shouted, "Get War Done!"

A gust of wind blew another tiny flag against his face, covering his good eye like the patch on the empty socket. The triangle stuck there. He giggled. Staggering about with his hands outstretched.

Mary watched him play a few seconds, then removed the flag.

"Did you see the way Private French thrust his rifle stick into the air and twirled it like a cheerleader," Cyclops gushed. "Control British Fish!"

"It was a stirring sight," Mary agreed.

Mark's marching feet were not only out of time with the other soldiers, but even with themselves. The Churchill radios compensated for the cacophony by blasting out a recording of feet that were in time.

A cold wind was blowing now though. The patriots were small in the distance. A dog howled. A woman was heard quietly weeping behind a nearby door.

"It's not an omen," Mary muttered. "It's not."

"They were a rag tag bunch Mrs French," Cyclops said, shivering now. Goosebumps on his scrawny legs. He mocked marching back and forth to try and warm up. Marched until Mary gave him a playful clip around the ear.

"Knock that off," she chuckled, pulling Cyclops in, in to a hug.

"Now, what do you want to do first?" she asked.

"I was going to take first watch on Private French's defensive barricade."

Mary raised her eyes to the sky and sighed.

"It would be an honour! They told us at school that the boys left are now something called Public Morality Officers.

It's my patriotic duty to guard our perimeter. I'm supposed to report anyone who undermines the will of the people."

"You're a good boy Cyclops. A smashing lad." Mary gave him a squeeze. "But how about we go and thrash the bigger boys who stole your egg? Then you and I have a slap up dinner?"

Cyclops wrapped his spindle arms around her hips and hugged. Mary wasn't sure, but she thought she heard him sniffling. Then his little body began to heave up and down with sobs.

"Don't worry about old Mark. The devil takes care of his own."

"I'm not worried about Mr French," Cyclops blurted. "I don't know the last time my mother hugged me."

"Now. Now. I'm sure it was this morning!"

"How could she?"

"Cyclops! You're a wonderful boy. I'd be proud to call you my own. I'm sure your mother feels the same."

"But she was taken away to a re-education camp yesterday. She smashed the front door of Jelly's with a brick and stole Margaret Thatcher."

He paused and pushed dirt with his feet.

"They took her away?"

"They said I had to pull myself up by my bootstraps. But I don't have any boots."

Mary grew very still and very tense.

"Will you look after me?"

Mary burst into tears. She knelt on the pavement and scooped Cyclops into her arms. He folded up in her embrace.

"You silly boy. If I'd only have known."

"I was told by a Lance Corporal Carrot that I couldn't tell anyone or I would be thrown out of Raylee. My mother has shamed the town. I'm a rotten egg from a bad hen, that's what he said."

Mary put Cyclops down and cupped his wet face in her hands. They looked into one another's eyes. It was not clear whose tears were fattest.

"I didn't think Mr French would let me see him off if he knew of my mother's crimes."

Mary tutted. Was she in danger herself, by association? She didn't care.

"Come on," she held out her hand. "Let's get you home and cleaned up. Afterwards we'll have supper. You can stay with me until your mother comes home."

Cyclops snorted, wiped the back of his nose with his torn sleeve. He took Mary's hand. She didn't care that it was covered in snot.

"I've been saving some food in case the war goes badly," she said quietly. "Squirreling it away day after day. I'm going to feed you until you burst."

"But what about thrashing the bigger boys?"

"We'll do that tomorrow. It will be cracking sport. They'll have forgotten all about the egg and it won't half come as a surprise!"

They hurried on.

"Can we skip to your house?"

"To our house Cyclops. Our house."

"Can we skip to *our* house?"

"I don't see why not."

Mary burst into a skip, still holding Cyclops' hand, and pulled him clean off his feet. He landed in a pothole and sprawled across it. After, when she had picked him up and dusted him down, they tried skipping again.

"One...two...three..."

"Get Skipping Done!"

THE END

Appendix A - The Official Government List of Who to Hate

1. Postmen.
2. Nurses.
3. Doctors.
4. Firemen.
5. Refuse Collection Men.
6. Anyone under eighteen.
7. Continentals.
8. The Woke.
9. Environmentalists.
10. The Irish.
11. The Scottish.
12. The Welsh (some).
13. Londoners (except Cockneys).
14. The Disabled.
15. People without Union flags on their houses.
16. Your next door neighbour.
17. Women.
18. Poor people.
19. Teachers.
20. Job Stealing Foreigners.
21. Refugees (ie, welfare scammers).
22. Pacifists.
23. Republicans (not those located in the USA, ie anti-monarchists).
24. Princes who marry foreigners.
25. Archaeologists (excepting any who are vaccine sceptics).
26. The sick.

27. Farmers.
28. Wine importers.
29. Anyone who suntans too readily.
30. Train Drivers.
31. Anyone who bans Easter.
32. Anyone who yearly engages in The War on Christmas.
33. Academics.
34. Students.
35. People who wore masks during the Pandemic.
36. Charity workers.
37. Veterans (who complain).
38. The childless.
39. Renters.
40. Early retirees.
41. Anyone who works from home who isn't in the Cabinet.
42. Avocado eaters. Avocado eaters. Avocado eaters.
43. Bishops

Appendix B - A list of confirmed miracles attributed to Winston Churchill (the potato).

1. Bunsen's Toilet Law - Prime Minister William Bunsen witnessed the eyes of the Divine Potato weeping blood as he sat with it in private contemplation in 10 Downing Street. A vision followed in which Bunsen saw Dover's port on fire, smoke spiralling into the sky over the English Channel, a flotilla of small boats beaching at Herne Bay, as inland heretics used the front page of The Daily Parrot, on which Bunsen and the Potato featured, as toilet paper.

That day Bunsen used his sovereign powers to outlaw the use of any edition of The Daily Parrot in a water closet. Only a supernatural tuber could affect a Prime Minister in this manner. This was Winston's first miracle.

2. The French Defeat at Agincourt - It was suspected from the moment of his discovery that Winston the Holy Potato was not bound by the usual boring rules regarding time and space. The subsequent discovery of (hitherto) lost papers by King Henry V, in an obscure abbey in Sussex, confirmed this.

The parchment is so miraculously preserved it appears new. In it England's King describes how he discovered a mysterious orb shaped rock in an Uxbridge field. The rock possessed a skin which "peeleth" under the fingernails to reveal a red, white and blue interior.

Henry goes on to describe feeling hit as if by heavenly lightning, his brain shaken so powerfully he feared he was possessed. And he was, by a desire to invade France, like any English king worth his salt.

When attendants sought to see the magical rock for themselves it had vanished.

It is without doubt the rock was Winston the Holy Potato. The miraculous nature of both the event itself, and the rediscovery of the record of it, are both miracles now attributed to Winston.

**Miracles 3 – 52 to be included in subsequent editions of this book.*

Appendix C – A full list of the problems the army was drafted in to solve during the summer of Winston's discovery.

1. When it became known that thousands of individuals were using the front page of The Daily Parrot as toilet paper the army was called in to force entry into any home on any street with newspaper samples in the sewage outlets. The police were already overstretched. Thousands of arrests were made. When it became clear the criminal justice system was already overstretched dealing with lawbreakers, the army was called in again. Many a squaddie became judge and jury that day and law and order was saved. The number of heretics sentenced to death has not been recorded, as it was judged unseemly to focus on minor details in a moment of national crisis.

2. Filigree Bunsen was a minor wife of William Bunsen. She is so labelled because the marriage only lasted for one weekend. The army was called in late Sunday afternoon when Filigree spoke to Bunsen in German and attacked him with a dessert spoon, stained with trifle.

It was obvious the young, blonde temptress was a saboteur sent by Brussels to destroy OUR Prime Minister. Berlin wasted its resources. How many years they'd spent training this agent are unclear, but it must have been in the double figures, or she could never have so deceived and seduced Bunsen.

By a stroke of fortune the army was present at the property, dealing with a plumbing emergency in the kitchens.

Captain Fortescue Fontelbrain is recorded by William Bunsen as having "rugby tackled the insane Teutonic assassin" to the floor, showing courage in the face of "her obvious, advanced state of pregnic insanity".

This is not the only thwarted assassination attempt against Bunsen. A full list will be printed after it is compiled. It will be a very long list.

Suggestions that Filigree was not a foreign agent, and instead driven to murderous rage by discovery of the Prime Minister "banging a parlour maid like a tin drum" in a little used WC are not to be believed. They were spread by The Enemies of the People, in order to undermine The Will of the People.

Reports that Filigree Bunsen freed herself and raced to the roof of 10 Downing Street, from where she hurled herself to the street below, are to be believed. She perished, along with her phantom pregnancy, on the spiky railings of sovereignty.

Appendix D – Bridges That Were Never Built - for which feasibility studies were commissioned.

1. The Bridge to America
2. The Bridge to Ireland
3. The Bridge to Jersey
4. The Bridge to Bridgend
5. The Bridge to Calais
6. The Bridge to Alaska
7. The Bridge to Antarctica
8. The Bridge to Malaga
9. The Bridge to Brugge
10. The Orchard Bridge from Westminster to Southwark

Appendix E - Spare Quotations

1. *"Blighty reached perfection in the 19th Century and has been wise enough to return."* - Cardinal Bogg, from the 'Sermon on the Spout' (Dover, May 5th, 2024 - Bank Holiday in celebration of the robustness of British sewage outlets.)

2. Prime Minister William Bunsen taught us to, *"…know an Englishman's home is his castle and his selective memory the unbreakable force garrisoned within. Mi Casa, mi castel."*

3. Prime Minister William Bunsen held aloft the vacuum-packed flounder and declared, *"This is a Great British vacuum, and we will live inside it!"*, to a packed hall of patriots and wild applause, before he added the obvious classical references to *"sunburnt, oily, muscly Spartans and bedsheet wearing, girly swot Athenians."*

4. *"0.9144 centimetres are no match for a solid 36 inches."*
- The Science of Sovereignty, by Everyman.

5. *"The average Briton shares 80% of their genes with the average potato. The potatriot shares up to 100%."*
- The Observations of Prime Minister Mark French (Collected), Prime Minister of The Democratic Monarchy of Great Britain.

Appendix F – Provisional List of Towns Excluded from Blighty's Swan Song

1. London - Reason given, "Treasonous Mayor".
2. Kirkwall - Reason given, "Secession".
3. Stromness - Reason given, "Secession".
4. Finstown - Reason given, "Secession".
5. Lyness – Reason given, "Lack of GPS data. Additionally, secession".
6. Dounby - Reason given, "Secession".
7. Twatt - Reason given, "Self-explanatory".
8. Cairston - Reason given, "Local by-law dating from the 10th century banning swans. Also, secession."
9. Birsay - Reason given, "Secession".
10. Brinian - Reason given, "Secession".
11. Saint Margaret's Hope – Reason given, "No hope. Also, secession".
12. Pierowall - Reason given, "Fire. Also, secession".
13. Orphir - Reason given, "See Lyness".
14. Sandwick - Reason given, "Clerical error, confusing Sandwick with Sandwich, which was visited. Also, lack of GPS data, local by-law dating from the 10th century banning swans and concealment of town under heavy fog on day chosen for visit. Also, secession."

Printed in Great Britain
by Amazon

33682432R00229